Nostalgia Kills

ALSO BY ROBERT WESTBROOK

Journey Behind the Iron Curtain
The Magic Garden of Stanley Sweetheart
The Left-Handed Policeman

Nostalgia Kills

A LEFT-HANDED POLICEMAN MYSTERY

ROBERT WESTBROOK

Crown Publishers, Inc.

New York

Copyright © 1988 by Robert Westbrook

Published by Crown Publishers, Inc., 225 Park Avenue South, New York, New York 10003 and represented in Canada by the Canadian MANDA Group

CROWN is a trademark of Crown Publishers, Inc.

Manufactured in the United States of America

Library of Congress Cataloging-in-Publication Data
Westbrook, Robert.
    Nostalgia kills.
    I. Title.
PS3573.E827N6   1988   813'.54   87-27263
ISBN 0-517-56763-6

10 9 8 7 6 5 4 3 2 1

First Edition

For Gail—with love and lust and laughter.

Prologue

Rome, 1970

The bathroom was fascinating. The first day they arrived at the Grand, Billy made his girlfriend wash herself in the bidet so he could see how it was done.

Now *that's* civilization, he thought. Something we don't have in L.A. Everything else about Rome, however, was a disappointment. He had come chasing the ghosts of Michelangelo and da Vinci, hoping to meet Fellini—for though he was a rock star, Billy Lion was no ignoramus. But all he had found here so far were Jack Daniel's (a fellow American) and girls who wanted to party with a star. He could have stayed in Los Angeles for that.

It was a late afternoon in August, and a heat wave had settled on the continent from the south of Italy to the Baltic Sea. Rome sat stifling in the sun, the wide piazzas and narrow streets empty of all but the most fanatic tourists, mainly Americans and Japanese. Why Maya Moon had wanted to come here at this time of year was beyond him.

Maya Moon had been his lady for nearly four months now, which was the most enduring relationship he'd had in years—since his career had taken off, really, about 1965. The reason this romance survived was, he supposed, that here at last was a girl who was intelligent as well as beautiful. Someone he could talk with. But coming to Rome in August was not so bright. A few more ideas like that and she could hitchhike home.

It was so hot that Billy took the bottle of Jack Daniel's into the tomblike coolness of the Grand Hotel bathroom, filled the great marble tub with cold water, and slipped inside. He could have simply turned on the air conditioning, but Billy did not like artificial air. He preferred real heat to artificial cool.

Real heat, he mused, wondering if he could turn the phrase into a song. He was so used to that: turning every little thought into gold. He would have to get unused to it now. He had left his band in shambles back in the States in the middle of a national tour. At this point, he wasn't even certain he had a career to return to.

Well, fuck it.

He reached for the bottle of sour-mash sipping whiskey. Jack was all right. Billy had been pretty drunk now for about a week, but that was all right, too. How did Maya Moon put it? *It doesn't matter what we eat or smoke or drink. Life is alchemy. What matters is to transmute the substance into God.*

What a lot of bullshit, he considered.

"New-age bitch!" he said aloud.

And where was she? She'd left in the morning to go shopping, but he'd stayed in the hotel to sleep and be alone. Three days earlier he had been going out, too. For a while it seemed the streets of Rome were safe, that no one would recognize him here. But just as he started to relax and enjoy himself, some crazy bitch who was a girlfriend of a guy who had once worked for him recognized him on the Via Veneto, and that was it as far as anonymity was concerned.

"Billy! What are you doing in Rome?"

Instantly he was visible, there on the street in person: Billy Lion. He was besieged by fans and a motley assortment of international youth who materialized magically from the semideserted streets, all of them asking for money.

"Hey, Billy, can you spare two hundred fifty thousand to help us build a utopian society on Ibiza? . . . Billy, I love your music. Could you finance my college education?"

Christ! Even the beggars made exorbitant demands. Fortunately, Maya Moon had been with him, and though she seemed fragile—a delicate blond beauty with green eyes, who looked somehow recently arrived from a distant planet—in this instance she'd shown more stamina than he had supposed. She had elbowed a German student firmly in the kidneys and led the way to a taxi. Billy was impressed. But he'd stayed in the hotel from then on.

He reached over to the side of the tub for the bottle of Jack Daniel's. "Mmm, eighty thousand watts," he said vaguely, wishing Maya Moon were here so she could roll him a joint. Christ, did he have to do everything for himself?

He set old Jack back on the marble floor harder than he intended, and the glass shattered. They certainly didn't make goddamn bottles the way they used to. He was lucky not to cut himself, but even so it made him feel very sad. Mournfully he looked down at his pale body in the tub. This caused him to feel even worse. Billy was nearly one hundred pounds overweight, and his last two album covers contained artwork rather than photographs. It was hard to imagine that at one time he had been incredible-looking. Writers had compared him to a Greek god. Just a few years back, in 1967, *Look* had called him the greatest sex symbol to hit rock and roll since Elvis Presley.

All gone. Gone the Dionysian curls, gone the Greek profile. He looked at himself in disgust. In the bathtub he looked like a bloated white whale. Horrible! He had a moment of panic: the white marble bathroom appeared to him suddenly as cold and merciless as a morgue, with himself dead meat on the slab.

Lord, he wished he hadn't broken that bottle of Jack Daniel's! It made him want to cry. But then, thank God, he heard the door open, and she came in, looking very cool and in command.

She was wearing the briefest minidress, which showed off the delicate curves of her thighs. She had on lots of jangling jewelry—bracelets and necklaces with an entire pantheon of occult symbols: goddesses and pentangles and crescent moons. Billy breathed in the scent of her, an intriguing combination of patchouly oil, marijuana, and sex.

"You look like a dimestore goddess," he told her. "You know that? A Salvation Army slut."

"Yes, Billy." The girl smiled mockingly, her eyes darting about the broken glass on the floor. "Having a little party, are we?"

"Yeah, a party," he said sullenly. "I broke the goddamn bottle."

"It's okay. I'll clean it up later," she said. "Look, I brought us back something nice to smoke."

"Yeah? So roll us a joint, why doncha."

"I got something better than a joint. I'll take off my clothes and bring it in for you."

Billy sighed. He felt inexpressibly weary.

Maya Moon went into the next room for what seemed like a long time. When she returned she was naked except for a pair of sandals, carrying a small pipe and a book of Grand Hotel matches. She carefully walked around the broken glass to the tub, handed him the pipe, and lit a match.

"What's it?"

"A mixture. Mostly heroin and hashish."

"I don't do heroin," he complained. "You know that."

"Come on, you'll like it. You're strong enough to ride a little horse."

She said this in a subtly erotic way, challenging him to the ride. Since they had known each other, they had often egged each other on to new and bizarre experiences. Billy inhaled the smoke, which hit him immediately, a solid wall of euphoria. The smoke was strangely sweet and heavy. He felt instantly paralyzed. He could hardly move, hardly breathe, and he would have been frightened except it felt so good.

The girl looked down on him, it seemed, from a great distance. Her eyes were like large glass marbles, serene yet unknowable. Though his body was paralyzed, his mind was wonderfully clear.

"Feel good?" she asked, her voice far away.

Billy could only smile. When her hand touched his leg, the sensation of skin against skin seemed to fill the entire known universe. He could visualize the pores of her fingers on the pores of his leg. Damn, he was stoned! Maya Moon's hand caressed upward over a forest of hairs. A finger found a testicle and traced a slow line up his cock. He responded immediately, terrifically horny, blood swelling into his cock—not so much an erection, more like a mighty tree, a redwood growing toward the distant heavens. God, he felt strange. The very room began to breathe.

Then her pink wet tongue touched his leg and began to trace the path upward where her hand had gone. He felt soft lips and a hint of perfect white teeth—soft flesh, hard enamel. The tree growing from the center of his body seemed to continue up out of the room through the clouds into a turquoise sky. So very pleasant. Now what was this new sensation?

Jesus, she was licking his balls! Her hands were beneath his ass, lifting him out of the water toward the paradise of her mouth. Her tongue took forever moving up the trunk of the tree. She lifted him completely out of the water, engulfed him with her mouth.

Billy Lion floated endlessly upward. But he had to giggle. This was really pretty funny. *Didn't she see what was happening?* As the center of his body moved upward, his head began to slip down beneath the surface of the bath. She was drowning him in her love.

Billy struggled momentarily with his arms, trying to lift himself out of the tub, up from the waters of bliss. But Maya Moon had one hand firmly on the center of his chest, holding him down. He could see her quite well: She was looking into his eyes with intense curiosity. There was love there, he thought strangely, but no mercy. The hand holding him beneath the water was firm as iron.

Yet it felt wonderful, the rhythmic motion of her mouth. A river was welling up inside of him, ready to surge out. Maybe it's better this way, he thought. God knows, I burned my bridges. . . .

His body shuddered. He saw a stone being dropped into the waters of eternity. The ripples continued outward until the waters were perfectly still.

Billy Lion, legendary rock star, drowned in the best orgasm he ever had.

Part One

1

On a wintry Friday morning in February, Nicky Rachmaninoff sat at his old Steinway upright piano trying to ignore a ringing telephone. He glanced up at the clock on the kitchen wall to see it was not quite eight o'clock.

He had been playing a Bach fugue, a piece that was beyond his skill as a self taught blues piano player. And yet he almost had it going, minus a few trills and turns no one would really miss. The music was flowing out upon the early morning with all its architectural purity and passion and logic. Wouldn't it be nice if the entire day could be just like this music of Bach? If he could, he would wrap it around him, wear it like a cloak to keep him safe when he entered that less than pure, less than logical, less than angelic place called Los Angeles.

But the phone kept ringing.

"Suck," he said wearily, a word Johann Sebastian Bach would not have recognized. Unfortunately, he knew exactly who was calling, for Nicky was a cop—not a musician.

"Rachmaninoff," he said into the receiver, wondering what piece of blood and gore and horror awaited his attention.

"Nicky, hi. Hope I didn't wake you, but the car's coming for me in a few minutes and I thought of a few last-minute things."

He had been wrong. This was not the station. It was Susan Merril, his ex-wife. She had left him ten years ago to become an actress and had succeeded beyond her wildest dreams. She had become a star.

"Nicky, I have it all worked out with Marymount. The school bus is going to pick up Tanya outside your house at seven-fifteen every morning. Okay? She'll be brought back around four-thirty every day except Wednesday—you'll leave a key for her, won't you?"

"Sure."

Tanya was their daughter, now twelve years old, the living result

9

of their having been married so long ago. She was about to come and live with him for the next six months, which was why Susan was calling from her mansion in Bel Air and had been calling anxiously several times a day for the past week.

"Nicky, on Wednesdays she's taking gymnastics after school. Did I tell you that already? You're going to have to pick her up yourself at four-fifteen. Are you going to manage that?"

"Yes, you told me, Susan. And yes, I can manage," he said patiently. "Hell, if I'm tied up, I can always send a squad car for her."

There was a significant silence from her end. Then: "You're not serious, are you?"

"What do you mean?"

"*Nicky!* Marymount's a *very* exclusive school. A lot of the girls are picked up by limousines. I don't know how Tanya would feel having a police car coming for her. Twelve's a *very* sensitive age, you know."

"I see what you mean," he reassured her quickly. "I'll manage somehow. If there are any homicides Wednesday afternoons, they'll just have to wait. Okay?"

Susan sighed ponderously. "I hope this is going to work out. I know what you're like when you have a case. The house could burn down and you wouldn't notice. . . . Are you on a case now?" she asked suspiciously.

"Nothing interesting," he said. He could have added truthfully: Not for a long time now had there been anything interesting.

"If you have any problems, you'll call me, won't you?"

"Of course."

Nicky did his best to be accommodating. It was complex dealing with an ex-wife. The issue of Tanya's coming to live with him for half the year was particularly sensitive and new. In the past, Nicky had had his daughter only every other weekend. The arrangement was not wonderful, but he had accepted it, mostly because Susan seemed so much better equipped to be a parent than he was. She had married again, a nice millionaire named Frank Fee who happened to be a TV star, too. Together they had just about everything people in Los Angeles ever desired: fame, money, a Rolls, a Bentley, a tennis court, an olympic-size pool, a great house in Bel Air, a duplex in New York, and a chalet in Switzerland for that occasional Christmas trip to the slopes. They were also both extremely good-looking and healthy. How could Nicky Rachmaninoff, a mere cop, compete with all this?

Yet, strangely enough, Tanya—at the age of twelve—decided to forsake all this wealth and Hollywood glory for fully half a year in an effort "to get to know my father."

How Susan must have laughed. "Get to know your father? Well, lots of luck on that one, kid!"

But Tanya was stubborn, and this question of getting to know her elusive father had become something of a quest. Susan had felt rejected, but she was meticulously fair. The transfer of parental authority, discussed endlessly for over a month now, was to happen this very Friday afternoon. After work tonight, Nicky would drive to Bel Air and become a full-time father for the first time in ten years.

He was, frankly, terrified.

Did he have enough blankets? Susan wanted to know. Did he remember Tanya's appointment with the orthodontist on the seventh? There was also the fact that Tanya had just begun to have her menstrual periods: She might be embarrassed to ask her father to buy Tampax at the store, so Nicky should be sensitive. He should be tactful.

Nicky listened to all this and more. He looked wistfully across the room at his waiting piano, and his gaze wandered idly upon a copy of this week's *People* magazine that was on the table by the phone. Susan was on the cover, dressed in white, looking very tan and gorgeous. She was certainly a classic California beauty. Her hair was blond, her eyes blue, and her limbs long and golden. Great wealth had given her a languid elegance she had not possessed as a policeman's wife.

The caption of the magazine cover, beneath her picture, read CAN SUSAN MERRIL REALLY BE 40?

The answer was no. Maybe twenty-six, maybe a young thirty. But forty—never. It gave Nicky a vaguely lonely feeling, as if he had gone on to middle age without her.

"Oh! The car's here!" Susan said suddenly. "Guess I got to go to work."

Work for Susan these days was a remake of the classic western *High Noon*. Susan was playing the Grace Kelly role opposite an Australian actor who was trying to be Gary Cooper. The resulting effort would eventually be fed to the American public as a TV miniseries. Somehow Nicky doubted it would be as good as the original.

"How's it going?" he asked.

"I don't know, Nicky. Everyone's fighting with each other—the producer, the director, even the damn cameraman can't get along with the set designer. The leading man is real edgy with me because

11

I wouldn't go to bed with him, and the writer's on my case because I've changed some of his lines—can you believe the nerve of the guy? I tell you, if they weren't paying me a million dollars, I'd quit."

"That's real tough, Susan."

She missed his tone. Irony was the last resort only of underpaid police detectives.

"And next week we're supposed to go to Arizona for some location shots, the *last* place I want to be," she complained. "I'm going to have to ride a fucking horse. You know I've always been frightened of horses, Nicky."

He made some vaguely sympathetic noises.

"Well, good luck with Tanya," she told him. "Love you."

"Love you, too," he responded. Then the phone went dead.

The house felt lonelier than before Susan's call. Nicky walked to the sliding-glass door at the far end of his living room and stared restlessly at a sky that was full of storm. So much for the pure and logical world of Bach. Out the window, red clouds glowed on the horizon and became darker to the west, toward the sea. It had been a wet February. Beneath the sky, the city of Los Angeles sprawled endlessly as far as the eye could see.

Nicky Rachmaninoff had quite a view of the city. He lived high in the Hollywood Hills at the very end of a dangerous little road called Sunshine Terrace, which rose up out of Laurel Canyon in a confused and rambling way. The Hollywood Hills had become fashionable, but his own house defied fashion—a ramshackle wooden cabin with many windows looking out upon a thicket of woods, a small meadow, and the city below. At night raccoons came to visit his garbage cans, and owls hooted from the trees. Occasionally he even saw deer. Sunshine Terrace was a fool's paradise, where they all imagined they were in the country.

Nicky's father had built this place, and his son remained—resisting offers from developers to turn the property into a flashy new condominium for swinging cinematographers and rising young starlets. Nicky's father had been a cop, too, just like him.

Of course, sometimes he thought he should sell and get on with his life someplace else. But then who would feed the raccoons?

Standing at the window, gazing at the city far below, Nicky felt time and memory trying to eat him up alive. Then the phone rang again. He assumed it was Susan calling back with some last-minute item. Maybe he was supposed to put birth control pills in Tanya's orange juice.

12

"Hi," he said in his relaxed Susan-voice.

But this time it was the station, and they had news for him of a mutilated body in a house in North Palm Drive.

This was turning into a swell day.

2

As head of the homicide squad of the city of Beverly Hills, Lt. Nicholas Rachmaninoff had long ago come to the conclusion that the entire town had died.

The pulse, certainly, was hard to find. People did not walk on the sidewalks. Children did not play on the lawns. Even the birds seemed muted by the presence of so much wealth.

The house on North Palm Drive, in the 500 block near Santa Monica Boulevard, was a good example of mausoleum architecture. The facade of the building was white and boxlike with a few elongated windows. Instead of a front lawn, there was a small, low-maintenance area of decorative rocks, from which a single cypress tree emerged as the only living thing. Two radio cars and an assortment of official vehicles were lined up by the curb, disturbing the heavy peace only slightly.

Nicky parked and walked up to the front door, where a uniformed cop nodded and let him in. The dead man lay at the foot of the stairs, at the far side of the foyer. It was a violent and bloody death. The back of the skull was dark with blood. The victim appeared to have fallen down the stairs, landing in a heap at the bottom, his legs spread in an unnatural way, as if he had had one final urge to do the split. He wore only a silk robe, which was partially open, revealing the horror that had happened to him. The dead man's genitals were completely missing. An enormous quantity of blood had flowed out of the pulpy wound before congealing on the white shag carpet.

Nicky had seen too many corpses in his almost twenty years as a policeman. He stared at the dead man for some time without turning to acknowledge the various lab people and colleagues who were already in the house. The victim's toupee had fallen off and lay on its own near an outstretched arm, like some small, furry animal. The man, in his mid- to late forties, was unfashionably overweight.

"Ah . . . Lieutenant?"

It was a uniformed sergeant, an older man with white hair and a pockmarked face. "We got the call half an hour ago from the maid," he said softly. "She's sitting over there. You want us to hold her or let her go?"

The sergeant gestured toward a young woman who was sitting rigidly on a strange-looking sofa in the nearby living room. The girl did not particularly look like a maid. She had brilliant red hair and wore a frilly black uniform that showed a great deal of leg. She might have stepped out of some soft-core French film.

"I'll speak to her in a second. Do we have an I.D. on the victim yet?" he asked, nodding toward the corpse.

"His name's Jay Jeffries. Murray's been telling me the guy's a VJ. Whatever the hell *that* is. A social disease, I think."

Murray was one of the white-jacketed lab technicians. "A VJ's a video disc jockey," he said without looking up from his work. "You'd know that if you weren't such an old fart."

"Like I was saying. A social disease," repeated the old cop. "You ever watch that shit, Lieutenant? All the guys wear lipstick and eye shadow, and the girls have orange hair."

Nicky did not answer. The name Jay Jeffries was trying to make a connection somewhere in his tattered memory. Probably it came from Tanya, who watched music videos fiendishly whenever she could—as much as Nicky's nerves allowed when she came to visit.

"Hey, Nicholas. You look lost in space."

Nicky glanced up to see Jason Whittle, chief of crime lab, standing near the top of the stairs. Jason had long white hair and looked like a cartoon image of a mad scientist. "Oh, hi, Jason," Nicky said without much enthusiasm. "How's it look?"

"Pretty straightforward, really. The guy was standing at the top of the stairs, about where I am now. Some unpleasant person came up from behind and shot him in the back of the head with a small-caliber handgun. We'll hope he died instantly, before he tumbled down the stairs to where you see him now. That's where the genitals were removed, with a knife that was not too sharp. Look, you can see where the skin was torn, rather than being severed cleanly."

Nicky did not look. "What time was he killed?"

"Let's say after eleven last night, and before twelve-thirty."

"Have you found the murder weapon?"

"No."

"How about the knife?"

"No, not that, either. We did find the genitals, however," Jason added brightly. "They were stuffed down the garbage disposal in the kitchen."

14

Nicky heard a violent retching sound behind him. He turned to see the red-headed housecleaner, who had been listening to this conversation from the living room. She was clutching her stomach and throwing up dramatically onto the shag carpet.

3

Nicky stood over the sick housecleaner, who was stretched out on a kidney-shaped black plastic sofa. Her skin was milky white, which went nicely with her curly red hair. The back of one hand rested on her forehead, like some fainting Camille.

"Sorry," she said, then proceeded to retch again.

" 'S all right," Nicky murmured. It was nice to know sensitive souls might get sick at the thought of a dismembered penis stuffed down a garbage disposal. Only a few feet away, a cop and a police photographer were swapping recipes for spaghetti sauce.

Nicky surveyed Jay Jeffries' living room while the girl caught her breath. A large oil painting of Elvis Presley hung over a fake fireplace of plastic logs. All the chairs and sofas were made out of the same slick black vinyl and looked as if you could slide right off them if you weren't careful. The coffee table in the center was actually a table-model video game called Ms. Kong. There was also a pink baby grand piano and a Hawaiian-style bar made of bamboo. Outside a sliding-glass door, a stubby palm tree shaded the calm turquoise waters of the pool.

The housecleaner was sitting up now. Her brief upset had not left a single hair out of place. She had lips as red as cherries, fingernails to match, and false eyelashes that were fluttery as little birds. At first sight, he took her to be in her early twenties, but he quickly revised this upward to early thirties. She was looking at Nicky with hard brown eyes, waving a long leg at him like bait.

"So you're the maid," he said dubiously.

"Well, actually I'm an actress," she said airily. "Just doing this between gigs."

"I see." Nicky took a small pad from the breast pocket of his brown corduroy jacket. "What's your name, please?"

"Nancy Normal."

He raised an eyebrow.

"Sandy Giannini," she admitted. "But everyone knows me as Nancy. . . . That's a line from a Beatles song. A joke—get it?"

Lieutenant Rachmaninoff did not smile.

"I see. . . . Now, Ms. Normal, what time did you get here this morning?"

"Eight," she said.

"Is that when you usually arrive?"

"Uh-huh. I've been cleaning for J. J.—uh, Jay Jeffries—every Tuesday and Friday morning for, oh, about a year now. I'm usually out by one, which is great—gives me plenty of time to go on auditions. I'm with the Winston Loom Agency, you know."

Nancy Normal wanted to talk about her acting career, but Nicky cut her off. In this town, you sometimes had to get ruthless.

Patiently, he kept at her until he had her story. Nancy Normal had met Jay Jeffries—J. J., she called him—at a party. They got to talking, probably over a coke spoon, and J. J. offered her a job. As far as Nicky could tell, she was something more than a servant and less than a friend. J. J. was generally at work when Nancy Normal cleaned his house, so after that party she rarely saw him—except on television. J. J. was the morning VJ weekdays at The Rock Channel, and Nancy liked to have his show going while she cleaned. It gave her energy, she said, so she could really boogie with the vacuum.

This morning she had arrived and the front door was locked. The key was in its usual hiding place, beneath one of the decorative white rocks near the door. Nancy said she opened the front door, saw the body, screamed, and called the cops.

Nicky had her show him where the outside key was hidden. Maybe it was important, maybe not. A lab technician was already examining the lock on the front door to see if it had been forced. Nicky gave him an inquiring look, and the technician shook his head.

"Was there anyone else who knew about the outside key besides you?" Nicky asked when they were in the living room again.

"I don't know. Probably. J. J. was a pretty major party animal, you know."

"No, I don't know. Tell me."

"Well, there were always lots of people around, coming and going."

"Even when Mr. Jeffries wasn't home?"

"*Mr.* Jeffries." She laughed. "You're sorta old-fashioned, aren't you?"

"Sort of," Nicky admitted. "Please answer my question."

"Yeah, well, as I said, people came and went, mostly girls, if you

16

wanna know the truth. It made it pretty hard for me, actually. Some mornings there'd be so many beer cans lying around the place, you just about needed a pickup truck to haul 'em off. J. J. was a real swinger."

"Could you give me any names of the people who were in and out of here recently?"

She shrugged. "Not really. I didn't want to get too involved. It was sort of a sleazoid scene, actually. I did my job, minded my own business. I was just the maid," she added ruefully.

Nicky had a feeling there was a lot he should be asking her. But for now, too many other matters demanded immediate attention. He tried one last question. "When you arrived this morning, did you notice anything unusual?"

"Yeah! There was a fucking body at the foot of the stairs."

Nicky smiled, model of patience that he was. "I mean besides that," he explained. "Something not in its normal place? A funny smell, perhaps?"

"Hey, now that you mention it, there *was* a smell."

"Yes?" he encouraged.

She seemed to be doing some kind of inner Stanislavsky memory exercise.

"It was like . . . like sex," she said at last.

"Could you explain that?"

"Like sex and gunfire, all mixed together," she told him, a bit too rapturously. "Come and cordite," she added. "Like someone really shot their wad."

The thought seemed to stimulate her. Nicky took her address so he might question her at a later date, and he sent her away fast.

4

"Lieutenant, there's a bunch of reporters outside waiting for some kind of statement, sir." It was the uniformed sergeant with the pockmarked face.

Nicky sighed. "Vultures," he mumbled.

"Pardon me, sir?"

"Let them wait."

Nicky wanted to browse through the house to try to get some sense of Jay Jeffries' life. He began downstairs, passing through a small dining room that had the appearance of being seldom used, to the kitchen beyond, dazzling white and clean. The kitchen contained every modern convenience, but it seemed to Nicky basically a sterile and unappetizing place. Part of the reason the room was so unappetizing right now was the contents of the garbage disposal. Two crime lab people in white jumpsuits were in the process of taking the sink apart, fishing out some very unpleasant bits and pieces with long tweezers.

He directed his attention away from the gore and toward the refrigerator. Nicky generally took refrigerators very seriously. This one revealed a man at war with himself. Low-calorie diet dinners stood next to chocolate marshmallow cookies; yogurt, grapefruit, and diet sodas alongside pastries and imported beer. Every bin and shelf was crammed to overflowing; you could feed an entire African village from this refrigerator for a week.

Of course, this was Beverly Hills. He sometimes imagined a book he would probably never write: *Certain Conclusions Regarding the Citizens of Beverly Hills as Revealed by the Contents of Their Refrigerators* by Lt. N. Rachmaninoff. The reader would discover the vast insecurity that lies behind wealth—the spiritual hunger that tries to lull itself to sleep with tidbits of lobster and liver pâté. Nicky closed Jay Jeffries' refrigerator door with some difficulty, squeezing a half-eaten turkey back toward the salmon mousse.

He left the kitchen gladly, passed through the dining room, and came again to the foot of the stairs. Jason Whittle gave him a pair of plastic booties to put over his shoes, as well as some latex gloves, so that he would not disturb any evidence. At the top of the stairs there was a small landing. Nicky paused here for a moment, looking down at the corpse.

This is where Jay Jeffries had been standing, naked except for his robe, with the killer behind him. An intimate tableau. Had they been coming out of the bedroom? One thing was certain: the person who murdered Jay Jeffries had been no stranger to be upstairs in his house late at night.

Standing at this intersection with death caused a shiver to pass through his body. Nicky turned and continued toward the master bedroom, which was off the landing to the right.

The bedroom confirmed what the maid had told him. Jay Jeffries had been a swinger. The room was set up for maximum pleasure of the senses. There was a large waterbed surrounded by mirrors on every wall and a mirror on the ceiling as well. Jay could lie on the bed and observe himself from five different views. The room also

18

had a number of electronic gadgets: quadraphonic speakers, one in each corner, and an expensive television console and videocassette player built into one wall, positioned so it could be easily watched from the waterbed.

The sheets on the bed were black satin, and they were in disarray. A zebra-striped bedspread lay where it had been tossed onto the floor.

Had Jay been having sex right before he was killed? Perhaps there was a nice fat pubic hair in these tangled sheets with a killer's name on it.

Nicky let his gaze fall at random about the room. On a bedside table he found copies of *Penthouse, Oui,* and other magazines less slick and more graphic. There was also a small bookshelf where Jay Jeffries had kept his video collection. Nicky did not expect to find any old Ingmar Bergman titles, and he was right. J. J.'s video library consisted of *Debbie Does Dallas, Deep Throat,* and others with names like *Cruisin' for a Bruisin', Vicious Virgins,* and *Babysitters in Bondage.* One of the tapes on the shelf was unmarked. It appeared homemade. Nicky took the tape out of its plastic case and slipped it into the VCR. The TV screen came alive.

The scene was this room. The camera was in close on the bed. A naked Jay Jeffries was frollicking with a young lady.

"Oh," she moaned, "fuck me with your big dick."

It was definitely grade-B dialogue. The girl looked like a hooker going through the motions of lust with less than total enthusiasm. Still, Jay Jeffries appeared to be enjoying himself.

Nicky fast-forwarded the tape, stopping every few seconds at a different pornographic vignette. Sometimes there were two women, at other times just one—but J. J. was always the star attraction, lounging in the center of the waterbed with a big grin. Nicky found it difficult to look at the man's luridly photographed erection without thinking about the contents of the garbage disposal downstairs.

He wondered who had taken these videos. Nicky saw no sign of any video equipment in the bedroom. Perhaps it had been set up on a tripod and had been recorded automatically? He noticed that the camera angle never changed, which might indicate the lack of a human operator.

He turned off the machine and slipped the videocassette into his coat pocket. Sometime later he would have to study this tape more carefully and find out the identity of the various people in it. If he were lucky, he might delegate the task to someone else.

This sad house was starting to weigh more and more on his spirits.

Nicky moved quickly now, glancing in the closet to find more clothes than any one person would ever need, and then into the bathroom, which was everything a Beverly Hills bathroom should be, complete with sunken tub, Jacuzzi, telephone, portable TV, two sinks, and enough drugs—uppers and downers—to meet the demands of any situation.

In the bathroom, Nicky also ran into a strange man in the mirror: tall, still good-looking (despite some wear and tear), peering back at him with dubious eyes. There was more gray in the unruly thicket of hair than he had noticed before. The stranger looked as if he could use a good long vacation in the sun. The brown eyes in the mirror also had too intense a focus and seemed to say to him: *Shit, what are you doing here, browsing through some dead man's bathroom? Don't you have a life of your own someplace?*

Nicky turned away from himself and walked back into the bedroom of Jay Jeffries, terminal L.A. swinger. He gave the room a final glance. Despite all the gadgetry and paraphernalia of pleasure, Nicky's verdict was that this was the domain of a lonely man.

Back at the top of the stairs, he noticed a grouping of framed photographs on the wall showing J. J. with a number of celebrities: sharing a laugh with Elton John; making funny faces with Madonna; looking quite debonair with Mick Jagger. They were the usual industry photos taken at various functions. In them, Jeffries appeared a slightly overweight figure, not handsome, not ugly—a person who would not be noticed in a crowd and whose smile seemed forced and hollow.

Nicky's glance wandered slowly across the wall, came to an older photograph, and froze.

"Christ!" he muttered. "I don't fucking believe it."

"What's that, Nicholas?" Jason Whittle asked from the bottom of the stairs. "Find anything?"

Nicky shook his head. What he had found completely altered the nature of this case, yet it would have been difficult to explain to Jason. At least he now knew why the name Jay Jeffries was so persistently familiar.

The photograph showed four young men with long hair gazing back at the camera with a combination of bemusement and arrogance. Jay was the second from the left. He was wearing a paisley shirt and a jacket without a collar. The picture must have been taken around 1967, when Jay Jeffries had been the drummer for a group known as the Perceptions.

This was back when even Nicky liked rock and roll, and the

20

Perceptions had been his favorite group of all. Just seeing the publicity still with the old hairstyles and clothes took Nicky on a fast trip back to his youth.

And then standing next to Jay Jeffries was the lead singer, that mad, self-destructive genius of rock and roll: Billy Lion.

5

Det. Sgt. Charles Katz—Charlie Cat to his friends—was standing by the foot of the stairs looking at the dead VJ when Nicky joined him.

"How's it, brah?" Charlie asked absently. The Cat was recently returned from three weeks in Hawaii and had been interjecting island slang into their conversations ever since. Today he was wearing a glossy green aloha shirt that showed bright tropical flowers intermixed with dancing hula girls. Just a few years back, a shirt like this would have epitomized bad taste, but Charlie assured him that right now it was very in. Very rock and roll.

"Man, this is brutal," Charlie said with some emotion, glancing over Nicky's shoulder toward the living room. It took Nicky a moment to realize the sergeant wasn't referring to the murder but to the decor of the house.

"Man, Elvis Presley above a fake fireplace!" he said mournfully. "Did you notice, it's one of those trick paintings where the eyes follow you around the room? I mean, speaking of deadly assault, this place is murder on the eyeballs."

"People wearing aloha shirts shouldn't talk about bad taste," Nicky told him.

Charlie sputtered indignantly and clutched his side to show he'd been shot down. Charlie was a clown. He was also Nicky's partner. Together they comprised two-thirds of the Beverly Hills homicide squad. The remaining third was Theo Oshimoto, whom they had recently recruited from traffic to help out with the paperwork.

"I wish people wouldn't find bodies so early in the morning," Charlie complained. "I mean, I was about to grind some breakfast —that's what they say in the islands, you know. You don't eat, you grind, brah. Pretty cool, eh?"

Nicky wasn't listening. He was staring at the corpse on the floor with renewed fascination.

"Jesus, I wonder what happened to him?" he asked quietly.

"Well, offhand, Nick, I'd say the guy's been murdered."

Nicky gave his partner a tired look. "I don't mean that. Do you know who this guy was?"

"Sure. Jay Jeffries, the world's oldest VJ. The guy could talk sixty miles an hour. He had a show five mornings a week on The Rock Channel."

"I mean before he was a VJ. Before all *this*," Nicky explained, gesturing with distaste to the gaudy Beverly Hills house. "He used to be a musician, the drummer for the best American rock band of the sixties."

"Jeffries was one of the Monkees?" Charlie asked. "No kidding?"

Nicky's mouth opened in surprise. "Not the Monkees, you asshole. The Perceptions."

Charlie said, "Oh." He didn't seem impressed. "So that was your favorite band, huh?"

"Yes, of course. It was the *only* American band that combined serious lyrics with great music."

Charlie looked doubtful. "Yeah? Well, personally I always found the Perceptions a little too arty-farty for my taste. Kind of hard to dance to, know what I mean?"

"Kind of hard to dance to," Nicky repeated. He was stunned. "Charlie, I never realized you were such a Philistine."

"Hey, Nicky, each to his own. Personally I never even listen to the lyrics, man. I just like to move the old bod, preferably in unison with some sweet slinky thing."

Charlie did a little dance step around the corpse. The burning question of which was the ultimate American band of the sixties caught hold around the room. The uniformed sergeant with the pockmarked face said it was the Four Tops, while one of the lab technicians suggested the Beach Boys.

"Bullshit," said the coroner. "The best American band of the sixties was the Moody Blues."

This was greeted with derisive laughter. No one liked the coroner anyway. "Those assholes were English," someone said.

"Hell they were!" protested the coroner.

"Hell they weren't," came the spirited reply. " 'Knights in White Satin' was recorded with the London Philharmonic. I mean, does that *suggest* anything to you?"

Nicky was amazed at what he had let loose. "Come on, let's get out of here," he said to Charlie.

"Where to, O Exalted Leader?"

"Let's try The Rock Channel. You know where their studios are?"

"Sure. In the valley, a few blocks from Warner Brothers. Hey, they got some pretty girls over there, I bet."

Nicky grunted irritably and led the way outside, where they were greeted by the hungry faces of the press. Microphones and camera lenses immediately converged upon them.

"Lieutenant Rachmaninoff, can you tell us the circumstances of Jay Jeffries' death?"

"No comment at this time."

"Do you have any suspects? . . . What was the murder weapon? . . . Can we get a photograph inside the house?"

All the questions came at once and merged together into a vague sea sound. Nicky muttered something about a possible statement later in the afternoon and kept moving through the crowd. The sky above them was full of dark clouds, alternating with shafts of fierce sunlight—a miracle sky full of storm and salvation. Charlie slipped on his tan raincoat over his aloha shirt, and Nicky turned up the collar of his brown corduroy jacket.

"Can you tell us if burglary was involved, Lieutenant?"

Nicky shook his head.

The palm trees along the street danced in the quickening wind.

6

Locals called it Black Beauty, though the real name of the building was Inter Stellar Village, after its main tenant, the Inter Stellar Group—an amorphous entertainment combine with long arms.

The building was the latest version of modern, with an open courtyard in the center and shafts of black glass and steel rising thirty-two stories above the valley floor, higher than anything surrounding it—looking down upon two movie studios, Bob Hope's backyard, a golf course, a freeway, and the endless ozone of suburbs and car lots that spread out into the smoggy horizon.

In the main lobby downstairs was an indoor waterfall that came cascading down a wall of shiny black marble. Even the directory was impressive. Black Beauty was home for The Rock Channel, two major record labels, several independent television companies, an insurance corporation, a brokerage firm, a bank, five restaurants, legions of layers, and more. The security on the ground floor was intense. Nicky used some charm and a little force to get him and Charlie shown up to the executive suite on the thirty-second floor.

They went up in a special elevator to the reception area at the very top of the building. Money whispered very loudly at these heights. A secretary with golden hair bade them sit on a beige sofa that was so soft it seemed to float. The young lady, who looked as expensive as the furniture, offered them coffee, tea, or perhaps a glass of champagne. She was a thoughtful hostess.

"That's you," Charlie told her. "Isn't it? I just know it is!"

He was looking at a Picasso on the wall behind her. The painting was from the cubist period—a naked woman with two noses and three breasts.

The girl glanced at the Picasso and smiled. "I only have one nose," she said.

"I'm wild about girls with only one nose," he confessed, leaning across her desk. Charlie just couldn't help trying. He was short, round, dark, and sensual—not exactly Robert Redford, but he did amazingly well with women. He was making some slight progress when a light flickered on her desk and she said they could go in now.

"You ever need some help with a parking ticket, you let me know, you hear?"

"Mmm . . . I like to park," she told him.

Nicky grabbed his partner's arm. The name on the door they entered was Bo Daniels, president of the Inter Stellar Group. The office was a corner suite with two entire walls of tinted glass, floor to ceiling, overlooking the sound stages of a movie studio far below. The thick beige carpet seemed to run off into empty space. A proud semicircle of a desk stood near the apex where the glass walls came together. The people in the room, however, were all gathered around a coffee table on sofas in the opposite corner.

The president of the Inter Stellar Group had stood up from an armchair and was coming toward them. He was not quite as impressive as his office.

"I'm Bo Daniels," he said, shaking hands. "You must be Lieutenant Tchaikovsky."

"Rachmaninoff," Nicky corrected.

Bo Daniels looked like a scrawny kid in need of a haircut, not the chief executive of a multimillion-dollar communications empire. He was dressed in ragged tennis shoes that had once been white, faded blue jeans, and a black sleeveless T-shirt that had PARTY NAKED written across the front in large white letters. The face was tan but unhealthy, half-hidden by a rock haircut, a mane of curly black hair that covered his ears and rolled partway down his back.

"So Jay's dead, huh?" he asked with a sigh. "Well, another one bites the dust," he added philosophically. "I've seen 'em come, I've seen 'em go. But Jay . . ."

"You were the guitar player," Nicky said.

Bo smiled thinly. "No, I played the drums for a while before Jay came into the group. But I could hardly keep the beat. I was the manager. Rick here played the guitar. You're lucky, Lieutenant. You've found all the old Perceptions gathered today. All the ones who are left."

Nicky had been so struck by the unusual appearance of Bo Daniels that he had not even glanced at the others in the room. Bo made some introductions.

"Rick Elsmore, king of guitar," he said grandly, gesturing to a lanky figure in a wrinkled white linen suit who was sprawled across a couch, languidly sipping on a Bloody Mary.

"Donny Meredith, monster of the keyboards. . . ."

Once the most notable member of the group after Billy Lion, now a dour middle-aged man beginning to bald, dressed in a blue blazer and gray slacks.

"And our oldest groupie, Marilyn de Malibu."

"Ms. de Malibu," Charlie said gallantly as he took her hand. She was a handsome blond, with closely cropped hair, somewhere in her forties. She studied the policemen with cool brown eyes, then looked away. Rick Elsmore and Donny Meredith hardly looked at them at all.

"Well, sit down, gentlemen, please," Bo suggested. "How about a coupla Bloody Marys? Frankly, we're all sitting around getting sloshed. This was supposed to be a business meeting to discuss the special award we're going to get at the Grammys in two weeks, but with J. J. dead . . ."

Bo Daniels wasn't a man to finish a sentence. Maybe when you were as rich as he was, you could let other people do that for you.

Nicky sat way back on a sofa and declined anything to drink. He noticed a large TV console next to the bar. The volume was off, but the picture showed what was either a rock video or an elaborate commercial for tight blue jeans.

"Can you tell me the last time you saw Jay Jeffries?" Nicky began. Not a profound question. Not "Have you found Jesus?" Or even

25

"Do you prefer Tolstoy to Dostoyevski?" Still, it was a question, and Nicky was annoyed when it wasn't answered.

Bo held up a hand for him to shut up while he simultaneously turned up the volume of the TV with a remote control on the coffee table.

"Gotta see this," he said. "Won't take a minute."

What Bo had to see was a close-up of an astonishingly pretty young girl, who was talking breathlessly about the videos that were coming up in the next twenty minutes—Prince, The Cure, Tina Turner, Don Johnson, A-Ha. She said the name of the last group as if she were having a small orgasm.

"Great!" Bo exclaimed, clapping his hands together. "Hot damn!"

Even the trio around the coffee table—Rick, Donny, and Marilyn de Malibu—looked momentarily less sullen and watched the TV screen with interest.

On the screen, the girl smiled charmingly, as if she knew everyone would have to love her. She had rich reddish-brown hair that fell about her face in many small ringlets. There were a few freckles on her pert little nose. All in all, there was a clean and windswept look to her, as if she had just come in from a long poetic walk on the beach. She was the girl next door and them some. The "then some" lay mostly in her eyes, which were an intense shade of deepest blue, nearly violet. It was a color you might see at thirty-five thousand feet if you looked out of your jet window upward to the heavens. The eyes dominated the TV screen, peering into the living rooms of America.

"All right!" Bo told everyone. "So what do you think? Huh?"

"Great," answered Rick, Donny, and Marilyn—nearly in unison, like a Greek chorus.

"Was I right? Or was I right?" Bo gloated.

"You sure were right, Bo," they told him.

Bo Daniels smiled complacently at Nicky. "You're going to be seeing a lot of this young lady—mark my words, Lieutenant. Her name's Unity Sphere. The next teen sex goddess of America."

"Wow," said Nicky. The girl on the TV screen was busy showing her perfect white teeth to the camera. She seemed very excited to be doing what she was doing. She spoke with a very slight lisp, but she was so sparkling, brand-new pretty that it hardly mattered.

"She's taking over Jeffries' show?" Nicky asked.

"Exactly. She was J. J.'s assistant. Occasionally we gave her special assignments, so she's been on camera before. But this is her first real break. Kinda exciting, huh? Frankly, Lieutenant, I think she's headed all the way to the top."

"How fortunate for her," Nicky said. "And for you, too, Mr. Daniels. Good thing J. J. had the sense to get himself killed."

Bo Daniels was watching the girl's lead-in to the next video, so he missed Nicky's remark. "Guess how old she is?" he invited.

Nicky studied the girl in the box. "Nineteen?" he offered. "Twenty?"

"*Seventeen*," Bo replied. "Can you believe it?"

"Isn't that awfully young to have her own TV show?"

Bo just smiled. "Not for this kind of channel," he said. "Guess the age of our average viewer."

"Seven?"

Bo scowled. "Twelve," he corrected. "That makes Unity a role model, you see. Someone the kids can relate to. All the girls want to look like her, all the guys fantasize taking her to their senior prom. Which makes her perfect, absolutely fucking perfect!"

"I see," Nicky replied. "How about J. J.? How fucking perfect was he?"

The president of the Inter Stellar Group emitted a great sigh. He shook his head sadly. "Look, I loved J. J. as a brother. I knew him, what—a quarter of a goddamn century, through more ups and downs than you can probably imagine, Lieutenant. Quite honestly, I gave him the show because he had his heart set on being a VJ, and I loved the guy too fucking much to say no."

"I can see friendship means a great deal to you, Mr. Daniels."

"Everything," Bo admitted. "We're all family here. Isn't that right?"

"That's right, Bo," said the Greek chorus.

"The problem with J. J., you see—he was just too old."

Nicky turned off the TV set with the remote control on the table. This was a serious accusation, and he wanted to deal with it without distractions.

In Hollywood, getting too old was even worse than murder.

7

Nicky needed to know how a radical rock group of the sixties had managed to catapult itself into a communications empire of the eighties. It seemed an unlikely situation, and Bo Daniels was only too happy to give the two cops a brief history of how it had come to pass.

In the beginning there were two friends, Billy and Bo, inseparable high school buddies who lived near each other in a quiet suburban neighborhood south of San Francisco. In 1962 they were the two oddballs of their class: Bo, the school's best student, seminerd, whose grades were too good; Billy, the school troublemaker, whose grades were lousy and who constantly asked rude and embarrassing questions of his teachers in class. Bo and Billy found each other at the end of an era.

It wasn't long before they started cutting classes to go into San Francisco to hang around the beatnik sections of North Beach, listening to Lawrence Ferlinghetti and black jazz. Billy's main hero was Jack Kerouac. Billy and Bo read *On the Road* aloud together and vowed to live just like Dean Moriarty. In this holy quest, they discovered booze and pot and cool bebop ladies who did some things the nice girls back in the suburbs would not have considered.

After high school Bo was accepted at U.C.L.A., and Billy—whose grades precluded the opportunity of a college education—followed his friend to the southland for the hell of it. They got an apartment together on the outskirts of the Westwood campus. The year was 1964. Billy decided that rock and roll was the mainline to liberation. American Zen. The apartment he shared with Bo soon became the focal point for endless parties, orgies of talk and offbeat ideas. Billy was a natural leader. A scene coalesced around his boundless energy, and out of his enthusiasm a rock group was born: the Perceptions. Billy saw music as the new alchemy that was going to take his whole generation to a place of love and freedom.

His ideas were in tune with the time. The musicians of the band were all U.C.L.A. students who were glad to exchange academics for rock and roll, sex, and drugs. Rick Elsmore had been in prelaw, Donny Meredith was from the film school, and Jay Jeffries was a fraternity boy who drifted into the scene one Saturday night and never left. None of them had had any musical training except Donny, who had played classical piano as a child. This troubled no one. They learned as they went along, picking up the necessary skills over the next five years. Billy wrote the lyrics, and the music rose— as Bo put it—from the "spontaneous combustion of stoned telepathy."

By late 1965, the Perceptions had become the house band for the prestigious Whisky à Go-Go on the Sunset Strip, and in 1966 their

28

single, "Streets of Love," had become the number-one hit around the country. It was a heady time. All things seemed possible. From 1966 to 1970, the Perceptions gathered fame, fortune, a string of gold albums, and an assortment of bad habits and expensive hobbies. Billy continued to be the artistic impulse, and Bo took care of the business. The two high school buddies from Northern California took their friendship a long, long way.

And then in the summer of 1970, Billy Lion died in a bathtub in Rome, and it was all over.

"Like a fucking rocket ship," Bo said. "There we were, rising toward the heavens, burning, burning . . . then *poof!* ultimate explosion, and there we were, coming down in flames."

Bo sat on the edge of the beige sofa, orchestrating the story with his hands. A strange little man in his PARTY NAKED T-shirt: it would be easy not to take him seriously. Yet Nicky could sense the obsessive energy and egomania of a true Hollywood tycoon.

"It wasn't just the drugs"—Bo was explaining about Billy's death —"it was the alcohol that did him in. Goddamn Jack Daniel's. He became so bloated the last few years, we couldn't even use his photographs on the albums. It was heartbreaking, really, but that's the way it is sometimes with genius, you know."

"What was the exact cause of death?" Nicky asked.

"No one ever exactly knew," Bo said carefully. "Heart failure is what the Italian authorities said. You see, it was such a hot day, and Billy was so overweight—he got into a tub of cold water, and it was just too much for him. His poor heart just stopped beating. Kind of ironic, really, when you consider all the abuse he did to himself—cold water got him in the end. But it was just the last straw. Billy was killing himself for years."

Bo leaned back again into the sofa. "I loved that son of a bitch," he proclaimed. "Well, for a few years it seemed that was the end of us. We made one more album with Donny singing the lead vocals— a hell of a good album, in fact—but no one wanted to listen to the Perceptions without Billy. Quite honestly, even if Billy had lived, I think we'd have had problems. By seventy-one, the whole hippie thing was dead on its feet. There was a new audience, and they didn't want revolution and all that crazy sixties shit. They didn't even want songs with long instrumental jams. Excess of every kind was out, and frankly, Lieutenant Tchaikovsky—"

"Rachmaninoff."

"Frankly, *I* saw it first. It was in the winter of 1972. Our fortunes

29

were at a low ebb. Everyone was broke. So I called a meeting with Donny and Jay and Rick. Right? And what did I tell you all?" Bo asked, looking at the lethargic figures on the couch. "Huh?"

Rick Elsmore appeared to be asleep. Donny Meredith gave a very small grunt. Marilyn de Malibu very thoughtfully rubbed her nose.

"I told 'em, let's not be fucking dinosaurs," Bo continued. "I said, dinosaurs die because they can't evolve, they refuse to accept new circumstances. So I asked 'em—do you want to die, or do you want to live? Do you want to be a miserable broke has-been *ex*-rock band? Or would you like to be fucking multimillionaires? And you know what the answer was?"

"I can't imagine," Nicky said.

"Everyone but Rick here said okay, Bo—let's live. Let's make money. Rick wanted to be a dinosaur, okay—we bought him out. Columbia had just given us twenty-five grand to cancel our contract with them, and that's all we had. We gave six thousand two hundred and fifty bucks to Rick—which lasted exactly three weeks, right, Rick?—and with the rest of the cash we set up a corporation, Lion Enterprises, Inc. The first thing we did was start to manage other bands. Seventies-type bands, all nice and polite and proper, bands that could have played the Republican National Convention. We didn't care. Within a year, we started to diversify. We bought an AM radio station in Dallas, then three months after that an FM station here in L.A. A year later we had a string of stations across the country and a record label in Philadelphia. By the end of the decade, the whole dream was beginning to come together. Musicians in our stable recorded on labels we owned and were played on our radio stations."

A nifty setup for a megalomaniac, thought Nicky.

"And then came the flash point," Bo said. "The big bang. You know what it was, Lieutenant? Rock television. Music videos. I mean, *flash!* Suddenly we were all this. Not just a corporation anymore, but Inter Stellar Village. And you know who thought of rock television? Whose goddamn idea it was? *Billy Lion's,* that's whose."

"How's that, Mr. Daniels?"

"Let me tell you—Billy was a fucking genius."

"You told me that already."

"No! I mean it. When I think of that guy's *monster* intellect, I'm staggered. Like totally in awe. Billy came up with the idea for music videos after he read that Huxley book, *Brave New Village. . . .*"

"*Brave New World,*" Nicky said.

30

"Whatever." Bo glowered. "This must have been about 1968. Billy said to me one night about three o'clock in the morning—he'd just come out with these *monster* statements, you see—he said, the two most potent forces in the twentieth century, after the atom bomb, are rock and roll and television. Put them together and you could control the world. That's what Billy told me. Does it boggle your mind, Lieutenant, that one person could be that fucking smart?"

Nicky smiled vaguely. He was fairly certain he had just heard Bo Daniels's innermost ambition. He would rule a teenage tomorrow beneath curly hair and a PARTY NAKED T-shirt, the emperor of Rock and Roll.

Nicky turned his attention to the reposing form of Rick Elsmore, who was stretched out on the sofa.

"Mr. Elsmore, I'm curious why you didn't join the others in forming Lion Enterprises."

"He was an asshole," Bo said, unwilling to give up center stage. "He would have been a millionaire now like the rest of us."

"Mr. Elsmore?" Nicky persisted.

Rick Elsmore opened his eyes. "I like being a dinosaur," he said briefly, then closed his eyes once more.

Bo laughed loudly. "You see! What a jerk. But we take care of old Rick anyway, even though he didn't have the faith. Don't we? We're just one big family. Billy was our founding father, so to speak, and we've stayed together through thick and thin."

"Through blood and booze," Rick agreed, not opening his eyes.

Donny Meredith snickered, and Marilyn de Malibu went to the bar to make up another round of Bloody Marys.

"Let's get back to Jay Jeffries," Nicky suggested. "Can you tell me what sort of person he was? Who were his friends? His enemies?"

"Hey, we all loved J. J.," Bo answered. "He was always the clown, the guy who made us laugh. What he was, Lieutenant—J. J. was a forty-four-year-old teenager. I guess he never grew up."

Nicky contemplated the idea of a forty-four-year-old teenager and didn't like it much. "His maid described him as a swinger," he said. "Judging from his bedroom, he seemed to have a fairly ornate sex life."

Bo Daniels lit a Dunhill cigarette in one fast, angry motion. "For Christ's sake, Lieutenant, this is Hollywood we're living. Life in the fast lane. J. J. was a big boy—what the hell do you expect?"

"Oh, I don't know. A little decency is always nice." Nicky was

31

puzzled by Bo's sudden belligerence. He decided to press the issue and see where it led. "For instance, Mr. Jeffries seemed to have an inclination to record his little orgies on videotape. Some of the girls looked awfully young—underage, I should say."

Bo snorted smoke through his nostrils in a good imitation of a dragon. "Damn it, you're not going to start a lot of muckraking, are you? Because if you are, I warn you, I'm *not* going to have the reputation of The Rock Channel dragged through the mud. I have friends, Lieutenant—important friends—who can bust your ass to meter maid if you start making unfounded accusations. You understand me?"

Nicky smiled blandly. He was beginning to understand what was bothering the great man. "Please, Mr. Daniels, if it's publicity you're afraid of, maybe we should continue this conversation back at the station. We have rooms there that are incredibly discreet. Isn't that right, Sergeant?"

"Most discreet," Charlie agreed. "No one ever finds out what goes on in *those* rooms."

Bo opened his mouth in shock. "Are you threatening me?" he demanded. "You hear that? They're *threatening* me!" he complained to his Greek chorus. "Well, let me tell you, gentlemen—I can have *ten* lawyers here in *five* minutes to take care of you guys."

"Fine, " Nicky agreed, standing up. "Tell them to meet you at the Beverly Hills police station. We'll be holding you as a material witness for a day or so. We'll certainly try to make you comfortable, though I can't guarantee—"

"Whoa, Lieutenant! Let's not get off on a wrong foot here. If we can talk off the record, maybe we can deal with this in a more informal manner. I'm an awfully busy man, you know. *Awfully* busy."

"Naturally, Mr. Daniels," Nicky reassured him, sitting down again. "No one wants to harass you. We only want to find out who killed Jay Jeffries."

Bo moaned self-indulgently. "I should have known that son of a bitch would be as big a pain in the ass dead as he was alive."

"What exactly was the problem, Mr. Daniels?"

"The problem?" the executive repeated in sheer exasperation. "Look, I'm no prude, but common sense must prevail. The Rock Channel has to be especially careful these days, with all the Jerry Falwell types in Washington, and what's her name—the one who's married to that senator? They think we're corrupting the nation, for God's sake! One false move and they'll shut us down."

"And Jay Jeffries' life-style didn't help much," Nicky suggested sympathetically.

"You can't imagine what I've been up against," Bo complained, leaning forward confidentially. "Hey, I didn't mind him knocking up sixteen-year-old girls and having to pay off their parents—no sweat, what are friends for? I could even live with the arrests for drunken driving, and the cocaine charges I arranged to have dropped. But Pubic Telephone, that was the last straw."

"I see. And what exactly was Pubic Telephone, Mr. Daniels?"

Bo looked surprised. "A rock band, of course. They are the people who threatened to kill him."

Nicky nodded sagely. "Why don't you start at the beginning, Mr. Daniels."

The tycoon gave Nicky a most crucified look.

"Well, it was like this. Three weeks ago I'm at home in my hot tub when I get a call from the station telling me I should turn on my TV quick. So I do that, and what do I see? Holy fuck, we're running some black-and-white monstrosity from this group, Pubic Telephone—which up to that moment, thank God, I had never heard of. The song's called 'The Punishment of Love,' and the video's all bondage stuff with Ginny Gina, the lead singer—that's right, her name rhymes with vagina—she's chained to the wall in a leather harness with her tits hanging out. You get the picture? I almost had a heart attack watching the thing. Just that morning there had been a big article in the trades about explicit sexual content in videos, how if the industry didn't start showing some sense, the government would soon be making our choices for us. So I get on the phone and I do some serious yelling. J. J. cries and begs and finally convinces me not to fire him until he can come over to the house and explain. So he comes over, I hear his story, and I give him one more chance—but maybe that was my mistake. Maybe J. J. would be alive now if I *had* fired him."

"What did he tell you?"

"He was in love, that's what he said. In love with Ginny Gina, who's sixteen or seventeen, I don't remember—jail bait, anyway. And of course Jay's in a real bind, as usual. It seems the girl's screwing him because he's promised to make her a big star. Unfortunately, Ginny has a real boyfriend, Tommy Torch, who's the keyboard player in the band. Tommy's putting up with the situation, hoping to get some mileage from it himself, his big break on The Rock Channel. Jay's made a hell of a lot of promises he knows he can't keep, but he's managed to string them both along for a month

33

or two, until it's obvious he's full of shit. So Tommy goes a little crazy. I mean, he's probably not too thrilled about Ginny screwing this dude in the first place. When he realizes he's being jerked around, he totally freaks out. He goes over to J. J.'s house in Beverly, knocks him around some, and says if he doesn't come through and play 'The Punishment of Love' the very next day on his show, Tommy is going to come back and kill him."

"Uh-huh," Nicky said, looking over to Charlie, who was taking notes furiously in shorthand. "You're certain this Tommy Torch character actually made a threat against J. J.'s life?"

"I'm not certain of any of it," Bo said. "All I'm telling you is what J. J. told me. The exact threat, if I remember, was that if J. J. didn't play the video, Tommy was going to cut off his balls and grind them down the garbage disposal."

Charlie looked up from his notebook, and the two policemen exchanged a glance.

"Mr. Daniels, do you know where I can find Tommy and Ginny?"

"I don't have the faintest idea, Lieutenant. I never met them, and I never want to. Kids like that are ruining the business."

Marilyn de Malibu spoke up unexpectedly. "The tape's still down in Studio A, Bo. It will have the credits on it and the address of their production company."

"There you are, then," Bo said, standing up to indicate the interview was at an end. "Marilyn, my dear, why don't you take these gentlemen down to Studio A so they can get the address of these unpleasant little punks who murdered J. J. And then we can be finished with all this."

Nicky stood up, followed by Charlie.

"You have any more questions, don't hesitate to give me a call," Bo said, offering his hand. "Good to meet you, Stravinsky. You too, Sergeant . . . sorry, I never caught your name."

"Mozart," Charlie told him. "But you can call me Mo."

8

Marilyn de Malibu led the way to the elevator. She had a brisk walk with a lot of sway in it. At one time she must have been quite a beauty, but now her features seemed a little hard.

"So tell me—what does the oldest groupie do around here?"

Nicky asked. She didn't seem inclined toward excessive conversation.

"I'm in publicity," she managed.

"Ah!" Nicky said as if this explained everything. "Can you tell me, Marilyn—was the threat against Jay Jeffries' life general knowledge?"

"Probably. I dunno," she said. "It's pretty hard to keep a secret in this place. The Pubic Telephone video attracted a lot of attention, so I guess people were talking about it."

"I see," Nicky responded bleakly. He wanted to believe the Pubic Telephone angle might lead to a quick solution. However, with a large number of people knowing about the threat, there was always the possibility that someone other than Tommy Torch had taken advantage of the situation for reasons of his own.

The elevator took them to the seventh floor, where Marilyn led the way down a long, uncarpeted hallway. They passed a door leading to makeup and came at last to a windowless room where there was a coffee machine, a line of chairs, and a television monitor. Pretty Unity Sphere was on the screen sharing some gossip with her viewers about Janet Jackson's love life. If people in this building were upset about Jay Jeffries' death, they were certainly doing a good job of hiding it.

Nicky and Charlie and Marilyn de Malibu stood in the waiting room in front of the monitor until the image of Unity Sphere was replaced by a commercial. The red light above the thick studio door blinked off.

"We can go in now," Marilyn told them, pushing open the door. The inner studio was a vast open stage divided into a number of individual sets—small habitats such as you might find at the Museum of Natural History: idealized living rooms, bedrooms without beds, dens, and game rooms, all missing a fourth wall and ceiling. Along with the sets was a jungle of cameras and cables and lights. The crew at the moment was busy relaxing, taking advantage of being off the air.

Unity Sphere was sitting in a perfectly pink bedroom, bathed in a wash of light from the rafters above. She saw Marilyn on the other side of the cameras, stood up, and hurried over.

"Well?" she asked, taking Marilyn by the hand. "Tell me, tell me! You know I can't *stand* the suspense. What did Bo say? Am I going to get the show?"

At this moment the girl didn't look like anyone's image of a future sex symbol, but more like a child the night before Christmas. She hung on to the older woman and actually jumped up and down.

"My dear, the police are here and want a word with you," Marilyn said quietly.

Unity's girlish energy faded fast. Her eyes followed Marilyn's glance toward the Law.

"Oh!" she exclaimed.

Her near violet eyes came to rest on Nicky. She studied him somberly as if she had never seen a policeman before, and Nicky looked back at her just as hard. Unity was smaller than she appeared on television—which is often the case. Her figure, however, was full and catlike and sexy. She was dressed in white—white tights and a kind of white muslin jersey that fell off one smooth shoulder and seemed to be held in place precariously by one perky breast. It was hard to say exactly where her beauty lay, except it was clearly brought into focus through her startling eyes.

"This is—"

"Lieutenant Nicholas Rachmaninoff," she finished. "Of course, I've seen your photograph in the papers."

The girl, for some reason, was blushing violently, making an obvious effort to recover her poise.

"You must think I'm horrid," she said. "God! Bouncing up and down at a time like this. Thinking about getting a silly TV show, when a man's been . . . murdered."

The pretty girl seemed to have to force herself to say such a horrible word as *murdered*. Nicky didn't blame her. "This is my assistant, Sergeant Katz," he said.

She seemed reluctant to take her eyes off Nicky and did so only for the briefest moment. Charlie, for his part, just about had his tongue hanging out.

"These men have come for the Pubic Telephone tape, my dear. Do you know where J. J. left it?" Marilyn put in. She seemed to be trying to speed things up.

Unity didn't seem to hear her. "You *do* think I'm horrid, don't you?" she asked. "All morning long I've been trying to feel sad about J. J.'s death, but I can't. I despised him, you see. Isn't that awful to say about someone who's dead?"

"Why did you despise him?" Nicky asked her gently. She looked as if she were about to cry.

"He was so crude. He always touched me and made disgusting jokes. For instance, whenever he saw me he'd make a big show of wiping his mouth with the back of his hand, and you know what he'd say? 'Come here, honey. I'm just clearing off a place for you to sit down.' Isn't that dis*gus*ting? And he said it to me *every* day!''

"This is a pretty tough world you've chosen," Nicky told her. "TV. Maybe you'd be better off going back to school or something. You could harden yourself more gradually to the real world."

"Oh, no!" she cried. "I couldn't do that. This is what I've always wanted. Anyway, you see, I'm an orphan. I don't have anything to fall back on. I *have* to succeed."

Nicky had a feeling it was time to get back to the subject at hand. "Now then, this video by Pubic Telephone . . ."

"Oh, yes. I'd better get that for you. I'm back on the air in three and a half minutes."

She turned and walked away with Marilyn at her side. Unity had a nice way of moving across a sound stage. All the crew smiled at her in a proprietary sort of way.

Nicky shook his head dreamily. "Jesus, seventeen years old," he said to Charlie. "Can you imagine being so young?"

"It's a young medium, television," Charlie answered. "And a young town. Pretty soon everyone over the age of nineteen is going to be shipped off to concentration camps outside of California."

Nicky was irritated by his partner's attitude. "Doesn't innocence get to you, just a little?" he asked. "Or has being a cop made you too hard?"

"In this case, I would tread very cautiously, my friend. This young girl's innocence is spelled u-n-d-e-r-a-g-e."

Nicky looked at Charlie in astonishment. "Jesus! What do you think I am? My interest in this child is completely—"

But she was coming back now, gliding through the room. "I hope you find whoever killed J. J.," Unity said as she handed him the plastic videocassette. The violet eyes again took him under intense consideration. "You must see such terrible things, Lieutenant Rachmaninoff. I don't envy you your job."

"Oh, it has its compensations." He smiled wanly. As Unity handed him the video, Nicky felt something else being passed into his hand. It was a piece of paper, which he palmed smoothly.

"Thirty seconds, Unity," someone called. "Places, everybody."

She gave him a final flash of violet, then hurried back to her perfect teenage bedroom beneath the bright lights.

"Oh, you must see such terrible things, Lieutenant Rachmaninoff!" Charlie mimicked as they walked away down the hall. He doubled over

in laughter. "Oh, Lieutenant Rachmaninoff, you big brutal cop, you!"

Nicky ignored him. In the elevator he opened up the piece of paper Unity had passed him with the videocassette. There was just a telephone number written hurriedly in pencil, and two words:

"Call me."

9

The true center of the Beverly Hills Police Department's homicide squad these days was a carefully restored 1959 sky-blue Chevrolet Impala, generally referred to as "The Yacht."

Charlie had found this vehicle in the station's basement garage, a black-and-white radio car left over from another era, which he had transformed over a period of six months into the envy of the department. He had even managed to gain official sanction for the project, convincing the bureaucracy that this would be the ultimate undercover car, since absolutely no one would believe such a machine belonged to the police.

When he was done, the Impala had a new V-8 engine, a heavily reinforced frame and suspension for high-speed driving, and numerous extras that were not available to the general public. Built into the dashboard was the latest multichannel radio-telephone from which they could talk to anywhere in the world. Hidden beneath the seats were two high-powered rifles, a shotgun, tear gas canisters, gas masks, and ammunition. Locked in the trunk was a very unregulation fully automatic assault rifle. They were ready for most of the sweet surprises the city of Los Angeles might offer.

Nor would they starve or lack for music. An expensive Blaupunkt sound system with four speakers and a graphic equalizer had appeared one day, as well as two ice chests in the trunk—one for liquids, the other for food. Charlie was very domestic in his own way. He had come up with the idea of a lunch kitty, where each of them put fifty dollars a week into a special envelope from which Charlie (never Nicky) would buy the supplies: an incredible assortment of deli items, fruit, mineral water, gourmet breads and cheeses, and imported beer. As Charlie often said, "We may be cops, but we don't have to be barbarians."

After leaving Inter Stellar Village, Charlie slipped a Mozart piano concerto onto the stereo and drove back toward Beverly Hills. It was early afternoon, getting on time for lunch. Friday was traditionally sushi day, and Charlie stopped off at a little place called Sushi on Sunset where their regular order was waiting for them—the sergeant occasionally dated one of the waitresses—and then they continued onward to have their midday picnic in an elegant little park near the Beverly Hills Hotel.

The had become connoisseurs of the small, seldom used parks of Beverly Hills, and this was one of their favorites. Usually when they stopped here, they sat on the manicured lawn near the old fish pond, where the fat carp glided in and out of the lilies. But today the sky had grown dark, and it looked as if the rain could come pouring down any moment, so they ended up eating out of the car with the curb door open. Charlie thought this was fairly uncivilized, but he puttered around in the ice chest and got things ready while Nicky made a few calls on the mobile telephone.

The first call was to Theo Oshimoto back at the office.

"Homicide," Theo answered happily, letting everyone know the grandeur of his position. Theo was a new addition to their department and he still thought of this as fun. Charlie had discovered him in the traffic department, an area Beverly Hills was big on. Officer Oshimoto had been one of the centurions of Rodeo Drive, patrolling the palm-lined streets in a three-wheeled motorcycle with a long antenna sticking out the back. Charlie thought he was funny, and it was his idea to move him up into homicide.

"You'll be our secretary," the sergeant assured him. "Answer the phone, take the messages, type up the reports. In a sense, *you* will run the department . . . since Lieutenant Rachmaninoff and I are hardly ever there."

Theo's presence in the office was the last part of the equation that allowed Nicky and Charlie to continually roam the streets in their sky-blue Impala—nomad policemen rarely seen at City Hall.

"Hi, boss!" Theo said agreeably. He was always agreeable, which sometimes drove Nicky nuts. "How are you on this beautiful day?"

"Mediumish," Nicky replied. "How are things at the office?"

"Wonderful, wonderful. Your beautiful wife just called."

"My *ex*-wife," Nicky reminded him.

"Yes, yes. So sad about that."

"Thanks, Theo. Now why did Susan call?"

"To say your daughter's orthodontist appointment has been changed to Wednesday the ninth at one o'clock."

"That's it? That's why she called?" Nicky was astonished. Had she really interrupted the filming of a major miniseries to call his office with this message? "What else is going on back there? Any *police* business, by some remote possibility?"

"Yes, various members of the press keep telephoning, requesting information regarding the deceased Jay Jeffries. I've been saying they should call back later this afternoon."

"Very good, Theo. Let me dictate a short statement you can give them. Let's see . . . 'The body of Jay Jeffries was discovered early Friday morning by his housecleaner. The exact time of death has yet to be established, though we believe it was approximately between eleven and twelve Thursday night. No suspects for the crime have yet been found, though the Beverly Hills Police Department is investigating several promising leads.' Blah blah blah. 'Anyone with information is urged to contact the homicide squad,' etcetera, etcetera. You know the routine, Theo. Just sound like you know a great deal but are not yet prepared to divulge your information to the press. You got it?"

Theo got it. Nicky hung up the phone. Charlie meanwhile had mixed up the hot green *wasabe*, cracked open two bottles of Japanese beer, and was arranging the sushi on a platter: all the octopus for him, the salmon for Nicky, and the tuna—which they both liked—divided between them. The sergeant very lovingly arranged the chopsticks and the small crock of soy sauce, or *shoyu*, as he called it more correctly. Sometimes Nicky felt like the last normal person in Beverly Hills.

When he phoned in to the scene of the crime, Jason Whittle and his team were just finishing up their work at the house.

"What's the fingerprint situation in the master bedroom?" Nicky asked.

"Good. We lifted clear prints from three different people. We should have some names for you by the end of the day."

"What about the bed?" asked Nicky. "Was Jay Jeffries having sex before he was killed?"

"Definitely. There were recent semen stains on the sheets and some vaginal fluids. We even have a few pubic hairs. We decided to take all the bedding downtown to the lab for a thorough analysis."

"Great. What about documents? Find any checkbooks? Maybe a nice safe-deposit key?"

"Yep. All of the above. There was a desk drawer downstairs with a variety of keys, insurance policies, savings books, all that sort of stuff."

"Why don't you send them directly over to Ethan," Nicky told him. Ethan Wright was one of the station's financial experts, whose resources were available to the various departments on a time-sharing basis.

Nicky listened to a few minutes of chatter, mostly of a highly technical nature, then spoke to the officer who had been in charge of the door-to-door questioning of the neighbors. Everything about this case was pointing to an early solution. A rich old matron who lived across the street from the Jeffries' house did not sleep much at night and spent a great deal of her life staring out her window. On Thursday night had seen two different cars come and go from the VJ's house. The first was an old car—a wreck, she called it—which brought a blond girl to the house a little after ten in the evening. The blond girl parked several houses down, but the witness saw her entering the victim's house. Half an hour later a new car arrived—this one a fancy sports car—depositing yet another woman, who was hidden beneath a wide-brimmed hat and a long coat. She parked in Jeffries' driveway for two or three hours, then left, still hidden by the long coat and hat. A few minutes later the blond girl came running out of the house, got into her car, and drove away.

The old lady across the street was a vigilant guard of her neighborhood. She was certain these were the only visitors Jay Jeffries had on Thursday night.

Nicky hung up the phone feeling that either he or Charlie would have to interview the old woman more thoroughly. In the meantime Charlie had finished his aesthetic arrangement of sushi and various condiments—including a small bowl of pickled ginger—on the seat between them. Nicky began to eat absentmindedly with his fingers.

"Use the chopsticks, for chrissake," Charlie told him, always one for proper form. "What are you, a barbarian?"

"Yes." Nicky growled.

"Well, what do you think?" Charlie asked after a while.

"It seems our suspect is a woman, apparently a blond. It will be interesting to see what color hair this Ginny Gina has."

"I meant the *tuna*. Pretty damn fresh, don't you think?"

Nicky glared at his partner.

"Okay," Charlie relented. "Let's talk about the case. It looks about as straighforward as it gets. I mean, the motive has to be sexual revenge, right? Cutting off someone's genitals is quite an angry statement. Most likely we're going to find the musicians from Pubic Telephone did the dirty deed."

41

Nicky gobbled up a California roll, a ball of sticky rice with avocado in the center. "Weren't you struck by a feeling of tension in that office, between Bo Daniels and the rest? There's something there I just don't trust—like enough plots and subplots to fill an entire shelf of southern novels."

"Maybe," Charlie admitted. "They've all known each other a long time—but that doesn't mean that one of them offed old J. J. Unless," he added with a smile, "it was the sexpot in Studio A. I mean, there's a motive. She kills J. J. so she can inherit his TV show. It's a Hollywood classic."

"That sweet little thing?" Nicky protested. "You're not serious!"

Charlie laughed wickedly.

"Maybe it was murder in the pink bedroom. Pubescent passions run amuck. . . . Anyway, don't look so glum—you big brute, you! We have Pubic Telephone and a witness that the last person to leave Jeffries' house was a blond girl. Not bad for the first day."

"Yeah, maybe."

As they ate lunch Nicky set forth an itinerary for the rest of the afternoon. He decided that they should split up to cover more ground quickly. It was Friday, and with his daughter coming tonight there would be no time to work on this case again until Monday. Probably the killer would get an extra weekend of freedom due to Lieutenant Rachmaninoff's domestic arrangements. So be it. At least he would do everything possible today.

Charlie would interview the old lady across from Jeffries' house, then start looking for the actresses in J. J.'s X-rated home videos. Nicky would track down the members of Pubic Telephone. The videotape Unity had given him listed credits for three musicians— Ginny Gina, vocals; Tommy Torch, keyboards; and someone who called himself The Bone on drums. The tape was produced by the band itself, whose address was a post office box in Topanga Canyon.

After lunch Charlie dropped him off back where he had left his Austin-Healey on North Palm Drive, and Nicky continued on his own down the length of Sunset Boulevard to the Pacific Coast Highway. He found he was glad to be by himself in the noisy solitude of his old car. As soon as he reached the ocean, the rain that had been threatening all day long at last began to come down. It rained so hard and fast the highway began to flood.

Nicky turned on his wipers to part the curtain of water and his headlights to pierce the gloom. Though it was early afternoon, the sky was touched with midnight.

10

Topanga Canyon Boulevard left the Pacific Coast Highway before Malibu, a winding two-lane road that headed up into the hills. Topanga had the reputation of harboring an eclectic population of aging hippies, school bus gypsies, winos, artists, and dropouts of every description. Mixed together with this were a few rock stars and assorted millionaires. Clint Eastwood was said to own great tracts of the surrounding hills, keeping them free from development. Nicky had once known a girl who was homesteading on his land—unbeknownst to the star—living in a tent with a pet lion. She had a very idyllic existence until the lion got hungry one night and ate a few neighborhood horses.

Nicky pulled into the small town center, parked, and made a dash through the rain for the post office, taking his place in a line of long-haired men and women, most of whom seemed to be buying food stamps and then driving off in BMWs and Volvos. Nicky got to the window, produced his shield, and requested his information. Within a few moments he was back in his car driving through the gray and liquid sky.

It took another half an hour to find the house. He drove up into the hills on a narrow dirt road scarred with deep ruts. The rain seemed to be coming down even heavier than before, turning the road into slush. Nicky wondered if he were going to have to be pulled out by a police tow truck. The address he was looking for turned out to be an old barn that was nestled at the end of a small valley. In sunlight, the place might have had some rural charm. Nicky parked beneath an enormous eucalyptus tree and took a moment to check his .38 Smith & Wesson revolver, spinning the chamber to make sure he had a full load. It had been several years since he had had to use this weapon, and he would just as soon never use it again. But he had learned to be careful.

He heard the sound even while he was still in the car: music was not quite the right word, nor was it quite random noise. The sound coming from the barn was electronic and totally unlike anything Nicky had ever heard before. It sounded like a radio gone berserk.

Nicky stepped out of his car into a deep mud puddle. He swore savagely and made a dash for the barn. An old phone booth stood

43

near the front door, apparently liberated from Ma Bell. The "L" had been removed so that the sign of the booth read: PUB IC TELE-PHONE. Nicky scrambled to a large sliding door and knocked loudly. The strange noise was louder than before, but he had identified it now—someone was experimenting on a synthesizer at a very high volume. Nicky knocked again but had little hope of being heard above the synthesizer and the storm. A rain gutter that must have been clogged suddenly freed itself, sending down a river of water directly on his head. Without waiting for an invitation, Nicky pulled open the barn door and stepped inside.

The barn was one enormous room, with mattresses and old sofas intermixed with speakers, mixing boards, amps, microphones, a drum set, and miles of electric cables. A wood stove burned in the center of the vast room, sending out waves of heat. On a nearby kitchen table, remnants of breakfast stood next to a plastic bag of marijuana and a graphic equalizer that had been taken apart. Everything lay in disarray. The barn reminded Nicky of artist's lofts he had known years ago when he was in college in New York. The word then was *bohemian. Beatnick.* He wondered what you called it today. *Postmodern punk? Renaissance skinhead?* Society was probably in a very bad way when you couldn't even find the right labels any-more.

A young man, dressed completely in black, stood at the far end of the room in front of a keyboard that had an impressive number of lights and dials on it. The musician had not yet noticed Nicky's presence. He had a mane of wild blond hair, and his sleeveless T-shirt revealed muscular arms. Standing over his synthesizer, he looked like a cross between Conan the Barbarian and some mad scientist at work. The noise inside the barn was deafening and mo-mentarily resembled church bells.

The young barbarian finally looked up as Nicky approached. He shouted something.

"What?" Nicky shouted back.

He pressed a button on his synthesizer, and the sound mercifully ceased. Now there was just the rain pounding on the roof.

"I said, does it sound like steel drums?"

"No," Nicky shouted above the rain. "More like church bells."

"Shit! I knew I shouldn't have smoked a joint. I had it, damn it, just the sound I wanted. Then I lost it somehow. It's in the fucking memory circuits, but I can't remember where!"

Nicky had to smile. He had had the same problem with police computers.

44

The blond musician looked as though it were entirely natural for Nicky to be there. "Look, do me a favor," he asked. "I'm going to try a lower cut-off frequency at the first part of the waveform, and then a quicker decay. Tell me if this sounds more like a steel drum, okay?"

The church bells came back with overwhelming volume but soon began to transform. Nicky watched the young man play with the various dials and listened to the different sounds emerge.

"What about that?" he shouted. They were standing close enough now that they could communicate by yelling into each other's ears.

"It's more like wooden mallets now," Nicky called back.

The musician kept fiddling, working for a more metallic sound. Nicky was surprised, but eventually he arrived at something that did indeed sound like steel drums. He smiled happily. Nicky flashed him a V. Then the musician set the program in the computerized memory banks so that it wouldn't be lost again.

Finally, he turned it off.

"That's quite an invention," Nicky said, impressed. "How much does a keyboard like this cost?"

"Five grand."

Nicky raised an eyebrow. He was beginning to appreciate how much money was tied up in this high-tech barn. The policeman in him wondered vaguely where the money came from. Certainly not from playing Saturday-night dance music at the local bar.

"You look wet, man," the musician said, noticing. "Want a hit off a joint?"

Nicky shook his head. How marijuana would help him get dry, he could not imagine. "Thanks," he said. "Not right now."

A girl came into the room from the bathroom. Nicky registered the fact that she was blond—though that might not mean too much, since blond was the official hair color of the state of California. She was wearing a terrycloth robe with obviously nothing on underneath. She was very pale, with dark smudges beneath her eyes, thick, pouting lips, and the fuzzy look of someone stoned on grass.

"Hey, Ginny, this is the drummer who's sitting in for The Bone tomorrow. Sorry, I didn't catch your name, man."

Nicky smiled thinly. "Well . . . it seems we got our signals crossed. Actually, you see, I'm not a drummer. I'm a cop."

Their manner, of course, changed at once. Nicky was sadly used to this. All eyes moved immediately to the open bag of marijuana on the table.

45

"I don't really care about your stash," he said quickly. "Quite honestly, I smoke myself sometimes." Why was he being so honest? Perhaps there was something about this barn that reminded him of his own rebellious youth? But the two kids only looked at him with utter hostility.

"You got some kind of ID?" the young man asked angrily. "How about a fucking search warrant?"

Nicky pulled out his wallet and showed his shield. "Look, I just want to ask a few questions. Nothing to get upset about. You must be Tommy," he said, bringing out the videocassette from his jacket pocket and looking at the credits again. "Tommy Torch?" he asked with a hint of amusement.

"Yeah. Where'd you get that tape?" Tommy asked sullenly. The girl was saying nothing at all. She looked far away, lost somewhere in her distant universe.

"I got this over at The Rock Channel," Nicky said, trying to gauge their reaction. "Jay Jeffries had it."

Tommy snorted his contempt. "That asshole," he muttered. "Fucking jerk. You'd think someone who'd once played for a great band like the Perceptions would have more class."

Nicky had had the same thought himself. Did they know J. J. was dead? He turned his attention to the girl.

"Will you tell me about your relationship with Jay Jeffries?" he asked.

Before she could answer, Tommy exploded.

"*Relationship?*" he sputtered. "Oh, this is too, too much! Ginny's been *fucking* old J. J. Okay? There isn't any goddamn relationship."

"I see. And just why are you fucking him, Ginny? Is it you're turned on by middle-aged guys with pot bellies and fake hair?"

"So he would play our goddamn video, asshole," Tommy interrupted once again.

Suddenly from Ginny: "Fuck you, Tommy. Let me talk for myself." She had a drowsy, sensual way of speaking, like a stoned southern belle. She turned her smudged and sullen eyes on Nicky.

"Why you wanna know about me and Jay?" she asked. "You some kind of pervert or something? The details get you off?"

"He's dead," Nicky said, watching both of them closely. "Like as in murdered."

Tommy was about to say something, but he froze comically with his mouth open. Ginny hugged herself and shivered.

"He was a creep," she said at last. "But it's weird to think he's dead. Man, that's trippy. . . . "

46

"How did you meet him?" Nicky asked. It seemed a long, long way from this barn in Topanga Canyon to Beverly Hills.

Ginny Gina hesitated a moment, then began. Nicky had heard stories like this before. A few months back, Ginny had been working as a cocktail waitress at a place in Malibu. Jay Jeffries had come in one night with a group of friends. He acted like the last of the big spenders, tipping twenty dollars each round of drinks. He assumed this gave him the right to pinch Ginny's ass and touch her breasts when she came over with her tray. He told her who he was, claiming friendships with Huey and Michael and the Boss. Ginny thought if she were nice, the VJ might take a look at their video. Perhaps he would even play it on his show. Maybe this was the break she and Tommy had been waiting for.

So she was nice. Very nice. She went back to J. J.'s house in Beverly Hills that night and did all the things he wanted. She even managed to get her video onto the VCR in the bedroom. J. J. said he loved it. "The Punishment of Love" was going to be a great hit. He personally was going to make Ginny a big star. Meanwhile she should relax and enjoy the party.

Thus it began. Jay was quick to invite her back for more nights of fun and games, but he was slow to follow through with any of his promises to help her career. Nicky wondered how a girl like Ginny could be so naive, but Hollywood was like that. Even the streetwise could be suckered in by the hope of being a star. It took Ginny and Tommy nearly a month to realize they'd been had.

"I bet you don't approve," Ginny asked bitterly.

Nicky paused before he answered. "It's not that I approve or disapprove," he told her. "It just makes me a little sad."

"Well, it makes me sad, too. But that's the way it is. We tried everything else. We made demo tapes, took them all over town. When everyone started saying you had to have a video, we got some friends together, rented some equipment, and we made a video . . . but where did it get us? Fucking nowhere. We couldn't even get an appointment with anyone in a record company to see the damn thing. I mean, we couldn't even get in the front door."

"It's that hard, huh?"

"It's fucking impossible," she said. "Man, we got some good songs, but no one will even give us a chance. At least J. J. actually looked at our video. When he said he loved it, Tommy and I felt real high, ya know. We started thinking maybe we had it made. That's why it was such an extra-special bummer when we discovered it was just a con."

47

"It must have made you angry," Nicky suggested.

"It sure did."

"I would have been," he told them. "Now tell me, I understand J. J. actually did play 'The Punishment of Love' one time on his show. How did you manage that?"

Tommy laughed, not a happy sound. "It's very simple, cop. I went along with Ginny one night when she was supposed to meet that jerk, and I told him I was going to kill the motherfucker unless he came through with some of the promises he'd been making."

"You threatened him?"

"Damn straight I threatened him!" Tommy was red in the face. "Look, man, as far as I'm concerned we had a business deal. He could get his rocks off with Ginny in exchange for helping the band. Okay? Only he welshed on the deal, man. Of course I fucking threatened him! I told him I'd cut off his goddamn balls unless he got us some air time quick."

Nicky narrowed his eyes. "Funny you say that, Tommy. Because that's exactly what happened to J. J. Someone cut off his balls, dick, the whole works. What do you say about that?"

As far as Nicky could tell, Tommy looked genuinely surprised. Nicky watched a quick succession of emotions pass over his face: shock, satisfaction, and then finally fear—when he realized what a damaging confession he had just made. As for Ginny, she seemed paler all the time. Nicky now turned his attention back to her.

"When's the last time you saw J. J.?"

"I don't remember. Maybe last Saturday night.'"

"What do you mean, *maybe* last Saturday night? Don't you remember?"

"Yes . . . no. Shit! Who keeps track of the days? I've been smoking a lot recently, ya know."

"How about last night? Do you remember that?"

She shook her head.

"What?" he insisted.

"No!" she shouted. "I didn't see him last night. I was here all night with Tommy. Now leave me alone."

"I'd like to, Ginny. It's just I'm having trouble with your story."

"Well, I'm telling you the truth."

"Hmm . . . look at it from my point of view. I've got this murder to figure out. My chief's going to be really pissed at me if I don't. Right now you two are my best suspects. Most cops I know would haul you into the station right now."

48

"Look, we don't have any motive," Tommy interrupted, trying to be reasonable. "He gave us our air time. That's all we wanted."

"Maybe," Nicky suggested. "Maybe not. I wouldn't be surprised if one of you wanted a little revenge for what he put you through. It couldn't have been too easy for you, Tommy, lying here in bed at night, thinking of your girlfriend fucking that slob."

Tommy almost seemed to stop breathing for a moment. He was standing very close and looking dangerous. Then he deflated and looked sad. "Don't give me your middle-class morality, policeman," he said wearily. "I'm way beyond jealousy. Ginny and I are more enlightened than that."

Nicky had to suppress a desire to laugh. If this were enlightenment, it had never appeared in a more shabby disguise.

He kept at them for another grueling hour. He worked on their alibi for Thursday night, but Tommy and Ginny insisted they were together, in the barn, going over new material. The third member of their group, the drummer, was up in Palo Alto for a few weeks on family business. That's why Tommy had initially mistaken Nicky for the friend of a friend who was supposed to fill in on drums for their club date next Saturday.

Nicky made them go through the entire story one more time. It was an intimate process, an interrogation, going into a stranger's life deeper than most people ever have a right to. Eventually they invited him to sit down, even offered him a cup of coffee. A cop was combination psychoanalyst, priest, and god.

Finally, he put it to them as plainly as he could: "Listen to me carefully. If either of you kids killed Jay Jeffries, tell me now. There may be extenuating circumstances. A good lawyer could get you off fairly light. But you got to level with me. The lab experts are going through his house, and if they find any sign that either of you were there last night, it's curtains. Understand? A first-degree murder charge."

"We didn't do it," Tommy said tensely.

Nicky turned to the girl. "No," she said. She looked horrified and sick. "I didn't kill him."

Nicky decided he believed them. Something was wrong here—he didn't know exactly what. His years of experience in listening to endless lies, confessions, alibis, and excuses had instilled in him a sense of what was true and what was not. Tommy and Ginny were withholding something from him. They seemed uneasy. Perhaps they were doing some drug deals they didn't want him to know about. But Nicky did not think they killed Jay Jeffries.

49

"Okay," he said, getting up at last. He took a card from his wallet. "This is my number. Give me a call if you think of anything I should know."

Nicky walked out into the pouring rain and somehow managed to drive back through the thick mud without getting stuck. He hoped he was right about Ginny and Tommy. Basically, he liked them. He had plenty of sympathy for the rebellious kids of the world. God knew, he had been one in his time. It still amazed him that he had joined the other side.

11

Nicky was nearly an hour late picking up his daughter, not an auspicious start to their six months together.

He sped back from the beach along the wet curves of Sunset, then up into the hills of Bel Air. The mansion that belonged to his ex-wife and new husband, Frank, was a large English manor house that sat splendidly on three acres of rolling lawns and forest. It was a movie set, circa 1940—a Hollywood imitation of an English estate but probably more comfortable than the original thing. Not even the queen of England had bathrooms like Frank and Susan's. The entire estate was surrounded by a thick, ten-foot-high stone wall, with a laser-beam security system completely encircling the property—for to be rich in Los Angeles was to be paranoid.

Frank met him at the front door, a stone archway large enough to drive a team of horses through.

"Hey, Nicky! Come in, kid. You look wet." Frank was actually a pretty nice guy for a big Hollywood star. A great paw of a hand settled affectionately on Nicky's shoulder, drawing him inside. He had a craggy, handsome face—a classic, chiseled-out-of-rock face. An honest-to-God matinee idol was old Frank. Nicky didn't hold it against him. He was older than Susan by about fifteen years, but his looks just got better with age.

Nicky had come to genuinely like Frank Fee. This could be an awkward occasion: ex-husband confronts present husband to take away stepchild—but it wasn't, because Frank was such a gentleman. As far as Nicky could tell, the man was a great oddity: a truly happy Hollywood star. He had made all the money in the world, had bedded three generations of leading ladies, and he didn't seem to have anything left to prove. Right now, he had found a secure resting place in a television series, portraying the evil patriarch of a fashion empire in an enormously popular prime-time soap.

"I can see you need a drink, kid," he said in his deep rolling bass. "Tanya's still packing, so why doncha come into the den and let me fix you up with a little medicine." Nicky didn't argue. "Anyway, there's something I sort of wanted to ask you," Frank said more softly, putting his big hand on Nicky's shoulder, leading him toward the den. They walked past the baronial living room, the dining room, the library, Susan's office, the exercise studio, the projection room, and the music room. You could get a lot of exercise being this rich.

"You hungry, Nicky? How about a sandwich?"

"No thanks, Frank."

Frank seemed suddenly ill at ease. Nicky could not remember ever seeing him like this before.

"You and me, Nicky—we've been friends, right?"

"That's right, Frank."

"I mean, it's not just that you were married to Susie before me—hell, I never got to know any of my other wives' ex-husbands. But you, Nicky, you're a big-shot cop, head of fucking homicide, and you know I've always respected you. I mean, it's like you're one of my heroes, Nicky—you know that?"

"Well, I'm pretty damn tough, it's true," Nicky said, wondering what this preamble was leading up to. "I give lessons to Charles Bronson."

They had reached Frank's den, a distinctly masculine place: leather armchairs, a blazing log in a stone fireplace, a glass gun case with a few shotguns and rifles, a well-stocked bar, and various souvenirs of films he'd made—including a zebra skin from Africa, an Indian headpiece, even a medieval suit of armor from some long-forgotten Hollywood epic. Modestly, on a bookshelf, stood Frank's single Academy Award.

Frank made two drinks, a hot brandy for Nicky and a Scotch and water for himself.

"*Chin-chin*," Frank said, clinking glasses.

"*Naz drovia*," Nicky responded. "Now what's on your mind?"

"Well, it's like this . . . a friend of a friend of mine was killed last night in Beverly Hills. I'm sort of trying to piece it all together. Find out who's to blame."

"You're talking about Jay Jeffries?" Nicky asked in great surprise. "*He* was a friend of yours?"

"Not J. J.," Frank said uncomfortably. "Though I knew him a little. My friend, actually, doesn't want his name thrown into the arena. He just wants to know who's responsible for J. J.'s death so he can . . . take appropriate action."

Nicky was so dumbfounded he could hardly speak. He had never imagined Frank in the role of a conspirator, and it took some getting used to. Frank, meanwhile, was sitting in his leather armchair crossing and recrossing his legs. He didn't seem to like this role either.

"It's like I owe this guy a favor," Frank said miserably. "But if I'm out of line . . . "

"No, I'm just a little surprised, that's all," Nicky reassured him. He realized that in all the years he had known him, Frank had never asked anything of him before. So Nicky quickly told him what he knew of J. J.'s death, describing the murder scene: upstairs at night; signs of sexual activity; the victim wearing nothing but a bathrobe, his back to the killer, to end up mutilated at the foot of the stairs. Nicky also mentioned the punk band that had made a threat on Jeffries' life, as well as his visit to Bo Daniels and friends at Inter Stellar Village.

Frank kept nodding, rubbing his big hands together, looking as grateful as a dog getting a bone.

"I'm sorry it's not really a lot of information, Frank."

"Hey, it doesn't matter. I'll tell my friend I talked with you. That's the main thing. A gesture of goodwill, you see."

Nicky studied the man. He had always considered Frank rich enough—and famous enough—to be beyond pressure of any kind. "Are you in some kind of trouble?" he asked.

Frank laughed. "Hell, no!" But the laugh wasn't entirely convincing. "This is just a matter of a little money. My friend, you see, has some pretty heavy change invested with Inter Stellar, and, well—he's just a little worried about the way things are going over there."

"How are things going over there?"

Frank ran a hand through his wavy, matinee-idol hair. "Well, not so good, apparently. The word is that Bo Daniels is kinda over his head. Inter Stellar grew just a little too fast. They have everything riding on The Rock Channel, but videos aren't doing as well as people thought they would. The ratings are down, and advertising, too. The feeling is, the wrong kind of scandal from a murder case right now could knock the whole empire out of orbit. Especially if there's something funny going on."

Nicky took a hit off his brandy, feeling the liquor warm up his insides. *Something funny going on over at The Rock Channel?* Yes, he had sensed it, the subtle odor of corruption.

"How well do you know Bo Daniels?" Nicky asked.

"Bo? Why, I've known the boy genius about ten years now, but not real well. At one point, we were talking about producing a film together, but it didn't quite gel. He's a pretty tough customer. People tend to underestimate him because he dresses like a hippie, but he created Inter Stellar from fucking nothing fifteen years ago, and you just have to look at that black tower to see how far he's come."

"But he's in trouble, you say?"

"That's the word, though I don't know the exact details. Hey, you want another brandy?" Frank asked, jumping up to play host.

Nicky did. He also wanted to hear a whole lot more about Bo Daniels. But this was not why he had come tonight. He stood up reluctantly. "No thanks. I'd better see how Tanya's coming along."

Frank walked with him back down the hall, looking very relieved the serious talking was behind them. "Hey, look, Nicky, we got to get together one night soon and do some carousing. Whad'ya say to that? I know some watering holes you won't soon forget."

Nicky thought getting too chummy with Frank was a little inces tuous, but he lied and said it sounded like fun.

"Oh, man! We'll go out and do some *serious* partying. Okay, pal?" Frank let out a small cowboy yell.

This was how Tanya found them. "You guys are sure having a great time," she remarked. "Hi, Nicholas."

This was what she called him now: Nicholas. About a year ago the word *daddy* had magically disappeared from her vocabulary.

He kissed her on the cheek. "Hi, munchkin," he said, then immediately regretted it. Tanya was not a munchkin anymore, she was a young lady. From age ten to eleven, she had gone through a temporary awkward phase, but now—at twelve—it was clear she was going to be a great beauty, like her mother. Tanya had perky blond hair, impish green eyes, and the beginnings of a womanly figure. The antennae of young men already wavered perceptibly when she was near. Fortunately—as far as her father was concerned —she still had braces on her teeth. Nicky sometimes felt that this mesh of stainless steel in her mouth was Tanya's last dwindling connection to her childhood, and for this he was glad.

53

"Frank's quite a guy," he said to Tanya as they were driving away.

"Uh-huh. He's *un peu gauche,* but he has a heart of gold."

Un peu gauche? Was this what Tanya was learning at the Marymount School for Girls?

A few minutes later, waiting for the light to change by the fire station on Sunset, father and daughter smiled at each other inanely and didn't know what to say. Nicky thought: *We're strangers, really, but this time together is going to be good.* He was going to learn to be a real full-time father.

"What's for dinner?" she asked. "I'm starving."

Jesus, he'd completely forgotten about feeding her.

"Maybe we'll go out tonight. Stop somewhere on the way home."

"Okay. Where?"

Yes, where do you take a child who's been to the Polo Lounge more often than most kids have been to McDonald's?

"McDonald's," he answered without missing a beat. Good thinking: Susan was a health fanatic and never allowed Tanya to eat fast food. "Is that all right with you?"

"Yeah! Radical!"

"Basically subversive," he agreed.

"Oh, Nicholas," she chided. "You're so silly."

12

Silly Nicholas was definitely not prepared for the extent of Tanya's social life. She was in the seventh grade this year and seemed anxious to prove she was not a child anymore.

The rock music started early Saturday morning, and not long after that the phone calls began. Tanya settled herself with the telephone on the living room sofa in a near impossible position (one foot on the floor, the other draped over the back of the couch), and she *talked*. Nicky didn't quite know what to do with himself, so he made a mild stab at cleaning up the house. He couldn't help but notice, however, that Tanya was talking about boys, boys, boys.

"Nicholas, can I invite my two girlfriends over today?" she asked between calls.

"Certainly, dear. Do you want me to pick them up?"

"No, that's okay. Bunky has a chauffeur, and she can pick up Kirsten on the way over."

Nicky had a feeling he was going to learn a lot about the upwardly mobile twelve-year-olds about town. "Listen, honey. I gotta make a few calls myself this morning . . . "

"*Oh!* I'm sorry. I don't mean to hog the phone."

"I know you're used to having your own line," said the polite stranger who happened to be her father. Actually, in Bel Air Tanya had *two* lines of her own, so she could stack up her friends on hold.

Nicky telephoned the police lab downtown. Jason was not there, so he spoke with one of his assistants, a lady by the name of Maggie O'Day. She told him that the bullet had been removed from the back of the victim's head and identified as a .32-caliber slug, fired from an inexpensive handgun. This last deduction was based on the microscopic markings on the slug, which indicated a cheap, slightly irregular barrel.

"How about fingerprints in the master bedroom?" Nicky asked. "Has the computer come up with any names?"

"Yes, Lieutenant. Besides the victim, of course, we have two women. First, Sandy Giannini, white female, born December sixth, nineteen fifty-five, five feet seven and a half . . . "

Sandy Giannini, he considered, drumming the table with restless fingers. Yes, Sandy Giannini was the real name of Jay Jeffries' maid, the redhead in the skimpy black costume who now called herself Nancy Normal. Nicky had lost a few sentences of the lab girl's recitation.

"What's that?"

"Her sheet, Lieutenant."

"She has a sheet?" he asked in some surprise.

"That's what I'm trying to tell you. A conviction for armed robbery, Trenton, New Jersey, July tenth, nineteen seventy-nine. It was a first offense—she held up a gas station with her boyfriend, who was apparently judged the real villain. She got a two years' suspended sentence."

"Her prints were in the master bedroom?" Nicky repeated. "How recent were they?"

"Impossible to say with complete accuracy. Anytime within the last three days, we believe."

Well, it would be expected to find the housecleaner's prints in the bedroom, Nicky imagined. Still, he was going to have to have another talk with Nancy Normal.

"The second prints belong to Virginia Langer, white female, five feet six, born July fourteenth, nineteen seventy, blond hair, hazel eyes, driver's license issued at Fresno . . . do you want all this stuff, Lieutenant?"

"Just tell me does she have a sheet, too?"

"Two juvenile convictions, one for shoplifting in Fresno, the other for prostitution in San Francisco."

"Maggie, as soon as we get off the phone, I'd like you to give a copy of everything you have to a driver to bring to my house."

"Yes, Lieutenant."

Nicky had a sinking feeling that Virginia Langer was Ginny Gina. It made too much sense. The age seemed about right, as well as the description. It would mean she lied to him, which made him unhappy.

"Incidentally, Lieutenant, some parts of the house had been deliberately wiped for prints—the doorknob to the master bedroom, the bedside table, and the kitchen sink downstairs—so we can't guarantee there wasn't someone else in the house we don't know about. However, with Virginia Langer we have definite evidence that she left her prints Thursday, the night of the murder."

"How's that?"

"Her prints were in the bathroom, on the sunken tub. We got a really nice one superimposed on a small particle of water that would have evaporated within a few more hours. Virginia Langer was also the last person to flush the toilet. They were all having sex, of course, and you know what *that's* like," she said—a little too warmly, Nicky thought, for a scientist. "Makes you want to go wee-wee more than usual."

"What do you mean, exactly, they were *all* having sex?" Nicky asked softly, because Tanya had just walked into the living room from the kitchen, munching on a peanut-butter sandwich.

"I'm sorry."

"What do you mean by *sex?*" he repeated more loudly than he intended.

Tanya opened her mouth in surprise and stared at her father. The girl from the crime lab giggled. "Oh, Lieutenant Rachmaninoff! With your reputation, I wouldn't think I'd have to tell you about *that*."

"Please. Ms. O'Day," he said wearily. "We are both city employees. I just want to know what happened at Jay Jeffries' house Thursday night."

"Well, it was rather a kinky scene, actually. It got pretty hot."

She proceeded to tell him about it. There was evidence—pubic hairs and the remnants of various body secretions—to indicate that Jeffries had sexual intercourse with two separate women on the night of his death. Nicky listened to the various technical details, which included a discussion of the spermicidal cream found in minute traces on the severed penis.

"Tell me this," he asked after a few minutes. "I'm interested in the sequence. Is it possible the women visited Jeffries at separate times throughout the evening, or was it a . . . ménage à trois?" he posed carefully, hoping Tanya's knowledge of French had not progressed to this point.

Maggie O'Day gave her little giggle. "Well, we're not certain of the time sequence, but the indications, at least, are not the classic ménage. The victim had intercourse with one woman on the bed and the second woman on the stairs."

"On the stairs?" Nicky asked incredulously. "They fucked on the *stairs?*"

Tanya almost dropped her peanut-butter sandwich onto the floor. Nicky tried to wave her out of the room, but she was not moving. No way.

"I told you it got hot," Maggie said. "Do *you* ever have fantasies of making love in unusual places, Lieutenant?" she asked huskily.

"No. . . . Good-bye, Ms. O'Day."

Nicky hung up the phone. "Listen here, young lady," he told his daughter sternly. "I will not listen in on your phone conversations, and you will definitely not listen in on mine. Is that clear?"

Tanya giggled. "But Father, dear, your phone calls are so much more interesting than mine. Boy! Fucking on the stairs," she added rapturously. "My virgin ears!"

13

Within half an hour a patrol car came to Nicky's house to deliver a packet of information, including a computerized photograph of Virginia Langer, taken from her California driver's license. Nicky stood in his driveway looking at the picture as the messenger drove away.

"Shit," he said gloomily. This wasn't what he wanted. Virginia Langer was indeed Ginny Gina. She had been in Jeffries' house Thursday night. She and Tommy had lied to him.

Nicky was wondering what he should do about this when a dazzling white Lincoln Continental limousine pulled up Sunshine Terrace into his driveway. A chauffeur in an elaborate uniform popped out of the driver's seat and opened a rear door for two young ladies to emerge. Tanya came outside just in time to make the introductions.

Bunky Baker was an overweight, preadolescent girl with large doelike eyes, thick glasses, and fuzzy brown hair. Her father, Tanya had told him, owned a chain of department stores. Kirsten Cooleridge, the second girl to step out of the limousine, was the pretty one. She was going to be a beauty, like Tanya, and was more developed than either of the other girls. At the age of twelve, Kirsten had knowing, world-weary eyes. Nicky could already see the future Beverly Hills matron lurking in the eyes of this little girl. She shook Nicky's hand and sized him up in a most unchildlike way.

Nicky did his best to shift gears from detective to parent. Actually, when Tanya made the introductions and came out with those magic words—"this is my father"—he felt a ridiculous surge of pride. He could hardly imagine that moments earlier he had been considering ducking off for a fast trip to Topanga Canyon to find out why that bitch Ginny Gina had lied to him.

Bunky and Kirsten spent some time admiring the rural nature of his house. Apparently, they had never before been exposed to anything less than a mansion.

"Gosh," Bunky enthused, "this looks like something out of *Grapes of Wrath.*"

Tanya quickly took her friends into her room and closed the door. Before long, the sound of girlish giggles emerged from the room. Nicky heard one of them shriek, "On the *stairs?*" Moments later, from the cassette recorder in her room, came the old Led Zeppelin song "Stairway to Heaven," accompanied by raucous laughter.

So much for the innocence of young maidens. Nicky paced his living room and wondered if he really was going to survive this weekend with his sanity intact. Here he had set aside the day, putting off his murder investigation so he could spend time with his daughter. But did she want him? No. She preferred to close herself up in her room with Bunky and Kirsten.

He decided he might as well do something constructive outside in the garden. He changed into his old work clothes, found a shovel by the back porch, and walked out into the feeble sunlight, past the meadow in front of his house, to a small fenced-in area around the side. The garden was hidden behind an oak tree at the far edge of the property. Nicky had not had a chance to do any work here for months, and the long weeds and hemlock were beginning to take over.

He raised the shovel above his head, then drove it down into the ground. All the smells were rich and damp. He turned the dark brown earth over, then raised the shovel again. Before long he felt a trickle of sweat near his hairline. He liked this. Up with the shovel, then down into the earth. He cut a long pink worm in two. So sorry, fella, but that's the way it goes.

After a while, his muscles began to ache. The shovel hit a large rock. Nicky picked up the rock and threw it over the chicken-wire fence. Gardening was supposed to soothe the savage beast, but it wasn't working today. Depression gnawed at him. He wondered things like what exactly his life added up to. He also wondered what he was doing with a shovel in hand when a murder case demanded his attention.

What he was doing, in fact, was growing marijuana. A fairly absurd thing for a cop to do, admittedly. He didn't even smoke marijuana anymore, hadn't for years. He gave it away as Christmas presents, mostly to Charlie and Frank. Given the current antidrug attitude in the nation these days, this little joke could easily cost him his job. And for what?

He knew the answer: he needed to take a risk like this, gamble with his career as though it didn't matter. The dope garden was just the last remnant of a once rebellious self-image. It was his youth itself he couldn't quite discard.

Nicky drove the shovel down into the ground one last time and then threw it away from him in disgust, as hard as he could. The shovel sailed over the chicken-wire fence and then went *clang!* against a tree.

"*Nicholas!* My God, what are you doing?"

He had not heard Tanya come down from the house. She was standing with another girl, and the sun was behind them, giving them both a golden halo shining directly into Nicky's eyes. He could tell the second girl was not Bunky or Kirsten, just from the shape of her. For a moment, with the light the way it was, it looked as if Tanya were standing next to an angel.

Nicky shielded his eyes against the glare and the girl came into focus. It was Unity Sphere, teen goddess. She was dressed in old blue jeans (very tight) and an oversized beige sweater. She didn't

59

seem to be wearing any makeup today, which made her look both younger and prettier than when he had last seen her at The Rock Channel. Though the sweater was baggy, two perky breasts were pointed his way like pistols. The violet eyes stared at him with a kind of friendly astonishment.

Tanya was the first to speak.

"It's not that my father's actually crazy, you understand. It's just that he's Russian," she explained. "And when you're Russian, you do mad things like dance and weep and sing and throw shovels at trees."

Unity threw back her head and laughed. Nicky walked around the outside of the fence to find the wayward shovel. It gave him a chance to catch his breath and gather his thoughts. Tanya was busy admiring Unity's hair—those lovely ringlets that fell softly about her face—asking where she had it done. Complaining at the same time that *her* mother made her go to Saks, which was the absolute pits, for chrissake. When Unity explained her hair was done each morning at The Rock Channel, Tanya was instantly agog in hero worship.

"The Rock Channel!" she cried. "How eternally fantastically radical! Are you . . . ?" Tanya could hardly dare to ask.

"I'm a VJ," Unity admitted. "Or at least, I have been since Friday. I just got my own show."

Tanya looked as if she were going to die. She said this was the most exciting thing that had ever happened to her, meeting an actual in-the-flesh VJ from Rock Television.

"But you must be used to all this," Unity objected. "With your mother and all."

"Oh, my *mother!*" Tanya said with great scorn. "She just does dumb old movies and stupid cop shows. It's not like rock and roll."

Susan would certainly get a kick out of this conversation. Nicky, shovel in hand, joined the two young ladies.

"You're quite a passionate gardener," Unity told him.

"Plants get me pretty excited," he admitted.

Tanya giggled. "Especially *these* plants. Do you know what Nicholas grows in there . . . ?"

Nicky took his daughter's arm. Firmly. "Dear, don't you think Kirsten and Bunky are wondering where you are? I tell you what. Why don't you look in the paper and pick out a movie. I'll take you all to a matinee in a little while."

"But I've seen everything, Nicholas," she complained.

"No, you haven't," he told her. "Anyway, this is business, dear."

"I guess I can take a hint," she said. Her look implied she knew exactly what kind of business this was. But she walked back to the house and left Nicky alone with Unity Sphere.

"I hope you don't mind my coming over. Actually I tried to telephone you all morning, but your phone was always busy. Then I noticed we're almost neighbors. I live right down the road in Laurel Canyon. So I thought I'd just stop by."

"Let's sit down and talk," he suggested.

He led the girl back up the path from the garden to the front meadow, where she sat down easily on the long grass. Nicky liked women who could sit down on a meadow without worrying about their clothes. Unity plucked a blade of grass and played with it, wrapping it around a finger like a ring. Nicky sat down next to her.

"I like it up here," she told him simply. "This meadow so high above the city."

The girl gazed off toward the world below. It was her windswept, poetic look. One thing bothered him. Yesterday, on television, Unity had spoken with a slight Valley Girl lisp. Today that was gone, with something more transatlantic in its place. It made him wonder who she really was.

"You're not from L.A., are you, Unity?"

She smiled mysteriously. "You don't think so?"

"Somehow, no."

"Well, you're right. I'm from across the sea. Far, far away. Hawaii," she added just as Nicky was imagining some mythically distant kingdom where all the girls were beautiful and had violet eyes.

"Honolulu?"

"No, the Big Island. I'm a country girl, Nicholas—can I call you that? It's much nicer than Lieutenant Rachmaninoff. I grew up on the slope of a volcano high above the sea."

"How ever did you find your way to this fair city?"

"Oh, that's a long story," she told him vaguely.

"I'm interested."

"Are you? Bo has an estate on the Kona coast, you see, sort of a combination recording studio and retreat for overly famous rock stars who want to get away from it all. I used to baby-sit his kids and take care of the horses, that sort of thing. My mother was a friend of his. When she died a few years ago, well . . . Bo took an interest in me. He brought me to Los Angeles and gave me a job. And so, here I am."

"How about your father?" Nicky asked. "Where is he?"

Unity was looking outward, past the city, past the ocean, someplace all her own.

"My *father*," she repeated speculatively, as if trying the word on for size. "My mother was awfully wild. *Your* generation," she added. "You know, free love and all that. Anyway, I never had the foggiest idea who my father was. One of the multitudes, I suppose. I'm quite illegitimate, you see."

She sighed, stretched, lay back on the long grass. Nicky had to suppress a desire to roll over on top of her. He reminded himself firmly that the girl was only seventeen, just five years older than Tanya.

"Unity, why did you come here today?" he asked in his official homicide investigator's voice.

She sat up, hugged her knees, and seemed to remember herself that she hadn't come to gaze at the sky and talk of the past.

"I was hoping you would call me. Weren't you intrigued by my little note? I *do* try to be intriguing, you know."

"I'm sure you are. I'm afraid I've been very busy investigating a murder."

"But maybe I can help you," she said playfully.

"Can you?"

She turned to face him, moving so close he could smell the girlish freshness of her skin. Her complexion at this proximity was just what he imagined it would be: perfect—though her lips were slightly cracked, maybe from too much kissing.

"It's the mob," she whispered dramatically.

"The mob, huh?"

"Yes, you know—the Mafia. The Cosa Nostra."

"I've heard of them," Nicky told her.

"*Well!* That's what this whole thing's all about. The mob's moving into The Rock Channel."

"I see. Can you give me any specifics?"

He was noticing that up close Unity's eyes were not a solid violet but were made up of passionate swirls of different greens and golds and blues.

"You don't think I'm serious, but I am, Nicholas. About five years ago, Bo realized he needed fifty million dollars to set up The Rock Channel, and he came up with this semibrilliant idea that there were people in this country who had that sort of money who were just dying to put it to use."

"Organized crime."

"Exactly. Bo made a deal with the devil. Basically what he runs is an Italian laundry. It's all drug money, millions and millions of dollars from cocaine and heroin."

"Who's his contact?"

"A hood by the name of Bushy di Sutro."

Unfortunately, Nicky knew who Bushy di Sutro was. Mob involvement in Hollywood was becoming a major concern.

"Have you actually seen Bo and Bushy di Sutro together?" he asked her.

She narrowed her pretty eyes. "Lots of times. That's what I'm trying to tell you. The whole deal was concluded in Hawaii, back when I was still the baby-sitter. I saw the whole thing come down. I can give you names, dates, everything you want."

Nicky had to admit he was getting interested.

"They talked in front of you?"

"Uh-huh. I was just something decorative in a bikini no one took too much notice of."

Nicky was quiet for a while, absorbing all this. "Why was J. J. killed, then?" he asked softly.

"J. J. didn't know about the deal with Bushy until just a few months ago. He thought The Rock Channel had legitimate investors. When he learned the truth, he went to Bo and tried a little blackmail—a million dollars to keep quiet. It was a dumb move, of course, but no one ever accused J. J. of being too terribly bright. Bushy just had him eliminated."

Nicky smiled vaguely. "It's an interesting angle. We'll certainly check it out."

"Why don't you believe me?" she challenged. "You probably believe that story about Pubic Telephone, is that it?"

"I didn't at first, Unity. Unfortunately, the evidence is mounting against them."

"What evidence?" she demanded, squinting her eyes at him.

Nicky frowned. He had a deep-seated cop's reluctance to discuss the facts of a case with a civilian—but the girl on his meadow was too young and pretty and earnest to be denied. He told her about the phone call he had just received placing Ginny Gina's fingerprints all over the shower and toilet in Jay Jeffries' bathroom.

"Hmm," she said, puzzled. "You're certain Ginny was there *Thursday* night? I mean, couldn't she have left her prints another time?"

He tried not to smile at her innocence. "Police labs are able to date fingerprints rather accurately these days," he explained. "There was another lady there as well we haven't identified yet. Apparently, it was quite an orgy. Jeffries was just messing around with the wrong two women."

"*Two* women," she said in some amazement. "Dear me, this town. . . . Well, what if they were working for Bushy di Sutro?"

Nicky shook his head. "It's a little farfetched. Actually, Mafia executions are generally very quick and businesslike. This whole thing with two women wouldn't be their style at all. But thanks for your information," he added gently. "I really do appreciate your coming forward."

Tanya poked her head out of the sliding-glass door from the living room.

"Nicholas!" she shouted. "I found a matinee over in Westwood. But we have to hurry. It starts in half an hour."

"I'll be right there," he called to his daughter. "Well, I guess we're finished," he said to Unity, helping her to her feet.

"One thing I don't quite understand," he added. "Bo Daniels has really given you quite a lot—he took care of you when your mother died, brought you over from Hawaii. Now he even hands you your own TV show."

"Yes?" she asked. "You're wondering why I'm ungrateful?"

"I'm wondering why you would feel a need to tell me about Bo's Mafia connections, yes."

Her violet eyes turned very intense. "Because it's true," she said, "and I don't like it very much, even if I find myself beholden to the man. Put it this way—I have reasons to be grateful to Bo Daniels, and reasons to be ungrateful, too. Besides that, I went through some soul-searching yesterday, after you found me jumping up and down with glee because J. J. was dead and I had a chance to take over his show. I mean, I looked at myself, and I didn't like what I was becoming."

"Nicholas!" Tanya called again from the living room. "We're going to be late!"

Unity took his arm as they walked slowly back toward the house. Nicky liked the natural way her hand felt there.

"One more thing," he asked her. "Where were you on Thursday night?"

She seemed momentarily shocked. Then she laughed gaily. "Oh, Nicholas! Are cops always so suspicious?"

"We are," he told her.

"Well, rest easy. I had dinner with Marilyn, and then we saw a double feature on Melrose. Two old Fellini films."

"Marilyn de Malibu?"

"That's right. We even ran into some friends of ours, and went to the Hard Rock Café afterward until nearly two."

"I'm glad," Nicky told her.

"Me too," she said.

At the house she turned and shook his hand. It seemed a rather formal gesture for someone her age.

"Good-bye, Nicholas. You're a nice man," she told him. "For a cop."

She turned and walked away. Nicky tried hard not to stare at her shapely rear.

14

The Austin-Healey raced down out of the hills toward Sunset, with the canvas top down and girls sticking out all over. Kirsten and Tanya squeezed together into the passenger seat, while poor Bunky was relegated to the back. She didn't seem to mind. Nicky had the impression Bunky was glad to hang out with Tanya and Kirsten on any terms and probably volunteered her father's chauffeur and limo as a way to be included in the group.

Nicky was approaching the intersection of Laurel Canyon Boulevard and Sunset, when the small electronic object in his coat pocket —a device not much larger than a cigarette lighter—began to emit a loud beeping noise.

"What's that funny sound?" Kirsten asked, her mouth full of gum.

"That's Nicholas's beeper," Tanya answered.

Kirsten giggled. "That sounds almost . . . *dirty*." Everything sounded dirty to Kirsten.

Tanya began to sing: "Jeepers, creepers, where'd you get your beeper? . . . " Giggles turned to laughter.

"Girls, *please!*" Nicky pleaded. The beeper was actually no source of amusement. It seemed degrading somehow to be summoned by a machine. Still, good bureaucrat that he was, he dutifully crossed Sunset and pulled up to the first gas station with a pay phone.

"Rachmaninoff," he told the communications operator. "What do you have for me?"

"Yes, sir," came an efficient female voice. "We have a message from Sergeant Katz. This came a few minutes ago. Hold on, please."

There was a short pause as the operator lined up the tape. Then the recorded voice of Charlie Cat:

"Nicky, I'm in a wee bit of a jam, old buddy. You think you could zip over to the Climax Massage Parlour on Berkley Place and give me a hand? Don't put out a code three, but get here quick, okay?"

The tape ended. Charlie definitely sounded in trouble. "Do you want a code three anyway?" asked the police operator. This would result in a half-dozen patrol cars being dispatched immediately to the officer in distress.

"No, I don't think so," Nicky replied cautiously. "Not yet."

Nicky hurried back to his car. "Uh, ladies, my partner is in a little trouble. I know this is a drag, but I got to dash over to Berkley Place for a moment. It's just a few miles away."

Tanya looked at her watch. "*Nich*olas, we'll be *late* for the *movie!*" she whined in several octaves.

Nicky flashed her a heavy look. He got back into the car, reached over Kirsten's legs to the glove compartment, and pulled out a red plastic emergency light that was attached to a long wire. Normally he would clamp this light onto the roof of the car. Today, he simply handed it back to Bunky in the rear.

"Here, hold this," he told her.

"Me?" she asked. "Really?"

"Yes, really. Hold it as high as you can. Let everyone know we're coming through."

Nicky fired the ignition and pulled away from the curb. He pressed down hard on his horn, ordering other traffic out of the way. It was a strange sight: a crowded sports car with Bunky in the back holding the revolving red light high in her right hand, like the Statue of Liberty. Bunky's face was radiant as they sped down the street. She seemed happy to be of use.

Berkley Place was a short cul-de-sac off La Brea. It was an alley, basically, fixed up to look quaint and old-fashioned. The Climax Massage Parlour resided in a renovated Victorian house that was supposed to recall the Gay Nineties in San Francisco. It stood next to a small real estate company that was trying to look like an English mews house. Both succeeded in appearing equally unreal in the early-afternoon light.

Nicky parked by a bright red fire hydrant that looked as false as everything else on this street. They were about fifty feet away from the entrance to the massage parlor. Everything was quiet.

"Where *are* we?" Kirsten asked.

Bunky peered down the street through her glasses. "Climax Massage Parlour," she read carefully. "My mother has a masseuse who comes to the house."

Tanya put her hands over her eyes and laughed.

"Now listen to me," Nicky said sternly. "Tanya, Kirsten, Bunky —I want you all to stay right here. You understand? I won't be a moment."

He left the car and began walking toward the Victorian building. Without warning, the front door to the massage parlor was flung open. Three ladies, in various stages of undress, appeared holding Charlie between them. Charlie was doubled over, as though he had been hit in the stomach. He was completely naked.

The massage parlor girls tripped the sergeant unceremoniously down the short flight of stairs. Charlie rolled down upon the sidewalk and groaned. One of the women screamed after him: "Don't you ever come back here! Pig! Cocksucker! We'll stick your head up your ass if you ever do!"

The door to the building slammed shut. Nicky ran up to where his partner lay and pulled him behind the cover of a nearby garbage dumpster.

"Are you hurt?"

"No. I'm okay. A little short of breath," Charlie gasped. "Man, those girls were something else."

"What happened, for chrissake?"

"Nicky, my friend, let me advise you against the Climax Massage Parlour. It's a fairly stressful place in which to relax."

"Damn it, Charlie. I was in the middle of taking Tanya and her friends to a fucking matinee. Now what the hell is going on here?"

Charlie looked hurt. "I was just doing what you asked," he complained. "I got the names of three of the actresses in J. J.'s home videos. There are only two more to go."

"Okay, tell me about it. Quickly."

"Well, this is maybe the tenth massage parlor I've been to since we split up yesterday. I'm getting a little rubbed out, actually. I got to this place about an hour ago. I asked for the Triple Delight."

"What's a Triple Delight?"

"It's when you get three girls at once. Once of them licks your balls while the second—"

"Okay, okay. Just tell me what happened."

"Well, you asked me what a Triple Delight was. Jesus! I was just doing it to save time. I thought if I could do three girls at once, I'd get the job done quicker."

"Sure, Charlie. You're quite the cop. By the way, do those girls have your revolver?"

"No, I left my gun locked up in the Yacht, which is in a parking lot nearby. I wanted to be able to undress without letting on I was a cop."

"Hmm . . . "

"Unfortunately, those damn girls aren't honest. You know what they did? While two of them had me, uh, occupied, the third was going through my wallet. They found my shield and freaked out. I mean, those chicks are fucking cop haters. One of them's really crazy. From what she was yelling, it seems they've been getting hit pretty heavy for payoff money and free sex. She said she wasn't putting up with it anymore. Man, I thought they were going to tear me apart. I was able to run down a hall and lock myself in an office, which is where I called the station. But they broke down the door. Does that sound like rational behavior to you? I tell you, this city is in bad shape when a policeman can't go into a whorehouse without getting beat up."

Nicky looked at his partner. He did not laugh. "I guess I'd better get your clothes back. Here, wrap up in my jacket for now."

Nicky started walking back toward the massage parlor.

"Hey, brah, I wouldn't go in there if I were you. I mean it. Those chicks'll tear you apart."

Nicky turned back to his partner, who now had his corduroy jacket wrapped around his waist like a towel. "You sure look cute, Charlie. What say we call up the reserves to get your clothes and shield back for you?"

Charlie looked miserable. "Got an extra gun in your car?" he asked. "At least I could keep you covered."

"Just keep yourself covered. I'll be right back."

Nicky walked up the wooden steps to the front door, and a woman's arm appeared with a neat bundle of Charlie's clothes, his shoes, and his wallet.

Charlie scowled at him. "That's the last time I'm going to do your dirty work," he said. "Next time you want to investigate massage parlors, you can do it yourself."

When Charlie was dressed, they began walking back toward Tanya and her friends in the Austin-Healey. "So did you learn anything from this fiasco?" Nicky asked him.

"Yeah. Three girls at a time is a little too baroque for my taste. I think from now on whenever I'm in the mood for group sex, I'll stick with two."

Nicky stopped walking and glared at Charlie.

"You *used* to have a sense of humor," Charlie observed, and when this got no reponse: "Okay. J. J. was well remembered at several places. Apparently, he paid very well for his little orgies. But everyone swore they hadn't seen him for at least a month before his death. Some chick at Cleopatra's Spa said she heard Jeffries had taken up with some singer who was putting out for free."

Nicky thought gloomily of Ginny Gina, who had lied to him. "How about the witness, the old lady across from J. J.'s house? Did you think she was reliable?"

"Ah, yes, Mrs. Dorfman. A delightful old hag. She's an import from New York City, where apparently that's what old people do with themselves—they stare out windows all day long. Her son-in-law, the periodontist, would like to put her in an old people's home, but they keep her around for guilt. It was really a lot of fun over there, Nicky."

"Charlie!"

"Okay, okay . . . Well, *I* believed her. I saw the window where her rocking chair is, and she has an unobstructed view of the Jeffries house. She maintains that two women—no more, no less—came and went on Thursday night. Mrs. Dorfman is pretty frail, though. Any kind of defense lawyer would have a lot of fun tearing her apart in court."

"Could she have dozed off, you think? Maybe the real perp showed up while she was asleep."

"We talked about that at some length, Mrs. Dorfman and I. She claims she never sleeps until three A.M., and then she's up by six, guarding the streets again. A very vigilant old lady. Very regular, too."

Tanya and her friends were waiting with bright eyes back at the car. "Here come our returning heroes," Tanya said. "Hello, Charlie Cat. Isn't it a little late in the season to be running about naked?"

Kirsten and Bunky were laughing so hard, tears ran down their cheeks. Nicky tried to stay well in the background.

"I know this may seem humorous to you," Charlie said solemnly, "but this is part of a very serious murder investigation."

"But why were you naked?" Tanya insisted.

"I was doing a little undercover work for your father. You girls wouldn't understand."

69

"Was that under-the-covers work?" Kirsten asked mildly.

"Yes, yes, it's all quite funny," Charlie agreed sadly. "To you I may be a mere policeman, your father's flunky. But I also happen to be a man."

"Oh! We could see *that!*" Bunky said enthusiastically.

15

Later that night, long after Bunky's dazzling white limousine had come back to Sunshine Terrace to take her and Kirsten home, Nicky sat on the edge of his daughter's bed.

"I'm sorry about this afternoon," he told her. "I guess I embarrassed you in front of your friends."

"It's okay. They thought it was great. Anyway, we only missed ten minutes of the movie. No big thing."

"You sure now?"

"Mmm . . ."

She made a warm little sound, snuggled closer to her teddy bear, and was instantly asleep. Nicky kissed her forehead, turned off the light, and left.

In the next room, Charlie was sitting at the old Steinway playing chords. He knew exactly three chords, which did not inhibit his self-expression. He had already made a serious dent in Nicky's wine supply.

Charlie began to sing:

> *"I'm goin' to Kansas City, Kansas City here I come,*
> *I'm goin' to Kansas City, Kansas City here I come.*
> *They got some crazy little women there, and I'm gonna get me*
>   *two, three, four—maybe a whole fuckin' bunch of 'em."*

Nicky crossed the room and put another log on the fire. The dancing orange firelight reflected warmly against the wood paneling in the living room. Sometimes on wintry evenings Nicky had the illusion of being high in the Sierras, far from the city below. It was a pleasant thought.

"Come on, Nicky. Play us a song," Charlie called out from the piano. "I haven't heard you play in ages."

"Not now. Tanya's trying to sleep."

"Oh," he said contritely, and stepped away from the piano. "Well, let's open up another bottle, shall we? Singing the blues is thirsty work. What's left in the old cellar, Nicky me lad?"

"Only jug wine."

"*Jug wine,*" he repeated distastefully. "How sad."

Without waiting to be invited, Charlie stepped into the kitchen and returned with the entire half-gallon bottle of Valley of the Moon Burgundy, as well as two wineglasses. He sat down on the sofa in front of the fireplace and poured.

"Here's to you, Nicky boy. May we survive in this strange and foreign land."

Nicky touched glasses. "Amen," he said. "Now, Charlie, getting back to the case for a moment—tomorrow I want you to start checking out alibis—the housecleaner, Bo Daniels, Donny Meredith, Rick Elsmore, Marilyn, even Unity Sphere. Lean on 'em hard, if you have to. I want to know where everybody was on Thursday night."

Charlie rolled his wineglass around in his hand. "What about this Ginny Gina character?" he asked. Charlie and Nicky had been discussing the case on and off throughout the evening, whenever Tanya was out of the room. Nicky had told him about the singer's fingerprints in the bathroom. "If I can make a suggestion, Nicky, what we should do here is arrest Ginny, charge her with first-degree murder, and scare the shit out of her. Maybe she'll tell us why she lied to you. She certainly knows who the mystery woman is who joined them for their little threesome on the stairs. The chances are Madame X is the killer. Maybe the two girls did it together."

"But what's their motive?" Nicky asked.

Charlie shrugged. "You know the motive. Ginny put out for Jay Jeffries, and he welshed on his part of the deal. The name of the game here is revenge. She even cut off the offending part."

Nicky was still skeptical. "I don't know. Ginny seems fairly practical to me, the kind of girl who's used to hard knocks. I just don't see her going off the deep end, especially since she eventually got what she wanted. I mean, Jeffries *did* play her song on his show. Right? Not only that, but two women makes the whole thing even more doubtful. Why should Madame X, whoever she is, get involved with Ginny's revenge?"

Charlie put his feet up on Nicky's couch. He was looking more and more comfortable. "Look at it this way, Nicky," he said. "A lot of people in this city walk around like a loaded gun, just waiting for

71

something to set them off. Maybe J. J. the lecherous VJ was like that for Ginny, the last straw in a long chain of events.''

Nicky stared into the hypnotic firelight. "Maybe," he said at last. "But I still don't like it. There's a piece missing somewhere. Shit," he added in disgust, "I'll pull Ginny in on Monday. We'll find out what's going on.''

"You don't think she'll run before then?"

"She better not," he said gloomily.

Charlie sat up on the couch. "Look, Nicky, why don't you let me pull her in tomorrow? We have enough to hold her a few days. Maybe you could even slip away from playing daddy a few hours and join us at the station.''

Slip away from playing daddy a few hours? Great! This would be Tanya's second day here, and already they had had one minor police action. Couldn't a policeman be a human being? Couldn't he have one damn weekend with his daughter?

Nicky filled up his glass and passed the wine bottle over to Charlie. "Okay, we'll give Ginny one more day. You can get the warrant tomorrow, and we'll arrest her first thing Monday morning. Will that make you happy?''

Charlie looked at Nicky in amazement. "Hey, I don't know why you're getting mad at me, brah. It's not *my* fault that the pieces fall the way they do." He lifted his wineglass for a toast. "Here's to the fox and here's to the hounds. May everyone have a most civilized Sunday before the shit hits the fan.''

Nicky had some trouble drinking to this but forced himself.

"One thing I keep forgetting to tell you," Charlie mentioned. "A curious little detail. None of the three people I spoke to who had been in Jeffries' little videos actually knew they were being photographed. The camera must have been hidden somewhere in the room.''

"What?" Nicky asked sharply.

"They didn't know they were being videoed," Charlie repeated. "One of the little gals was pissed as hell. She said she would have asked for more money.''

Nicky stood up and began to pace the living room floor. "I wish you had told me this right away." He was frowning.

"Charlie, will you do me a favor? Stay here with Tanya for an hour or so. I need to take another look at that house on Palm Drive.''

"You think . . . ''

"Yes, I think. If there's a hidden camera in the bedroom, maybe it was recording whatever went down on Thursday night.''

16

Nicky drove down from his hilltop to North Palm Drive in the flats of Beverly Hills and let himself into the dark and lifeless house. He turned on as many lights as he could find, to dispel the eerie feeling of being there by himself at night. The place still smelled subtly of death. The eyes of Elvis Presley looked down upon him from above the fake fireplace and followed his progress to the foot of the stairs. Nicky stepped over the chalk marks where the body had been and bounded quickly up the stairs. On the top floor, as below, he turned on every light switch he passed.

The master bedroom was as gaudy as he remembered it, with the elaborate waterbed surrounded by mirrors on every wall. Nicky tried to recall from which angle the pornographic videos had been recorded. He began tapping on the mirrors, listening for a hollow sound. He found the spot very quickly, a square of glass that sounded different from the others. He was tempted to simply smash it in. Only the thought that he might destroy the recording equipment on the other side kept him looking patiently for the proper access to the hidden cavity.

Fifteen minutes later, he found it. The clothes closet had a false wall at one end, with a sliding panel that led to the secret chamber. Jay Jeffries' television studio was about the size of a telephone booth. A video camera rested on a tripod, pointing through one-way glass onto the bed in the next room. Nicky wondered vaguely what you said to the carpenters when you were designing something like this. Probably as little as possible. He found there was indeed a cassette cartridge inside the camera, which he ejected and brought around to the television equipment in the bedroom.

It was almost too much to ask for that this cassette would reveal what happened Thursday night. In his haste, Nicky had trouble finding the buttons on the VCR. At first, nothing happened at all. High-tech wizard that he was, he had forgotten to turn on the actual TV set.

Finally the scene sprang into view. Nicky turned off some of the lights and sat down on the edge of the waterbed. On the televison screen, Ginny Gina was cavorting with Jay Jeffries in a variety of ways. He felt strangely embarrassed to see her this way. She looked terrible, scrawny and unhappy.

Every now and then, Nicky touched the fast-forward button. At one point—changing from the classic missionary position to a style more generally favored by four-footed creatures—Ginny's mask seemed to fall. Nicky had to freeze the frame for a moment to look at her face more clearly: for one brief moment, as her partner was looking in another direction, all Ginny's despair showed itself on her face.

Then she turned toward J. J. and smiled.

Nicky had to do some more fast-forwarding. This was simply too painful to watch. When he took his finger off the button, he was startled to see a new person in the tableau. This had to be Madame X, J. J.'s mysterious second visitor on the night of his death.

Who was she going to turn out to be?

She stood in the foreground, fully dressed, partially obscuring the bed. Her back was to the camera, so that all Nicky could see was a long black coat and wide-brimmed black hat. Then she moved a few inches, so that Nicky could see J. J. alone on the bed.

But where had Ginny gone?

He reversed the tape, trying to find the beginning of this sequence. It took a few minutes of fiddling before he located the exact end of the earlier sequence. The last frame was of Ginny lying on the bed, while the VJ reached over to the lamp on the bedside table. Probably he had turned off the switch that controlled the video camera, because there was a clear jump in time to the next event. The woman in black suddenly popped into view, her back taking up the frame, then moving aside to show Jeffries alone on the bed. Nicky turned up the volume, trying to hear her voice. But the sound quality was the most amateurish part of this whole production, and he could not hear much. The phrase "Let's do it on the stairs" stood out and was followed by laughter. Then the lady in black disappeared. Jay Jeffries lingered for a moment by himself on the bed, then he reached toward the remote control by the bedside lamp. The screen went blank. And that was all there was.

Nicky reversed and played the sequence several more times, hoping to be able to identify Madame X. But she never showed her face, not even a glimpse of her profile, and the only distinguishing words about doing it on the stairs were still too blurred to be able to recognize the voice again, should he ever hear it.

It was almost as if Madame X were aware of the video camera in the room and used the stairs as a ploy to get away from its close scrutiny. If that were true, it would imply someone who knew a great deal about Jay Jeffries' private life.

Nicky turned off the recorder and television set and put the tape in his pocket. Perhaps the police lab would be able to ungarble the sound and get a better voice I.D. on the lady in black, though Nicky was not optimistic. The lady had not been dumb. She had been clever to leave no clue of herself behind.

The only person who might be able to identify Madame X was Ginny. This gave Nicky a sudden anxious feeling in the pit of his stomach. He wandered into the bathroom, trying to imagine when she had taken her shower, leaving her fingerprints there. What if she had been in bed with J. J. on that fatal night, when suddenly the door downstairs was opened by someone who knew him well? Someone who had the key to the front door or knew where it was hidden outside, and also knew the house well enough to be aware of the concealed camera in the bedroom.

Madame X is coming up the stairs. What would Ginny do? Maybe she would run to the first place for safety, the bathroom— and hide there until the unknown intruder had left.

Was this it? Nicky stood in the bathroom playing his game of "what if." Ginny would be naked and a little miserable, perhaps wrapped in a towel waiting for the late-night visitor to leave.

Did she put her ear to the bathroom door to find out what was going on in the next room? What did she hear?

But perhaps it wasn't like that at all. The old woman across the street could be wrong about both women being in the house at the same time. That would change everything. If so, Ginny's little frolic in the VJ's bed could have been hours earlier than the visit from Madame X.

Nicky walked back into the bedroom, turning off lights behind him. It was time to pay a visit to City Hall.

17

The Beverly Hills City Hall was a ponderous phallic tower erected in simpler times. The police station was in one of the new wings, close to the fire department and behind the public library. Beverly Hills was still small enough to lump everything together like this, though the cops complained about noisy fire trucks, and sometimes old women wandered into the police station trying to borrow a book. In civic government, nothing ever ran as smoothly as you might wish.

Inside, the police station was much like its counterparts everywhere: bulletproof glass, institutional hallways, typewriters clacking, computers, narrow offices, and cops lounging around looking both self-important and a little bored. Saturday night was always a busy time. By the front desk, Nicky saw an unlikely gathering of humanity: a tall woman in a mink coat who was shouting at a short bald man, while a uniformed officer stood referee between them. There was also a Vietnamese boy in rags who didn't seem to know English and a Yuppie couple who had just tried to sneak out on their dinner bill at The Bistro.

Among this assortment of humanity—walking toward him at just this moment—was Maj. Wesley McGroder, the new chief of police. Actually, Major McGroder had been chief for a year and a half now, but to Nicky he would always be the *new* chief, more impersonal and bureaucratic than the old. Chief McGroder had closely cropped gray hair, narrow eyes, and a vaguely military bearing.

"Lieutenant, come here a second. I want to talk to you."

The chief was flanked by the Beverly Hills D.A. on one side and someone from the mayor's office on the other, all of them splendidly dressed in evening wear, passing through the station after some important function somewhere. Nicky put on his most reliable expression and went over to see what the chief might want.

"This new case of yours, Rachmaninoff—what's the name of the victim?"

"Jeffries, sir. Jay Jeffries."

"Yes, that's the one. A man by the name of Bo Daniels called me this morning to see what kind of progress we're making."

"Yes?" Nicky asked vaguely, wondering what the point of this was.

"Well? What kind of progress *are* we making?" asked the chief.

Nicky had to concentrate on retaining his reliable smile. This was exactly the sort of thing he hated about the new chief. His predecessor, Dave Molinari, would never have put any pressure on him just because some big shot wanted a case solved fast. McGroder often behaved as if they were in some kind of service industry in which the customer was always right.

"Actually we're going pretty good," Nicky said, conveniently taking on Charlie's position rather than his own. "We have a good suspect, a girl who lives in Topanga Canyon. It's conceivable we may make an arrest as early as Monday."

"Good work, Lieutenant," the chief said, then turned to the

D.A. "You see, I got a fucking genius at the head of my homicide squad."

Everyone smiled nicely at the compliment. Nicky had been called a genius before. In this town, everything was exaggerated, and everybody loved you madly—as long as you were successful. Nicky had a reputation for unorthodox procedures, but he got the job done. If he were ever to fall on his face, though, Chief McGroder would be the first to turn against him.

"We'll have lunch sometime," the chief said pleasantly.

"I'd love to, sir," Nicky replied. "That'd be swell."

"Tell you what, Rachmaninoff, you bring me in a killer on Monday and I'm going to make damn sure you get some tickets to the Lakers game next weekend. Whad'ya say to that?"

Boy, oh, boy! Nicky hardly knew what to say. Sports events bored him to tears, but he could kiss ass with the best of them. He grinned, he gurgled, he said that was fucking okay. As soon as he was on his own again, walking down the long corridor to his office, he wanted to puke.

Theo was in the office. Though it was late Saturday night, it was hard to drag him away from this place he loved. Nicky found Officer Oshimoto with his feet up on the desk hanging up the telephone. There were remnants of a sushi dinner spread out near the typewriter. Theo was short and frail, with a delicate birdlike face and luminous brown eyes. Any lady cop in town would probably have been able to beat him arm wrestling.

"So how's it going, Theo?" Nicky asked gently. He always had a feeling that if he spoke too loudly Theo might break.

"Oh, very good, Lieutenant. A quiet Saturday night, no bloody bodies so far, sir. But I'm ready for action if needed," he said. Theo was always terrifically polite.

"I bet you are, Theo."

Nicky sat down on the edge of the desk. "How'd you like to do a little surveillance job for me in Topanga?" he asked.

Theo lit up. "Oh, Lieutenant Rachmaninoff! You don't mean it? A chance to get out into the field—a chance to do some *real* detecting!"

"Well, you know—surveillance is usually somewhat boring," Nicky cautioned him.

"No, not to me!" Theo protested. "To me it will be fascinating."

Nicky explained the fascinating job he had in mind: Theo would drive in his own car to the barn in Topanga Canyon, park off the road, and spend the night watching the house. Charlie would relieve him in the morning, and then the two of them would take six-hour shifts until Monday—at which point they would haul Ginny Gina into the station. Nicky wanted to know who came and went. If Ginny left, the surveillance person should follow her.

Nicky walked out of the station and drove home feeling that he had made a reasonable compromise. Ginny would be kept under close wraps until Monday, and if he were lucky—very lucky—he might actually be able to spend an uninterrupted Sunday with his daughter.

18

It rained hard during the night. The tail end of the storm unburdened itself upon the city and then drifted slowly inland. Nicky woke to bright Sunday sunshine pouring in his bedroom window. Birds were chirping in the trees outside. Someone—could it possibly be Tanya?—had put a Vivaldi concerto grosso on the stereo in the next room. A smell of fresh coffee and bacon gently pervaded the air.

There was a knock on his door. "Good morning, Nicholas. I have your coffee," Tanya called.

"Mmm, thanks." As soon as he tried to sit up, he felt terrible. His head weighed in at a thousand pounds. Someone had filled his mouth with dry cotton.

"Are we feeling chipper this morning?" Tanya enquired. She put his coffee next to a half-finished bottle of beer.

"You know what you look like?" she said. "An old gangster on the run."

"I don't know why you say that," he told her, scratching the unshaved stubble of his beard. "What time is it?"

"About ten."

"Charlie still here?"

"No. He left about an hour and a half ago, he said to relieve Theo someplace. I gave him some coffee to take with him."

"Thanks."

"Don't mention it. You guys were sure cute last night."

Nicky rubbed his forehead. "I'm sorry, honey. Were we very loud?"

"Only when you started singing 'Satin Doll' around three in the morning. But I was impressed. You were almost on key."

78

In the living room, an impressive number of empty beer bottles were scattered about the room. They had hit the beer when the wine was gone, and somewhere in the wee hours Charlie had invaded Nicky's home-grown stash of marijuana. Nicky had a feeling this was probably not a good environment for a young girl, but at least it balanced out her Marymount education and her protected life in Bel Air. Tanya actually seemed to be enjoying herself immensely. It was not every day that a girl her age could find herself at such a moral and physical advantage over the older generation. She was fairly gracious about it. She even cooked her father breakfast.

"Well, Tanya, what shall we do with ourselves today?" he asked. "This is your day entirely. We'll do anything you want."

She thought a moment.

"Why don't we drive over to Paradise Cove and fish off the pier?" she suggested.

"Really?" He used to love doing this with her when she was quite a lot younger. In recent years, however, she had preferred more stimulating activities, like going to Disneyland or the movies.

"You're certain you're not just doing this for me?" he asked.

"No, honestly. I'm in sort of an herbal mood today."

"Herbal" was one of Tanya's pet words and covered a lot of ground. Generally, it described the preferences of the generation that flourished after Eisenhower and before Calvin Klein.

Nicky loaded up the car before she could change her mind, finding their old fishing poles at the back of the carport, and they set off to the beach. It was perfect Sunday weather, bright and clear, and the ocean was a deep ultramarine with frothy whitecaps stirred by the wind. They drove without talking very much, listening to rock music on the radio, each in their own thoughts. The Pacific Coast Highway passed the road to Topanga Canyon, and Nicky wondered only briefly how the surveillance was going there. Paradise Cove was another twenty minutes up the coast. There was a picturesque though expensive trailer park, as well as an old wooden pier jutting out into the ocean. It was a peaceful spot, almost herbal, despite the fact that it had been used repeatedly as a location for films and TV shows, most visibly as the spot where James Garner had parked his trailer in "The Rockford Files."

Nicky liked fishing mostly as an excuse to be near the ocean. They walked out to the end of the pier where the water was deepest and cast their lines down. The breeze was tangy fresh and carried no hint of smog. They fished in a companionable silence as the afternoon colors deepened and the ocean surface became flecked with gold. It was a rare afternoon. Nicky took an inner snapshot of himself and his daughter side by side on the pier. He locked it away in his heart as something he knew he might come back to one day.

"You hungry?"

"Mmm . . . okay."

They bought hot dogs, potato chips, candy, and soda. They fished, they ate, they stared out to the endless horizon. They didn't catch a thing, but it didn't matter.

Why, then, was he not at ease? He kept picturing a long black coat, a wide-brimmed black hat. *Let's do it on the stairs,* said the spider to the fly.

Nicky's thoughts swam around a vague circle of ideas: sex, murder, rock and roll, money, power, and life in the sun. The circle of thoughts kept returning to Ginny Gina, for Ginny was only twenty minutes away in Topanga Canyon, and she would be able to answer a lot of questions. Nicky hated mysteries; that's why he was a detective. It went deeply against the grain to be fishing here when there was a case hanging at such a delicate point.

After an hour or so, some teenagers joined them at the end of the pier. Their portable music box was screaming rock music that set his teeth on edge. One of the teenage boys was giving Tanya the eye. Christ, didn't he realize she was only twelve? Maybe Tanya would smile and show the braces on her teeth. Unfortunately, she kept her best profile pointing his way and managed to look ever so much like a young Grace Kelly.

"When I was a teenager, we brought guitars to the beach," he said grumpily. "Not fucking radios."

"Yeah, and you were all probably stoned on LSD," Tanya said. "Very creative."

"Hey, I'm not saying we were perfect. But we tried."

Ten minutes later, Nicky made his only catch of the day. He snagged an ancient aluminum can, genus Budweiser. The boy who had been ogling Tanya thought this was very funny. "Boy, I wouldn't mind catching a cold six-pack of those fish!" he said.

"Asshole!" Nicky muttered

The boy was lumbering over their way. He had just been waiting for some clever opening to get his hands on Tanya.

"I think it's time to leave," Nicky said. "It's getting late. And the damn ocean's polluted with beer cans and radios."

Tanya just laughed. She had always been a precocious child.

"What a silly Nicholas," she said mildly.

Yeah, silly Nicholas. Terrible Nicholas. Nicholas the compulsive, who could not even relax on Sunday and go fishing with his daughter.

Driving home on the coast highway, he turned left on the road to Topanga Canyon and drove with a strange sense of urgency to see what was happening at Ginny and Tommy's barn.

19

Topanga Canyon looked vastly different from the last time he'd been here in the rain. Today the rolling countryside was vivid with color—green hills against blue sky, with bright yellow wild mustard swaying in the breeze.

"Where are we going?" Tanya asked. She said it in a way that implied *nothing* her father might do would surprise her anymore.

"I just want to check on an operation I have going here," he told her. "Won't take long."

"Hmm, last time you said that we had to rescue Charlie naked from outside a whorehouse."

"Tanya, it wasn't a whorehouse. It was a massage parlor."

"Same difference."

Nicky pressed harder on the accelerator so that they were driving faster than they should, racing along the curves. Tanya looked at him strangely. He forced himself to slow down.

In an attempt to get her interested in this small detour, he described Ginny and Tommy and their high-tech barn full of amps and synthesizers. Tanya refrained from making any comment. They drove past the rustic village center and up deeper into the canyon, to where the dirt road took off from the pavement. There was still runoff here from the rain and ruts in the road thick with mud. As Nicky approached the old barn at the end of the road, he saw Theo's light blue Honda half-hidden down a side road, nestled against a field of long grass. Nicky slowed down and pulled alongside. His plan—such as it was—was to leave Tanya with Theo for a few minutes while he went into the barn to light a small fire beneath Ginny and her boyfriend. But there was no one in the car.

"Is this it?" Tanya asked.

"I don't know," he said slowly. "I'm going to take a look."

81

He walked up to the empty Honda. The door on the driver's side was hanging open.

"Can't find your cops, Nicholas?" Tanya asked merrily.

Nicky frowned, eyes scanning the long grass and brush by the side of the road. Instinctively, he unzipped his jacket.

"Maybe Theo's at a massage parlor," Tanya suggested.

"Shut up, Tanya," he told her softly. He had never told her to shut up before, and Tanya was so astonished she did just that.

Nicky's moving line of vision traveled up the road and then stopped. He walked a little ways and looked into the deep brush. A foot was sticking out of the tall grass at a very unnatural angle. Tanya was walking around the Honda to where her father was standing.

"Don't come any closer," he told her.

She didn't understand. "What's the matter, Ni—"

He took hold of her wrist firmly, keeping her in place behind the protection of his body.

"Nicholas, you're hurting me," she complained.

He forced her backward around the empty Honda toward his Austin-Healey. He was looking about like some wild animal, scenting the breeze for danger.

"Daddy, what is it?"

"Shh . . . there's something wrong here, honey," he whispered. "I want you to get in our car and lie flat on the floor. You understand? Do exactly as I say."

She started to object, then changed her mind. Her father had just pulled out his snub-nosed .38 revolver. Never in her entire life had Tanya seen him bring out his gun like this, as though he intended to use it.

Nicky jogged back to where he had seen the leg in the grass. He eased back the safety on the Smith & Wesson and let the gun lead his way into the long grass. A few steps were enough to see it all. Theo was lying facedown on the ground. His hands were bound behind him by police handcuffs, probably his own. There was a small entry wound at the back of his skull. Nicky wanted to move Theo's mouth out of the mud, but he knew it was best to touch nothing. The mud wouldn't matter much anyway because Theo was very dead.

Nicky found it hard to breathe. He felt a cold sweat on his forehead and a warm thud in his ears he realized was his own heart. Theo had been overwhelmed with apparent ease, bound, and executed. Nicky took in the scene with dreamlike clarity. He stared at the dark red blood on the green grass. A caterpillar was climbing over a lifeless arm.

Tanya meanwhile was lying on the floor in his car. Nicky wondered what in hell he should do. He ran, half crouching, back to the trunk of his car where he kept a loaded shotgun locked for just such an occasion as this: *because you never knew when a Sunday outing with your daughter might erupt into a damn bloody massacre, the prepared father travels this city fully armed.*

"I'm beginning to feel sort of ridiculous," Tanya called. "Can I come up for air, or something?"

"Stay down," he told her, pumping a shell into the chamber of the shotgun.

"Shit," she muttered.

Where had she learned language like this? Nicky laid the shotgun against the car and hurriedly put up the canvas top, latching down the two clamps at the top of the windshield. In his haste he pinched his index finger, drawing blood.

"Fuck piss hell!" he swore with passion.

Tanya shook her head in disbelief. "And what did *you* do last Sunday?" she began, mimicking an invisible friend. "Well, I—"

"Tanya, listen to me very carefully. I have to take a look at the barn. I want you to stay exactly where you are. Don't make a sound —and keep hold of this, okay? In case there's trouble."

Tanya's mouth opened stupidly. Nicky was handing her his .38 Smith & Wesson revolver, butt first. Growing up as a policeman's daughter, the main taboo had always been that she was never, under any circumstances, *ever* to touch Daddy's gun. He had let her fire the gun exactly once, when she was seven years old and had expressed some curiosity about it: he'd driven her up into the mountains and let her aim at a tree. The kickback had almost sprained both her wrists—he had wanted her to experience what an ugly and powerful thing a .38 revolver actually was.

Now she hesitated to take the weapon. "It's all right," he said gently, slipping it into her hands. "Look, honey, I know this is heavy. I think that whatever happened here is over, but I'm just being very careful. You understand?"

She nodded.

He studied her face to see if she was holding up. She was. She looked uncomfortable, crouching on the floor of the car, but Tanya was basically too stubborn to fall apart under pressure.

"Okay. Now I'm going to check out what's happening inside the barn. I have a bad feeling the people are dead in there, but they might just be wounded and need help. However, if you hear gunfire . . ."

"Yes?" she asked, her green eyes very large.

"If you hear gunfire, I want you to get away from here as fast as you can. I'm leaving the key in the ignition. I've taught you how to drive this thing, so here's your chance. Go back the way we came, find a phone, dial nine one one, and get help. If anyone tries to stop you, use the gun. Here's the safety catch—see where I'm pointing? Leave it on unless you're in danger. If you have to shoot, hold the gun with both hands. Don't worry about aiming down the barrel, and don't hesitate, not for a second. Just point and shoot and then get the hell away. Okay? Only you're not *really* going to have to do any of this because there's not going to be any trouble I can't handle. I just feel better preparing for the worst."

"Jesus Christ," Tanya said, "Kirsten's not going to believe this!"

"That's right," Nicky told her, trying to smile. "You'll be the envy of the seventh grade. Well, here goes."

He took the shotgun and dove into the long grass by the side of the road. The field separating him from the barn was about twenty-five yards wide, wet and messy with mud. He ran, half crouching, forcing a path through the thick growth, feeling the grass slap against his face.

Beyond an old stone wall was a small garden where baby marijuana plants had recently been started. Beyond that, the barn stood in utter stillness with the sliding door half-opened. Nothing moved. Nicky took a deep breath, jumped over the wall, and ran across the open garden to the side of the barn—stopping near the half-open door, listening, waiting for his racing heart to slow down. There was still no sign of life.

At last, gathering himself for the unknown, Nicky eased slowly toward the open door and peered inside.

He saw synthesizers, speakers, amps, the refrigerator, the kitchen table. His eyes scanned the room until they came to . . .

He looked away quickly and walked soundlessly inside the barn, the shotgun held before him. He thought he'd better check out the bathroom. The door was closed. He stood in front of it, gathering himself, then kicked viciously at a spot slightly to the side of the handle. The door flung open with a loud crack. His gun covered the room, but there was no one inside.

84

At last he lowered the shotgun and turned his attention back to what remained of Ginny Gina and Tommy Torch. He could hardly bear to look.

They were dead, of course. In a way, he had known that from the first moment he had seen Theo's leg protruding from the grass. They were dead, tied to the straight-backed wooden chairs, executed with a bullet to the back of the skull with the same unyielding efficiency as poor Theo back in the field.

Nicky felt a weight of sorrow upon his chest. It wanted to strangle him, but he knew he couldn't let it. Tanya was still on the floor of the car; she would be worried about him. He walked back to the front door and called out to her.

"I'm all right. It's all over," he shouted. "You hear me?"

"I hear you," she shouted back, her voice fragile and incredibly reassuring coming across the meadow.

"Stay where you are," he called. "I'm going to telephone this in, and we'll get the hell out of here."

He walked back inside the barn and spent a grim moment examining the two corpses, trying to see if they had offered any resistance to death. As far as he could tell, they had died like Theo—without protest. Nicky sighed and felt too old. There was a wall telephone he had seen near the refrigerator. He used his shirt-sleeve like a glove so he could pick up the receiver without disturbing any prints. It was simply force of habit. He doubted if the person or persons who had done this job had left any prints. The logistics of taking out Ginny and Tommy and Theo with apparent ease implied a level of professionalism that completely altered the nature of the case.

He heard a noise behind him and spun around. It was Tanya standing in the doorway.

"Don't—" He wanted to yell for her to get away, hide her eyes, run, *don't look*. But she was already inside the door, her face as pale as ice, staring at the dead young musicians tied in their chairs.

He had a sudden and terrible thought that this moment marked the exact end of Tanya's childhood. But he let her stay. She had been part of this, and it seemed she had the right. He was glad that at least Ginny and Tommy had not been too grossly disfigured by the bullet wounds.

"Don't touch anything," he told her, which was unnecessary. Tanya had not moved an inch since coming into the barn.

Not taking his eyes off his daughter, Nicky dialed the operator and asked to be put through to the Topanga station. He got a sheriff

85

whose interest in the conversation gradually increased until he was asking questions in a terse, staccato voice. Nicky hung up. He walked over to Tanya and gently pried the .38 from her right hand. She spoke at last.

"Who did this?" She was angry. Nothing in her well-protected life had prepared her for this final injustice: that someone could simply tie you to a chair and shoot you dead.

Nicky did not say a word. He knew Tanya would not like the answer: *I killed them, dear. Because I wanted to go fishing with you and not deal with this case. Because I said it was Sunday, and Monday would be soon enough. I thought I could be a normal human being for a change and have the weekend with my daughter. But I was wrong, as you see before you. Quite a price to pay for a small mistake—three people's lives.*

He said only, "Come on. It's over."

He put his hand on her shoulder and guided her outside. They walked back to the car without saying a word. Nicky reversed back up the road to where he could turn around, then he headed down into the canyon.

It was a strangely beautiful late afternoon. The sun was getting low, casting long shadows, while the old two-lane highway seemed like a soft ribbon gently wrapped around the green hills.

They came to a long rise where they met a convoy of police cars racing toward the direction from which they had just come. There must have been something about the sound of sirens that made Tanya realize what she had seen was real. She began to cry.

Nicky just kept driving toward the sea.

The Ghost of Rock 'n' Roll
(1)

When the rain stopped, Cowboy left his small hotel room near Hollywood Boulevard and headed out to the streets.

He was a gaunt, ageless figure with shoulder-length hair that was a color somewhere between dirty blond and white, a floppy mustache, elaborate sideburns, and watery blue eyes.

Cowboy, they called him on the streets, after his buckskin jacket, sharply pointed boots, and Stetson hat.

He had lived in this neighborhood a long time, watching it grow worse over the years, full of pimps and pushers, hookers and con artists and thieves—people whose dreams had long since given out. They were drawn to the gaudy neon, along with the tourists from out of state: Hollywood Boulevard. In the sunlight, the old buildings looked inexpressibly small town and shabby, but at night you could still be fooled by the glamour of the lights. Cowboy knew it well. He nodded to Liza, the toothless bag lady who claimed to be a descendant of the last czar of Russia. He said hi to Wally the Wino and Denise the Black Prostitute, who was really a man. There was also Geraldo the Pimp, Jimmy the Holy Roller, even Buddy the Cop.

"Morning, Cowboy," they all said. They all knew him. Or thought they did.

The sidewalk was studded with stars. Cowboy walked over Clark Gable and Jean Harlow, Robert Taylor and Myrna Loy. He took a right turn near Bing Crosby into the Dunkin' Donut shop and sat himself down at the counter. Hilda, the teased blonde with penciled-in black eyebrows, gave him a cup of coffee and two chocolate doughnuts without having to be asked.

"Hey, Cowboy. Long time no see." She grinned.

This was what Hilda always said. It was supposed to be witty, since Cowboy stopped in here several times a day.

The AM radio near the cash register was on to a golden oldies station, thinly playing the old tunes minus any bass. The Beach

Boys were followed by Neil Diamond and then the Supremes. Then, with his second cup of coffee, there it was—"Streets of Love." A song he knew well.

It still did something funny to the pit of his stomach to hear Billy's voice coming over the radio after all these years. It was like entering a time warp.

"Hey, here's your friend, Cowboy," Hilda said.

Cowboy studied the surface of his black coffee, not encouraging conversation. Some years ago he had told Hilda he had known Billy Lion—knew him well, as a matter of fact—and from then on Hilda always said "Here's your friend" whenever a Perceptions tune came on the air. Probably she didn't believe him any more than anyone believed Liza the Bag Lady was really related to the last czar of Russia—but on the streets, people let you have your illusions.

Cowboy glanced up the counter to see if anyone had heard Hilda's comment. Probably he was paranoid, but strange things were happening recently. Fortunately, the doughnut shop was not crowded. There were few people at the counter, and most of them had their faces buried in newspapers, minding their own business.

Someone put a hand on his shoulder. Cowboy jumped and spun around. It was Timothy, a frail old man in a torn raincoat. Timothy was a flasher.

"Whoa there, Cowboy. Didn't mean to startle you," Timothy said. "Just wanted to ask you, though . . . did I ever tell you about the time Elvis Presley was going to make me a star?"

"Sure, Timothy. You've told everyone that story lots of times."

"Well, Elvis was really a very down-home sort of person, just plain folks, you know," Timothy began. Cowboy could have told the story word for word—how Timothy, working as an extra on the film *Love Me Tender,* once had a ten-minute conversation with Elvis Presley that had grown into the central event of a lifetime. Cowboy stood up abruptly and put some money down on the counter for Hilda.

"Gotta go now, Timothy," he said. He felt guilty about the crestfallen look in the old man's eyes.

"Jeez, Cowboy. Sorta in a hurry today, huh?"

Cowboy reached in his wallet and pulled out a twenty. He was one of the few street people who ever had any money, a mystery he never explained.

"Here, buy yourself a new raincoat or something," Cowboy told him, and made a fast escape out to the street. With long strides, he covered the distance from Bing Crosby to Mary Astor, walking west toward Highland. At first, he didn't admit to himself that he knew where he was going. But he was going where he always went, two or three times a week.

On Highland, Cowboy turned up toward the park near the entrance to the Hollywood Bowl. This was his destination. Cowboy sat down on a hard green bench at a spot where he could see the gentle curve of the amphitheater. It was hard to believe how many years had passed since that night in 1967. Cowboy could still close his eyes and see it: the smoke of marijuana rising into the night sky, the colored lights, the rows filled with long-haired young people in their bright crazy clothing, everyone going wild—girls throwing bras, even panties, onstage.

Hard to believe now, over twenty years later, seeing this spot in the bright mundane sunshine. The Perceptions' Hollywood Bowl concert was the event of a lifetime. He and Captain Sunshine, who was the road manager, did the sound. Together they put up the largest sound system ever created to that time—a mountain of speakers driven by 80,000 watts of power. It was a mad gesture to an extravagant time. They said you could hear Billy's voice all the way to Beverly Hills. Afterward, so many neighbors complained that new laws were passed to restrict the volume of further concerts at the Bowl. It was all downhill after that.

"Damn it, Billy, you checked out at the right moment, old friend. You wouldn't have liked the eighties very much, I can tell you that."

He often talked to Billy these days, which was strange—because when Billy was alive, Cowboy hardly had said a word. He had been the listener.

In those days, Cowboy had been a twenty-year-old Green Beret who had served eighteen months in Vietnam. AWOL in San Francisco, stoned on acid, he had managed to get backstage at the old Avalon Ballroom, wearing a cowboy hat to hide his military haircut, finding himself unexpectedly face to face with Billy Lion.

"Hey, Cowboy, where you coming from?" Billy had asked. And that was his name from then on. Billy took the AWOL Green Beret under his wing, gave him a job on the road crew, and took him on tour.

Billy was the best friend an AWOL soldier ever had. Understood everything, did old Billy Lion. But the time was short and over fast. The Hollywood Bowl concert was the climax, but even then the end was in sight.

Cowboy remembered the fight in Billy's dressing room after the show. J. J., Donny, Rick, Bo, and Billy—all of them screaming at each other, saying terrible things.

Cowboy lit a cigarette, stood up from his bench, and wandered off thoughtfully toward Hollywood Boulevard. Normally, coming to the Bowl had a quieting effect on him. It was his way to get back in touch with Billy—almost like going to church. But today there was no quiet in his heart. Angry voices, hatred that would not die, seemed to follow him down the years.

Part Two

Nostalgia Kills

1

Sunday night, some hours after the Topanga Canyon killings, Lt. Nicholas Rachmaninoff pondered the meaning of responsibility.

He didn't know what to do with Tanya. By the time they got back to Sunshine Terrace, her teeth were chattering and she had a frozen, faraway look in her eye. Not knowing what else to do, he got her into a hot bath, made her a lemon drink that had a very healthy wallop of brandy in it, and then bundled her off to bed. He wished he had something brilliant to tell Tanya about the meaning of life and death. Lacking such wisdom, he merely rubbed her back for a long time until her trembling gradually turned to quiet breathing and he knew she was asleep.

When Tanya was taken care of, he took care of himself. He turned off the phone, removed the tiny battery from his beeper, and brought the rest of the bottle of brandy with him out to his front meadow.

He sat down heavily in the long grass and looked out at the terrible city that stretched before his feet in a carpet of twinkling lights. The night was wet with dew, but his thoughts were in too much turmoil to notice.

He took a swallow of hard brandy.

He felt like: a. an utter failure;
b. a lousy father;
c. a lonely bastard not capable of a long-term relationship with a woman;
d. not even much of a cop.

Nicky wallowed in his deficiencies as the level of the bottle went down. He thought of his father, Sgt. Samuel Rachmaninoff, who had gotten himself killed answering a silent alarm to a liquor store hold-up in progress but had never gotten one of his colleagues killed. Not the way Nicky had done to poor Theo.

He raised the bottle to his lips. There was only a quarter of an inch left, but suddenly he felt too miserable even to drink. Theo was dead. Ginny was dead. Tommy was dead. Everything was falling apart, and he—self-indulgent monster that he was—just sat here drinking brandy. *Well, fuck it.*

Nicky Rachmaninoff stood up, staggered toward the edge of his meadow, and flung the bottle as far as he could out to the abyss of the city below.

It wasn't until the bottle had left his hands that he cried: "Oh, God! Now what have I done?"

There were people down there, houses, roads, and cars. In his mind's eye, he followed the bottle's progress through the air, somersaulting head over tails toward disaster below.

Add this to the list of deficiencies: e. The man cannot even dispose of garbage properly!

Whom would he kill now? He envisioned the brandy bottle smashing through the window of a moving station wagon full of children. He saw the station wagon losing control, slamming into a lamppost.

This was the exact moment Nicky truly and finally learned the meaning of responsibility. It was like a flash of faith, an insight, a turning point. Here it was, truth in a bottle: *Everything you do affects everything around you, precisely.*

Nicky heard the bottle land softly in the not-so-distant brush. He sat back in the grass and cried.

2

The second night, Nicholas Rachmaninoff discovered sex was better than brandy, if you were a man hell-bent on salvation.

He kept at it until they were covered in sweat and could hardly move anymore. She called him a crazy-wonderful Russian beast.

"God, Nicky! I don't believe what you're doing to me!"

She had to bite down on the sleeve of her sable coat to keep from crying out and waking Tanya in the next room. At last they rolled apart, hearts beating loudly, legs still intertwined. After a while, she giggled.

"You always knew my erogenous zones," she told him. "Even back in high school."

"Well," he said modestly, "we learned together."

Susan Merril sat up from the bed of pillows they had created in front of the fireplace. Her shoulders were bare, golden in the reflected firelight. The rest of the living room was dark, hidden in shadows. Susan had arrived some hours earlier dressed in old jeans, a T-shirt with USA FOR AFRICA written across the front, and a twenty-thousand-dollar ankle-length coat of silver Russian sable. At this moment, the jeans and T-shirt along with bra and panties were scattered across the living room floor, while the fur coat was serving as a blanket. Nicky and Susan lay beneath the soft sable with their toes sticking out.

"More wine?" she asked.

"Mmm . . ."

She stepped out of their makeshift bed, and Nicky watched her walk naked into the kitchen, coming back with the bottle. She was an elegant woman, Susan Merril, particularly without clothes. He knew she liked the firelight, though, thinking it would hide the flaws like the fact her left breast hung just slightly lower than the right, due to Tanya's preference to this side back in the nursing days. A good Hollywood actress was always studying lighting and angles. She snuggled back under the fur and looked at Nicky earnestly with her blue eyes.

"So what do you think?" she asked. "You and me lying here like this?"

"Sort of blows me away," he admitted. "Like a heavy dose of déjà vu. Reminds me of a high school chick I used to know who really knew what to do in the backseat of a car."

"Clown," she said languidly, resting her head on his chest. Gently, he stroked her wild blond hair. Nicky was lying on his back, full of postcoital thoughts. Wondering, for example, if he was ever going to be able to look Frank in the eye again. This was not the first time he and Susan had made love since their divorce ten years ago. They had had a few for old times' sake scattered here and there across the years—though not often, and not for a long time. And it had never been like this—thunderbolts and violins—not since the very early days of their love.

This encounter, whatever it meant, had begun in the afternoon with Susan phoning him at the station. She had just read the newspapers and was incredulous that Nicky had placed their daughter at the scene of this week's most spectacular multiple murder. Susan was so upset she'd managed to have her call interrupt a closed meeting with Police Chief McGroder and the mayor.

At that point, it hadn't looked like they'd be ending up the evening in bed together.

"You son of a bitch!" she had shouted over the line. "How *could* you, Nicky? You always cared more about your job than you did for any of us—but this time you've gone too far."

Nicky had managed to calm her down a little—not easy with the mayor and the chief looking on with bemused tolerance. Susan's phone call had been just one more hassle in an already impossible day. A cop killing set many wheels in motion, and this Monday had been an endless succession of meetings with various officials—sheriffs and district attorneys, medical examiners and bureaucrats from all over town. This was definitely not the time to have a fight with his ex-wife. Nicky had suggested she stop by his house that evening to discuss the matter in private. He'd thought it would be a good idea if she saw how Tanya was doing for herself.

Actually, Tanya was doing better than Nicky had any right to expect. Monday morning he'd told her she didn't have to go to school if she didn't want to. Tanya had sat at the breakfast table looking every inch the tragic heroine. But it soon was obvious she couldn't *wait* to get to school to tell Kirsten and Bunky and all her friends about her amazing Sunday.

The school bus had come, and she'd kissed him before running off.

"I love you, Dad," she'd said.

Magic words. She wasn't even calling him Nicholas anymore.

When Susan arrived Monday night, in her old blue jeans and sable coat, Tanya was in a heavy telephone mode, too busy in her room to give her mother much attention. By now the Sunday adventure was ancient history. As far as Nicky could tell, the conversation on the phone seemed mostly back to boys.

"I guess Tanya's all right," Susan said wonderingly.

"The young bounce back," he told her. "It's the middle-aged you have to worry about."

Nicky cooked dinner, with Susan's help. They dragged Tanya away from the phone long enough to eat. At the dinner table she said things like "Gosh, it's great to see you two together again" and "This almost feels like a real family, don't you think?"

After dinner, Tanya said she was going to turn in early. She yawned dramatically and said she was so exhausted *nothing* would keep her awake.

"Subtle, isn't she?" Nicky said.

Susan flashed him her sly pussycat smile.

They were sitting side by side on the sofa, looking at old photo albums from their marriage, when a friendly hug led to a friendly kiss. In moments, hands were groping at bras and working at zippers. There was a rapid deployment of clothing on the floor, skin against skin, hard into soft, man into woman. There was also an attempt to do this without much noise, so their innocent daughter in the next room wouldn't know what the grown-ups were up to in front of the fire.

"I've missed you, Nicky," she said, very relaxed, after it was over. She rested her wineglass on his chest. "You're the anchor in my life, you know."

"Bringing you down?"

"No, keeping me safe. I guess it's because I've known you so long, before I was famous. In this business, it's so easy to lose your way. But you . . . you make me remember who I really am."

He didn't encourage her to talk. He was afraid of what she might say, where it might lead. But she kept talking anyway.

"I mean, Frank doesn't *really* know me. Not like you do, Nicky. Frank and I always have a wonderful time, you know. With him, life's a party all the time. He's never depressed, never down. I needed someone like that after you. Or I thought I did. But my marriage with Frank's never gone deeper than the surface. I'm not sure I even love him . . . maybe I never did."

"Well," he said evenly, "you two certainly are photogenic. Maybe the most photogenic couple in Bel Air."

"All on the surface," she repeated solemnly. This clearly was Susan's evening to get below the surface. She started telling him amazing things. She hadn't had a really good orgasm in years—not like the ones she had had tonight. Not only that, she wasn't even certain she wanted to be an actress anymore. There was that much doubt and indecision in her life.

"Oh, Nicky, sometimes I miss the old days. I really do. It was so much more fun *wanting* to be rich and famous than it actually turned out to be."

"Yeah." He sighed. "Being a celebrity sucks."

He began nibbling on her calf, working his way up her thigh.

"Nicky, be serious! I'm trying to talk to you."

He took a small nip at the soft place along her inner thigh. "Yum yum," he said. "This *is* serious. I haven't eaten an actress for days."

She gave a little shriek of laughter, which changed abruptly to a soft moan.

"You're an animal," she told him.

"A beast," he agreed.

It was fun being with Susan again. Years rolled away, and he felt almost young again. He had to remind himself it didn't mean much —just a trip down Memory Lane.

3

On Tuesday morning, Nicky learned two important facts:

First, the Beverly Hills murder Thursday night was definitely linked to the Sunday massacre in Topanga Canyon. Jay Jeffries, Theo, Ginny, and Tommy had all been shot by the same .32-caliber handgun, whose slightly irregular barrel left small grooves on the bullet—or striations, as they were called by the lab—which made the slug as identifiable as fingerprints.

The second piece of news was that none of this need concern him anymore. The investigation of both sets of killings had been taken away from the Beverly Hills homicide squad and given to the Los Angeles County Sheriff's Department instead.

Nicky and Charlie learned this at a meeting with Chief McGroder a little before noon on Tuesday. Nicky had seen it coming. In Los Angeles the various police agencies held sway in the cities, but the sheriffs ruled the hinterland—the far-flung reaches of the county, a lonely empire of highways, oil fields, beaches and bars and rowdy coastal communities—all the vast unincorporated tracks of land like Topanga that no on else dared to claim. The sheriffs were not famous for their cooperation. They wore cowboy hats and six-shooters, and Lord help anyone who got in their way.

Tough guys like that could hardly think of a place like Beverly Hills without a smile. With careless superiority, they informed Chief McGroder that they would be taking over all aspects of the murder investigation.

Of course McGroder could have protested, but the chief was only too glad to give it away.

"This is a lucky break," he explained. "The sheriffs have the resources to do this right. I know you guys are gung-ho to avenge Officer Oshimoto's death—and I don't blame you; no, I don't blame you at all. But that's all the more reason to keep this entirely impersonal. This way no one can accuse us of any wrongdoing."

This way, also, Beverly Hills could return to being a nice polite rich person's police force, unmarred by violent crime, keeping the streets safe for multimillionaires.

Charlie and Nicky came out of the meeting quietly, unable to look at each other. They wandered slowly through the maze of corridors back to their squad room, which seemed diminished and shabby and very desolate with Theo gone. Nicky was worried about his partner. Charlie and Theo had been close. On Monday, Nicky had tried to keep Charlie too busy to think about it too much, sending him out on a variety of errands while he himself was detained with the various officials of death. But now the case was gone, and the only job before them was to gather all the paperwork they had done on the Jeffries murder and send it over to the sheriffs in Topanga.

Nicky sat at his desk gazing out the window at the strangely arabesque design of the post office next door. He felt momentarily out of steam. He thought of Susan's golden body in the firelight. When she'd left early in the morning, she'd said she wanted to see him again. He didn't know what he thought exactly about having an affair with his ex-wife.

Charlie suddenly kicked Theo's desk savagely with his foot. Nicky turned sharply to see Charlie's eyes streaming with tears.

"Damn you, Theo!" he cried. "How could you go and get yourself killed!"

Charlie had been going through Theo's desk and had just come across the first few pages of a book they had been planning to write together: *A Guide to the Sushi Bars of Southern California,* by Charles Katz and Theo Oshimoto. They had not gotten far in this vast project, but coming across the notes they had made was just too much for Charlie to bear.

Nicky stood up and closed the door so the guys in robbery next door wouldn't hear. Cops were not supposed to cry, not even in a place like Beverly Hills.

"Damn it, Nicky! How can you just sit there like that? What kind of cold bastard are you?"

"Go ahead. When you're finished, we'll talk about what we're going to do."

Charlie laughed bitterly, wiping the tears from his cheeks with the back of his hand. "What the hell do you mean? There's nothing we can *do*—we've been dealt out of the game, brah, in case you haven't noticed."

Nicky stared at his partner without comment. He brought his

fingertips together into a kind of cathedral. "Tell me about yesterday," he said at last. "Let's go over some of the alibis."

This had been Charlie's assignment on Monday—to check out the whereabouts of everyone they knew so far in this case, for both Thursday night and Sunday afternoon.

"Why bother, Nicky? What's the bloody use?"

"Humor me."

"Okay." Charlie sighed. "The alibis."

He took out a small notebook from his shirt pocket. "First off, we have the great man, Bo Daniels. He seems to be in the clear on both occasions. Thursday night, he and his wife, Kitty, were on a jet from Hawaii to L.A. They arrived a little before midnight, and a limousine took them directly to their beach house at Trancas. On Sunday, they were at the beach house all day. In the late afternoon, Bo and Kitty had a little family barbecue with their two kids and a vice-president of Fox who lives next door. Very chummy. And Nicky, you know that sexy little thing?"

"Unity Sphere?" he guessed.

"Yeah. The rumors are she's Bo's mistress. Apparently, Mrs. Daniels knows all about it and doesn't mind. Bo's such a great man, you see, everyday morality just doesn't apply."

Nicky frowned. Although he had been vaguely suspicious there was a sexual connection between Bo and Unity, he was disappointed to have it confirmed.

"Now Rick Elsmore—here's a guy who knows how to party. Thursday night he had dinner at Spago's, then spent the rest of the evening club hopping—The Roxy, Tramp, the Palomino—all favorite haunts where he's well known. After hours, he ended up at a private party over at the Château Marmont that was given by some English rock star. . . . Now Sunday afternoon, at the time in question, Rick was in a small recording studio in Hollywood, a place called X-Wave Sound. He's doing some session work with a group called Rude Cousin. They all have pink hair and white faces. Very creative, I'm told. Donny Meredith was there as well—it seems Donny is producing this great work of art."

"Where was Donny Thursday night?"

"At his home on Mulholland Drive, with his wife, Andrea. Apparently he's the early-to-bed type, unlike Rick. Now we get to the ladies you asked me to check out, and here's where things start getting murky."

"Murky?"

100

"Yeah. First of all, Marilyn de Malibu—whose real name, incidentally, is Janet Weinburger—lives with Nancy Normal, née Sandy Giannini, the maid."

"No kidding. They're roommates?"

"They're lovers, Nicky. Marilyn and Nancy are gay. Now Thursday night, Marilyn had dinner with Unity at a little place in Westwood. They say they saw a double feature afterward and then had a drink, but I don't have any confirmation of that."

"What about Nancy Normal?"

"Nancy went out on her own. I get the impression she was a bit unhappy about her girlfriend having dinner with Unity. So she went shopping and then saw a movie by herself. No witnesses. So she's a contender. She could have knocked off J. J. easy."

"Where was she Sunday afternoon?"

"Ah! Now here's where we have some interesting contradictions. Both Marilyn and Unity said they were together with Nancy in the hot tub at Unity's house in Laurel Canyon. Makes you wish you were a bar of soap, huh? I spoke to Ms. de Malibu separately, and her timing is different. She says the hot tub party was Sunday *morning* and that she and Nancy left Unity's house closer to noon. They had a fight driving back to their apartment in Westwood, and Nancy got out of the car in Beverly Hills. So none of the three women really has an alibi for Sunday afternoon."

"Hmm . . . did Marilyn say what her fight with Nancy was about?"

"Jealousy. Everyone lusts for sweet Unity Sphere. Nancy thought Marilyn was ogling the girl too much in the hot tub, and Marilyn didn't like the way Nancy put suntan lotion on Sweetie-Pie's back."

Nicky was staring out the window at the post office again, always a source of inspiration.

"You know, Charlie, when I left Topanga Sunday afternoon, I was convinced the whole thing had been done by a couple of really slick professionals. But one girl—one especially attractive girl—could have done the job easy. All she had to do was get rid of Theo first. She could have simply walked up to him in the car—Theo would have been delighted for the company—gotten the drop on him, ordered him into the bushes, and shot him with a silencer. Then she could go to the barn to take care of Ginny and Tommy. No one would have been suspicious of a pretty woman until it was too late."

Charlie hit his desk with his fist. "Damn it, Nicky, can't you see it? Theo probably smiled at her! He was probably *polite* to his fucking killer!"

"Let's go over your movements Sunday," Nicky suggested.

"We've done that already."

"Well, let's do it again. Maybe you missed something."

"Okay, Sunday . . . I woke up at your house with a very dry mouth and a headache. Your angelic daughter made me a cup of coffee, and I drove out to Topanga. I got to the barn around nine and found Theo asleep in his car. I sent him home and told him to come back at five. So I took up my position, and it was all a big zero. Nothing happened at all until noon, when Ginny came out of the house to inspect her marijuana garden. Tommy came out to see what kind of day it was. He pissed in the bushes, and then he went back inside and started playing music, if you can call it that. Ginny was outside for maybe an hour, and then she went inside. I never saw either of them again, and there were no visitors. Theo came back early—at three—that damn guy was just too excited about doing 'real police work' to stay away. Shit, Nicky! He wouldn't have been killed if he'd listened to me and returned at five as he was supposed to. No fucking killer would have gotten the drop on me . . . but Christ, I was still hung over from the night before, and he was so eager, so I left him there. I was going to catch a little nap, get something to eat, and come back at ten . . ."

Charlie's voice trailed off into the mist.

"So you left him at exactly what time?" Nicky persisted.

"Ten minutes past three. I checked my watch."

"And Tanya and I got there at four. That means the whole thing was done within fifty minutes. The perp was damn close to both of us."

The two men fell silent with this thought. Nicky was thinking he had probably passed the killer on the highway. The phone rang.

"Yeah, homicide," Charlie said with no energy at all. He made a nasty face into the receiver and stuck out his tongue to the invisible caller as he passed the phone. Nicky had a feeling he knew who was on the line.

"Yes, Chief?" he inquired politely.

"Lieutenant, would you come into my office for a moment? There's a gentleman from the FBI who wants a word with you."

"Certainly, Chief."

Nicky hung up the phone and stood up. Charlie was back to

staring at Theo's old desk with a dead look in his eyes. Nicky thought he'd better find something to keep him occupied while he was gone.

"Look, Charlie—get on the computer and see if any of our suspects happens to own a thirty-two-caliber gun, okay?"

"Our *suspects*," the sergeant repeated pessimistically. "Jesus, Nicky. It could have been anyone. Maybe it was just a prostitute, for chrissake, or someone we don't even know about yet."

"Then we'll find out," Nicky said. "We're going to solve this one, Charlie, I promise you."

Charlie looked up with his sad brown eyes and didn't say a word.

"I promise you," Nicky said again. Then he went to see what the FBI could want.

4

Inspector Dwight Jones was tall and black and cool. He wore a charcoal-gray pinstripe suit, a pink shirt with French cuffs, and a burgundy tie. His black shoes had a mirror shine. His eyes were cold.

Chief McGroder made the introductions, then sat back behind his weighty desk. The chief's office was large and splendid, and there were a number of framed photographs on the wall: the chief with Glenn Ford, the chief with Nancy Reagan, the chief with Joe Montana. In each case, the chief seemed very thrilled to be in the company of someone so famous.

"Well, Lieutenant, I bet you're going to laugh when you hear this! The sheriffs aren't getting your case, either. Ha! Ha! Aren't they going to be pissed? The FBI's taking over the entire thing."

Nicky looked at the dapper FBI inspector, who was busy adjusting his burgundy tie. He didn't seem terribly impressed by the police department in Beverly Hills.

"What's this all about, Inspector?" Nicky asked.

Inspector Jones smiled nastily and crossed his long legs. He seemed to find it amusing that someone so far beneath him should be asking for an explanation. Nicky was beginning to get awfully fed up with self-important people.

"What if I were to tell you, Lieutenant, that the Mafia has come to Beverly Hills?"

"Not the Mafia!" Nicky gasped. "First the Iranians, now the Cosa Nostra. Let's hope we get a few good pizzerias out of it, at least."

Inspector Jones was not amused. "Let me spell it out for you, Rachmaninoff. For the past two years, we've been conducting an extensive investigation—an international probe, in fact—into the relationship between organized crime and the entertainment industry."

Agent Jones spoke very distinctly, managing to make it seem a little humorous that he should be explaining himself—like a college professor giving a lecture to a chimpanzee.

"Basically, Hollywood has become a very big laundry for drug money from back east. Now I'm sure we would all appreciate help from the Beverly Hills homicide squad in resolving this dire situation. However, we have a rather delicate sting operation going on. We also have several undercover operatives in rather sensitive positions. So what we're asking you, quite simply, is to back off. Leave this to us. You don't even know the good guys from the bad."

Nicky leaned back in his chair.

"Organized crime, huh?" he asked, remembering what Unity had told him. "But why kill Jay Jeffries? He was just a harmless, hedonistic little VJ. A has-been from the sixties."

The inspector sighed darkly. "Greed," he said. "Corruption. Mr. Jeffries got himself caught in an internal power struggle between those wishing to control the di Sutro crime family. And I'm afraid that's all I'm prepared to tell you, Lieutenant."

Nicky tried to picture this but couldn't. It sounded quite simple, but it didn't feel right. "But Jeffries was killed by a woman," he objected. "We found evidence to suggest he even had sex with his killer—that doesn't sound like a Mafia hit to me."

"Oh, some of the best hit men *are* women these days," the agent said in an offhand manner. "It's quite the equal opportunity field, you know. And as for the little fucky-fucky—well, it doesn't surprise me a bit. Frankly, the new generation of gangsters—they're a little flaky, not as serious as the old. Why, most of them are almost Yuppies."

The inspector looked at his gold Rolex wristwatch. "Well, time to get to work," he said, rising from his chair. "So you'll leave this to us, won't you, Rachmaninoff? Too many cooks in the kitchen, you know, and all that . . ."

"Just one more question."

"I'll try."

"You're saying that Bushy di Sutro is laundering mob money through The Rock Channel, and that Jay Jeffries somehow got involved? Is that it?"

Inspector Jones arched a left eyebrow and looked very smug. "I don't believe I said that, Lieutenant. No, I don't believe I mentioned Bushy di Sutro at all."

Nicky stood up. He had an absurd desire to take the FBI man by his elegant pinstripe suit and shake him until information came pouring out. "But why Tommy and Ginny and Theo?" he pleaded. "Why did they have to die?"

The inspector seemed to grow more and more pleased with himself. "I told you, Rachmaninoff, leave this one to us. The bureau has the situation well in hand."

"Fuck you do!" Nicky exploded. "If you had the situation in hand, Theo Ushimoto would be alive right now."

"Rachmaninoff!" cried Chief McGroder, aghast a mere cop would insult the mighty FBI.

The inspector's eyes became narrow slits. "So you think you're a wise-ass, Rachmaninoff—some hot-shit cop who's *even* been married to a Hollywood actress? Well!" He made it sound like a sexual deviation. "Yeah, I know all about you, Lieutenant, and let me tell you something—you couldn't find your dick if your mama handed it to you on a silver spoon."

The situation was deteriorating fast.

"Gentlemen, *please!* This isn't getting us anywhere," Chief McGroder bemoaned.

Inspector Jones and Nicky Rachmaninoff were squared off, standing face to face a few mean inches apart. The FBI agent was nearly two inches taller than Nicky and some hard pounds heavier. He did not look nearly so refined as he had earlier on. Nicky thought his best bet would be to knee him in the balls, without warning—very hard—then a swift karate chop to the windpipe. Then run like hell.

To Nicky's surprise, Inspector Jones suddenly smiled, though it was not a smile to warm the heart. "Listen here, dumb shit," he said sweetly. "What if I were to tell you that one of your very closest palsy-walsies is a major Mafia figure?"

"Bullshit," Nicky snarled.

The inspector laughed with glee. "Oh, this be good! I'm referring to your ex-wife's new hubby. How that grab you, baby? Yeah, a major Mafia figure, and all this time you didn't know diddly shit. That's right—I'm talking about Mr. Frank Fee."

5

Nicky was so preoccupied on his way back to his office, he took a wrong turn and drifted toward the jail before he saw what he had done.

Frank? he thought. *Frank just couldn't be involved with this!*

Nicky thought back to when he saw him last Friday. He had to admit, Frank *had* seemed worried, not his normal carefree self. And he had asked questions about J. J. But involved with the Mafia? This was turning into a bad hallucination.

Nicky shook his head mournfully. The sergeant outside the jail block was giving him a funny look, so he turned around and slowly made his way back to his own squad room.

Charlie's mood had improved dramatically in the time he'd been gone.

"Oh, Nicholas, you sly son of a bitch. Bull's-eye, brother! Right to the fucking heart!"

Nicky looked at Charlie with no comprehension at all. "Huh?"

"I've found it, that's what. Guess which one of our beauties owns a nice inexpensive Remington thirty-two-caliber automatic?"

Nicky shook his head hopelessly.

"God, Nicky, you look like you just dropped in from Pluto. Marilyn de Malibu—our ex-groupie lesbian from publicity, who doesn't have a very good alibi for Thursday night and Sunday afternoon—*that's* who. What do you think of that?"

"What do I think?" Nicky asked. He sat down at his desk without answering his own question or Charlie's and made sure the Beverly Hills Post Office was still there outside his window. It was.

"Hey, Nicky—did McGroder give you a lobotomy?"

Nicky brought his attention in from where it had been wandering on the street, and he told Charlie about his conversation with the dapper Inspector Jones from the FBI, leaving out the part about Frank. He couldn't quite bear to pass that information on yet.

Charlie was chuckling in a very nasty way. "Ha! I bet the sheriffs are just gonna *love* being upstaged by the FBI! Boy, oh, boy."

"That was McGroder's reaction, too," Nicky told him.

Charlie stopped chuckling. He didn't want to have anything in common with Chief McGroder. "So where does that leave us? Maybe we can solve this one ourselves, Nick—whad'ya say? Up-stage the sheriffs, the FBI, fucking *everybody*."

"Don't get carried away," Nicky warned him. "He who lives by the ego dies by the ego. Anyway, if this case really is a Mafia deal, we're not going to get too far on it, just the two of us. The area of investigation is too large."

"Yeah?" Charlie challenged. He was wound up. He sat down on the edge of Nicky's desk, grinning fiendishly.

"Beverly Hills is still the damn key," he said. "We find out who killed J. J. and we'll know who got Theo. Organized crime can have Hollywood, for all I care. Just give me Theo's killer and I can walk away from the rest."

Nicky gave his partner a hard look. "If we stay on this, we could both find ourselves back in uniform giving tickets to jaywalkers—you know that, don't you?"

"Nicky, no one's going to blame us for trying to find out what happened to Theo. He was our guy, for chrissake. I mean, if you don't take care of your own, where the hell are you?"

"Employed," Nicky told him.

"Hell, we get kicked off the force—we can always open up a restaurant. Make tons of money. So what do you say?"

Nicky was trying to think. His brain felt like oatmeal, and it didn't help to have Charlie hovering over him.

"Tell me, Charlie—you have any friends in the sheriffs' department?"

"Yeah, sure. There's a captain I know, Marty Gorn. We were in a transcendental meditation class together over in Westwood."

"You're kidding."

"No, honestly. This was about five years ago. Sheriffs have an especially heavy load to transcend, but Marty's a pretty good guy. For a Pisces. We get together for dinner every now and then, usually Indian food."

"That's good," Nicky told him. "What I want you to do is call your friend and find out what the sheriffs' lab came up with in Topanga. They had two days there, so they must have learned something beyond the gun match-up. While you're doing that, I'll go have a chat with Marilyn de Malibu about thirty-two-caliber revolvers."

"All right, Nicholas! We're still in the game, huh?"

"I guess so," he said. "Until they deal us out for good."

6

Nicky took his Austin-Healey out onto the congested freeway, around the side of the Hollywood Hills into the flat sprawl of the San Fernando Valley. The black glass towers of Inter Stellar Village stood gleaming in the midday sun. Nicky was beginning to suspect black was an appropriate color for the building to be.

Unfortunately, Marilyn wasn't there. A pleasant young man in a tan uniform told him Ms. de Malibu had called in sick that morning.

As long as he was there, Nicky tried to see Bo Daniels, then Unity Sphere—but they were out as well. At least that's what the nice young man told him, and with Nicky's investigation being what it was, he thought it best not to try and bluff his way through.

Instead, he drove back on the freeway to West Los Angeles, from where he had just come, and then to Westwood, where Marilyn shared a high-rise condominium with her girlfriend, Nancy Normal. Nicky might have telephoned ahead to make certain she was home, but he was hoping for a surprise confrontation.

The condo was all steel and glass and glitz. It had a pretentious lobby with the largest chandelier Nicky had ever seen. There was also an unpleasant doorman with white gloves who rang the ladies' apartment and reported there was no one at home.

Nicky wondered what to do next. When in doubt, you may as well eat. He happened to know a great drive-in not far away on Santa Monica, a place that was greasy all the way to its soul. He did sneaky things like this when Charlie was not there to stop him.

He ordered a double monsterburger, large fries, and a chocolate shake, which was delivered to his car window by a teenage girl on roller skates. He lingered lovingly on each taste, the delicate combination of salt and grease and catsup. Tomorrow it would be back to avocado sandwiches on earth bread, but today he would throw caution to the winds.

He flagged down the mobile waitress.

"How about an order of onion rings?" he suggested.

"Why not?" she replied. The waitress wore an orange minidress and appeared to be about sixteen. She had nice legs, though her complexion could stand some improvement. Probably she ate here, too.

It was soothing to get back to one's roots. Children of Los Angeles had some traditions after all. Maybe Chinese people felt like this coming across a really good bowl of rice. For a born-and-bred Californian, it was old Cadillac fins, "Crusader Rabbit," French fries, and rock and roll.

Nicky ate more and more slowly. Images of Susan played through his brain like a home movie. From the first time he had seen her long ago in the hallway at Hollywood High to last night in front of the fire. He also thought about Frank.

He couldn't finish his monsterburger. He hardly touched his onion rings when they came. The waitress on roller skates glided by with a faraway smile, and he knew coming to the drive-in had been a mistake.

He threw the remaining food into the garbage, doing a nice dunk shot from his car window. Nicky's stomach growled. He belched.

He supposed his body was trying to tell him that somewhere along the way he had grown up.

7

Unity Sphere lived in a cute little bungalow in Laurel Canyon beneath the trees. The house was painted white with blue trim, with wooden shutters on the windows carved with hearts. There were also boxes full of brightly colored geraniums and a small elf by the front door. Sleeping Beauty could live here and be happy.

In the driveway stood a not-so-cute motorcycle, a big old Harley-Davidson, the kind the Hell's Angels liked to ride. There were neighbors not far away on each side of the house, a Swiss chalet to the left and a modernistic glass box to the right.

Nicky rang the doorbell. From inside the bungalow came the first four notes of Beethoven's Fifth Symphony. There was no answer, so he played the melody again. He waited a moment, then rapped sharply on the front door with his knuckles.

The door had not been completely closed, and it swung open a few inches. Nicky made an instinctive police move, jumping to the side of the doorway and reaching for his gun. He wasn't sure why he was suddenly so nervous. He thought of Theo.

"Hello? Anyone home?"

There was no answer. He pushed the door fully open with the tip of his revolver and peered cautiously inside. From where he stood, he could see the entire living room. He had an impression of potted plants, macramé holders, candles, and brightly polished wood. Everything was neatly arranged: a rocking chair in front of a stone fireplace, a couch covered with Guatemalan material, various posters on the walls. But there was no Unity.

"Hello?" he called again. The only answer was the sound of his heartbeat in his ears.

One of these days I'm going to get killed doing shit like this, he considered. He walked into the house slowly, the .38 leading the way. Every few steps he stopped and listened and looked around. From the center of the living room, he could see a kitchen, a small dining alcove, and a bedroom that contained a big old-fashioned bed with a thick eiderdown on top.

Nicky lowered his pistol, though he still kept it in his hand. He liked Unity's bungalow. Everything was girlishly clean, bright, and optimistic. On a table by a rocking chair he noticed a paperback copy of *Siddhartha* opened and lying facedown.

He spent some time examining the titles on her bookshelf. She had almost all of Herman Hesse, from *Damian* to *The Bead Game.* There was also a heavy dose of Carl Jung: *Man and His Symbols; Memories, Dreams, and Reflections.* Some American Indian stuff, like *Seven Arrows.* D. H. Lawrence, Tolstoy, Dickens, and books of poetry. Could this really be the house of a teenage VJ from The Rock Channel? Nicky was impressed. The girl was not only pretty and young, she was apparently intelligent as well—a lethal combination.

Nicky was taking this all in when he heard a sound from outside the French door at the rear of the house, a sound like a board groaning under pressure. He raised his gun and stood very still. After a moment he walked noiselessly to the rear door. He turned the knob as quietly as he could. Then he threw himself against the door, tumbled on through, and came up into a crouch, ready to fire.

"Police!" he cried. "Freeze!"

He wasn't certain who was more startled—the woman or himself. She was completely naked, standing by a hot tub that was built into the redwood deck, dripping water and shivering with surprise.

But it wasn't Unity, whom he had come to see. Nicky's revolver was pointing straight to the heart of Marilyn de Malibu, whom he had been looking for earlier.

8

At least there was no need to search her for a weapon. Marilyn de Malibu stood defiant in her nakedness, hand on hip, glaring at him angrily. She was a handsome woman, making it look good to be forty: tanned, hard cool features, with hair so short and molded it made her head a piece of sculpture.

She was not, however, a natural blonde.

"You can get dressed," Nicky told her, putting away his gun.

"I'd prefer to get back in the tub," she said.

"By all means." Sophisticated California cops like Lieutenant Rachmaninoff hardly thought twice about interrogating attractive female suspects in hot tubs.

He sat down on a wooden bench and took out a small spiral notebook. The redwood deck overlooked a small stream whose opposite bank rose sharply upward, covered with thick brush and pine trees, giving the backyard complete privacy. The afternoon sun found a path through the canopy of tall trees, slanting down on Marilyn in the hot tub like a spotlight from above.

"Seen any wood nymphs lately?" Nicky asked.

"Huh?" She gave him a look that was supposed to make him feel he was a creep, then flicked on the Jacuzzi to tune him out. Nicky reached forward and turned off the switch. It was a battle of wills. The water jets gurgled and farted to a halt.

"Fuck!" she said nastily. Nicky had a feeling she didn't like him much.

"Life's sure a bummer," he told her sympathetically. "Cops harass you in the hot tub. And California's supposed to be paradise."

"Look, do you think you could get to the point? You're sort of weird, you know."

Nicky smiled. "Okay, let's start with Unity," he said agreeably. "Perhaps you can tell me where she is?"

She shrugged. "I dunno."

"Take a guess," he suggested.

"She's probably at the studio taping next week's shows. She's going to Hawaii with Bo for a few days, so she has to get ahead."

"Really? I was just over at Inter Stellar Village, and they told me Unity wasn't there."

"Yeah? Maybe they didn't want you around," she sneered. "I mean, no one's exactly thrilled to host the police."

"It's a burden to be popular," Nicky admitted. Marilyn didn't smile back. She stared at him with no curiosity, wishing only that he would go away.

"Unity lets you use her house while she's not here?"

"Of course. She leaves a key for me under the elf. You can ask her if you like."

"I will. Tell me, why didn't you answer the door when I rang the bell?"

"I was undressed, that's why. Then I heard someone sneaking around inside the house. I got scared."

This seemed reasonable enough. Nicky decided it was time to get to the heart of the matter.

"Marilyn, you own a thirty-two-caliber Remington automatic. Will you please tell me where this gun is now?"

"How should I know? I haven't seen it in months."

"Is that so? When did you see it last?"

"It was in my bedside table. It just disappeared one day."

"Just disappeared?" he repeated skeptically. "Did you report the theft to the police?"

"No. Should I have? Frankly, I was glad the thing was gone."

Nicky sighed. "When you own a deadly weapon, you have a responsibility to keep track of it."

Marilyn made a big show of making herself more comfortable in the hot tub, resting her head backward on the wood. "Responsibility was never my main bag, you know. Anyway, who cares about my gun?"

"I do," he told her. "Interestingly enough, Jay Jeffries was killed with a thirty-two-caliber handgun. So were Ginny Gina, Tommy Torch, and Officer Oshimoto."

Her eyes flickered with momentary interest, then went dead. Her attitude annoyed him.

"Well, there must be millions of guns like that," she said.

She was right, of course. There were millions of cheap little handguns just waiting to shoot people dead. Nicky made her go over her alibi for last Thursday night, but it was just as Charlie had told him: dinner in Westwood with Unity, then two Fellini movies, then some club hopping. Marilyn gave the names of two different people who would vouch for their presence at the Hard Rock Café, where they

112

were having a merry time between eleven-thirty and midnight, while Jay Jeffries was not having such a merry time being emasculated and killed.

On Sunday, she said she and Nancy and Unity spent the morning lounging around the hot tub here, drinking Margaritas. It was quite a jolly group.

Nicky consulted his notes.

"Okay, according to Nancy's statement, you spent the afternoon too, not only the morning. She says you two left a little past four, and that you had a fight on the way home, so that she got out of the car in Beverly Hills."

Marilyn laughed. "That crazy chick! Did she say that? Well, I'll tell you—one Margarita and Nancy doesn't know what city she's in, much less what time warp she's in. It was more like noon when we left here—ask Unity if you don't believe me."

"I will," Nicky told her. "I'm also going to check out these names at the Hard Rock Café."

She shrugged. Marilyn de Malibu acted like a woman who had seen everything and was not impressed. She closed her eyes and tilted her face upward to the shaft of sunlight coming through the trees. It was a hard face, with lines coming downward from the mouth. She floated up luxuriously upon the water, determined to show how relaxed she was.

"I've got nothing to hide," she said.

That was true. She seemed to be offering her body for inspection, though Nicky had a feeling if he made a pass at her, she'd probably kick him.

"Tell me about Nancy Normal," he suggested.

Marilyn opened her eyes reluctantly.

"You want to know what we do in bed?"

"Not particularly," he answered. "When did you meet her?"

"A couple of years ago."

"Where?"

"At one of Bushy's bashes. He chartered a yacht, and a whole bunch of us sailed to Catalina and back—back and forth for three days, actually. It was like totally first class, you know. Live music, private cabins, all the dru . . . all the *drinks* you could ever want. By the time it was over, Nancy and I were in love."

"Gee, will the fun ever end?" Nicky wondered. "Now when you say Bushy, I presume you're referring to Bushy di Sutro, notorious gangster?"

113

Marilyn scowled. For a moment there, she had looked almost friendly.

"Hey, I don't know what the guy does for a living," she protested. "Bushy's just a dude who likes to have a good time."

"I see, and Nancy—is she a friend of his, too?"

"Well, nothing special. There must have been seventy-five people on the boat, you know. Mostly music people. I don't think any of us were especially *close* to Bushy or anything. I mean, we were just there to bop."

"Sounds like a fascinating cultural experience," Nicky told her. "Can you remember if Jay Jeffries was on board?"

"J. J.? Sure, he never missed a party if he could help it. He was an Aquarius, you know. Very social."

"Thanks. That may come in handy. Now how exactly did Nancy end up becoming J. J.'s maid?"

"Well, that didn't happen until later. Nan was feeling kinda bored and restless—nothing much was happening with her acting career, and she wanted to do something useful. It was supposed to be just a temporary sort of thing. J. J. really needed some help with his house, you know. The guy was a slob."

"Why didn't he just go to an agency?"

Marilyn shrugged. "Who wants strangers in your house?"

"I see. Are you aware Nancy has a police record in New Jersey—under her real name, of course? Sandy Giannini."

"Oh, wow!" she cried. "An enemy of society! Sleeping in *my* bed, no less."

Nicky decided to change directions. "Tell me about your relationship with Unity. You seem to be very close."

The question seemed to disturb Marilyn. She stepped briskly out of the hot tub and wrapped herself in a terrycloth robe that was hanging off the branch of a tree.

"Unity's straight," she said with hostility. "Our relationship's strictly platonic. So you can keep your dirty mind to yourself."

Well, well! At least he was getting through.

"Tell me about her."

"Why should I?"

"Because if you don't, I'm going to haul your ass down to the station, where life is not so pleasant as this bucolic backyard."

Marilyn didn't seem impressed by his easy banter. "Unity's just a kid," she said. "Why don't you leave her the hell alone."

He narrowed his eyes in his most menacing way. "I don't know.

She looks like a killer to me. The baby-faced ones are usually the worst."

Marilyn snorted her contempt.

Nicky didn't mind it that she was gay. But not to have a sense of humor—that was fatal.

"Look," she said, "I've known the kid since she was seven years old. She's like a daughter to me. The girl's an absolute angel. She wouldn't hurt a fly."

"Yeah?"

"Honestly. Listen, I met Unity on the Big Island ten years ago when Bo was building his place over there. She was sort of a lost lamb, you see—her mother was a junkie, hardly able to take care of her. So we all more or less adopted her. Me and Bo and Donny and J. J. and Rick. I mean, the child was so pretty and bright and her mother didn't even feed her half the time."

"So you all took care of her?"

"That's right. If I act defensive about her, it's because maybe she's the best project we took on. The only really good thing we've done since Billy died."

"Very philanthropic of you, I'm sure. What's her real name, by the way?"

"That's it. Unity Sphere."

"Come on."

"No, really. Her mother was a big hippie and all. She gave her daughter a creative name. Maybe it's the only thing her mother gave her. So you see, that's why we all got so excited the other day when Unity did so well taking over J. J.'s show. When you find a bird with a broken wing, and you fix it—well, the little bird becomes more special to you than the others."

Marilyn de Malibu was capable of some poetry after all, even if she didn't have a sense of humor. She had seated herself on a canvas deck chair, the terrycloth robe wrapped tight, looking at Nicky with some misgivings.

"Can I go now?" she asked. "I mean, not that I'm not having a wonderful time and all . . ."

"Just a few more questions," he promised. "Let's get back to the fight you had with Nancy on Sunday afternoon. What was that all about?"

"Oh, it was dumb. Nancy was jealous. She always thinks I have the hots for Unity. She doesn't understand it's just a mother-daughter thing between us. So we were driving back through Beverly Hills, cutting south from Sunset to Santa Monica. I came to a stop sign and Nancy just got out of the car. Slammed the door hard. I called to her to get back in, not to be so stupid, but she just kept walking."

"And this was what time?"

"I told you, we left Unity's around noon. Maybe it was twelve-fifteen when Nan split from my car. Monday morning she came back to our pad in Westwood. She had a hell of a hangover."

"Where did she say she was?"

"She told me she spent the night with a guy. Nan sometimes likes to swing both ways." Marilyn gave her famous shrug. "It doesn't bother me much. I do it myself sometimes when I'm desperate."

"Did she tell you the name of the man she was with?"

"Rick Elsmore."

"You mean the guitar player?"

She nodded.

This was one hell of a tight-knit group, Nicky thought. Very incestuous. He didn't know what to make of it all.

"Let's talk about Jay Jeffries some more," he tried. "When's the last time you saw him?"

"I guess it was Wednesday. He was coming out of Studio A after doing his show."

"How about the time before that?" Nicky asked. "When's the *second* to last time you saw him?"

"Yeah, I remember that. It was Tuesday night at The Bistro. I don't usually go to those dumb Beverly Hills places, but it was Nan's birthday, and she wanted to see some celebrities. We were both surprised to see J. J. there at a table across the room. I don't think he saw us. He was having dinner with some actor guy—can't remember his name. They seemed to be arguing about something. I remember saying to Nan that old J. J. looked kind of upset."

"Try to remember the name of the actor he was with," Nicky asked. Already he was getting a bad feeling in the pit of his stomach.

"Let's see. It's that guy with that Mount Rushmore sort of face."

"Frank Fee?" Nicky suggested. "Is that who J. J. was having dinner with?"

"That's right," she told him. "The guy with the big smile. Frank Fee."

9

That evening, Nicky sat at his piano playing the blues. There was no Bach in him tonight. A syncopated shuffle turned into a slow boogie-woogie, his left hand slinking up and down the bass while his right hand tapped out some mighty funky triplets high up in the treble.

He could keep this pattern going for hours, while his mind drifted far away. He sure felt blue. In a mood like this he could look at yet another fire in the fireplace, yet another glass of red wine within easy reach of his hand, and meditate upon the useless repetition of it all. Only tonight there was no lovely Susan lying naked before the fire beneath a sable coat.

In the kitchen, Tanya was finishing up the dinner dishes. In Bel Air there were servants to do work like this, and Tanya was not allowed to lift a finger. As a result, she thought washing dishes was fascinating. Nicky wondered how long it would last.

Tanya hung up her towel, turned off the kitchen light, and came into the living room looking very satisfied.

"That sure makes me feel like a real person," she said. "A real person living in a real world."

"I feel that way, too, sometimes," Nicky told her. *And it sucks*, he might have added—but didn't—because the young must be protected in their illusions.

She kissed him on the cheek. "I'm going to get into bed and read Jane Austen, Dad."

"Sounds purifying," he said.

"Dad?" she asked hesitantly. "Are you and Mom getting back together?"

Nicky hit a wrong chord and stopped playing. He sighed. He took a swallow of wine. "Gee, that's a hard one," he said. "We'll always love each other, of course. In our own way. No matter what happens."

"You certainly *sounded* like you loved each other last night."

"Tanya! You were supposed to be sleeping."

She smirked. "Yeah, but who could sleep through *that?*"

Tanya skipped merrily into her bedroom, leaving Nicky clutching an empty wineglass.

He stood up, paced his living room floor for a few minutes, then walked outside, took a few breaths of air—then came back inside and stared at his telephone.

What the hell was he supposed to do: with Susan, with Frank, with the murder case he was no longer part of?

He knew he was going to have to call Frank, and the prospect was not inviting. He braced himself by opening a bottle of Burgess Cabernet Sauvignon. When difficult things had to be done, he might as well have a really good glass of wine in hand. Prepared at last, he dialed the unlisted number in Bel Air.

Susan answered the phone, which was exactly what he was afraid would happen. He tried to disguise his voice.

"Is Frank Fee there, please?"

"Nicky, hi, is that you?"

"More or less," he admitted.

She giggled naughtily. "Did you feel as deliciously relaxed as I did today?"

"I'm sure I would have," he told her, "if I hadn't had to deal with the FBI and Chief McGroder and a whole lot of people being killed."

"Have they been nasty to you, darling?"

"Well, it could have been worse, I suppose. I could have had a horrible day *and* been sexually unsatisfied. That really would have been the pits."

"Thank you, dear. That's a very romantic thing to say."

"Look, Susan, I'm actually calling to speak with Frank. Is he home?"

"No, he went out around eight. God, Nicky, are you two going to fight it out for my hand? How exciting!"

He sighed. "Frank's name came up in connection with a case. It's probably nothing, but I have a few questions for him."

Susan was silent for about the space of five heartbeats. "Frank's in some kind of trouble, isn't he?" The coquetry was gone from her voice. On demand, Susan could be very practical.

"Now, Susan, I didn't say that."

"You don't have to. I can tell from the way he's been acting the past few weeks. A few times I've actually caught him looking worried. It's not like him at all."

"Well, don't you worry," he told her. "Not yet, at least. I'm sure there's a very simple explanation. Meanwhile, I'd appreciate it if you'd leave a message for him to give me a call."

"Okay. I'm sure he'll get back to you tomorrow."

"Uh, Susan . . . tonight would be better yet."

There was another short pause from her end. "Are you going to tell me what this is all about?"

"I think it's better I talk with Frank first. As I said, it's probably nothing."

"You think so? Look, Nicky, when Frank went out tonight, I gave him a hug, and it was the strangest thing—I could swear he was wearing a gun under his arm, like you do. He sort of pushed me away so I wouldn't feel it, but it was too late. You should have seen the way he looked at me. I mean, for a second he looked just plain desperate. And then he turned away so I couldn't see his face."

"Did he say where he was going?"

"No. A white Rolls came for him. He said he'd be back late."

"Okay. Well, thanks, Susan. Talk to you soon. . . ."

"Nicky, don't go yet. One more thing . . . about last night. Was that just hit and run, or do you want to see me again?"

It was his turn to be silent. He tried to speak, but the words got strangled in his throat. He took a long swallow of wine instead.

"Well?" she demanded. "It's a simple question, Nicky."

"Is it?" he wondered. "You know I'm nuts about you, Susan. But there's my alienation to think of, and my freedom to be lonely and depressed a lot. I worry about those things, you know. Then, of course, you come from the wrong side of the tracks."

"Wrong side of the tracks? Nicky, be serious."

"I mean it. The wrong side of Sunset. Sends shivers up my spine. I try not to be prejudiced, but this is deep stuff. An ingrained fear of the rich and famous, even though I find you all so fantastic in bed."

"Nicholas Rachmaninoff, stop acting like a clown."

She slammed the phone down. Love was certainly a many splendored thing. He poured himself another glass of wine and stared at the telephone some more.

Why was Frank carrying a gun? He picked up the receiver and dialed the records division at the Beverly Hills police station. He asked the operator to check out gun registration for a Mr. Frank Fee, whose street address he gave in Bel Air. Nicky hung on to the receiver for the few minutes it took the operator to run the request through the computer.

"Here it is, Lieutenant. Frank Fee. He registered a three fifty-seven Beretta on October twelfth of last year. It was purchased at the Hollywood Hobby Shoppe on Wilshire Boulevard. Anything else I can do for you, sir?"

"No. That's quite enough," he said wearily.

Nicky wandered out onto his meadow in front of his house. It was a clear night and he could see the millions of twinkling lights of the city far below.

Oh, the folly, the folly of it all.

A .357-millimeter pistol was the European equivalent to a .32. This put Frank right square in the middle of his investigation, in a more important place even than he had occupied before.

10

Jay Jeffries was buried Wednesday beneath a smoggy sky. His small rectangle of eternity was a hundred yards from an eight-lane freeway, so that the minister's fine words of wisdom had to compete with the roar of diesel trucks and the blast of passing car radios.

The cemetery was called Forest Lawn. If there had ever been a forest here, it was long gone. But there was lawn, acres of it, green as Astroturf, dotted with headstones and marble crypts and many small interdenominational chapels from which one could sit and meditate upon the traffic below.

Nicky had borrowed a tie from Charlie for the occasion. The tie had been crumpled up in Charlie's desk. It was a twenty-five-cent Salvation Army special with swirls of bright rayon colors. Charlie said it was very new wave trash. Nicky wore it around a blue Levi's workshirt and underneath his ever-present brown corduroy sports coat. Charlie, unfortunately, had to miss this sartorial event. A television actress had committted suicide overnight, and someone had to stay in Beverly Hills to create the illusion the homicide squad was functioning as normal.

Nicky arrived after the funeral had begun and stood at the rear of the group looking down from a small knoll. He estimated perhaps fifty people gathered before the gleaming white coffin. Nicky spotted Stephen Stills, wearing a velvet jacket, standing next to Joni Mitchell, who was in leather and lace. Most everyone seemed to have crossed the age of forty—aging hipsters, gray in the hair, survivors of the sixties and the once resplendent L.A. music scene of which Billy Lion and the Perceptions had been the leading edge.

Neil Young, who still looked strangely boyish, was standing near Donny Meredith, Billy Lion's once-upon-a-time keyboard player. Donny was wearing a dark suit. His hands were thrust in his pockets, and his shoulders were a little hunched over. Donny looked as if he had seen too many funerals in his time. Nicky felt that way, too, sometimes.

Bo Daniels was standing near the coffin, and he was dressed in a dark suit as well. It almost made him look like a grown-up. Bo was standing between two pretty ladies—Unity Sphere on his left and an older woman on his right, who Nicky took to be Kitty Daniels, Bo's wife. Unity was dressed in soft gray wool, á la Ralph Lauren. Mrs. Daniels, a brunette with a proud build, was stunning in black. The three of them together—husband, wife, and teenage mistress— made a nice family grouping.

Nicky's eyes came to Marilyn, who was holding hands with the redheaded ex-housekeeper, Nancy Normal. Next to this fine couple stood his naughty quasi relation, Frank Fee, who had not returned his telephone call. Frank was wearing enormous dark glasses in an effort to conceal his famous face, but Nicky was not fooled. Just a few days ago Nicky would have been astonished to find him in this crowd, but now he took it as a matter of course. Frank was standing next to a tall man in a three-piece suit who might be taken for a stockbroker or a banker. The man was balding on top but had two unruly clumps of hair bushing out around the sides, like Bozo the Clown.

Call him that, however, and you'd probably end up dead, for this particular Bozo was Bushy di Sutro, notorious gangster. Nicky had seen photographs of the man in a thick file back at the station. As Nicky watched, Bushy whispered something in Frank's ear, who listened and nodded sagely.

Nicky was about to come down from his knoll and edge up closer to Frank and Bushy, when he noticed FBI Inspector Jones standing between him and his goal. The inspector was looking his way with a scowl that could shoot down a satellite from the sky.

Nicky smiled sheepishly and shrugged his shoulders. Inspector Jones did not smile back.

Nicky made a point of turning away from the FBI man and putting attention where it more properly belonged—upon the young minister who was conducting the graveside service, dressed in slacks and a bright rayon shirt. The minister was talking about death in a casual, friendly sort of way, as though God were an impresario who finally brought you in from the road. Nicky imagined he must be from one of the newer denominations.

"Hey, ya got a light?" came a voice from behind.

Nicky could smell the newcomer before he turned to look at him. The aroma was like a bar at closing time: stale cigarettes, booze, and exhaustion. It was Rick Elsmore, once the guitar player for the Perceptions. He was wearing the same white suit Nicky had seen him in last Friday in Bo's office. The suit looked as if it had been slept in and used generally as a place for people to wipe their hands. Rick's blond hair was ragged, his eyes were unfocused, and his face was a diary of hard times. Out of thin, bloodless lips a joint was dangling, waiting for some kind soul to provide a match.

Nicky glanced back over his shoulder to Inspector Jones, who was watching this encounter with interest. What the hell. Nicky produced a match from his coat pocket, and in a moment the musky smell of marijuana drifted upward to the smoggy sky. Inspector Jones narrowed his eyes thoughtfully, taking in the full extent of Lieutenant Rachmaninoff's rebellion.

At least Rick was happy now. He sucked in the smoke with sweet contentment and exhaled with a sigh.

"Yeah," he said dreamily. "What a trip is life!"

11

Marijuana seemed to have a beneficial effect on Rick Elsmore, sobering him up a bit. His eyes came slowly into focus on Nicky's face.

"Hey, don't I know you?" he asked suspiciously. "Yeah, you're Rrr-Rachmaninoff the Rrr-Russian spy."

Rick seemed to get a lot of enjoyment out of rolling his R's. Nicky was frankly surprised the musician had managed to remember his name.

"Not a spy," he corrected, glancing meaningfully at the joint. "A cop."

Ricky offered the joint. "Wanna hit?"

"I think not."

"Hey, suit yourself. But if you want to improve your playing, Rrr-Rachmaninoff, you should smoke a little Mary Jane. Getcha more in tune, ya dig?"

"My playing?"

"Yeah, piano—right? That's your instrument, ain't it?"

Nicky was astonished. "How do you know I play the piano?"

"Oh, is that a secret? I though everyone knew that. Rrr-Rach-maninoff, the piano-playing cop."

"Who told you that?"

"Bo."

"*Bo?*"

"That's right, the big man himself. After you left his office Friday, he made a few phone calls about you. Checked you out a little downtown. What he decided, you see, was that any cop who's daffy enough to play the piano probably wouldn't cause him too many problems."

"Oh, he thinks that, does he? What kind of problems does he think I'm going to cause?"

Rick shrugged and took another drag. The roach was very small now, and he had to hold it delicately with his fingertips.

"Hey, I don't know what the big man worries about. I don't have those kinds of problems, you know. The responsibilities of being a captain of industry, pillar of society, etcetera—though you probably couldn't tell that by looking at me."

Nicky smiled. There was something about Rick Elsmore that appealed to him.

"Tell me something," Rick said. "Why does someone like you, a guy who can play the piano, do something stupid like waste your time being a cop?"

This was a very good question, one that Nicky had asked himself more than once. Under the present circumstances, however, he passed it off with a vague smile.

"Rick, let me ask *you* a question," he countered. "Try to remember last Sunday night and tell me what you were doing."

The guitar player scratched his head. "Ah, yes, I remember. Drinking and fucking. That's what I was doing Sunday night. Sticking it here, sticking it there, sticking it most everywhere."

"With whom?"

"With whom? Why, you cad! And I thought you were a gentleman, Rachmaninoff!"

"Please. A young woman gave you as her alibi for where she was Sunday night. I want to know if your story corroborates hers."

"Gad, *alibi . . . corroborate . . .* what kind of words are these? Have we just tuned in to 'Perry Mason'?"

"Rick, this really would be a great help."

"Oh, well, then. Scruples be screwed. I'll kiss and tell. Her name was Nancy, and she calls herself Normal, though frankly I found her

123

a bit subnormal to my taste. Fortunately, I was too drunk to remember it well. It's just a blur of limbs and tongues, you know. Did she really give me as an alibi? That really is a first."

"What time did you get together on Sunday?"

"Time?"

"Was it afternoon? Night? Late night?"

"Late night, I think. Outside the window, I remember a profound darkness."

Nicky tried to imagine this as testimony in court and couldn't. Still, Nancy was not quite off the hook after all. She could have done the dirty deed in Topanga, then gone to meet Rick afterward.

"Can you be more exact?" Nicky asked. "Did Nancy come over at six o'clock? Seven? Ten?"

Rick Elsmore shook his head at all the above. He swayed on his feet and seemed to be fading fast. The marijuana had given him a short burst of energy, but now he was sinking into an alcoholic stupor.

"Billy . . . so damn sorry." The words came thick and full of self-pity. Nicky wasn't certain he heard them right.

"Billy? Don't you mean J. J.?"

"Naw, Billy . . . we sold him out . . . handful of gold . . . no wonder . . ."

Rick began staggering up the hill, away from the funeral.

Nicky followed him. There was nothing like trying to get the truth out of a drunk. "No wonder what?" he asked.

Rick Elsmore sat down heavily on a grave and laid his head against the stone marker. Nicky Rachmaninoff knelt down close to his ear. The smell was terrible.

"No wonder what?" he insisted gently.

"It's the ghost," he said. The words were barely coherent. The phrase sounded more like "Idsa ghosh." Rick closed his eyes and seemed to be falling asleep.

"The ghost?" Nicky whispered in his ear. "What ghost?"

Rick said the next words very clearly, then began to snore.

"Yeah," he said, "the ghost of rock and roll."

12

The crowd was drifting back toward their cars. A few small groups stayed and talked quietly among themselves. Funereal tones prevailed as the expensive people posed with one another against the too green lawn.

Nicky watched the crowd break up with a feeling of frustration. He wished Charlie were here to help him, for there were too many people he needed to talk with and no way to cover them all. Donny Meredith and Stephen Stills had located Rick Elsmore sleeping on a grave and were helping him to his feet. Marilyn and Nancy Normal were smoking cigarettes and standing in a circle of friends. Unity Sphere was getting into a big black limousine with Mr. and Mrs. Bo Daniels. She looked up and saw Nicky across the crowded cemetery and flashed him a brief, enchanted smile. Then she got into the car and was gone.

Nicky was meditating upon her when he noticed FBI Inspector Jones charging his way. He decided he'd better move fast. He ducked behind a miniature Parthenon and jogged in the direction of Frank and Bushy di Sutro, who were slowly walking toward a gleaming white Rolls-Royce.

"Hey, Frank! Wait up!"

Frank turned and put a great fake smile on his Mount Rushmore face. Nicky knew damn well old Frank had been hoping to sneak off without this confrontation.

"Hey, Nicky! What a surprise to see you here."

"Isn't it, Frank?"

"Do you know the Bush?"

"Only by reputation," Nicky answered coldly.

The Bush, as Frank called him, stood with an innocuous smile in his dark three-piece suit, trying to look harmless. He was tall, maybe six feet three or four, with mild brown eyes, a floppy mustache, and a small moist mouth. He was the first gangster Nicky ever saw who wore an earring—a single diamond stud in his right lobe, which occasionally caught the light and dazzled like a small star.

Embarrassment made Frank more effusive than ever. Making the introductions, he elevated Nicky from honorary brother-in-law to full brother *and* best friend.

"Oh! I've heard so, so many nice things about you, Lieutenant Rachmaninoff!" Bushy said enthusiastically, offering a limp and flabby hand. Bushy spoke with a pronounced lisp, transforming Nicky's name to *Wok*maninoff.

"So Fwank has been keeping you all to himself, has he? The cweep!"

Frank had an arm around Nicky's shoulder as if he were afraid to let go. "Yeah, this kid and me go way, way back."

Nicky thought guiltily of Susan.

"Isn't it a shame about poor J. J.? Poor whittle fuck," Bushy said, shaking his head at the capricious gods. "Of course, I believe in we-incarnation myself, so death doesn't hold quite the same terrors"—pronounced *teh-was*—"it does for the average man."

"That must be useful in your profession," Nicky mentioned.

Bushy laughed as if this were quite the joke. Frank laughed, too. They made a jolly group as they continued walking slowly toward Bushy's splendid white Rolls-Royce, where a uniformed chauffeur stood waiting. The chauffeur was even taller than Bushy, a muscular giant with a head too small for his size. Even from a distance, Nicky could see the bulge of a weapon under his arm. This formidable person was eyeing Nicky hungrily as someone he might one day have the pleasure to tear limb from limb.

"Won't you join us, Wokmaninoff? It would be wovely if you could. We're all going to a whittle party at Bo's beach house. A wake, you know, for poor ole J. J."

This was a hard offer to pass up. However, there was his car to consider. When you owned a classy automobile like his, you couldn't just abandon it upon the wormless fields of Forest Lawn. He glanced back along the line of parked limousines, Mercedes, and BMWs to see his own ancient Austin-Healey waiting like a faithful friend. Someone else was waiting by his car, someone who was not a friend —Inspector Jones, who seemed to want a word with him. Nicky decided he might leave his car after all.

The inside of Bushy's limousine was like an old-fashioned men's club, paneled with dark polished wood with seats of comfortable leather. There was an Oriental carpet on the floor and a vase with a single pink long-stemmed rose near the concealed bar. There were also a few modern touches, such as built-in television, telephone, and stereo.

"Oh, I do enjoy teasing the FBI," Bushy said enthusiastically as the Rolls drifted past an irate-looking Inspector Jones. "Pwobably it will pwove my downfall, but a man must have some fun. They've been twailing me, you know, for two years now. The stowies I could tell you, Wootenant! Last July, they twied to sell me a million dollars of cocaine. Their lastest scam is to try to lure me into kiddie porn. . . . I pwetend to go along, you know, just up to the point where they're about to close the deal. Then I back out at the last second. Oh, it's fun, I tell you, to see their faces!"

"I'm glad you're enjoying yourself."

"Oh, I do! I do! And now we must have a dwink to celebwate our new fwiendship. Fwank, would you mind pwaying bartender? I'm hopeless, you know, utterly hopeless with glasses and corks and all those silly things."

It made Nicky sad to watch the subservient role Frank seemed to have with the gangster. Frank, for his part, did his best to avoid direct eye contact. Nicky declined a drink and also said no to the smoked salmon and caviar appetizers that magically appeared from a small refrigerator near the TV. Bushy had a glass of champagne and gobbled up the food. Frank skipped the food but went heavy on the Scotch. L.A. drifted past the tinted windows.

"Mr. di Sutro," Nicky posed, "I understand heavy amounts of mob money are being laundered through The Rock Channel and the Inter Stellar Group. If you're in any way responsible for the four murders last week, I'm going to nail your ass to the wall. There won't be enough left of you to send to San Quentin."

"Oh, Wootenant! So vicious, so bwutal. But you're tewibly out of date, deah man. We don't kill people anymore. Why, the Mafia's just a boring business association these days. Sort of a Lions Club."

Nicky laughed unpleasantly.

"Oh, how can I convince you? It's quite mahvelous, dahling, how in Hollywood you all have such a glamowous picture of the Mafia. You imagine James Cagney and Marlon Bwando and all sorts of womance and Technicolor and wonderful shootouts at the end. Ah! If wife only were wike the movies!"

Nicky gave the gangster a long cold stare.

"Well, I admit, of course, our pwocedures were—shall we say?— a whittle more colorful in the past. But you know what they say: At the woot of evewy gweat fortune is a gweat cwime. It's as twue with the Wockefellers as it is with us. But once you've made your fortune, the place for the next killing—ha! ha!—is Wall Stweet. Isn't that wight, Fwank?"

127

Frank was staring out the window, doing his best to disappear. "I don't know, Bushy," he mumbled. "Money's never interested me all that much."

"Ah, well, you're an awtist, Fwank. No wonder. But the west of us have to make a living as best we can—and that's all the di Sutro family is doing these days. A whittle investment here, a whittle investment there. So boring, weally, but we muddle along."

"Mr. di Sutro . . ."

"Please call me Bushy, Nick. Wet's be fwiends."

"Mr. di Sutro," Nicky repeated. "My understanding is that Jay Jeffries was threatening to go to the FBI if you didn't pay him off. He had become quite a thorn in your side."

Bushy neatly devoured a piece of smoked salmon. It was a predatory gesture.

"Look, Wootenant, be weasonable," he suggested. "Assume for one fantastic moment that J. J. was attempting to blackmail the di Sutro family—what would we do? Would we kill him in the middle of Beverly Hills, cut off his genitals, leave the poor man in a puddle of blood to be discovered by the gweat Wootenant Wokmaninoff? No, we would not. Why call so much attention to ourselves? If we had decided J. J. must go, he would have had a heart attack after some nice dinner someplace. Or he would have hit his head in the swimming pool. Perhaps he would have fallen asleep smoking in bed —oh, there are so many ways to die! But he would *never* have died in a manner which guaranteed maximum publicity. Quite fwankly, publicity is not in our interest at all."

Nicky followed the logic of this. Bushy's eyes absolutely glistened with delight as he had begun to imagine the various accidents that could befall a man.

"So who killed J. J. if you didn't?"

"We don't know!" Bushy cried with some animation. "It's all vewy distwessing. Fwankly, we wish the answer to this whittle widdle as much as you do, Wootenant. Many of our Hollywood fwiends deal with us only because we have managed to convince them that the new Mafia is weasonable, wesponsible people—just businessmen with quite a bit of money to invest. We're on *your* side now, the side of law and order."

"That's quite stirring, Bushy."

"I'm absolutely sincere," said the gangster, putting his hand over his heart for emphasis. "Now I have to show you something. I was sent a threatening note yesterday. It may be nothing, but . . ."

"You have it on you?"

"Yes, as it happens."

Bushy took out a billfold from his breast pocket and produced an envelope, addressed to him at his bungalow at the Beverly Hills Hotel. Nicky unfolded the paper inside. The short message had been written on a word processor.

> *Bushy di Sutro,*
>
> *Justice has a long arm. J. J. wasn't the first and he will not be the last. You will need eyes in the back of your head to see—*
>
> *The Ghost of Rock and Roll*

Nicky read the note several times. This was the second time in an hour the Ghost of Rock and Roll had come up. Nicky did not believe in coincidence. The use of Jeffries' nickname, J. J., seemed to indicate someone from the inner circle.

"So melodwamatic, don't you agree?" Bushy asked him. "The Ghost of Wock and Woll! I mean, weally!"

"Do you have any idea who could have sent this?"

"Not a clue."

"I'd like to keep this note, if you don't mind."

"Absolutely. I'm completely at your disposal, dear Wootenant Wokmaninoff. We must work together, we must trust each other now."

"Yeah? Why's that?" Nicky asked.

"Because we're family, *that's* why," Bushy told him, astonished the policeman couldn't see such a simple thing. Then he laughed, throwing back his head to reveal sharp white teeth.

"Oh, you don't *know*, do you, Wootenant? This is weally *too* tewibly amusing, is it not? Pay attention, pwease. Fwank's dear mother, Angelina di Sutro, was my auntie. So Fwank and I are cousins, and you, dear Nicholas, what are you? My cousin, too, perchance!"

Nicky looked sharply to Frank, who was leaning so hard against the car door it appeared he might suddenly jump out onto the freeway. Nicky was tempted to give him a push.

"Isn't it a welief to discover you're not alone in the world?" Bushy was asking rapturously. "You and me and Frank and Susan—and dear, sweet wittle Tanya. All of us joined together in an eternal circle, our woots weaching back to holy Sicily. . . . So welcome, cousin Nicholas. Welcome to the Mafia!"

Nicky accepted a double Scotch, no water.

13

Bo's beach house was at Trancas, an expensively pretty bay a few miles north of the Malibu Colony. The house was a Mediterranean villa, a faded yellow mansion with a roof of Spanish tile sitting behind a line of gentle sand dunes almost at the end of Broad Beach Road.

It looked to Nicky the sort of place where you might imagine an aging movie star going slowly mad. Bougainvillea and honeysuckle were climbing up the walls, trying to work their way inside the house. A line of cars was already parked up and down the road. Bushy's chauffeur pulled into a small walled courtyard and let off his passengers by a heavy wooden door. Then he drove back to the road to join the rest of the limousines.

Inside, the booze was flowing and people were having a good time meandering through a series of high-ceilinged rooms. The house could have been furnished by Busby Berkeley, a particular Art Deco style Nicky generally thought of as Early Beverly Hills. There were a lot of curved couches, pastel colors, and peacock plumes emerging from large pots. Those who had gone to the funeral wearing coats and ties now were removing them and rolling up their sleeves. Some of the women were kicking off their shoes. This wake was going to be serious business.

Bushy was immediately absorbed by a group of young men who seemed to know him well. Perhaps they were comparing the size of their guns. Frank tried to slip away as well, but Nicky took him firmly by the arm.

"Hold on, good brother, best friend. I think it's time you and I had a little chat."

"Gee, Nicky, I'm awfully thirsty. Can't we have a drink first?"

"I think not. What you and I got to talk about is too important to have our minds clouded by alcohol."

Frank didn't like this, but he allowed Nicky to lead him through a side door onto a patio, past a kidney-shaped swimming pool, and onto the beach itself.

"Jesus, Nick, isn't this far enough? I'm getting sand in my shoes."

"Better than bullets in your belly. Come on, Frank, I want to walk down by the water where no one can sneak up on us."

"Getting a little paranoid, aren't you, buddy?"

Nicky didn't bother to answer but led the way in silence over the hundred yards of clear white beach to the edge of the water. It was low tide, and a stretch of wet sand gurgled and popped with the small holes of little creatures. Seagulls made their lonely cry, and the ocean itself was wild and full of foam. Ordinarily Nicky would be glad to be here by the edge of the continent, looking out upon the not yet completely polluted waters of the Pacific.

"Okay, hand it over, Frank."

"Hand what over?"

"Your gun, Frank. The three fifty-seven Beretta you're trying to conceal under your arm. What I should do is haul your ass off to jail to teach you a lesson—you know that."

"Gee, Nicky, you're not being too friendly for an old friend."

Frank was very reluctant to hand over his deadly toy. Nicky waited patiently with his hand out until the gun was in his palm. He took out the clip, emptied the bullets into his pocket, then stuffed the pistol into his belt.

"This is like a bad dream. I never thought in my wildest fantasies I'd ever find you on the wrong side of a murder investigation."

"Hey, it's not quite *that* bad, Nick. I haven't actually shot anyone yet."

"Oh, that's good! Susan and Tanya are going to be *so* pleased about that, Frank. Now tell me—is this true about you being Bushy de Sutro's cousin?"

Frank bowed his head. "It's true," he said faintly.

"For chrissake, why didn't you ever tell me? Does Susan know about this?"

"No, no one knows. Look, when I first came to Hollywood in the late forties, it wouldn't have exactly helped my career. I got used to keeping it my big dark secret. Anyway, it's a complex situation, kinda hard to explain."

"Great! Well, you'd better start trying, Frank."

Frank sighed. "Nicky, please. This isn't easy." He sighed again, like an old tire deflating. "My mother, you see, was Icepick di Sutro's favorite daughter, the baby of the family. He absolutely doted on her, until at the age of nineteen, twenty, she started acting pretty wild—hanging out with a fast crowd in Greenwich Village, smoking reefer, doing all sorts of things good Italian girls weren't supposed to do. Finally, she ran off with a trumpet player who had a gig down in Miami. She got pregnant—me—and had to get married. The marriage lasted less than six months, but my grandfather never forgave her. She was totally stricken from the family records, no one was allowed to mention her. Icepick was a very strict and old-fashioned kind of man, you understand."

"How quaint."

"Nicky, please, I'm trying to explain how I grew up in a kind of special position. I was related to all these heavy-duty *mafiosos*—I was of them, but not of them—and there would never be a place for me in the Families' business. Officially, no one was supposed to have any contact with us—we were cut off—but relatives would sneak over to visit. Eventually, I met just about everyone and became friends with some of the kids my age, which happens to be the generation that's running things now."

"This is true?"

"It's true. Cross my heart. I grew up and everyone encouraged me to get the hell out of New York, so I came to California, changed my name, and became an actor. Occasionally some of the people I used to know would come out to Hollywood and look me up. They all thought it was a big deal I had become a movie star—these are simple people, Nick—and I gotta admit, I sorta enjoyed them in a funny way. I'd fix up some of the boys with starlets, and it would all be kind of palsy-walsy and fun.

"Anyway, I stayed in touch. Sometimes a year or two would go by where I wouldn't hear from any of them at all. Then, about six or seven years ago, things began to change. Hollywood was becoming important for them businesswise. The general feeling was that Las Vegas had absorbed about as much dirty money as it could stand, and that the feds were putting too much heat on things there. So there was this bright idea that maybe Hollywood was an ideal place for them. It's hard to account for all the loose money that changes hands in this town, and a producer who's trying to raise thirty million dollars for a film does not give a shit where the money comes from. I tell you no lies, Nicky. Half the producers I know in this town would go out and kill schoolchildren if they thought it would finance their latest script. And for the Family, man, thirty mil is fucking nothing. Hardly more than carfare. So what we got here is a beautiful marriage."

"Sounds more like a shotgun wedding," Nicky muttered.

"No, listen, Nick—there's something positive to all this. A guy like Bo Daniels can get a vision that America's ready for a TV station that shows nothing but music videos, and *flash*—there's the

Family with fifty, sixty million dollars begging for a way to get back into circulation. It's a situation where everyone wins. Even if some of the projects fail, the Family's got a nice accountable tax loss to help square their situation with the IRS."

"What part have you been playing in all this, Frank?" Nicky asked, not too pleased about the beautiful marriage.

"Nothing heavy, honestly. Introductions, that's all. You see, at first, when the di Sutro family wanted to expand into the entertainment business, they really didn't know anyone out here. In Hollywood, as you well know, having the right contacts is everything. So I was able to bring people together—people who had a vision with people who had the money to make the dreams come true. I kinda felt I was performing a necessary service. For example, six years ago I introduced Bo Daniels to Bushy di Sutro."

Nicky's knees felt weak. "So almost single-handedly you've been responsible for bringing organized crime into Hollywood. Is that what you're telling me?"

"Hey, it's not quite like that," Frank said sheepishly.

"No? Well, at least I understand why you've been carrying a gun. What surprises me is that you're still alive."

Frank studied a small crab that was moving sideways by his feet. "Look, I wish I could make you understand how this all happened. Five, six years ago—when Bushy came looking for favors—what I was, Nicky, was extremely bored. I mean, I had thirty movies behind me, and a bunch of TV, and I was about as rich as I ever cared to be. There weren't any more challenges. My accountants had my money invested in all these boring shopping malls and real estate developments, stuff like that, and I was beginning to feel like some kind of damn institution. Frank Fee, Inc."

"So then you had a chance to play cops and robbers, and it made you feel young again?"

"Well, maybe it was like that, yeah. Mostly I wanted to do something real, Nicky. All my adult life I felt I'd been playing at things. So this appealed to me. I swear, I didn't feel like I was doing any real harm. A lot of times I directed cash toward some really artistic projects. Two of them won Academy Awards," he said proudly.

"How wonderful. And how did they pay you for your services?" Nicky asked bitterly. "Maybe a nice numbered Swiss bank account of your very own?"

"No, they only gave me little presents, I swear. I wasn't in it for the money, you know, as much as the satisfaction. Mostly I was assured that if I ever needed anything—and I mean *anything*—all I had to do was say the word. I know you think I'm crazy, Nicky, but I swear to you—until Jay Jeffries got killed, the whole thing seemed real harmless. I felt like I was dealing with the United Way."

"Or something," Nicky put in. "Let's talk about J. J., then, our mutilated VJ. I understand you had dinner with him at The Bistro not long before he was killed. What was that all about?"

"You heard about that, huh? Well, it was J. J.'s idea. Actually, as I told you last week, I hardly knew the guy. He phoned me Monday over at Fox, said he had to see me, that it was urgent. Quite honestly I wasn't thrilled, but it was difficult to say no. I suggested The Bistro hoping it would make the whole thing more pleasant. J. J. sounded pretty desperate, you understand."

"Let me get this straight. This is Monday of last week, three days before J. J. was murdered?"

"Exactly."

"And you had dinner that night?"

"No, I couldn't make it until Tuesday."

"Okay, then, Tuesday night. *Two* days before he was killed. What did he want to see you about . . . Frank?"

Frank was staring at the incoming surf, shaking his head. "You know I'm not allowed to talk about Family business, Nicky. *Omerta*, you know. You're really putting me in a hell of a spot."

"That's tough, Frank. Maybe I should tell Susan about all this?" Nicky threatened. "Won't she be delighted to learn she married into the Mafia! Anyway, aren't you forgetting what Bushy said? I'm part of the Family now—eh, *paisan?*"

"I guess that makes it all right, then." Frank still seemed dubious.

"Well?" Nicky pressed.

"Well, J. J. was upset because someone was trying to set him up, he said—make him look bad in front of Bushy."

"In what way?"

"Somehow Bushy got the idea that J. J. was collecting evidence about The Rock Channel's connection with the di Sutro family, getting together a big folder of names and dates and payments to turn over to the FBI."

"And this was true?"

"No. J. J. swore on his oysters Rockefeller that he was doing nothing of the kind. He said he had known all about Bushy for years and couldn't give a damn if he were Mafia or not. The whole thing was absurd. All J. J. wanted was to party."

"Why did he come to you?"

"He thought I might have some influence with Bushy, that I could convince him there was no secret folder, that J. J. was completely innocent."

"I see. Had Bushy actually made any threats against him?"

"Not really. Bushy merely mentioned the ancient Sicilian custom —people who informed to the police had their dicks cut off and shoved inside their mouths."

Nicky smiled grimly. "I can see why J. J. was upset. First Pubic Telephone threatens to put his dick down the garbage disposal, then the Mafia says they're going to stick it in his mouth. If I were J. J., I'd leave town in a hurry."

"Look, Nicky, I talked to Bushy on Wednesday, and he said he knew J. J. wasn't the sort of guy to cause any problems. The mention of the old Sicilian custom was just to shake him up a little, make him realize where his interests lay. The whole thing was like a Halloween joke. Actually, the Mafia doesn't do stuff like that anymore."

"No? I wouldn't be too certain of that, Frank."

"Besides that, Nicky, be logical—where did J. J.'s dick finally end up? Huh?" Frank asked shrewdly. "In the mouth or down the drain? I mean, *that* should tell you something."

Nicky gazed longingly at the far horizon. A few pelicans were circling beyond the breakers, making an occasional ungainly dive down for dinner below. Nature was a big restaurant in which the strong ate the weak.

14

"Prokofiev! Just the person I want to see. Let's go into my office where we can talk."

Nicky turned to see Bo Daniels bearing down on him. They were standing in Bo's crowded living room, normally a spacious place with many large windows overlooking the ocean. A buffet table had been set up at one side of the room, heavily laden with food. As soon as they had come back inside, Frank had made his way to the bar. Nicky had declined the offer of a drink, but he had been edging toward a large bowl of prawns on ice when Bo Daniels found him.

"Come on, Prokofiev, it's too noisy in here even to think."

This was true. The party had grown in size and volume since he and Frank had taken their walk. There were many more people stuffed into the beach house than had attended the funeral itself. Nicky looked back wistfully at the bowl of prawns. Bo took his arm and led the way out of the living room, down a long corridor to a comfortable office. Bo had changed clothes from the suit he wore at the funeral to his more usual gear: black jeans, tennis shoes, and a T-shirt that had upon it the words PRESSURE MAKES DIAMONDS.

But there were smudgy dark circles beneath Bo's eyes, and his flesh had an unhealthy pallor. Bo sat down behind a vast white desk and gestured for Nicky to make himself comfortable in an armchair.

"Well, Lieutenant, tell me—are you making any progress on the case?"

"Yes and no," Nicky replied. He decided this wasn't the right moment to confess he had no case anymore. "We certainly have been learning many intriguing details about The Rock Channel's relationship with organized crime."

"There, I *knew* that was going to come up!" Bo cried, pounding a fist down on his desk. "Just my luck right now, when things are a little shaky with our sponsors. You'd almost think someone's out to get me, I swear to God."

"Maybe J. J. was killed to hurt your ratings?" Nicky suggested.

Bo took the question seriously. "That's a thought," he replied. "Isn't it?"

"Let's talk about Bushy di Sutro. He's one of your major investors, I understand."

"Yes, of course. But I never knew the money came from the damn Mafia. I mean, he didn't exactly introduce himself that way, did he? He simply told me he represented a group of investors from back east—people who wished to be anonymous—who were looking to put some money into the entertainment industry. What was I supposed to do? Say no?"

Bo went on at some length about how innocent he was and how unfair it was that everyone was out to get him. Was a grocery clerk, he asked, supposed to find out where each dollar bill came from that someone has handed him? Of course not. Then why should he, poor misunderstood tycoon that he was, have to check each and every penny some investor wished to hand over?

One thing he had to say, though—the Mafia was wonderfully easy to deal with. They were always on time, they didn't hassle you for fifty copies of every document, they were men of vision willing to take a chance.

Nicky listened to as much of this as he could stomach. "Tell me about the Ghost of Rock and Roll." He produced the threatening note Bushy di Sutro had given him during the ride from Forest Lawn. Bo read it carefully and handed it back.

" 'The Ghost of Rock and Roll' was the name of a song Rick wrote in 1971 for an album we never made. It was when the Perceptions were still trying to make it without Billy."

"What was the song about?"

"I don't remember the exact lyrics, but the general idea, you see, was that rock and roll was dead—it died along with Billy Lion in 1970. Kind of a defeatist attitude, if you ask me. And hell, if you think about some of the giants of the eighties, like Lionel Richie, like Madonna . . ."

"Mr. Daniels, please. What else did the song have to say?"

"Well, it was sort of weird. I told Rick at the time it wasn't exactly going to soar up the charts. Rock and roll was dead, you see, but the Ghost was going to come back one day like some Old Testament Jehovah and destroy all the false prophets. That was the general tone. Those who had betrayed the spirit of rock and roll were going to die in some kind of psychedelic flood of electric guitars that would make forty days and nights of rain look like fucking nothing. To tell the truth, Rick was pretty strung out on LSD when he wrote the thing. This was before he discovered booze."

"Who knows about this song, Mr. Daniels?"

"Why, all of us. Danny, J. J., Rick, and I. We actually recorded it and about three other tunes for the album, before we decided it was time to face up to the inevitable—no one gave a shit about the Perceptions without Billy Lion in the group."

"Do you think anyone still has a copy of 'The Ghost of Rock and Roll'? I'd like to hear it."

"God, I don't know. I don't have a copy, that's for sure. Maybe Rick still has it around someplace. Of course, you can always ask Unity. She might know."

"Why Unity?"

"Well, she's sort of our resident expert on everything concerning the Perceptions. About a year ago, she came to me with an idea about doing a video biography of the group. I gave her access to all the old stuff—Billy's journals, some of the half-finished recordings and rare film clips. All that sort of stuff. As a matter of fact, she's put together a fantastic ninety-second montage from the material for next Tuesday."

"Next Tuesday?" Nicky asked. "What happens then?"

Bo looked at him in utter astonishment. "The Grammys, of course. The Perceptions are being presented with a special achievement award."

Bo shook his head at the idea of an ignorant cop who had to be told when the Grammys were going to be.

"You're all going to be there?"

"*Yes*, we're all going to be there, Lieutenant. Where else would we be, for chrissake? This is a very big honor, you know, a special achievement award—not for just one damn song, either, but for the tremendous and lasting influence the Perceptions had on the course of rock music."

"I see. Is Bushy going to be there as well?"

Bo sighed. "Yes. Frankly, I tried to discourage him. Under the circumstances. But the Bush wants to bask in some of the glory, you know. I guess he's paid enough for the privilege."

Nicky was contemplating this new information when there was a little tap on the office door. Bo's wife stuck her face inside without waiting for a response.

"There you are, Bo. Someone said they saw you heading this way."

"What is it, dear? You know I don't like to be disturbed in my office."

"Lionel Richie's here. I thought you'd want to come out and say hello."

Bo jumped up from behind his desk. "Damn! When did he arrive? Has someone offered him a drink yet? Prokofiev, I'm sorry but we'll have to talk another time."

Nicky stood up. "Maybe tomorrow," he suggested.

"No, can't tomorrow. I'm fantastically busy. The day after that I'm flying to Hawaii for the weekend—gotta get some rest before the Grammys, for chrissake. Call my secretary anytime after Tuesday. She'll arrange something. . . . Well, what are you waiting for, Lieutenant? Didn't you hear, for chrissake? Lionel Ritchie's here!"

15

Back in Bo's living room, there was orgy in the air. The lights were low. Loud music thundered from the stereo speakers. Nicky caught a glimpse of Frank at the far end of the room, a drink in one hand and a blonde in the other. The girl seemed very young. Frank was listening to her, peering down the front of her dress. It gave Nicky a bleak, unlovely feeling: Frank cheating on Susan, Susan cheating on Frank, and himself somewhere in the middle.

"Hey, there! Having a good time?" came a voice in his left ear.

Nicky turned to see a painted woman: white skin, red hair, red lips, sharp fingernails, eyelashes like a Venus's flytrap. It was Nancy Normal, the decedent's maid. She seemed fairly drunk and—to his horror—very flirtatious.

"So tell me about yourself," she said, hinting at all sorts of future intimacy. "Who is this enigmatic policeman, this most mysterious Lieutenant Rachmaninoff?"

"Enigmatic?" Nicky wondered. "What a big word."

"Oh, I went to college, I did." She giggled. "Before they kicked me out."

"Where was that?" Nicky asked pleasantly. She had come asking about him but like most people really only wanted to talk about herself.

"Bard," she told him. "Very arty-farty, you know. But I was too wild to be constrained by a liberal arts education. I wanted to experience everything, you see. All the pleasures of man—and woman."

Nancy made a big show of turning eye contact into sexual volleyball. "Have you ever slept with a man?" she asked him.

"No," he admitted. "I'm probably not as adventurous as you."

"Ah, you need someone to free you from the shackles of convention, Lieutenant. Personally, I like to feel if I want to make love to a man—I will. To a woman, yes, also. To a flower, to a child, to a tree—yes! yes!"

"How about a Saint Bernard?" he wondered.

Her eyes opened very wide, then she laughed. "Oh, you're wicked! We could have lots of fun!"

"Yes, I'm sure. Now, Nancy, I understand you held up a gas station back in New Jersey—was this also in a quest of experience?"

"You know everything about me, don't you?"

Nicky smiled modestly.

"The gas station was after Bard," she told him, "and before Hollywood. You see, I was having an affair with this very brutal man who liked to do quite dangerous things. He convinced me that an armed robbery might be very exciting. Unfortunately, we were caught, which turned out to be *not* so exciting. My parents were extremely upset. I had to come to California just to get away from them.''

"And this was—when?"

"Oh, ten years ago. Doesn't time fly when you're having fun?"

"So for ten years you've been . . .''

"Acting, mostly. Experiencing emotions."

"I see. And have you had any luck getting parts?"

"No." She sighed. "This is a hard town. But Bushy's promised to help me."

"Bushy?" Nicky asked. "Why would he help you?"

"Oh, you policeman, you!" She laughed slyly. "You're *working*, aren't you, poor darling. Come on!" she cried, shaking her body, raising her arms. "Let's dance!" Nancy Normal slithered to the thumping beat.

"No, I don't think so," Nicky protested.

"Loosen up, Lieutenant! Free yourself!" she cried. She collided with another dancing figure, a lady she seemed to know well. "Martha!" she shrieked. "How the fuck are you?"

Nancy danced off merrily with her new partner.

More and more people were dancing now, including Frank and his young blond friend. The entire room seemed to be writhing to the beat. Through the haze, Nicky had a glimpse of Unity Sphere, who was sitting on a sofa next to an absurdly handsome young man. The young man had an implausible mane of long hair and a shirt that was open clear to his navel. He was leaning very close to pretty Unity, saying something in her ear. They both laughed. Nicky felt a strange sting of jealousy.

He also felt it was time to leave. This wasn't his scene, no place for a lonely policeman. He looked up from his thoughts to find Donny Meredith's eyes upon him from a dozen feet away. Donny gave him a small, knowing smile, then turned to talk with some friends. It reminded Nicky that the keyboard player was someone he needed to talk with, but for now he'd had his fill of this glitzy gathering.

Besides, it was nearly six, and Tanya would be wondering where he was. Nicky walked off down the hallway and tried a few doors until he found a bedroom with a telephone. He dialed the communications room at the Beverly Hills station and left a message to be put through to Charlie to come and pick him up. Quickly. He also asked the communications operator to phone Tanya and say he would be a little late. Meanwhile, she should eat out of the refrigerator and do her homework.

140

There was some time to kill. Nicky couldn't stand the idea of returning to the party, so he stepped out a side door and made his way past the swimming pool to the beach.

Night had already fallen with the suddenness of late winter. The sound of the crashing surf was wonderfully soothing after the man-made noise of the party. Nicky mounted a sand dune and inhaled the fresh salty tang of the ocean wind. It was cold, but he didn't care. The grandeur of the beach made up somehow for the desperate shabbiness of human beings. A crescent moon was sitting fat and sassy above the waves.

"Antisocial, aren't you?" came a voice from behind.

He spun around, startled. He had not heard her come up behind him. Unity Sphere was standing close by. She was smiling and looking achingly lovely in the moonlight. She was also bearing gifts.

16

The glasses made a nice clink as they touched—a delicate sound that stood out distinctly against the rolling thunder of the ocean.

Moonlight and champagne and Unity Sphere seemed a dangerous combination. The girl's eyes glittered with reflected silver, and her skin in this light looked like cool, perfect marble. She was definitely a girl to make your heart beat faster. She was also about three years too young even to be drinking champagne.

"I was afraid your friend inside was going to catch pneumonia," he told her, "what with his belly button sticking out and all."

She grinned. "You mean David?"

"Is that glitter boy's name?"

"Jeez, Nicholas, don't you know anything? That was David Lee Roth."

Nicky raised his eyebrows. "Sorry. Should that ring a bell?"

"This is incredible," Unity said. "David Lee Roth's an enormous rock star. Don't you follow these things, Nicholas?"

"Well, I only know the ones Tanya likes," he admitted. "She must not be too hot on this Tommy Lee Jones person."

"David Lee *Roth!* God, Nicholas, I'm worried about you. Maybe you have a cultural disease."

"Yes," he told her. "That must be it."

"You're a funny sort of person," she said. "Come on. Let's take a walk and I'll work on your education."

"Gee, and that used to be my line."

Unity kicked off her shoes, finished her glass of champagne, and threw it carelessly over her shoulder into the sand. She took his arm with one hand, held the bottle of Taittinger by the neck with the other, and they took off down the beach. "I bet you're the sort of person who doesn't like rock music after nineteen seventy. All the good stuff was in the fifties and sixties—is that what you think?"

"Not exactly."

"Well, what, then? Tell me what you think, Nicholas."

"Okay. For what it's worth—no, I don't think music was better in the fifties and sixties. Probably it's the other way around. Musicians are better educated than ever—I'm sure they can play circles around the old guys. It's just . . ."

"Just what?" she encouraged when he stopped.

"Back then it was happening for the first time," he said. "When Elvis got up and shook his hips, no one had ever seen anything like that before. Today Billy Idol can get up and do the same thing maybe better, but who cares? At this point, it's just an imitation of an imitation."

They had stopped walking and had turned to face each other.

"So what you're saying is it's the *first* time that's important?" she asked. "Like losing your virginity?"

"More like falling in love," he told her. "But yes, for the first time. Basically, music has only been repeating itself since about nineteen seventy. That's a long time for things to be recycled."

"Don't you think there are eleven-, twelve-year-olds—like Tanya —who are discovering rock and roll for the first time? For them, isn't it the same as when you first heard it in the fifties?"

"That's partially true," Nicky admitted. "But cultural movements have a life of their own. A birth, a midlife, a death. Like the Big Band era—great music, but it ran its course, got sort of flimsy, and finally ran out of energy. That's what's happened to rock and roll. It's time for something new—a new generation with new music and something revolutionary to say. Because that's what rock and roll used to be, but hasn't been for a long time now."

"Ah!" she said. "The next phase. Do you know how many people there are in this town who are trying to figure that out? What you're saying is absolutely true, Nicholas. All the record executives have known it for years. There are people who are paid fantastic amounts of money just to sit around and prophesy what's going to happen next—and yet no one really knows."

"Maybe they're trying too hard," Nicky suggested. "Anyway, it seems to me that when the new thing happens, it's not going to come from record executives. It's going to come from the heartland, the way it always does."

"Exactly," she cried, delighted with this conversation. "Not only that, but the record executives aren't even going to recognize it when it happens. They're all wrong, Nicholas. They've got the whole thing backward."

They came shortly to where the beach ended, a promontory of rock that blocked their way. Nicky took a swig of champagne from the bottle and passed it to the girl.

"You're very critical of the music business," he told her, "for an insider."

"Well, I have to earn a living. I'm quite practical, you know. I have to be. But that doesn't mean I have my eyes closed."

Right now, Unity's eyes were very open, staring at the surf with intense concentration. "What you said about the heartland, Nicholas . . . if you could find such a place, and you went out to it and listened—really *listened*—what do you think you would hear?"

"I'm not sure." Nicky found himself smiling at her youth and intensity.

Unity took another hit off the champagne and passed it over. "Well, *I've* listened," she told him. "About six months ago, Bo gave me some money to travel around the country and just report back to him what was going on. This is the way his mind works, you see. He thought, I'm a teenager—right? Maybe I can find out what's going to happen next with the youth market, so he can tap in on it and become even richer than he is. So I just bummed around and went places like Omaha and Sioux City and Detroit and Chicago and New York. I listened and I listened, and you know what I heard?"

"What did you hear, Unity?"

"*Nothing*," she told him with flashing eyes. "There's nothing going on, no new music, no new thoughts. The entire country's hypnotized, drugged out in front of their TV sets. Just a land of electronic zombies who are ultimately controlled by people like Bo Daniels."

"That's a pretty cynical attitude," he told her, "for one so young."

Unity started walking again, back toward Bo's beach house. Nicky followed after her with the champagne.

"Music television was supposed to be the new thing," she said. "The new art form, music and imagery combined. Who knows, maybe it could have been something if anyone had ever given it a chance. But from the beginning, it was just a big mind fuck. Do you know the first thing Bo did when he actually got the go-ahead from that slimy creep Bushy di Sutro? He spent a million dollars on a market research survey to find out what The Rock Channel should be. Bo figured out the age group, the economic status, everything he needed to know about his target audience. Then he hired a staff of psychiatrists to come up with ways to appeal to their subliminal fantasies. I mean, talk about *Brave New World!* Even the sets are designed for maximum appeal to a twelve-year-old's basic fantasies. The sad thing is that people don't even know they're being brainwashed."

"Brainwashed is a strong word for it," Nicky said, trying to be reasonable.

"You think so?" Unity flashed. She had gotten herself quite worked up about all this, and for a moment she looked at Nicky as though he might be Big Brother.

"Let me tell you something, Nicholas. There are soft-drink commercials we show at The Rock Channel where every thirty frames or so there's a single-frame image of a naked woman. It goes by so fast the conscious mind doesn't even know what it has seen. But the image registers subliminally, just enough to mysteriously identify a certain product with sexual pleasure. Does this sound like a brainwashing technique to you?"

"This is true?"

"Absolutely. If you come into the studio sometime, I'll show you some of these commercials and let you freeze-frame on some pretty X-rated stuff. Television has turned this country into a psychological dictatorship, and it's been so subtle and effective people don't even know."

Nicky hardly knew what to say. It wasn't that he didn't agree with her—he did. But he kept visualizing Unity in her pink bedroom on the set at The Rock Channel, talking excitedly about Prince and A-Ha with just the right lisp and just the right look to make a very big hit with the twelve-year-olds.

"Maybe you should find yourself a new line of work," he suggested kindly.

"Yeah? Like what?"

"I'm sure you'd be a dynamite baby-sitter."

She stopped walking to glare at him.

"Just kidding," he told her. "I do that a lot, to mask my real feelings."

The glare turned slowly to a smile.

"Maybe I could be a cop," she said. "How about that, Nicholas? Would they hire me?"

"Maybe," he told her. "Why don't you tell me about your relationship with Bo Daniels?"

They were walking again, and she gave him a sideways look. "You want to know if he's fucking me?"

"Well, I would probably have phrased it more elegantly. The man seems to have some hold over you."

They walked a hundred yards before Unity said another word. Nicky was beginning to wonder if she had forgotten him.

Then she said:

"I used to. Fuck him, that is. When I was younger."

"*Younger?*" Nicky was alarmed.

"Eleven," she said. "Twelve. It was all over by the time I was thirteen."

Nicky stopped walking. "Son of a bitch!" he said. "That's terrible."

She sighed. "I know it sounds that way. Actually, I was rather advanced for my age. Bo didn't stand a chance."

"You're saying that you seduced him?"

"Well, yes. Look, Nicholas, I know you'll probably find this distasteful, but I learned at an early age that I had a certain power over men. I also had a very practical streak in my nature—I had to, with my childhood being what it was. So I knew a good thing when I saw it. On the one hand, there was my mother living in a shack in the cane fields. And on the other, there was Bo Daniels living in a mansion on the beach, with people like Elton John and Paul McCartney flying in to record their latest tune. It wasn't a very hard choice to make. All I had to do was sit in Bo's lap in just the right way, and be adorable, and sort of . . . wiggle."

"Wiggle," Nicky said, feeling some distress.

"I can wiggle pretty nicely," she told him. "Want to see?"

"I'd be scared to death," he told her.

She laughed. "Are you a prude, Nicholas?"

"It's much worse than that, my dear. I'm a romantic."

"Ah, then you'll be glad to know the hanky-panky stopped when Bo adopted me."

"*Adopted* you? Are you serious?"

"Sure. Didn't you know that? Bo and Kitty Daniels are my legal guardians. They did that when my mother died, when I was thirteen."

145

As they talked, the breakers rolled in and out, making their eternal thunder. Not far up the beach, Bo's beach house was visible behind the sand dunes, the windows warm with light. Fragments of music and laughter drifted across the dark sand and became lost in the roar of the surf. A sharp breeze came up, and the girl snuggled closer to him for warmth.

It was decidedly pleasant walking with Unity Sphere, talking about music and larger cultural issues. Probably they should be talking whereabouts and alibis and hard facts. They were nearly back to the beach house, and Charlie would arrive soon to take him back to Sunshine Terrace, where his daughter was waiting. Ever since he had been on this case—officially and otherwise—Nicky had felt he was running out of time.

"Tell me about Marilyn de Malibu," he asked. "You all seem to be great buddies and give each other alibis all the time. I ran into her at your house yesterday."

"Yeah, she told me. She thinks you're a pervert."

"She thinks *I'm* a pervert! Whatever for?"

Unity smiled. "Didn't you grill her in the hot tub?"

"In this case, *boiled* is a better description. Actually, I was my usual gentlemanly self. I hardly peeked. So tell me about her."

"What can I say? Marilyn's earthy, sensible—a nice lady. She's been my friend for a long time, since I was real little. She's always been very supportive. Almost motherly, I guess. When I arrived in L.A., she showed me around, took me under her wing. Sometimes I like having a woman friend to talk with, where sex is not an issue."

"Isn't it?"

"Never. Marilyn's never even made a hint of a pass. I mean, the vibe isn't there."

"Are you aware she owns a gun?"

Unity shrugged. "Doesn't everyone in this town?"

"Do you?" he asked in return. Innocently.

She laughed. "No. I have other weapons."

"I bet. Now how about Nancy? How does she fit into your group?"

"Well, Nancy's kinda a dingbat, really. She and Marilyn have been together a couple of years. Generally, I try to see Marilyn by herself, but it gets a little sticky at times."

"What time did Marilyn and Nancy leave your house last Sunday?"

"About two, I think."

"Great!" Nicky told her. "Marilyn said noon, you say two, and Nancy said around four. The three of you would be a lot of fun in a court of law."

"Is it important?" Unity asked him. "We were drinking Margaritas, and we smoked a few joints. Sunday's the one day of the week none of us have to look at the clock too carefully."

"What did you do after they left?"

"I took a nap. I was exhausted. I woke up and it was dark. I opened a can of soup, read *Siddhartha* for about half an hour, then went to bed for real. Am I a suspect, Nicholas?"

"Actually, I'm just fishing," he said wearily. "I don't know what the hell I'm looking for. Just hoping something will turn up to make this all clear."

He did some more fishing as they walked the remaining distance to Bo's house. What was her last conversation with J. J. about? (He was trying, as always, to get her to come over to his house one night. She, as always, said no.) Did Marilyn dislike men? (No.) Nancy? (Nan swung both ways.) Had she ever met Tommy Torch or Ginny Gina? (No, but she enjoyed their video.) Did Marilyn ever mention her .32-calibur handgun was missing? (No.)

They came at last to the sand dune where they had begun. Unity's shoes lay where they had been discarded. The bottle of French champagne was nearly gone. All good things must end. Nicky took a swig and handed the rest to the girl.

She raised the bottle to her lips.

"Tell me about 'The Ghost of Rock and Roll,' " he said.

The bottle jerked. He was certain he had startled her. Then she smoothly finished the last drops and tossed the bottle over her shoulder, in the general direction of the house.

"You shouldn't litter," he told her. "It's a crime."

She held out her wrists to be handcuffed.

"Let's get back to 'The Ghost of Rock and Roll.' "

"It's a song, of course. Rick Elsmore wrote it for the last album that was never released. Why do you think I should know about such things, Nicholas?"

"Bo told me you're an expert on the Perceptions. I gather you have access to all the old files and memorabilia."

"Uh-huh. I'm doing a documentary, or trying to. Now that I have a show five days a week, it's not going to be so easy to find time."

"Do you have a copy of 'The Ghost of Rock and Roll'? I'd like to hear it."

"No, but I know where it is—it's in the master vault over at Inter Stellar, along with other stuff from the old days."

"Could you get it for me?"

"Certainly, Nicholas. But why?"

A hundred yards away, Nicky watched the silhouettes of two men walking across the beach from Bo's house to the surf. He wondered briefly what bit of intrigue was taking place.

"Nicholas, tell me—why are you interested in 'The Ghost of Rock and Roll'?"

He returned his attention to the girl.

"Oh, it's just a long shot. Probably nothing. Who do you think knows about the song?"

"Well, just a handful, I guess. All the remaining Perceptions, of course. Bo and his wife. People like Marilyn, who were hanging around at the time. Probably a few record executives and engineers."

"Tell me, Unity, in your research—have you come across any skeletons in the closet? Something someone might feel a need to . . . avenge?"

"Ah, I'm beginning to get your drift," she said with a smile. "Well, I don't know. Neither Bo nor any of the Perceptions are exactly nice people. There's a lot of old feuds and band politics, that sort of thing. But there's nothing I'd call a skeleton in the closet. Unless, of course . . . well, you've heard the rumors about Billy, I suppose."

"What rumors?"

"About his death."

"No. Didn't he die in a bathtub in Rome? An overdose or something?"

"Or something," she said. "There are theories galore. I'm surprised you never heard them. You see, Billy's death was kept secret for seven days. He died August tenth, nineteen seventy, and the first announcement didn't come until the seventeenth, one day after he was buried in a small cemetery outside of Rome."

"That's strange. Why the secrecy?"

"No one knows. Bo flew to Rome on August eleventh, and he was the only one of the inner circle actually to see the body. His explanation of the delay is he didn't want to turn the whole thing into a media circus. He wanted the luxury to mourn his friend's death in private a few days before the press got wind of it."

"Hmm . . . a noble sentiment, but it doesn't sound like Bo Daniels."

"Exactly. And because of the delay in announcing the death, a number of rumors got started. One of them is that Billy didn't die at all. Some of his die-hard fans say Billy got tired of being famous, so he simply arranged his death to get away from it all. The other rumor is that he was murdered."

"Murdered? Jesus, what did the autopsy say?"

"There never was an autopsy, Nicholas. There was only a death certificate stating that William Lion, American singer, died of heart failure due to extreme intoxication. That's all."

"No autopsy?" Nicky objected. "But that's absurd! There's always an autopsy with suspicious deaths, especially when they happen to young people."

"Maybe in America," Unity told him. "But not in Italy, not in the summer of nineteen seventy, in the middle of a heat wave when most Roman officials of any stature were out of town on vacation."

"Well, damn, I can see why there'd be speculation," Nicky muttered. "It's hard to imagine someone as famous as Billy Lion dying in such an obscure way. Of course, the doctor who signed the death certificate might be able to put any rumors to rest."

Unity shook her head. "The doctor who signed the death certificate died of cancer in nineteen seventy-eight. Two policemen as well as the house detective at the Grand Hotel reputedly saw Billy's body —but all of them are dead as well. Nineteen seventy's a long time ago, Nicholas."

"This is really astonishing. How did you learn all this?"

"I made some phone calls to Rome. I thought maybe in my documentary I'd be able to resolve the ambiguity surrounding his death. But I guess no one will ever know for sure what happened."

"Well, thanks," Nicky said distantly. First there was Pubic Telephone, then the Mafia, and now a suspicious death many years in the past.

Unity had him fixed in the gaze of her violet eyes. "I bet you'll figure this all out . . . if anyone can."

He smiled. "Thanks," he said. "I'm glad someone believes in me."

"Maybe I can help you, Nicholas. I know a lot about these people. I've been studying them most of my life."

She was standing awfully close. Nicky felt the way a positive piece of iron does when it comes in close proximity to a negative charge. The air was full of disturbed ions.

"You know, I've always been attracted to older men," Unity was telling him.

"It's our broader sophistication and world-weary wisdom, I suppose?"

"What it is, I've always been looking for the father I never had."

"I can understand that," he said understandingly.

"Probably it works out both ways," she said. "The older men . . . well, they get sort of a free trip back to their youth."

"That's quite a deal," Nicky admitted. He was scanning the road nearby for any signs of Charlie's car. He had a feeling Charlie better get here damn quick. He turned back to Unity to find she was even closer. Just inches away. The air was scorched between them. Hormones were doing high kicks a few inches below his solar plexus.

There is a point of magnetic attraction where the negative and positive come slamming together out of control. What could one policeman do against such universal force?

Their lips met, mouths open, thighs pressed as close as they would go.

"God, I want you," she moaned, working on his belt buckle.

"Me too," he admitted.

A motion down by the edge of the surf caught the corner of his eye. The two figures he had noticed earlier seemed to be conducting some kind of religious ceremony, waist deep in the surging water. At this moment, the larger figure was holding the smaller one beneath the waves—a strange time and place for a baptism.

What was wrong with this picture?

Nicky had a feeling he'd have been much better off if he were the sort of person to kiss with his eyes closed. Lovely Unity had just slipped a nubile little hand into his underpants, which was a very pleasant sensation.

"Fuck," he said sharply.

"Yes, Nicholas," she told him, trying to pull him down to the sand.

"Look, will you excuse me a moment," he said vaguely, breaking away from her. He took a few steps toward the ocean. *"Hey!"* he shouted to the figures. "Stop that!"

The larger figure holding the smaller figure beneath the waves jerked around and began to run wildly out of the surf toward the beach. It was the gesture of a guilty man.

"Stop! Police!" he shouted—a great line when it worked. The figure pulled out something shiny from his pocket and began to run away. Nicky chased after him, forgetting his belt was undone. He managed only a few yards when his pants fell down to his ankles, sending him tumbling headfirst toward the sand.

"Damn!" he cried, staggering in a last crazy dance to keep his balance—when a stream of fire burst from the nozzle of a gun, accompanied by a heavy roar. Nicky fell hard, feeling the twang of a bullet cut the air directly overhead where he had just been.

It wasn't the first time he had been saved by a woman's hand, Nicky mused briefly—before he got a mouthful of sand.

17

Nicky pulled up his pants, pulled out his .38 revolver, and wiped the sand from his eyes.

"Are you all right?" came Unity's voice behind him.

"Stay down," he told her.

The man who had fired at him was running away down the beach. Nicky gathered himself and made a quick sprint to the edge of the surf, where the smaller figure was sitting in the shallow waves, sputtering and rubbing his eyes. Nicky jogged into the cold water and took him by the arm. It was Rick Elsmore. Nicky hauled him roughly out of the surf onto dry land.

"Who attacked you?" he asked.

Rick coughed and seemed dazed. "Boy, oh, boy!" he muttered "That's the last time *I* take drugs at a party!"

Nicky left him and started running after the retreating gunman. The moon had risen, and there was enough light to guess the large figure might possibly be Gweg, Bushy di Sutro's giant of a chauffeur, but Nicky couldn't be sure. Whoever he was, the gunman had a fifty-yard advantage that he managed to keep as Nicky chased him along the edge of the wet sand. They ran like this for nearly a mile. Nicky was breathing hard, and there was a pain in his side. He was beginning to think he wasn't going to get much farther, when the figure cut suddenly to the left, running up from the ocean toward the sand dunes and the quiet beach houses that lay beyond. Nicky ran at a diagonal toward the spot where the gunman was heading and was able to narrow the distance between them.

The man turned and fired. Nicky fired back, but it was wasted motion. The figure hesitated briefly, then made a dash for a two-story house, jumping over a picket fence into the front yard. From inside the house, behind closed curtains, came the sound of a TV game show. Someone had just won a new convertible sofa and was going for the rest of the living room.

Nicky had lost sight of the gunman and was approaching more cautiously. He found a gate and slipped inside the yard, coming to a halt by a Ping-Pong table. A small dog began barking furiously nearby.

A shot rang out, shattering the glass windbreaker near his head. Nicky fired back, down a short pathway that led to the side of the house. The lights inside the house went off suddenly, leaving the game show to continue mindlessly in the dark. Nicky saw the gunman break cover, making a sudden dash from behind a patio table toward the garage at the rear. He fired again, ineffectually. The small dog was barking like crazy now, making itself hoarse. Nicky could see it, a little white French poodle showing its teeth at him in a very menacing way. The dog was small but very brave.

A bullet tore into the side of the house, sending a shower of splinters down upon his head. Nicky fired back. The French poodle, well to the right of where he aimed, yelped, spun around, whimpered once, and died.

Nicky had just killed someone's pet. He had to face it: He was one of the worst shots the Los Angeles police had ever known. Back at the academy, his scores on the firing range had almost kept him from graduating, though at the time he had been quite proud of his inability. For he was going to be a new kind of cop, one who didn't rely on force. Who reasoned with criminals in an enlightened sort of way. A true peace officer.

The figure fired at him again. It made Nicky very angry. He crouched and returned fire. A potted geranium hanging on a macramé holder exploded into a jumble of pieces. The plant, alas, had been hanging a good ten feet to the left of his aim. Nicky was beginning to feel like a home wrecker.

"Come out with your hands up," he yelled sternly. "You can't get away!"

The figure answered with another shot, then broke cover to flee down a narrow pathway toward the rear of the house. He was trying to escape onto Broad Beach Road.

Nicky ran after him, passing through another gate. He had a glimpse of someone hiding behind a Mercedes-Benz sports car. Nicky fired. The bullet shattered the car's right headlight and passed through into the radiator. In the silence that followed, he

152

could hear the steady drip of escaping fluid. In the distance, police sirens wailed mournfully in the night, coming down the Pacific Coast Highway toward Trancas.

The gunman and he exchanged another round. The car's windshield burst into a milky web of cracks. Nicky certainly was inflicting a lot of damage. He fired again, but his gun was empty and made only a dry click.

Nicky stepped backward into the shadows, melting behind the corner of the garage. He tried to hear what the gunman was doing, but in the darkened house someone had just answered a question correctly and the audience was going crazy. When the applause died down, Nicky heard footsteps coming his way slowly from the carport. He had a feeling he was a dead man. Tanya was going to be without a father. Susan would have an ex-ex-husband.

Then he remembered: He had stuffed Frank's gun down in his belt.

Was it still there? No. He had put it in his coat pocket when he started necking with Unity. But the gun was empty. He had unloaded the clip and put the bullets in the other pocket.

The footsteps stopped by the corner of the garage. The gunman must be listening for him, wondering where he was. Nicky quietly retreated farther down the side of the house, until he rounded the corner of a small toolshed. This was where he would make his stand. His hands were shaking. He pulled out Frank's .357 Beretta automatic and slid out the clip.

The footsteps were coming again, walking cautiously down the path where he had just been. Nicky found the bullets in his right-hand pocket. His numb fingers began pressing them into the clip. At first they wouldn't fit. He was trying to put them in backward. He corrected himself and began putting them in the proper way.

The footsteps stopped, very close. Nicky had succeeded in getting three bullets into the clip, and he figured this would have to do. He jammed the clip into the butt of the gun and peered out from the corner of the toolshed, the gun raised in front of him.

There was a man less than ten feet away, pointing a heavy automatic his way. But the man was the wrong shape—short and round, not the person he had been chasing down the beach.

"Nicky?" came a hoarse whisper. "That you, brah?"

It was Charlie Cat.

"Jesus, where is he?"

"Where's who?"

"The guy I've been chasing, for chrissake!"

"I didn't see anyone. He probably got away in the brush across the road. The sheriffs are a few minutes behind me—maybe they'll spot him."

"How the hell did you get here?"

"I was coming to pick you up when I heard the radio call that there was gunfire at this address. Some guy started shooting at me. The fucker really murdered the Mercedes I was hiding behind. . . . Nicky, you all right, brah?"

Nicky was kneeling by the side of the path, throwing up into a patch of petunias.

The Ghost of Rock 'n' Roll (2)

*I*n the window looking out on Hollywood Boulevard, twenty-five color television screens all showed the same scene:

A dozen elderly men and women, dressed in tweed jackets and wool skirts—members of the West Hollywood Poodle Association—solemnly marching on the sidewalk outside the municipal phallus of the Beverly Hills City Hall.

Many of them had their dogs on a leash, poodles of various sizes and colors—pink, white, blue, gray, and brown—all extensively coiffeured. Each one carried a placard on a pole, proclaiming the purpose of this vigil.

STOP POLICE BRUTALITY AGAINST DOGS, said one. WHAT IF IT HAD BEEN YOUR PET? asked another. POODLES NEVER HURT ANYONE, said a third. And finally, getting more personal: DOG KILLERS ARE WORSE THAN BEASTS. And, SEND RACHMANINOFF TO PRISON, THROW AWAY THE KEY!

Cowboy watched the TV images, standing outside the store window. He took an unfiltered Lucky Strike out of his buckskin jacket and lit it with a brief flare of his Zippo. He sucked in the smoke thoughtfully.

"Man, what bullshit!" he muttered to the twenty-five television sets, exhaling a thin stream of smoke. Cowboy knew of winos who had their throats slit and attracted considerably less attention. Quite casually, he began to consider how he might blow up this building containing the electronics store—where he would put the charges.

The fantasy gave him a few moments of real pleasure. The building was old and wouldn't present much of a challenge. About three pounds of plastic, he judged. The front door had an after-hours slot for the return of video movies. He could slip his little gift right through the slot, then detonate either with a timer or remote control. The whole front end of the building would cave in.

Just imagining it, Cowboy felt a warm pleasure creep up his spine. It had been like this a quarter century ago, watching his first bridge go in Vietnam. It had been like this as a child in Buffalo, New York, putting cherry bombs together to make bigger and bigger explosions. Cowboy liked to blow things up.

Night was falling on Hollywood Boulevard. The street lit up with neon. XXX-rated films announced themselves seductively as cars drifted by looking for action, up and down the boulevard, cruising sharks.

Cowboy saw a clock in a window of a store that sold vibrators and lingerie. It was seven forty-five. He walked faster so he wouldn't be late, though he was tempted to turn around, go to the bus station, and buy a ticket out of town.

There was a letter in his pocket, only a few lines, but threatening. Very threatening.

> *Dear Wayne Peterson,*
> *Be at the public telephone by the box office of the Holly-*
> *wood Bowl (555-6600) tonight at eight sharp.*
> *The Ghost of Rock and Roll*

The letter had been hand-delivered, slipped under the door of his hotel room, waiting for him when he woke up that morning. It had to be from Rick Elsmore, he presumed—who else would sign himself that way? But Cowboy didn't like it at all. The threatening part was the use of his real name, Wayne Peterson. No one had used that name in twenty years, and he would just as soon never hear it again.

Someone had found him after all these years. Cowboy turned up Highland Avenue and reached the phone booth a few minutes early. He lit another cigarette and waited nervously. The phone rang exactly at eight.

"Hello, Wayne. It certainly is good to talk with you after all this time."

"Who is this? Rick?"

"This is the Ghost of Rock and Roll—can't you tell?" The voice laughed, causing a brief flurry of feedback. Someone was trying to disguise his voice by speaking through a PA system with too much reverb and distortion added. It was amateurish but effective. Cowboy couldn't even tell if the voice belonged to a man or a woman, especially with the feedback ringing in his ears.

"Turn down the damn treble," Cowboy said grouchily. "And make sure your fucking microphone's not facing into a speaker."

"Ah, you always were the electronic whiz, weren't you? The Perceptions were really very lucky to find you."

"This *is* Rick Elsmore, isn't it? Having a bit of a joke, aren't you?" The voice laughed again, causing more feedback.

"If you're not Rick, you've got to be Donny. Right? Donny fucking Meredith! Mr. Keyboards himself."

"Oh, Wayne." The Ghost seemed saddened by these efforts to guess its identity. "You owe rock and roll quite a lot, don't you? I've come to collect on that debt. After all, rock and roll saved your life."

"Billy Lion saved my life," Cowboy corrected.

"Ah, yes," said the Ghost. "What a sight you were, Wayne. A twenty-year-old Green Beret, AWOL and stoned on acid. I remember when you showed up backstage at the old Avalon Ballroom in San Francisco. You were wearing that silly cowboy hat to try to hide your military haircut. Poor boy, you really didn't want to go back to Vietnam, did you? You told me you would do anything if I would hide you, let you join the tour. *Anything!* Well, this is it. I've come to collect, Wayne."

Cowboy tried to laugh, but it sounded hollow even to him. "Man, this is getting a little too far out, you dig. Let me get this straight— you're telling me you're the ghost of Billy Lion, come back from the grave. Is that it?"

"That's it, Wayne. That's it exactly."

"Okay, then tell me something, Billy," he challenged. "That first night at the Avalon Ballroom, I told you a secret I never told another living soul. We were alone in your dressing room. So what did I tell you, Billy? What's my secret?"

"Wayne, you told me you were walking on a jungle trail in Vietnam, just you and Captain Linderman. The captain was leading the way, and you shot him in the back. You killed him, Wayne, and then you returned to the base and told everyone you had been ambushed by the Vietcong. That was the secret you told me."

"So what did you do?" Cowboy shouted, because he was getting really scared, and he was hoping there was some explanation for this, though he couldn't imagine what it would be.

"Easy, Wayne. . . . You remember, I kissed you on the forehead and held you in my arms while you cried. I told you you were the sorrow of America. Then I helped you change your name and your identity, and I gave you a job on the sound crew and took you around the country with me. I stood by you and kept your secret, because I was a revolutionary, too. I was the only friend you ever had, wasn't I?"

Cowboy couldn't see through the tears that were running down his face. He made small choking noises into the receiver.

"They betrayed me, Wayne!" the voice said, suddenly harsh. "They took my dream and sold it cheap. Look what rock 'n' roll's become —a business conglomerate, controlled by goons and gangsters. Every bright dream we ever had of changing the world, now all greed and lust for power."

Cowboy wiped the tears from his eyes and tried to regain his composure.

"But don't you worry, Wayne. You and I together are going to take care of these people who destroyed our dream—aren't we?"

"What do you mean?"

Cowboy listened as the Ghost of Rock and Roll explained exactly what he meant. Cowboy said it was mad. Impossible to do it all in time.

The voice rang off for reasons of security, setting up a new rendez-vouz at a different pay phone in one hour's time. It took three such conversations for Cowboy to be convinced the plan was not so mad after all.

At the end of the last call, Cowboy was strangely exhilarated. Yes, it could be done. He had all the materials close at hand, and causing things to explode was really absurdly easy, as long as you had the proper tools. The hard part was getting the explosives in the right place, and the Ghost said he would take care of that. This promised to be the biggest bang he ever made.

They were going to destroy the inside of the Shrine Auditorium next Tuesday night. In the middle of the live presentation of the Grammy Awards. Right there on national TV.

Part Three

Rachmaninoff's Blues

1

*I*t didn't take Tanya Rachmaninoff very long to come to the conclusion that Unity Sphere was exactly the person she wished to be when she was seventeen.

Unity picked her up Thursday afternoon after school in a candy-pink 1970 Porsche convertible, about the coolest car Tanya had ever seen. Fortunately, a whole group of girls was standing by the front drive outside the main building at just that moment. Unity had the top down, rock music playing, and was wearing a pair of dark aviator glasses that made her look sexy, romantic, and mysterious all at once.

"Gosh, who's *that?*" asked Bunky.

"It's my friend Unity. You know, the VJ from The Rock Channel," Tanya threw out quite casually. "We're going shopping."

"Cool!" Bunky said.

It was a golden afternoon, blue sky, a crispness in the air. Tanya departed Marymount like a celebrity. Unity was a fast driver, aggressively changing lanes, handling the curves of Sunset Boulevard as though she were doing the Grand Prix. Tanya decided this was exactly the way she would drive one day. By the time they reached Neiman-Marcus in Beverly Hills, Tanya had mastered Unity's slightly mischievous smile, as well as her way of cocking her head a little when she listened to stories.

They didn't stay at Nieman-Marcus very long. They had come because Tanya could use her mother's charge account, but after ten minutes of roaming the aisles, Unity scrunched up her nose disdainfully.

"Neiman-Marcus is really *too* Beverly Hills," she said. "I don't see you in any of these clothes, Tanya."

"No, me neither," Tanya agreed, scrunching up her nose in the same way. "Actually, I can't *stand* Beverly Hills."

Unity mentioned a small boutique over on Melrose, and Tanya

was ecstatic. Her mother never took her to places like that, and her father's idea of shopping was to cruise the army surplus stores.

The boutique on Melrose was called The Lost Angel, and Tanya had never seen anything like it. The salesperson—if you could call him that—had curly hair down to his shoulders—and actually offered *both* of them a glass of white wine. His name was Byron, and Unity seemed to know him well. In fact, Byron walked casually in and out of the dressing room when they were changing, bringing them new things to try on, and no one seemed to think this was at all amiss.

"Don't worry, he's gay," Unity whispered, probably because Tanya was not succeeding in appearing as offhand about the situation as she wished.

Actually, if she had a body like Unity's, she wouldn't care who saw it. But in her case, it was more a matter of hiding what she *didn't* have.

"I wish my tits would get bigger," she said, scowling at her image in the three-sided mirror—trying on a really beautiful silk blouse that would be superb if it only protruded a bit more in front.

"They will, Tanya. Just wait a year or two. You're going to be gorgeous."

"God, I hate being twelve sometimes," she complained. "Most of the time, as a matter of fact."

Unity didn't laugh at her, which was something Tanya really appreciated. In fact, she took Tanya in her arms and gave her a warm hug.

"Don't grow up too fast, sweetheart," she said. "Take it from someone who didn't have much of a childhood at all."

Now what did she mean by that? Tanya longed to ask her about her life, because there seemed to be some mystery about her—but she didn't want to be rude. Unity ended up buying the beautiful blouse for her as a present, though Tanya tried to say no—because it was a hundred and seventy-five dollars, and she didn't know if Unity could really afford it or not.

By the time they drove away from The Lost Angel in the candy-pink Porsche convertible, Tanya was nearly exhausted with pleasure and her many impressions of the afternoon. As they drove up La Cienega toward Laurel Canyon, one of her favorite Phil Collins songs came on the car stereo, engulfing her in sound—as if she were in some wonderful movie and this were her own personal sound track, turning everything around her into magic. Tanya wished fervently that the song would never end.

They came to a red light, and another convertible—a new Alfa Romeo—came up alongside of them on the right. There were two young men, good-looking, in their early twenties, definitely giving them the eye.

"Hey, you—blond pussycat—I'm in love!" the driver called.

God, he's speaking to me! Tanya thought wildly. She didn't know where to look.

"Oh, have mercy, baby!" he was saying. "Gimme your phone number, you sweet little thing!"

The light changed to green and Unity accelerated up La Cienega, but the Alfa Romeo stayed alongside. Tanya was blushing violently. "God! What are we going to do?" she asked.

Unity gave her mischievous smile. "Well, my dear, we could run, or we could let them catch us," she suggested. "Sometimes it's a lot more fun to let them catch you, you know."

Jesus! Tanya didn't want to mention that her own experience in being caught by men was extremely limited. In fact, the farthest she ever got was last summer with David Feinstein, who succeeeded in getting a hand beneath her bra. But it ended abruptly when she opened her mouth at the wrong time, just as David was leaning forward to kiss her, so that the end of his nose banged against her braces and actually started to bleed.

The two young men in the Alfa seemed a lot more sophisticated than David Feinstein, however. Right now they were getting bolder in their suggestions, mentioning some of the things the four of them might do together if the ladies would be kind enough to join them in their hotel room at the Château Marmont.

"They're kinda cute," Tanya told her new friend. "But I don't think they have much *savoir faire.*"

"Exactly what I was thinking," Unity agreed. "Hold on."

Unity stepped sharply on the accelerator, pulling in front of the Alfa and making a sudden right turn onto Santa Monica. The young men in the Alfa howled in delight and took off in hot pursuit, but they were no match for the Porsche. Unity cut dangerously in front of a delivery truck, made a sudden right turn, then came around the block back to La Cienega. By the time they began heading back toward Sunset, there was no sign of the Alfa Romeo. The two girls laughed all the way up Sunshine Terrace to Tanya's home.

"Boy, that was the best afternoon ever," Tanya said.

"We'll do it again," Unity told her. "I promise."

"Gee, you've been so wonderful. I'm almost embarrassed to ask, but there's one more thing . . ."

"What, Tanya?"

"Well, the Grammys next week . . . now tell me if I'm asking too much . . . but do you think, I mean—is there *any* chance . . ."

"You want me to get you a ticket?"

Tanya lit up. "Could you? I know it's asking a lot. But, God! To actually *be* there at the Shrine Auditorium!"

Unity frowned. "Well, I don't know, Tanya. The tickets next Tuesday are incredibly hard to get . . . but I'll try, okay?"

"God, that would be too amazingly fantastic! *Really?*"

"Sure, why not? I bet I can scare up something. Tell you what—give me a call next Monday afternoon and I'll let you know. I'd tell you sooner, only I'm going to Hawaii tomorrow for the weekend."

"Boy, Hawaii for the weekend. You sure lead an exciting life," Tanya said enviously.

Unity smiled, but there was no mischief in this smile, Tanya thought. There was sadness around the edges. "Well, I have to keep someone company," she said. "It's part of my job, you see."

Tanya wondered about that as she watched Unity's Porsche descending down Sunshine Terrace. She imagined all sorts of things: rich men, tragic lovers—elegant beds where a beautiful young woman must keep someone company while she pined for someone else.

Tanya sighed at the fullness of it all, then went inside the house, to stand before the bathroom mirror and practice Unity's last sad smile.

2

Nicky Rachmaninoff spent most of that night fighting gunmen in his sleep. It was exhausting work, and the pay was not terrific.

He found himself running upon a barren desert landscape in the silver moonlight, chasing a man he once killed—a little fellow by the name of Lawrence Ferguson, who was back from the grave and ready to play cops and robbers some more.

Lawrence managed to stay a dozen feet ahead of him no matter how hard Nicky ran. They were in a valley that sloped gradually upward, so the running was not easy. Occasionally Lawrence looked over his shoulder and fired a shot back at him. Nicky returned fire as he ran, but they never hit each other—nothing happened except a growing anxiety that this was all in vain. They ran, fired their guns, and ran some more, and they never got anyplace at all.

Then, quite without explanation, Nicky was on a darkened beach, still running, gun in hand. Only now his pants were down around his ankles, because he had been interrupted from doing something he shouldn't have been doing with a girl who was too young. Guilt was now added to anxiety, as well as a feeling this probably was going to kill him, because the pants hobbled his efforts, and a new, more serious adversary—a large walking figure—was running circles around him, taunting and firing ever closer to the mark.

Nicky hobbled in this manner into a parking lot outside of a liquor store where a robbery was in progress. A teenager had just come out of the store. He was clutching a few ill-begotten candy bars, a six-pack of soda, and also a big lethal shiny .45. Nicky had stumbled upon this scene in his dreams before. His father, Seargent Sam Rachmaninoff, was just stepping out of his black-and-white cruiser, responding to the silent alarm, pulling out his gun. His father's partner, Dave Molinari, was more wisely crouching behind the cover of the open car door.

The tableau stopped for a moment, the three different realities arranged under the harsh streetlights in a kind of ultimate triangle: the teenager with his stolen goodies and gun, his father and partner in their cop uniforms looking very official and concerned—and Nicky, the observer, with his pants down to his ankles, watching this history unfold.

Unfortunately, he knew the ending too well.

"Hold it, Dad!" he cried, "This guy's going to kill you."

The teenager and the two cops turned their attention now on him. They all seemed to know he didn't really belong there.

"You disappoint me, son," his father said sadly.

Then the teenager and the two cops all turned their guns his way —and fired.

Nicky awoke with a start, finding himself in his bed at home. The clock on the table said three fifty-four. In the bed next to him, Susan turned in her sleep, sighed, and was still again. She had dropped by last night, and one thing had led to another. Only this time, everything was out in the open. When Tanya said good night, she had added, "See you in the morning, Mom." Quite casually. The womenfolk apparently had it all figured out, while the menfolk were still guessing.

Nicky slipped out of bed, careful not to wake her. He found his thick terrycloth robe and went out through the living room to the kitchen, where he located a can of beer.

Psst went the can as he pulled the pop-top. At four in the morning, sounds like that took on a certain Zen finality. A small eruption of foam gurgled forth. Nicky took a long swallow to drive away sleep and bad dreams. The beer tasted thin and watery. It was domestic brew, something he had never heard of before but had been on sale at his local supermarket, $3.99 a twelve-pack. There wouldn't be any Beck's for a while, because the worst had happened. That afternoon Nicky had been suspended from the police force, without pay, for an indefinite period of time, while an investigation of his actions was under way.

Susan came into the living room wearing one of his shirts and nothing else. She turned on a light, probably feeling it was wrong to sit in a darkened living room at four in the morning drinking beer.

"What are you thinking?" she asked him.

"A square peg in a round hole," he told her.

She sat down next to him on the sofa. "Honey, you can put your peg in my hole anytime."

He tried to smile. It was an effort.

"You feel like talking?" she asked.

"I don't know. What the hell is there to say?"

Susan was into personal growth, and feelings, and expressing oneself. Nicky was into beer. He got another cheap one from the refrigerator.

"Nicholas Rachmaninoff! I'm going to shake you," she said, "until you shout or cry or protest or make *some* sign that there's a person in there who's upset."

"Us dog killers don't have normal feelings like the rest of you folk," he told her.

Susan was studying him, a finger held to the side of her head, as if he were an interesting exhibit in a museum. "Killing the dog upsets you, doesn't it?"

"I don't give a shit about the dog," he said. "I *hate* poodles. I would like to take every goddamn French poodle in all of Beverly Hills and gas them to death."

"That's right," Susan said, nodding her head. "Let it out, Nicky. Don't be afraid to be ridiculous."

Nicky sighed and slid backward deeper into the sofa. "Jesus, all these loony-tune people out picketing in front of the station, making a lot of noise—the media has taken it up as a kind of heart-wrenching example of police excess. *And,*" he added glumly, "the

166

dog's owners are suing the Beverly Hills Police Department for fifteen million dollars. Mental anguish, you know. Fifteen million dollars' worth."

"They won't get it, Nicky. It's absurd."

"Absurd or not, the case will probably take a year in court and finance the new wing of a law school by the time it's done. Meanwhile, Chief McGroder is much too concerned about the negative publicity to let a monster like me anywhere near City Hall."

"It's a tough break," she admitted. "What about Charlie? Is he the head of homicide now?"

"No. Charlie's clean, but they don't trust him much. Captain Rosencrans of the major crimes squad has taken over homicide until internal affairs sorts things out. Where the wheel stops, no one knows."

They sat quietly for a while, side by side. Nicky knew he was being abrasive, but he was glad of Susan's company.

"Can I say something?" she asked. "This is probably selfish of me, but I'm glad you're off the force. I was always worried something would happen to you—and you know, Nicky, you never really fit. You were always too sensitive to be a cop."

Too sensitive to be a cop! Oh, how his father would howl with laughter!

"Nicky, listen to me—I've been thinking about you and me and Tanya and our different jobs, and I have some ideas."

She told him about her ideas. They were both of them fed up with Los Angeles, each in their own way—why not get the hell out? Susan, Nicky, and Tanya: a family again, as they were meant to be. Maybe they could buy a nice little ranch in Utah, near the Redfords, perhaps, so they wouldn't feel too isolated. It would be wonderful for Tanya, all that country air. Probably they would have to buy a small Lear jet so Susan could commute to Hollywood when she had a movie to do or a TV show. But that would be kind of fun. Nicky could even learn to fly it if he wished.

She'd build a music studio for him in the woods, where he could play the piano all day long and compose serious music. They would raise horses and sheep and have a vegetable garden. Nicky could grow a little dope. Every now and then they might take a trip to China or Paris or East Africa. They could really relax and get into the simple life.

Nicky told her the simple life sounded great. All you needed was tons of money.

She smiled and said *that* was what was so simple: she did.

167

He didn't know what to make of it. Ancestral Russian guilt told him something was wrong here, but he was hurting and his defenses were down. Actually, he was less tempted by money than what the shirt she was wearing kept opening to reveal—her body. Some way into her raptures of country living, he picked her up, carried her back into the bedroom, and showed her what nature was all about. Later, she lay in his arms and fell asleep while he stared at the bedroom ceiling, watching the gray light of dawn slowly creep into the room, listening to her rhythmic breathing by his side.

He had to admit, unemployment wasn't bad so far. Maybe he'd let Susan build him a music studio in some perfect forest, far, far from L.A.

She certainly could afford to take care of an ex-policeman with modest tastes. Hell, if worse came to worst, Susan could even pay for the French poodle he had killed.

3

They left him at his piano the following morning. First Susan, who had to hurry over to Warner Brothers to do voice-overs for her latest TV miniseries. Then Tanya, in her blue-and-white uniform, off to face the perils of a Catholic education.

Nicky was left to play the blues. It was his first day of unemployment, a day of hazy sunlight and semismog. He began a slow shuffle in the key of C, slipped up into the key of C sharp, then D, then continued chromatically until arriving back at C again. He managed to kill a whole hour this way.

He stopped playing and made himself a cup of coffee, pouring a few fingers of brandy into it rather than cream. You could do this sort of thing when you were unemployed: play the blues in every key and drink brandy at nine-thirty in the morning. Nicky had a premonition time could slow down, even stop, and he would be the last to know.

The irony was that now, for the first time, he actually had some theories about the series of violent events that had begun with Jay Jeffries' death and had led most recently to Rick Elsmore's evening swim at Trancas. Not that he had any answers, but he had the right questions to ask—definitely a step in the right direction.

It made one want to do something more active than sit around at

168

home playing the blues and drinking coffee spiked with brandy. One wanted to do something, one did. Nicky even had a pretty good idea how he might begin.

He hardly realized the exact moment he stopped playing the piano. He caught himself in the familiar motion of strapping on his shoulder holster, taking out his brown corduroy coat from the closet, and finding his wallet and car keys on the bedroom dresser.

He tried to stop himself walking out the door, remembering his tenuous position as a suspended cop.

"This is ridiculous," he told his Austin-Healey.

But being ridiculous had never stopped him before.

4

The Sunset Marquis was a small hotel off the Strip that was popular with the music crowd. The lobby was done in soft pastels, and there was a baby grand piano in one corner. There were two doormen in livery of greenish brown, young men with winning smiles and long hair, probably hoping to be discovered. It was the sort of place where everyone was chic and on the make and good-looking. Nicky had a feeling they wouldn't accept your reservation here unless you could prove you met these qualifications. He was able to get Rick Elsmore's room number by showing his detective's shield to an assistant manager behind the front desk.

He took the elevator to the second floor and knocked on the door to 211. There was no answer, so he knocked again.

"Yeah . . . coming," came a growl from inside.

The door swung open to reveal a very bedraggled Rick Elsmore. His eyes were pink and unfocused. His blond hair stood outward in a chaos of directions, like a storm at sea. He was stark naked: a pale, emaciated body with a large erection.

"Oh, it's you," he said. "I thought it was the maid."

Nicky followed a pair of bony buttocks into a pink living room. The place was an opulent mess. Three ice buckets were lined up by the door with bottles in them upside down. There were full ashtrays and empty beer cans and clothes covering every surface and chair.

"Have a seat," Rick told him. "I'll throw something on."

Nicky removed a woman's bra from a chaise longue and sat down.

169

Through the open door to the bedroom, he caught a glimpse of a girl in Rick's bed.

"Up and at 'em, honey pie," Rick pulled the blanket off the bed and slapped her bottom.

"Rick! You're a big meanie," she cried.

"Yeah, but I got an important Russian impresario in the next room who wants to talk with me about my upcoming tour of the Soviet Union. You don't want to stand in the way of international relations, do you?"

Rick took a sheet off the bed and came back into the living room with it draped around him like a toga. The girl followed in a moment wearing pants but no top. She was in search of her bra, which Nicky handed her gallantly.

"You . . . speak . . . English?" she asked carefully.

"When I have to," Nicky replied.

Rick kept her moving. She giggled as if it were all a big joke, but before she knew it, she was in the hall.

"Getting rid of women is a great art," Rick announced, rewrapping his makeshift toga and sitting next to a telephone. "How about some breakfast, Rachmaninoff?"

"No thanks. I'd rather talk about who tried to drown you Wednesday night."

"Oh, come on. Civilized people have elegant meals before serious conversation. Anyway, this is all on my wealthy benefactor, Bo Daniels."

Rick would not be put off. He picked up the phone and dialed room service. "Fuck, it's busy," he complained, slamming down the receiver.

He got up, went to the curtains, and pulled them open. A sliding-glass door opened onto a small balcony that overlooked the pool and restaurant below. Rick gathered the toga around him and shouted down to one of the waiters.

"Hey, Warren! Send me up two orders of eggs Benedict, two screwdrivers, and a bottle of Moët."

"It's better you skip the drinks and have a pot of coffee instead, Mr. Elsmore," the waiter shouted back.

"Here's what I think of your coffee!" Rick opened his toga and exposed himself to the lunch crowd below. There were a few small screams and some laughter.

He came back into the room. "This place is getting too middle class," he explained.

The phone rang. Apparently it was the front desk. "Yeah, yeah, keep your pants on," Rick said into the phone. "Okay, *I'll* keep my pants on."

He slammed down the telephone. "It's getting damn hard to be a free spirit these days, Rachmaninoff, I swear to God. I remember a party Janis Joplin threw here—it must have been sixty-eight. There were people fucking in the damn hallways. Billy and I and Janis dropped acid together and spent eight hours, the three of us, in her bathtub making up these incredible songs. One masterpiece after another. Only the next day none of us could remember a single thing about them. A pity—those were songs to change the world, Rachmaninoff! Songs to usher in a new age. If I had had a tape recorder in that bathtub, maybe things would have been different."

Rick shook his head mournfully, as if he were still trying to remember the lost songs that would have changed the world.

"Let's get back to Wednesday night," Nicky suggested. "And the unkind soul who tried to drown you."

Rick sighed. "I've been a bad boy, Rachmaninoff. Too many drugs. The last thing I remember is dropping acid in the limo coming from Forest Lawn to the party. I thought it would wake me up, you see. Didn't want to miss J. J.'s wake, for chrissake."

"How loyal. And the party?"

"A vague blur. Some psychedelic flashes—that's all, I'm afraid."

"Can't you remember anything about leaving the house and walking down to the beach?"

"Well, there were a whole bunch of goblins dancing around me like I was a maypole, I remember. I didn't like it much. That's when the archangel appeared and told me there was salvation in water."

"I see. Can you tell me anything about this figure?"

"Jeez, I don't know. He had wings, a pretty nice halo. Just sort of an average archangel, I guess."

"Was he a big archangel? A small archangel? Medium-sized, perhaps?"

"Big," Rich answered with finality. "Very big."

"And he suggested you go down to the water?"

"That's right. We started singing 'Sea Cruise' together. You remember that song? We sort of danced over the dunes, down to the edge of the water, looking for the big white boat that was going to take us away. I remember feeling deep joy."

"Naturally. And the angel? Would you recognize him again?"

Rick seemed very distraught. "Probably not," he admitted. "Not

171

unless you gave me enough acid. And even then—well, as you probably know, Rachmaninoff, angels come and go."

Nicky thought he might leave this subject for a while. "Let's talk about ghosts, then," he suggested.

"Yeah, that's a heavy topic." Rick nodded. "Ghosts will fuckin' kill you."

"Will they? How about 'The Ghost of Rock and Roll'?"

Rick raised an eyebrow. "You mean my song? Jesus, why's everyone asking me about that old thing?"

"Everyone? Who else has asked you about this, Rick?" Nicky was most curious to know.

"The big man himself, Mr. Bo Daniels. Woke me up this morning at the ungodly hour of ten o'clock. Pretty damn inconsiderate, I told him. But that's our Bo. Only thinks about himself. He was at the airport with succulent young Unity on their merry way to Hawaii, to work on their suntans for next Tuesday night. Fairly shallow of them, if you ask me."

"What did Bo want?"

"Didn't I tell you? He wanted to know if I had the master tape of 'The Ghost of Rock and Roll.' He said he wanted to hear it again, that maybe it had some commercial potential after all."

"What did you tell him?"

"Hey, I said, 'No way, José.' Do I look like the sort of dude who goes through life burdened with useless mementos of the past?"

"So that's all Bo wanted—to see if you had a copy of the song?"

"Well, when I said no, we bullshitted awhile about where it could be. I told him it was kinda funny, but J. J. was asking about the song a short time before he was killed."

"Yes? Tell me about this."

"Yeah, this must have been ten days before J. J. made the great departure. He got sort of a threatening letter that was signed 'The Ghost of Rock and Roll.' "

"You sure?" Nicky asked. "Did you actually see the letter?"

"No, he read it to me on the phone. He thought maybe I sent it as a joke."

"Did you?"

"Hey, I don't have the time for frivolity, Rachmaninoff. I'm too busy with my vices."

"Do you remember the letter, what it said?"

Rick shrugged. "Just the usual thing a ghost might want. Justice. Revenge. Personally, I think it's about time."

There was a knock on the door. "Room service," came a waiter's voice.

"Who do *you* think wrote that letter?" Nicky asked.

"Hey, that's easy, man. Just like I told J. J. Billy's back from the dead, and he's getting even with all the sons of bitches who let him down."

Like Nero, Rick gathered his toga around him to let in the waiter with the breakfast tray.

"Retribution," he whispered dramatically, signing the bill for breakfast. "Yea, the Day of Judgment draws nigh. And I've been expecting it for a long, long time."

The waiter popped open the bottle of Moët et Chandon.

5

When the waiter had departed, Rick Elsmore held up the bottle of champagne in a kind of salute, and he began to sing:

> " *The music was love, light of our youth,*
> *And we were like angels, living in truth.*
> *Before it was bargained and dealed and sold,*
> *Like a girl who once loved you, who's left you for gold.*
>
> " *But those who betray the dreams of the young*
> *Will endlessly suffer the evil they've done.*
> *Yeah, none of your power and none of your gold,*
> *Will hold back the vengeance of the Ghost of Rock and Roll.' "*

Rick sang in a raspy Bob Dylan-like voice. The song was fairly tuneless, and Nicky could not quite imagine it on Top Forty radio. Rick came to what seemed to be the chorus:

> " *The Ghost of Rock and Roll—*
> *Damn your soul for growing old!*
> *Remember all those dreams you sold,*
> *Damn your soul, rock and roll!' "*

Rick Elsmore sang the chorus a few more times, ending in a dramatic whisper: " 'Damn your soul, rock and roll!' "

Nicky smiled carefully. "So that's it, Rick?"

"Well, that's all I remember. Actually, the song went on another twenty minutes or so. I figured it would fill an entire side of the album. There was going to be a long instrumental break—I was hoping we could get the London Philharmonic for it, with over-dubbed guitars, you see, screaming above the orchestra—kind of like rockets in flight over a doomed landscape. But we never got that far into production."

"Tell me," Nicky said, "if Billy came back from the dead—what exactly would he wish to revenge?"

"Isn't it obvious? I mean, Billy would take one look at Inter Stellar fucking Village and totally freak out. What we've become—Bo and J. J. and Donny and me—is everything Billy despised. Like the whole message of the Perceptions was fuck the establishment, throw away your money, take off your clothes, dance, sing, fuck, do exactly what you like—*but do it for free.* Do it for love."

"It's easy to put down money when you have three gold albums in a row," Nicky suggested. "You guys must have been rolling in cash at one time."

"Ahem—there were *four* gold albums in a row," Rick corrected. "And there was money, sure—but in those days we spent it faster than it came in, especially Billy. He just gave it away—sometimes thousand-dollar handouts to bums on the street. The guy was a real revolutionary, all the way to the core. That's why he'd think he was fucking dreaming if he saw what we've become."

"There must have been some areas of disagreement between him and Bo Daniels, then," said Nicky.

Rick laughed heartily. "Oh, that's good. *Disagreement!* What it was, between Bo and Billy, was total war. Especially toward the end. If you ask me, Billy didn't die of any heart failure in that Grand Hotel bathtub. I don't know how he managed it, but somehow—I know in my soul—Bo killed Billy. As surely as Cain murdered Abel."

"But isn't that like killing the golden goose?" Nicky objected. "If Bo's as concerned with money as you suggest, he wouldn't murder his star attraction. Without Billy, the band went under in less than a year. It was the end of the road."

"It was the end of the music," Rick said, "but the beginning of Inter Stellar. Anyway, Bo didn't have much of a choice, because Billy quit. He simply flew off to Europe in the middle of the last tour. Not a lot of people know that. The official word was he got sick and had to cancel the rest of the tour due to medical reasons. But that wasn't it. Billy just didn't want to be a rock star anymore. He said it was boring. Can you believe that? *Boring*."

"So he ran away to Rome?" Nicky said, frowning. "I still don't see what Bo would gain by having him dead."

Rick leaned forward. He had the mad Nero look in his eye again.

"Bo was looking ahead, way ahead—ten years, twenty years, all the way to Inter Stellar Village and The Rock Channel. Alive, Billy Lion had become a liability. Unpredictable, you see. A real embarrassment. He was saying strange things to the press, like rock and roll was finished and it was time to get on to something new. Dead, on the other hand, Billy made a great legend, joining the ranks of Jimi and Janis. So you see, Rachmaninoff, Bo was simply protecting his investment. The goose had laid all the golden eggs he was ever going to, and it was best to get him out of the way."

Nicky had been working on his eggs Benedict. "That's an interesting theory, Rick. It's a pity it could never be proved."

"Yeah. Bo cleaned up after himself all right. Billy was buried before anyone had much time to investigate. If I were you, Rachmaninoff, I'd try to find the girl Billy ran off with. She'd be able to tell you what happened in Rome, if anyone can."

"There was a girl?"

"Naturally. With Billy there was always a girl."

"Who was she?"

Rick shook his head. "I don't know. It was hard to keep track of Billy's love life. You could ask Bo, of course—he flew to Italy when it happened. But I wouldn't believe anything that fucker told you."

"Didn't anyone else from the group go to Rome when Billy died?"

"I *wanted* to, you know. But I just couldn't do it," Rick told him painfully. His hand was shaking as he brought a glass of champagne to his lips. "Let me tell you a secret. Billy Lion was a god. He was too pure to survive on this planet. Do you know what it's like to be touched by a god, Rachmaninoff? To have your youth lit up by a miracle? Billy made me into something . . . and then he went away. And nothing's been any goddamn good ever since."

Nicky sensed he was losing him. "Rick," he pleaded, "tell me. Did anyone else besides Bo Daniels go to Rome around the time Billy died?"

"Yeah," Rick said heavily. "Donny was there."

"Donny Meredith?"

"That's right. Mr. Keyboards himself."

6

Donny Meredith lived in an old-fashioned California ranch house off Mulholland Drive near the top of the Hollywood Hills. There was a large willow tree shading the front door and well-tended flower beds around the side. The place had a tranquil, orderly feel to it.

Nicky was about to ring the doorbell when he heard piano music cascading from inside. Someone was playing Bach extremely well, a fugue Nicky had himself attempted but had never been able to master. The pianist inside was so good, Nicky supposed this might be a recording—until the music stopped and the player repeated a phrase.

Nicky rang the bell. The piano stopped for a second time. In a moment, a Filipino houseboy opened the front door. It had been a very long time since Nicky had known anyone with a Filipino houseboy. He presented his card and was led inside.

Donny Meredith was seated in a large living room that was furnished in a California-French provincial mode. There were many nice, expensive things in the room, but the nicest was a black Steinway concert grand piano, polished to an impossible gloss. Donny himself was in a nearby armchair wearing a silk dressing gown, slippers, legs crossed, looking at Nicky with slight contempt. He had a cold, aristocratic face, skin stretched tightly on a delicate skull. His eyes were bemused and skeptical.

"I enjoyed the fugue," Nicky told him, smiling. "That's always been one of my favorites, Number Five in D Major," he added unnecessarily. Might as well show the guy he wasn't the only one with a little culture.

Donny Meredith managed to look just a little more bemused and contemptuous. He managed this by raising one eyebrow a quarter of an inch. "Oh, you know Number Five, do you?"

"I've played at it a bit," Nicky admitted, "yes."

"Please, Lieutenant—I'd love to hear you," Donny said, gesturing toward the piano. It was a challenge, gauntlet thrown.

Nicky knew he was being damn foolish. However, Steinway concert grand pianos are very hard to resist. He sat down on the hard bench and laid out a fat chord to get the feel of it. The action was creamy, the tone unspeakably rich—and this was just a G triad. He shuddered to think what an A-flat major seventh would sound like. Nicky launched into the Bach fugue, going for an epic, heroic sound. Certainly the instrument helped him—or perhaps it was the fact he was too competitive to fail this little test—but the fugue came out effortlessly.

"I'm impressed, Lieutenant!" Donny told him. "Really, you must be L.A.'s first Renaissance policeman."

Nicky shrugged, trying not to show he was thrilled. Donny had to assert his one-upmanship by making a few suggestions about the timing of sixty-fourth notes, but that was all right. Sixty-fourth notes were a bitch to play, and by the time Nicky sat down on the sofa the two of them were almost on a friendly footing.

"I understand you don't perform anymore?" Nicky asked after Donny had ordered coffee from the houseboy.

"No, I've had enough of stages, Lieutenant. They don't interest me anymore."

"So that's why you produce records now for other people?"

"Ah, you heard about Rude Cousin? Yes, young musicians often come to me, and sometimes I let myself get involved in their projects. Rude Cousin is quite an intriguing group, very experimental. The music is horrible, of course, but I think they have somthing to say. Billy would have liked them."

There it was: *Billy would have liked them.* It struck Nicky as quite incredible that after nearly twenty years everyone in this group still thought in terms of what Billy would have liked and what he wouldn't have liked. The shadow was long.

"I'd like to ask you some questions about Billy, as a matter of fact." Donny shrugged, as if the subject were long exhausted.

"I'm interested in his death," Nicky pressed. "I gather you flew to Rome with Bo at the time he died?"

"No, Lieutenant, I didn't get there until *after* the funeral. Bo went first, I followed later."

"Why was that?"

Donny Meredith ran a hand through his thinning hair. He didn't appear happy to dredge up the past.

"Look, you have to picture the way this happened. Billy had been gone for about two weeks. He just disappeared one day, right in the middle of a tour. We were all very pissed. Then someone in London called Bo to say there had been a story in an Italian newspaper that an American rock star had died in his hotel room. It was all very vague, and no one really knew if it was Billy or not. Bo simply flew over to check it out."

"By himself?"

"That's right. Actually, we were trying to keep it secret."

"You were still hoping the Perceptions might get back together?"

Donny sighed. "Yeah, I guess so. Looking at it now, I can see we were fooling ourselves. Anyway, Bo telephoned me from Italy and said, yes, the story was true—Billy was dead. He asked me not to tell anyone."

"Why was that?"

"Well, there were legal complications—we still owed Columbia two albums, for instance. Bo wanted a few days to figure out some kind of strategy before the shit hit the fan."

"I see—and *that's* when you joined him in Rome?"

Another sigh, deeper and longer. "No, I waited a few days. You see, at this point I was really torn apart. I stayed around L.A. going crazy for a few days, and then finally got a plane across the ocean. I figured I had to see if the son of a bitch were really dead."

"And was he? You actually saw his body, I mean?"

"No, I got there the day of the funeral. I only saw the casket being lowered down."

"So everything you know about Billy's death, you only heard secondhand from Bo—is that it?"

"That's right."

"I see. Tell me—Rick said Billy had a girl with him at the end. Do you know who she was?"

"I don't know. There were lots of girls. Billy was the sexy one. The rest of us got his rejects."

Bitterness, Nicky thought. My, my.

"But you don't know who went to Rome with him?"

Donny shook his head. "Bo sent her away, maybe he could tell you who she was. She was gone by the time I got there."

"Tell me, Mr. Meredith—is there any chance it was Marilyn de Malibu?"

"Marilyn? Maybe, though I doubt it. Marilyn and Billy had a scene together back around nineteen sixty-seven, but by the end Billy wasn't speaking to her any more than he was to the rest of us."

"No one speaking to one another," Nicky wondered. "It's hard for me to imagine people playing such wonderful music together and hardly on speaking terms."

Donny gave a bitter laugh. "You've never been in a band, Lieutenant. The stress of being on the road, living out of suitcases for months at a time, always being together—it can have you at each other's throats. Things were getting bad with us even before the Pontiac disaster—but that was the last straw. After that, no one even tried."

"What exactly was the Pontiac disaster?" Nicky asked.

"They wanted to use one of our songs for a television commercial —it was 'Streets of Love,' our biggest hit."

"That sounds fairly simple," Nicky prodded. "Lots of money, too, I imagine."

"Yeah, well, Billy wasn't going for it. He was outraged we were even considering such a move. He said it was against everything the band stood for."

"Okay, so how were these questions decided? Did Bo Daniels have the final say, or was it Billy?"

"No, we all did. We had set ourselves up as quite the miniature democracy," Donny said with a sarcastic laugh. "We thought of the band as a commune—everyone had an equal vote and an equal split of the profits. We were all very idealistic, you see—in the beginning."

"So you voted?"

"Yeah, we voted, and Billy lost. It was four against one."

Nicky leaned back in his chair and narrowed his eyes. "You know, I'm a little surprised to hear that," he said. "Especially after the way you all talk about him, as if he were a god. Didn't any of you take Billy's side?"

Donny Meredith stood up from his chair and wandered to a window. He was no longer the arrogant figure he had appeared when Nicky had arrived. Now there seemed a weight on his shoulders, making him slump forward.

"No, not one of us sided with Billy," he said in a hoarse voice.

"I don't understand."

Donny spun around from the window. "It was money!" he cried. "We were all fucking broke! I know that's hard to understand— here we were, the top American band of the late sixties, everyone imagined we were rolling in money. But by nineteen seventy we were all living way beyond our means. Rick Elsmore, for chrissake, had just totaled his *second* Rolls-Royce. I was overextended trying to buy this house. J. J. had a new yacht and a drug problem to take care of—and none of us ever considered how nasty the IRS could be when you hadn't paid your taxes. The end was in sight."

"Sounds like it," Nicky said sympathetically.

Donny was pacing now, waving his hands in angry gestures. "Look!" he shouted angrily. "The youthful idealism was gone. Okay? It got lost somewhere in the hardships of the road. I wanted something solid out of all those years—something that would last. The fucking money for the commercial sounded pretty damn good. Can you blame me?"

"Nine out of ten people would have done the same thing," Nicky said mildly. "So the commercial was made?"

The keyboard player seemed to deflate until he was sitting down again. "Wrong," he said. "Billy outfoxed us. He got so outrageous in Florida, you know—he took out his dick at a concert and started waving it at the audience. The little stunt got him arrested, and we had trouble getting auditorium dates for a while. After that, Pontiac dropped us so fast, it was like we were poison."

Donny laughed a little too wildly. "Oh, Billy! You motherfucker! You sure had the last laugh!"

"But did he?" Nicky asked. "Mr. Meredith, do you think it's possible Bo Daniels murdered Billy in Rome?"

Donny stopped laughing. He took a few breaths and shook his head. "Christ, I don't know. If you're asking me if Bo is *ruthless* enough to do something like that—I'd have to say yes. However, Bo was in Los Angeles when it happened, right? He didn't fly to Italy until after it was over—so how the hell could he have done it?"

Nicky stood up with a vague smile. "Thanks, Mr. Meredith. I appreciate your time—and also what you told me about the sixty-fourth notes. I'll be sure to practice that."

"Yeah. Get yourself a metronome. Start out real slow, work up to speed gradually," he said mechanically.

"I'll do that. Now one more thing. Have you by any chance received a threatening note from someone who calls himself the Ghost of Rock and Roll?"

Donny looked up sharply. Without a word, he walked across the living room to a desk, opened the drawer, and took out an envelope. It was neatly typed.

> *Mr. Keyboards,*
>   *You've been riding high, but rock and roll never forgets. Justice is coming. Prepare to die.*
>   *The Ghost of Rock and Roll*

Nicky read the message and slipped it into his coat pocket.

"When did this come?"

"About three weeks ago."

"Did you tell anyone about it?"

"No, I just put it away. When you're in the public eye, you get a lot of strange things in the mail."

"But this was sent to your correct street address. Do you have any ideas, Mr. Meredith, about this Ghost of Rock and Roll?"

Donny had risen again and was staring out a window, his hands clasped behind his back. He shook his head slowly.

"Who the fuck knows?" he said. "I just hope he gets it over with fast."

7

Nicky was playing the blues again, not his usual G-C-D configuration but tonight something a little more sophisticated, something in E flat, a Chicago kind of blues with shifting chords and strange notes. He was in that sort of mood.

He had called a reluctant Charlie and told him to phone Rome and use his restaurant Italian to find out from Interpol the official cause of Billy Lion's death, why there'd been a mysterious one-week delay, and the name of the woman who was with Billy when he died. Unless there was a lead from seventeen years back, the case was stalled and so was Nicky.

His living room on Sunshine Terrace glowed warmly with firelight and candlelight. There were flowers on the tables. A woman's touch was obvious here. Susan was in the kitchen washing the dinner dishes with Tanya beside her, drying and putting away. Tanya was telling her mother stories from school, chatting as merrily as a little bird.

This was Susan's third night here, and she was still going strong, though there were signs that the less than palatial aspects of Sunshine Terrace were getting to her. Just this evening, she had ducked into Nicky's bathroom and come out two minutes later, wrapped in a towel and dripping water.

"Nicky! There are frogs in your shower!"

"Yes?" Then, realizing this was apparently not *comme il faut* with the Bel Air set, added, "They're only little tree frogs. But we can

181

poison them if you want. Or shoot them, or something. I have a knack with getting rid of unwanted animals."

"Yuck," she said. "One of them jumped on my foot, and I nearly died."

So much for the simple life.

After dinner, she brought up the subject again of where the three of them might eventually live—meaning definitely not *here*.

Tanya voted quickly for Paris. Susan was for a more spread-out approach: a nice duplex on Central Park in New York, the ranch in Utah they were considering the other night, and a bungalow at the Beverly Hills Hotel for those times they "absolutely had to be in this deadful town."

"And where do *you* want to live, Nicky?" Susan asked him as an afterthought.

"Chicago," he told her.

The two ladies exchanged worried looks, then smiled, evidently deciding Nicky was joking. Well, they would work it out between them and put Nicky on the right plane when the time arrived.

At the piano, Nicky was singing: "Oh, I'm going to Chicago, I'm going to Chi-cago . . . "

He was just coming to his favorite part, the walk-up, chord by chord—F minor, G minor, A-flat major seventh, A diminished, all the way to a momentous B-flat seven that had a flat nine and a sharp five—upon which the entire song hung like a boulder resting on a pebble, wanting to rush off the dissonance to E flat again.

Exquisite. *God, I'm getting pretty good,* he thought.

"Nicky, you sure are getting pretty good," Susan called from the kitchen.

"Thank you, thank you," he called back.

The phone rang, and Susan answered it.

"Yes? . . . Oh, *Frank,*" she said in a loud, unnatural voice. Nicky stopped playing.

"You got my note?" she was asking. "Yes, Frank . . . I'm sorry, too. But I guess we both know this has been coming for some time."

Nicky took Tanya into her bedroom, to give Susan some privacy. Tanya was unhappy to miss the conversation. She sighed and lay upon her bed in a corpselike pose, with her hands folded across her breast. Nicky sat down by her feet.

"So, munchkin, what do you think of all the changes?" he asked.

"I think it's great, Dad. Only . . . "

"Only what?"

"Only I can't imagine you living in a duplex in New York, or some ranch in Utah."

"Hmm, you don't think I'm sophisticated, is that it?"

"No, it's just you're so awfully set in your ways. Sort of like an old bear."

"An old bear, huh?" Nicky was not too pleased with the image.

"A *nice* old bear," she modified. "And this house is your cave, you see. Your territory. I just can't imagine you anyplace else."

Nicky smiled. "Well, my dear, maybe it's time I wasn't such a creature of habit. Maybe it's time for something new."

"*I* think so, Dad. I think it would be good for you."

It was astonishing to have a daughter who was old enough to tell you how to live your life. He hugged her impulsively and whispered into her ear: "Whatever happens, I love you best."

"I love you best, too," she whispered back. "And Dad . . . do you think I can ask you something?"

"Yes, sweetheart?"

"*If,* by any remote chance, I was able to get a ticket to go to the Grammys next Tuesday, do you think—well, what I'm asking is, *could* I? Would you let me go?"

"The Grammys? Well, gosh, dear—I'm not sure that's a very good place for a twelve-year-old. Anyway, I'm sure the tickets are impossible to come by."

"Honestly, Dad, I'll *die* if I can't go. Unity said *maybe* she could get me in. She's going to be there filming for The Rock Channel, you know. She would keep an eye on me, really, Dad—Unity's my absolute best friend I ever had!"

Unity her best friend? Nicky had a feeling he had missed something somewhere.

"Look, dear, I'll have to think about this. Anyway, the Grammys . . ."

He was about to say the Grammys were nothing but group masturbation, a big circle jerk, and she'd be better off staying at home. He was searching for a more delicate way to put this when Susan came into the room.

"Damn, Frank's awfully upset, Nicky. He wants to talk with you," she told him. "I know this puts you in a terrible spot, but you can talk with him—make him realize it's all for the best. Won't you?"

Tanya meanwhile was jumping up and down on the springs of her bed. "Can I go, Dad? I swear, I'll be so good for the rest of my life. . . ."

"Maybe," he told her. And to Susan: "Why don't you stay here with Tanya. I think I'll manage this phone call better alone."

"Is that a *yes*, maybe—or a *no*, maybe?" Tanya was asking.

Nicky closed the door on both of them. He wondered if Sherlock Holmes had a chaotic home life. Of course not! People left Sherlock alone to play his violin. The lucky bastard could concentrate on logical deductions.

"Hello, Frank?" he said cautiously into the receiver.

"Nicky, thank God! I've got to see you."

"Sure thing. Look, I'm really sorry about all this with Susan."

"Susan?" he cried as if he had never heard of her. "Will you just get here, Nicky, please?"

"Well, sure, Frank. I can be in Bel Air in about twenty minutes."

"No, not Bel Air," Frank protested. His nerves seemed shot, and he was shouting into the phone. "Let's meet at The Bistro. I'll make a reservation for half an hour."

"Won't it be difficult talking there?"

"No, Nicky—it's a public place. Safety in numbers, you know. They wouldn't dare gun me down in The Bistro!"

"Frank, what the hell are you talking about?"

But Frank had hung up. Susan came out from Tanya's bedroom as soon as she heard Nicky put down the phone.

"Well?" she asked.

"Well, he sounds a little insane, actually," Nicky told her. "He wants to see me tonight."

"I thought he might take it hard," Susan said sadly, shaking her beautiful head. "He didn't sound violent, did he?"

"It'll be all right, Susan. You go on to bed, and I'll try not to wake you when I come in."

She moved closer, put her arms around his neck, and rubbed her thigh against his.

"Oh, Nicky, you're so good to do this for me." She spoke in the little-girl's voice she only used when they were alone. "Wake me when you come in, and I'll make sure you fall asleep feeling very, very relaxed."

8

The Bistro had remained consistently the most fashionable restaurant in Beverly Hills for a great number of years now, while places like Spago's, currently in vogue, came and went with the passing of the tides. The Bistro's lasting popularity was a mystery. The place was ponderous and dark, the food mediocre, and the prices astronomical. Essentially this was what Beverly Hills was all about—a town where people paid for labels rather than quality. Rich people, alas, were always getting ripped off. You could get upset about this, probably, if you tried hard enough.

Nicky Rachmaninoff, fortunately, was free of labels himself. It didn't bother him the way the parking attendants at The Bistro gave his ancient Austin-Healey a look of infinite scorn. They didn't realize he had spiritual riches inside and that there was fifteen million dollars' worth of woman waiting for him in his bed.

"Take real good care of this machine, boys," he told them, "and there might be fifty cents in it for you."

They didn't even smile. It was grim going through life without a sense of humor.

Nicky entered the dark, crowded restaurant, where he was instantly recognized by the busy maître d'—a man who looked like an aging Italian movie star and whose real job was to know who's who. A policeman, even a suspended policeman, had some advantages after all. Or perhaps the maître d' simply recognized raw power, innate courage, and sensitivity—seating these people first? Nicky rather hoped so.

Nicky followed the maître d' through the downstairs room. At each table, faces looked up for a fraction of a moment to see who was arriving. *Is he important? Can he help my career?* they seemed to ask. And seeing the answer was no, they instantly dismissed Nicky from their minds.

He was led at first to one of the best tables near the front of the room, since Frank had made the reservation. However, since Frank had not arrived yet, Nicky was able to arrange a transfer—to a booth in a quiet little corner near the rear, where generally people without any notable fame or fortune were hidden away.

Would he care for a drink while he waited for Mr. Fee? Coffee,

185

Nicky replied. He figured this could be a long night. After two refills, Mr. Fee had still not arrived. Nicky began to tap his index finger impatiently against the table. For a while he killed time by turning his tap into a measure, then dividing it by two, by four, by eight, sixteen, thirty-two—and finally the unattainable sixty-fourth note. He was just beginning to visualize it when he saw Frank coming into the room.

Frank was very drunk and made a grand movie star entrance a little too grandly. He seemed to know everyone at the restaurant, passing from table to table shaking hands, giving people hugs, waves, and kisses. Frank got a little carried away by the latter, nearly tumbling into a lady writer's fettuccine while trying to kiss her hand. Nicky was relieved when he made it across the room and slid into the leather booth next to him.

"Damn, it's good to see you!" he bellowed. His eyes were red from heavy drinking. He looked away from Nicky's measuring gaze, closing his eyes for a second and leaning his head against the booth. "I know I'm a mess. Fucking hell, you got your gun with you, Nicky?"

"I'm armed," Nicky replied. "I hope you're not."

Frank was breathing hard, like a runner who had just finished a marathon. "God, let's get a drink," he said, trying to catch a waiter's eye.

"Frank, what the hell's happening?"

Frank could only look at him stupidly from the big drunken vat of all his problems. "How's Susan taking this?" he asked sadly, putting a big paw on Nicky's shoulder. "I haven't been home for two days, you know. My poor little girl's been waiting for me all alone in that big lonely house. . . . God, I'm a piece of slime!" Frank put his head into his hands and groaned.

Nicky thought he wouldn't tell Frank just yet that his poor little girl hadn't exactly been waiting the last two nights in the empty Bel Air mansion.

A waiter had appeared, hovering above them with a polite expression of expectancy.

"Just in time," Frank told the man. "A double Black Label, rocks on the side. What'll you have, Nicky? You hungry? You thirsty? What?"

"Mr. Fee will have coffee, a bowl of soup, and a big basket of bread. I'll take a refill of coffee, too, when you have a chance," Nicky told the waiter.

"Make it a *large* single," Frank told the waiter with a wink. "Didn't you take care of me last week? We're friends, aren't we?"

"Give him coffee," Nicky insisted more firmly than before.

The waiter looked from one man to the other and seemed about to implode. He was not programmed to say no to people, especially movie stars. Nicky had a sense he was about to lose this tug-of-war, so he pulled out his shield. "I'm a cop," he said, which wasn't precisely true at the moment. "You serve this man an alcoholic beverage and I'll have this restaurant shut down. You'll lose your job. Your children will probably starve."

The waiter smiled insanely and hurried off.

"God, I wish you hadn't done that, Nicky." Frank sighed. "Life sure used to be more fun, back in the old days."

"Frank, tell me—do your problems have something to do with Bushy di Sutro?" Nicky was reduced to playing twenty questions.

"Bushy di Sutro, yeah," Frank repeated mechanically. "Yeah, Bushy, that's right," he said again. "If he's alive, he'll probably kill me when he hears I've come to you. *That's* what disturbs me," Frank replied. "You know, I sure could use a drink."

"Frank, I'm fascinated—why wouldn't Bushy be alive?"

Frank shrugged, then whispered in Nicky's ear, "Maybe he'll convince the don he's been loyal, at least. That way they'll just exile him to Bolivia or someplace."

"The don decides, does he? Are we speaking of the head of the di Sutro family?"

"Shh! Keep your voice down," Frank said nervously, looking about wildly. "Yeah, Bushy's been recalled," he whispered. "To New Jersey."

"That sounds serious. But why, Frank? Why?"

Unfortunately, the maître d' appeared at just that moment, a concerned expression on his distinguished face. "Everything all right, Lieutenant Rachmaninoff?"

"Wonderful," Nicky told him. "Mr. Fee and I are having a splendid nonalcoholic evening."

"I'm going to die without a drink!" Frank pleaded. "You'll bring me a Black Label—won't you?"

"Ah, it takes a good friend to say no, Mr. Fee," the maître d' said diplomatically. "Now, Lieutenant, can't I get you something to eat? We have a splendid veal tonight, sautéed with a sherry cream sauce, topped with fresh asparagus and lobster. We called it Veal Academy Award." He beamed.

"What I'd like is a tuna-fish sandwich, side of fries."

The maître d' started to object, then quickly took out a small notepad instead. "Whatever you wish, Lieutenant. Would you like that on wheat, white, or rye?"

"Rye, I think. Lightly toasted—a little mayo, hold the lettuce."

The man hurried off to the kitchen to fullfil Nicky's special whim. Hollywood could really be a fun place when you had a little pull.

9

" 'S mistake," Frank said, standing up suddenly, lurching dangerously toward his soup. "Lesh get the hell out of here."

Nicky managed to get hold of Frank's belt, by which he pulled him back into the booth. "But we haven't dined yet," he complained. "Be reasonable, Frank—if you eat your soup and tell me what I want to know, well—maybe I won't tell Susan about the blonde at Bo's party the other night. Maybe I won't hand you over to the FBI. How's that for a bargain?"

"Nicky! Why're you being so mean to me?"

"It's tough, isn't it, but there it is."

Actually it was not uncommon for a witness to seek him out, then clam up at the last moment. Human beings were full of contradictory impulses. Nicky judiciously allowed Frank a bottle of beer with his bowl of soup, alternating kindness and threats, letting it be known that what the right hand gave, the left could take away. Beer had a positive effect on Frank. He looked dramatically to the right, then the left, then moved his mouth very close to Nicky's ear.

"The person you're looking for is Sandy Giannini," Frank whispered wetly. Nicky had to move back.

"Who?" The name was vaguely familiar.

"Everyone knows her as Nancy."

"Oh, yes. Nancy Normal. Are you telling me the maid did it, Frank?"

"She's Bushy's niece," he said, smiling stangely, as if this told the whole story. He pronounced *niece* more like *neesh*.

"A large family," Nicky said with some admiration. "But why would Bushy's niece end up working as a maid for Jay Jeffries?"

"It's a long story, Nicky."

Frank made it longer by naming each of Bushy's seven brothers and sisters. Bushy's third-to-youngest sister, Claudia, married a cheap hood by the name of Gino Giannini, who distinguished himself by attempting to embezzle Family funds.

Sandy Giannini, who would one day become Nancy Normal, was the oldest daughter. Sandy continued to disgrace the Giannini name by becoming something of a hippie, majoring in modern dance at Bard, and eventually being expelled for all kinds of inappropriate behavior, including the seduction of a faculty wife.

She nearly retrieved her lost reputation by getting involved in a gas station hold-up, but then shortly afterward she decided she wanted to be an actress and, like so many hopefuls before her, went west in search of glory. When the old don heard this, he asked never to hear of Sandy Giannini again. Girls from proper Mafia families did not go to Hollywood to become actresses.

"Please, Frank, this is fascinating—but can't we sort of fast-forward to the next reel?"

"Hey, I'm trying, Nicky. As soon as Nancy got to Hollywood, she looked up Uncle Bushy, hoping he would pull some strings for her, help her get a foot in the door."

"And what did Uncle Bushy do for her?"

"He didn't make any promises. Said he'd watch her a while. He invited her to a few parties to see how she'd behave—even lent her some money once—but he didn't go out of his way or nothing, you understand."

"Sure, I understand. And one of these parties was on a yacht—a three-day bash going back and forth to Catalina?" Nicky inquired. "And that's where Nancy met J. J. and Marilyn and the other nice people at The Rock Channel?"

"You know about that? *That* was a party, Nicky. I kid you not."

"Did Bushy arrange for Nancy to get her job with J. J.?"

"As a *maid?* You kidding? The Giannini side of the family might be in disgrace, but Bushy would never rub her face in the dirt. No, Nancy got the job herself—guess she needed the money. Her acting career definitely was going nowhere. Bushy thought it was pretty flaky, actually—someone who almost had a college degree being a maid. Said the American dream must really be going sour."

"Yes, yes—tell me, did Bushy change his mind at all and become more friendly toward Nancy, say, the last three months or so?"

"Yeah, I guess so. I remember a while ago he said maybe cleaning house was teaching Nancy old-fashioned virtues—making her more domestic, you know."

"I'm going to puke, Frank."

"Well, these guys are conservative, Nicky. As far as they're concerned, there are two kinds of women, and the *good* kind are at home taking care of the house and children. Anyway, about three weeks ago, Bushy gave me a call and asked if I could get Nancy a part on my show. Nothing major, you know—just a little part, but something regular, every week. Hell, I said I'd try. But you know us stars —we don't have the kind of pull we used to. Now everything's controlled by the conglomerates. . . ."

Nicky was frowning intensely, nodding his head. "So something happened to drastically improve Nancy's approval rating with Bushy di Sutro?"

"It wasn't something that happened, Nicky," Frank told him, looking very embarrassed. "It was something that was *going* to happen."

"Nancy agreed to kill Jay Jeffries, is that it?"

Frank covered his face with his hands. "God, I hate this!" he moaned.

"J. J. didn't like it much, either," Nicky reminded him. "Gee, and just the other day, Frank, you were telling me how innocent your buddies in the Mafia were. Just your average all-American business. Sort of a Lions Club, you said."

"Nicky, I *thought* so! I swear to God until yesterday I believed hits and contracts and all that sort of thing were part of the distant past. I didn't know, Nicky!" he cried. "I didn't *know!*"

"There, there," Nicky told his friend. "Now what happened yesterday, Frank, to open your eyes?"

"I've been an asshole, Nicky. Tell me I'm an asshole, for chrissake!"

"You're an asshole, Frank."

"I'm just an old drunk. I'm scum. I can't even begin to tell you this sordid tale without a drink—a double, please, if there's a God in heaven."

Nicky snapped his fingers, and a waiter instantly appeared. "A drink for Mr. Fee," he said grandly. "And for me—I'll have a dish of chocolate ice cream."

10

What happened yesterday to open Frank's eyes began with an urgent telephone call to his dressing room at 20th Century-Fox. Uncle Bushy had to leave town quick. He was in big trouble. It was essential that Frank meet him right away.

Fortunately, Frank was off for the rest of the afternoon—was about to have a soothing rub, in fact, from Ula, his blond Swedish masseuse, but he would forgo this pleasure to help a family member in distress.

Frank met Bushy at the parking lot of Saks Fifth Avenue in Beverly Hills. The feeling was that two more Rolls-Royces in the parking lot there would not attract any particular notice. Frank left his burgundy convertible and got into the back of Bushy's white limo, where they were hidden discreetly by tinted windows. That was where they had their talk.

Bushy wondered if his dearest friend and good buddy would take care of a few loose ends for him while he was out of town. He gave Frank a briefcase with several million dollars cash in it, as well as a key to a bank deposit vault in which (should worse come to worst), Frank would find his last will and testament. Bushy was leaving most of his fortune to Nancy Reagan's Just Say No program, and he rather hoped Frank might present the gift to the First Lady personally. Perhaps there could be a Bushy di Sutro scholarship for disadvantaged boys and girls who managed to turn their backs on drugs? Or maybe a Bushy di Sutro Rehabilitation Center in his hometown in New Jersey?

"Frank! I don't care about Bushy's philanthropy," Nicky cried in quiet distress. "Can't you just stick to the facts?"

"But, Nicky, the facts aren't enough. They won't tell you the real man, the flesh and blood—the fact that, yes, Bushy is one dangerous son of a bitch who'd kill both of us without a thought if he felt it was to his advantage. But there *is* some good in him, I swear to God—even though, yes, he *did* hire Nancy to kill J. J., mutilate him, and grind his genitals down the garbage disposal."

Nicky sighed. "Please, Frank—why did Bushy want J. J. out of the way? And why did it have to be done so gruesomely? And why, for chrissake, did Nancy ever agree to such a thing?"

191

"As I understand it, Bushy got a tip that J. J. was collecting evidence linking The Rock Channel to organized crime. He was getting ready to go to the FBI."

"Wait a second," Nicky objected. "We've already covered this. Bushy knew all about that and didn't take it seriously."

"That's what he wanted us to believe. However, he was scared to death. The FBI's been trying to nail Bushy for years—the few bits and pieces J. J. could supply would have been enough to send him away for the rest of his life."

Nicky played with his chocolate ice cream. A film producer had stopped by the table for a moment, and Frank instantly put on his most congenial manner. The producer had a script he wanted Frank to read, and Frank pretended this was the best news he'd heard in years.

"This seems a little hazy," Nicky said when the producer went away. "Who exactly gave him this tip that J. J. was about to turn traitor? I can't see it, honestly, myself."

"Don't know, Nicky. Bushy didn't discuss it. He only said the rumors had become impossible to ignore."

"Was this an anonymous tip?" Nicky asked suspiciously. "Maybe signed something strange—like the Ghost of Rock and Roll?"

Frank shook his head. "Bushy didn't tell me, and I swear, I didn't ask. If you want to know the truth, I didn't want to hear *any* of this. But the Bush—well, he was leaving me with his affairs, and I suppose he was making an attempt to unburden himself."

"Frank, are you crazy? What he was doing was trying to implicate you in his crimes—get you too involved to back out."

"I never thought of that," Frank admitted sheepishly. "I was just trying to be helpful."

"Great. To get back to Uncle Bushy—he told you he went to Nancy for help?"

"Yeah, with Nancy's job in the house, he felt the, uh, contract could be easily arranged. He told her if she did this one thing for him, she'd be back in the good graces of the family forever. Besides that, Bushy would make her a star."

"Gee, where have I heard that line before?"

"Nicky, she agreed to do it. Actually, Bushy was a little surprised how *eagerly* she agreed. Nancy was always looking for kicks, you know. Sort of a kinky lady, if you ask me."

"Definitely not normal," Nicky agreed. "So the mutilation was Nancy's idea—a little extra kick?"

"No, Bushy suggested that. It was supposed to send you in the wrong direction, make you think those kids from Pubic Telephone did it. Or maybe even a random sex crime."

"Wonderful."

"Nancy *did* improvise a bit—made Bushy damned nervous, in fact. She screwed J. J. before she killed him. I guess she thought it'd be sort of a turn-on."

"Lovelier and lovelier." Nicky scowled. "She, uh, had this sexual encounter on the stairs, I presume—knowing there was a secret video camera in J. J.'s closet?"

"Jesus, I guess so. Bushy didn't tell me that part. What a town, huh? Anyway, Nancy didn't do a very clean job, apparently. Maybe she was having too much fun to be careful. In fact, she didn't even check all the rooms in J J's house to make sure no one else was there."

"Ah, J. J. was not alone," Nicky said, nodding. "Ginny Gina was hiding in the bathroom all the while the murder was taking place?"

"Right. Incredible, isn't it? This is where Nancy really went off the deep end. The next day, she heared about Ginny being in the house, and she—"

"Hold on a moment—how did she hear about that?"

"Jeez, I don't know, Nicky. I'm just telling you what Bushy told me. Without his authority, she decided to go over to Topanga Canyon and get rid of the witness—killing a cop in the process, making the whole thing look like a Mafia hit—exactly what Bushy *didn't* want. He was furious. He told me the Mafia's image had been set back two decades by, quote, that dumb cunt's behavior."

"Hmm, so I presume the Giannini side of the family's still in the doghouse, huh?"

"Yeah, and Bushy along with them, by association. The old don back east sent for him to explain himself. When Bushy got on the airplane last night, he was a frightened man. Me too, Nicky. I'm the man who can't say no."

"Yeah, Frank."

"You believe me, don't you?"

"I believe you, Frank."

"All right! This calls for a drink!"

It called for a couple of drinks, as a matter of fact. A film director and his actress wife were passing by, and Frank shouted for them to join him in a round. Nicky sat quietly, not listening to Frank and the director going over the week's box office receipts, trying to decide what the elusive public was looking for these days.

Nicky felt overwhelmed by depression. Part of the lousiness was the fact that Inspector Jones of the FBI was apparently right about the whole affair: just a small Mafia comedy of errors—deadly errors, where people like Theo Oshimoto got killed because they were in the wrong place at the wrong time. Whatever happened to Billy Lion in 1970 probably had nothing to do with this at all.

Or did it? Wasn't there something more—a whisper, a ghost, a malicious intelligence behind all the events, causing bad things to happen?

Nicky sighed. Another depressing thought: He knew he was going to have to go with Frank's story to the FBI. If he could, he would find a way to leave Frank out of it. But something had to be said, because Bushy needed to be punished, and Nancy Normal—née Sandy Giannini—had to be punished, too.

Thinking of Nancy gave Nicky an uncomfortable feeling. Where was she now? he wondered. Standing shamefaced next to Bushy di Sutro before some wizened old don, listening to a moving lecture on the new Mafia?

Nicky began to tap absentmindedly on the table. There was a flurry of sixty-fourth notes racing time against his heart. With dawning panic, Nicky decided that for Nancy Normal time was running out fast.

11

After pouring Frank into a taxi outside The Bistro, Nicky Rachmaninoff clamped his emergency light to the roof of his Austin-Healey and raced down Wilshire Boulevard toward Nancy's condominium in Westwood. He wondered what they did to suspended cops who went around acting as if they were still on the force. But the thought that he was too late angered him and made him drive all the faster.

He left his car with his official police business card in the window, jogged into the garish lobby, and flashed his shield at the white-gloved doorman.

"Police emergency," he said briskly, running beneath the massively gaudy chandelier to the elevator.

He pressed the button for the sixteenth floor, impatiently watching the lights flick past. The elevator let him out into a windowless, thickly carpeted hallway. Nicky ran quickly to the door of 16-D, the apartment Nancy shared with Marilyn.

He tried the doorbell. There was no answer, so he tried again. *So what do you do now, hot shot?* He rapped sharply on the door with his knuckles. He caused himself some pain, but there was still no response.

Nicky stared at the closed door, wondering what he'd find inside. Of course—here was a wild thought—he could be plain wrong. Nancy and Marilyn could simply be out enjoying dinner or a movie, maybe a nice stimulating lecture at U.C.L.A.

If he could get the door open, he would know for sure. He took out a credit card from his wallet and tried to slip it into the crack. Charlie was very good at opening doors with credit cards and bobby pins. Nicky was not. After five minutes, he managed to break his brand-new MasterCard in two.

He sighed. This really was getting him nowhere. He rang the doorbell a few more times, just so he could feel totally useless. If he were still officially employed, he might try to get a court order to get the door opened, but that was no longer an option for Lieutenant Rachmaninoff. Still, he was not going to be defeated by a damn door.

He pulled out his .38 Smith & Wesson, aimed at the lock, briefly visualized the ranch that was waiting in Utah, and pulled the trigger.

The explosion in the narrow hallway was intense. When the smoke cleared, he saw he had shot the core of the lock completely away. This was certainly more effective than carrying a spare key. He reached into the hole, sprang the lock, and walked inside the apartment, gun in hand.

"Hello!" he called, just in case they hadn't heard him yet. He moved cautiously into the living room, past a glass table and pink couch, past a rubber plant and stainless-steel chairs. He caught a reflection of himself in a mirror: *Man with gun entering apartment with trepidation.*

He smelled it before he knew where it was coming from—the peculiar musky-sweet heavy smell of violent death, getting stronger as he approached the master bedroom.

He pushed open the final door.

Nancy and Marilyn were both naked. It looked as if they had been in bed reading. Nancy was lying on the floor near the foot of the bed, one foot caught in the sheets. Marilyn had tried to save herself by hiding under the blankets, but blankets don't make a very effective shield against bullets.

It was another violent, terrible scene, capturing the innocent as well as the guilty in its web. From the look of it, they had been dead at least twenty-four hours. Had Bushy killed them himself? he wondered. Or was it hired help? It made Nicky very unhappy.

He walked back to the living room and picked up the telephone, using his jacket to keep from disturbing any possible prints. Sirens were already approaching the building along Wilshire Boulevard. Someone had clearly not liked the sound of gunfire in the hallway on the sixteenth floor. Before having to deal with the Westwood police, there was someone he very much wanted to shout at.

He dialed the FBI building downtown and asked to be put through to Inspector Dwight Jones. He was told the inspector was not available, but he could leave a message. From the electronic beeps on the other end, he knew he was being recorded. He liked that.

"You can tell Inspector Jones that the lady who killed Jay Jeffries and Theo Oshimoto and Ginny Gina and Tommy Torch is massively fucking dead herself, on the floor of apartment sixteen-D at the Wilshire Star, along with her girlfriend, who had nothing to do with it at all."

"Who's this calling, please?"

"And you can tell that asshole that if he was any kind of detective at all, instead of some egomaniac fashion model, he could have stopped jerking off long enough to keep some of this shit from happening."

Nicky found his hand was shaking. There were lots of spiteful things he had in mind to say to Inspector Jones of the FBI, but when it got right down to it, the inspector hadn't really been any more stupid than he had been himself. The whole case was just a bloody waste.

"Who is this?" the FBI operator asked again, more sharply this time.

"This is Lieutenant Nicholas Rachmaninoff," he said wearily. "Tell that fuckerhead he'd better get down here to Westwood before the local fuzz start making tracks with his precious case."

Nicky put down the receiver in time to greet four uniformed cops, who were flooding in the front door with drawn pistols.

"Easy, guys," he told them. "Believe it or not, I'm one of you. Sort of."

12

It was dawn by the time the Westwood police and Inspector Jones were finished with him. Nicky told his story twenty times. Eventually, he was allowed to get into his Austin-Healey and drive home.

It was a murky dark Saturday morning, and the rain started as he reached Sunshine Terrace. The days were long gone when he could miss a night's sleep and not notice it. This morning he felt like a steam roller had passed over him. He could tell from the way Susan was looking at him that he wasn't exactly her idea of a knight in shining armor. He told her what had happened.

"So it's over," she said finally, leading him into the living room as if he were helpless to find any more directions for himself. "What are you going to do now? Are you going to quit?"

"Yeah," he said, trying the words on for size. "I guess I'll quit. The department sure as hell doesn't want me anymore."

Susan sat down next to him and put a hand on his knee. "That's good, Nicky. I know you can't see it now. I know it's going to be a difficult transition to civilian life, but you're going to be glad in the end. You know that, don't you?"

"Yeah. Who wants to go through other people's garbage and get shot at and have to deal with stupid bureaucrats and French poodles?"

"That's right, Nicky," she told him encouragingly. "I'm going to take care of you."

"Yeah," he said again, dreamily.

So it was all over. The killers had been punished, even—Nancy Normal was dead, and Bushy di Sutro had disappeared from Hollywood, probably for good. His fate—and perhaps The Rock Channel's—lay in the hands of the FBI. Somewhere out there was a professional gunman who had executed Marilyn and Nancy, but you could never get all those guys. He thought again about Theo Oshimoto and his foolish enthusiasm and wished that justice could somehow be more final. He also thought about the bright and manipulative person who had caused all these violent events to occur —starting a rumor here, a rumor there. Sending an occasional poisonous letter signed the Ghost of Rock and Roll.

"You want a cup of coffee, Nicky?"

"Sure," he said.

"No, I'm going to give you some tea instead, and pack you off to bed. What you need is sleep."

"Sure," he said, always agreeable.

Since last night, he had had a funny feeling that all the parts of the puzzle were there, spread out before him. If only he could see it correctly.

At least he had remembered who he had told about Ginny being in the bathroom when J. J. was being killed. It was Unity, who had come to his house shortly after he had learned about Ginny's fingerprints in the shower. Of course, Unity had seen Nancy the following morning in her hot tub, and the information could have been easily dropped. Still, he would have to ask her whom she had been talking to.

"Can I make you some breakfast, Nicky?"

"No, I'm not hungry."

Susan put her arms around him. "Sweetie," she said, "it's all going to be different now, you'll see. Just you and me and Tanya. It's time we were all together, you know. Tanya won't be a child forever."

"That's it!" he said, standing up.

"Yes, it *is* it," Susan told him earnestly. "Why, Nicky, already you look better."

"God, Susan, I don't know how I could have been so stupid not to see it earlier."

"Well, it was my fault, too, Nicky," she said. "I never should have left you in the first place."

Susan didn't know they were talking a different language. Nicky had just figured out the series of murders that began with Jay Jeffries.

"Child" was the key word, unlocking the door. Nicky did some fast arithmetic, and the mystery was solved. He knew who, and he knew why.

When Susan left to brave the frogs in the shower, Nicky picked up the phone and made an airline reservation for Hawaii.

The Ghost of Rock 'n' Roll (3)

Oh, Billy.

Remember, you said that rock was the revolution that would roll down the establishment? We'd go to the barricades with electric guitars. Assault the status quo with sound.

What kind of world is this, anyway? So much injustice. The strong prey on the weak. The rich get richer. Who will say no to all this if not the young?

Oh, Billy. You thought you'd gather up the young, and the flood of revolution would cleanse the world. Flowers would grow in the cracks of the pavement. Lives would be spent freely, exploring love.

It looked that way in 1969.

It sure was a good idea.

But, Billy, if you could see the young people today, you would weep. You would pull your hair and howl.

Cowboy had not been this worked up for a long time. Billy was back, and everything was going to be okay.

He had spoken with the synthesized voice on the telephone twice more on Thursday, working out the final details.

"Jesus, why didn't you give me more time?" Cowboy complained. "This is crazy—only five days to carry out a project of this size. Why didn't you call me a month ago?"

"Because I just thought of it," the voice replied.

"Come on, man. You're joking!"

"No, I mean it. Just a sudden inspiration. Like why not clean the slate—wipe the blackboard—start again. I just thought of it last week."

Cowboy howled with laughter. This was good. This was the way things used to be, the kind of spur-of-the-moment madness Billy always generated.

199

"It *is* you, isn't it?" Cowboy asked, finally daring to hope—really hope—that what had been lost so long had finally come again.

"Ahem, yes, it is. I believe it's really me," the voice said, with just the right intonation—and the funny way Billy had of putting *ahem* in front of grand pronouncements.

Cowboy wanted to meet in person, but Billy said no. There would be time for that later. Right now, there was too much to do.

A key had arrived in the mail at Cowboy's hotel early Friday morning, along with an envelope containing five thousand dollars cash. There were going to be some expenses. The key belonged to a self-storage locker on Vermont Avenue, where Billy had left what would become the outer casings of the five devices that were to be made.

The camouflage was clever. Two of the bombs would be inside portable TV cameras. Two more would look like battery power packs. And the last, which was to be the most powerful, simply a metal equipment case. The video camera, power packs, and case were all stamped with the official logo of The Rock Channel. Where Billy had managed to obtain this equipment, Cowboy did not ask. His job was only to fill the insides with explosives, then return them to the storage locker by midnight Monday.

Saturday, he had a bit of a crisis, realizing he did not currently possess enough matériel for a project of this size. He rented a van and drove down to San Diego, where there was a marine sergeant he had dealt with before. The man was not a revolutionary—he was a crook, the main part of his operation being the smuggling of heroin into the country on government planes. But the marine sergeant could sell you anything short of a cruise missile, and the plastic explosives Cowboy required were no problem at all.

While in San Diego, Cowboy stopped at Sears and bought a color TV with remote control. He also visited an electronics store for the rest of his needs, which were not many. For one who had the skills, the tools were not hard to find.

Saturday evening, Cowboy drove back from San Diego on Interstate 5, feeling good about his progress. He would spend tomorrow making the devices themselves and have them back in the storage locker Monday morning, hours before his deadline.

On the freeway, a light rain began to fall. Headlights reflected against the slick pavement. Cowboy turned on the van's AM radio, listened to the music, and talked with Billy Lion—a conversation that had been going on inside his head for twenty years now.

∞∞∞∞∞∞∞∞∞∞∞∞∞

Oh, Billy. Damn, it's good to have you back.

Take this guy on the radio right now. It's funny, I was into him for a while. Thought he might be the real thing. Then he went and turned one of his love songs into a beer commercial.

Can you believe it?

I mean, what sort of person can take a love song and turn it into a beer commercial? No one seems to even notice these things anymore, Billy. Love songs and beer commercials are interchangeable. You can screw your wife or buy a Toyota.

And the scary thing, Billy—not a whisper of protest from the young. It's like the world's been sold out from under us, and no one minds.

And the people we used to know, Billy, they're all fat cats now. They're logs jamming up the river. They're shit clogging up the plumbing. But you and I, Billy, we're going to clean the pipes.

This is the revolution, baby, returned from the grave.

When the Shrine Auditorium blows Tuesday night, the whole damn music establishment will have to start again from scratch.

Part Four

Almost
Paradise

1

Nicky slept fitfully at thirty-seven thousand feet above the Pacific Ocean. He was having a nice dream about Susan: They were teenagers again, discovering sex in the back seat of his old Chevy, high on a darkened street they used to visit in the Hollywood Hills. The radio played softly, sweet songs of youth.

Then the dream changed. The girl in his arms was no longer Susan, but Unity Sphere. This gave him an anxious feeling.

"It's okay, Nicholas" she told him, sensing his unease. "We're seventeen and we're in love. What could be better?"

He was still troubled.

"What about Susan?" he asked.

Unity only smiled. "Ah, Susan got old without you. Too bad for her."

Nicky woke to find himself a middle-aged man, somewhere in transit between Los Angeles and Hilo. He flagged down a stewardess and ordered a can of beer. It was Saturday night. He had wanted to catch an earlier flight, but a few things held him up—such as waiting for the results of Charlie's phone call to Interpol and dealing with Susan. The latter had not been easy. In order to leave Tanya, officially in his care, he had to convince Susan that rushing off to Hawaii was actually a life-or-death situation.

She was skeptical. "You've got to stop running around like this," she told him.

"Absolutely," he promised. "Except for this one last time."

"You'll always say that. . . . Anyway, I don't want to go back to Bel Air. What if Frank's there?"

"Stay here," he offered. "My house is yours, however humble."

"I might have to get rid of the frogs in the shower," she warned. "I may even give your sofa to the Salvation Army and buy you something new."

"It's a deal," he told her. "But you can't kill the frogs. Tanya will

205

help you put them in a jar or something. You can let them out by that nice pond across from the Beverly Hills Hotel. They'll like it there."

"All right, Nicky. Of course, everything else is understood, isn't it?"

"What everything?"

"You and me. We'll get married as soon as my divorce is final."

"Right."

"And you'll resign from the police department . . . Nicky?"

"It's a deal."

"You'll rent out this cabin—it will give you a nice income of your own—and we'll go live in the country, someplace where you can do what you should be doing—playing the piano."

"Sold," he said. "Anything else?"

"No, but we'll put this all in writing, so you can't wiggle out of it when you get back from Hawaii."

"Aw, Susan . . ."

"I mean it, Nicky. If you want me to take care of Tanya these few days—and I'm *not* going to let you take her with you—you have to put this all in writing."

Nicky had to comply. What else could he do? He would solve this case, but it would be the last one. His life had been dealt and sold. *And not a bad life,* he kept reminding himself.

At least now he was on the scent, closing in for the kill. This was fly now, pay later. But he might be dead by then, so why worry?

At least he would get the Ghost of Rock and Roll.

2

Not long after dawn, the island of Hawaii came into view: emerald hills sloping up from the ocean toward a distant volcano. The ocean was turquoise, transparent, milky green near the shore. From the air Nicky could see the coral formations underwater. There was something new and unformed about this landscape. Nicky looked out his window for the smoke and flame of creation, but the volcanoes were hidden beneath the massive rain clouds of the interior.

The jet flew parallel to the coast, down into the clouds, and came to rest on a runway lined with palm trees that actually looked like they belonged there.

Nicky stepped off the plane into a steamy tropical morning. The breeze was warm and caressing, scented with distant flowers. It was a heady atmosphere for a smoggy city boy.

"Aloha! Welcome to the Big Island, Lieutenant," came a friendly voice. Nicky turned and saw a large, brown-skinned policeman in full uniform, smiling like crazy, gun on hip, flowered lei in hand. This was one of Charlie's friends, Sgt. Kioni Pahinui, come out to meet him. The sergeant put the lei over Nicky's head and led the way to the baggage area. Most of the airport seemed open to the outside. Nicky enjoyed being decked with flowers, but he felt more secure when he had fetched his overnight case with the .38 revolver and extra rounds of ammunition inside. You could never be too careful, not even in paradise.

Sergeant Pahinui helped Nicky rent a car. He had an auntie who worked for one of the companies. Afterward, they stood in the parking lot going over a map of the island. The sergeant wrote down the names of two hotels, several restaurants, and a bank—all of which employed aunties and uncles and cousins who would be glad to help him in any way. Also, he gave Nicky the name of the police chief in Kona, as well as some information Charlie had asked for on the phone.

"You need anything, you give me a call, Lieutenant. Any time. When you get back, we'll go fishing, brah, okay? We'll take out a coupla six-packs and suck 'em down, eh?"

Kioni Pahinui had an open, childlike face and a belly that went on forever. He also had a high little laugh. *Tee-hee!* he said. Nicky felt he could like it here.

He drove north, through Hilo itself, and then up the lush Hamakua coast, passing in and out of squalls of rain. He had rented a late-model Toyota Tercel that hummed like a little sewing machine. Before reaching Waipio Valley, Nicky took the cut off toward the Parker Ranch, driving up the slopes of Mauna Kea into the high country of the interior. The landscape changed from tropical to pastoral and reminded him strangely of Northern California. This was cattle country up here, broad green plateaus with the lines of the earth always moving upward, toward the ever-higher ground of the volcano hidden in the clouds, whose sides would be covered with snow.

After two hours of driving, Nicky came to the small town of Kamuela, his first stop. He used Sergeant Pahinui's name to get an interview with the police chief there, then drove out of town to visit an old Japanese schoolteacher, now retired. The schoolteacher directed him next to a middle-aged hippie, who lived on what was clearly a marijuana plantation. The middle-aged hippie, the Japanese schoolteacher, and the Hawaiian police chief told him nothing completely new. They merely colored in the picture.

After Kamuela, the land changed abruptly from green pastures to arid desert, complete with cactus and burning sun. Hawaii was a place of extremes. Nicky stopped, removed a layer of clothing, then drove down off the slope of the volcano toward the leeward coast.

The Kona side of the island was different from what he would have imagined Hawaii to be. It was a moonscape of barren brown earth and black lava flow, with the ocean sparkling on the right-hand side of the road, an impossible shade of deepest blue.

Nicky consulted his map. He drove along the coast for another forty-five minutes before locating a small private road. The road led into a dusty valley, then to a small oasis of palm trees and tropical vegetation on the beach. In the center of the well-cared-for grounds sat a magnificent house of black lava stone, glass, and teak.

Nicky parked by a small waterfall, crossed a wooden bridge over a stream filled with carp, and rang a bell by a wooden gate. In a moment, a Japanese servant opened the gate and looked at him inquiringly.

"I'm here to see Mr. Bo Daniels," he said.

3

Nicky was led through a garden courtyard surrounded by a series of low buildings. The landscaping seemed more or less Japanese: tropical flowers and paths wandering among streams, wooden bridges, and stone Buddhas. He passed a swimming pool that was designed to look like a natural lagoon, a tennis court surrounded by coconut palms, and a bamboo pavilion on the beach.

The beach was spotlessly white and sloped down to meet a coral lagoon whose jewellike water was a dozen shades of blue, from creamy turquoise to ultramarine, depending on the depth.

The water was so clear Nicky could actually see large fish gliding beneath the glassy surface. Fifty feet out, someone with a snorkle was floating languidly upon the surface near a small island of protruding reef. The swimmer's feet suddenly arched up into the air, and the figure slithered gracefully down into the depths. Even from this distance, Nicky could recognize the nice curves of those legs.

"Well, well, it's Rimsky-Korsakov," came a voice.

Bo was swinging in a hammock in the shade of a palm tree, with a telephone by his side. He had a few days' growth of beard on his face, and he was wearing ragged old cut-off jeans. Somehow he succeeded in looking mostly like a rich city slicker trying to pass as a castaway. Bo spoiled the effect of his own paradise.

"Rachmaninoff," Nicky corrected.

"Pardon me?"

"The name's Rachmaninoff." Nicky had come to Hawaii to set things right, and he might as well start with the basics.

"Well, you don't have to get touchy," Bo replied. "A perfectly natural mistake if you ask me. Anyway, what can I do for you?"

Nicky looked offshore to see the girl coming up to the surface. The diving mask was turned his way, reflected the sun, then she disappeared again to join the other mermaids in their play.

"Ah, Mr. Daniels, I'm afraid I have some bad news for you. Marilyn de Malibu was killed last night along with her girlfriend, Nancy."

Bo nodded at his telephone. "Yeah, I heard," he said gloomily.

"Mr. Daniels, it's my belief that you're going to be soon on the list. Someone's killing off all of you left over from the Perceptions."

Bo sighed. "I wish people would leave me alone," he said.

Nicky gazed out to the lagoon but could see no sign of the swimmer.

"You're a killer, Bo," Nicky said out of the side of his mouth. "You killed Billy Lion eighteen years ago in Rome."

"*Killer*, did you say? You think Billy was murdered?" Bo laughed sourly. "Come on, Lieutenant! And I thought you were more the type to believe Billy was actually still alive someplace, writing poetry in Bora-Bora. Or reincarnated as the new Dalai Lama. Believe me, I've heard them all. But murder . . . come on, Stravinsky, gimme a break!"

"Rachmaninoff," Nicky insisted.

"You come into my perfect paradise, you disturb my peace with some cock-and-bull story, I'll call you any name I want."

"Mr. Daniels," Nicky continued patiently, "your old school friend died at a very opportune moment for you, didn't he?"

Bo was stunned. "What are you talking about, Rachmaninoff?"
Nicky felt he was finally making progress.

"I'm saying that by the summer of nineteen seventy the Perceptions were finished. Billy had quit the band, and he was determined to ruin you financially. You had Billy killed because he was dangerous, and with Billy out of the way there was no one to object to diverting profits from the band into your new dream. Your entire empire, Bo, is built upon Billy's murder, and now someone's coming after you to bring your house down."

Bo placed one bare foot on the ground as if to steady himself. "Oh, boy," he said. "I knew this was going to be one of those days. Tell me I'm dreaming."

"You're awake, Bo, and you're a lousy son of a bitch."

"But this is too absurd, Rachmaninoff. I don't deny I profited from Billy's death—I profit from everything. That's still quite different from having him killed. First off, it's impossible. I was in Los Angeles when he died, at the other side of the world. Tell me, how was I supposed to manage his death from six thousand miles away?"

"Ah, yes," Nicky said. "That brings us to the fatally lovely Maya Moon."

Both men glanced automatically to the lagoon, where the girl with the snorkle was moving in slowly, face down, toward the shore.

"What do you know about Maya Moon?" Bo asked uneasily.

"I know she was considered lovely. She was also Billy's last girlfriend. She went to Rome with him, and she was with him when he died. After that, you supported her the rest of her life, from nineteen seventy to when she died four years ago."

Nicky took out a notebook from his breast pocket and flipped open to a recent page.

"You sent a check for twenty-five hundred dollars every month to Maya's account at the Bank of Hawaii in Kamuela. That's a lot of generosity, Bo. I figure there's a pretty good reason for it."

Bo stood up from the hammock and began pacing. "This is unbelievable," he said to himself. And then, to Nicky, "So you're saying I *told* Maya to kill Billy—is that it? But for God's sake, why should she do that for me?"

"Because you made it worth her while financially. Besides that, you controlled her. I don't know exactly how. But I suspect you're very good at controlling people. You got Maya Moon in a place where she'd do anything for you at all."

Bo looked at him in astonishment, then began to laugh. "Oh, that's funny! You had me worried for a moment, Lieutenant—but this is really too much! The idea of *anyone* telling Maya what to do is just too ridiculous." He laughed to show how ridiculous it was. "I mean, the chick was absolutely nutsy-cuckoo. You could hardly *talk* with her, much less tell her what to do."

There was something authentic in Bo's laughter that disturbed Nicky. He decided to take a chance. "Then why did you make her disappear from the Grand Hotel?" He didn't know this for a fact, but from the slight flush that had appeared on Bo's face, he figured he had struck a nerve.

"That's a lie," Bo exclaimed. "Who told you that?"

Nicky pretended to consult a page in his notebook, which actually contained his L.A.–Hilo flight information.

"Now Mr. Daniels, I'm afraid you have quite a lot to explain here. Billy Lion died August tenth. You arrived in Rome August eleventh, then immediately telephoned Donny Meredith in Los Angeles telling him to keep Billy's death a secret."

"Yes, but—"

"Then you spent the next six days covering your tracks, rearranging evidence, getting the main witness—Maya Moon—out of the country, and even making certain Billy was buried quietly before an autopsy could be ordered. Only then, on the seventeenth, did you call a press conference announcing Billy's death." Nicky closed his notebook with a sigh. "This doesn't look very good for you, Mr. Daniels. Not good at all."

Bo was driven out of his hammock by sheer agitation. He was pacing now. "This is incredible," he said to himself. "Look, Lieutenant, you've got to picture the way this happpened. I got to Rome the day after Billy died, and Maya was so stoned on acid she was nearly catatonic. The hotel people had found her naked in the bathroom, talking gibberish, sitting on broken glass with Billy dead in the tub. I mean, it was like the end of the world in there. *That's* the reason I kept his death quiet for a week. I wanted to get him buried before the media could come in and make a big shocker of it. Publicity like that wouldn't have helped anyone, not Billy or anyone who loved him. It was like the end of the world in there," he repeated grimly, shaking his head.

Nicky listened.

"I know I'm supposed to be the bad guy," Bo said. "The people you talk with probably tell you that Billy was this great spiritual

211

person, this wonderful wounded genius who only cared about music —while me, I'm supposed to be some schmuck, only in it for the money. Well, okay, I accept that image. *Someone* had to keep it all together. Toward the end, you can't believe how crazy it got. I mean, Billy and Maya—they weren't on planet Earth anymore. Once in L.A., when they were living at the Tropicana, they cut each other's wrists with razor blades so they could drink each other's blood—this was supposed to make them true spiritual mates. They probably would have killed each other, but they were so drunk and stoned they passed out before they could do too much damage.

"And *that's* what it was like. That was the end of the glorious sixties. People make such a big fuss about it, but it was totally crazy, I tell you. If Billy finally died in a bathtub, it's a miracle he didn't die a hundred times before. I mean, who really knows what kind of games Billy and Maya were playing in that bathroom? I don't, that's for sure. I don't even think Maya really knew. Maybe she killed him —I had my suspicions, to tell you the truth. But she was on Venus or someplace—afterward, she didn't even remember being in Rome that whole time. She thought she was in Katmandu. For years, she'd look up in sort of a daze and ask where Billy was . . . and that's what it was like," he finished.

Bo ran out of words. He sat back down on the hammock, staring out to sea.

"Tell me," Nicky asked, "why did you take care of Maya for the rest of her life?"

Bo looked at him as though he were nuts. "For chrissake, Lieutenant, don't you know *that?* It wasn't for Maya's sake I gave the money. It was for *her.*"

As if on cue, Unity Sphere gathered herself out of the lagoon, taking off her fins and mask. She stepped out of the ocean like Venus emerging from her bath. There were probably fish weeping to see her go.

She was wearing a very small bikini, bottom only. Her breasts were bare, nipples firm in the tropical breeze. She didn't try to hide herself but posed a moment, tan and healthy, showing off her lissome grace. She held up a net bag with something wiggling inside.

"I have our dinner," she called.

Bo was beaming, just to see her standing there on his beach, so young and pretty and barely clothed.

Nicky had to admit she was a lovely girl, this daughter of Maya Moon and Billy Lion.

4

"Aloha, Nicholas! What a surprise," she told him. "Are you on vacation?"

Unity set down her fins, mask, snorkel, and black diving gloves. The net bag she carried was wiggling full of lobsters whose antennae were poking through the holes, furiously trying to understand their new environment. The girl handed the bag to Bo. She seemed extremely pleased with herself.

"Some of these lobsters are too damned small," Bo told her. "Jesus, you want to get me slapped with a five-hundred-dollar fine?"

Unity threw back her head with a laugh, showing her fine white teeth.

"But the young ones are the tastiest, Bo," she told him. "*You* should know that."

"You should put some clothes on," Bo grumped. "I've told you not to walk around like that."

She laughed again—made sure Nicky got one more good look at her, and then put on a vividly colorful silk blouse that was lying on a chair.

"Bo's so provincial," she confided to Nicky. "Come on, I've got to take tonight's din-din to the kitchen. I'll show you around the estate."

Bo didn't seem happy about her disappearing with Nicky, but she flashed him a look. Apparently, Unity got everything she wanted in this household. Bo leaned back in his hammock with a resigned sigh.

She led Nicky down a garden path lined with carnivorous-looking tropical flowers.

"You're looking sort of grim, Nicholas. Hawaii will be good for you," she said. "How long are you here for?"

"That depends on you."

"On me?" She flashed her violet eyes flirtatiously. "Well, well," she said.

She led the way up a verandah, into a large living room, and down a hallway, into an expansive, old-fashioned kitchen. She gave the bag of lobsters to two cooks, who made a great deal of fuss over both the girl and her catch. Unity Sphere seemed generally beloved in this kingdom by the sea.

213

From the kitchen, she gave him a tour of the main house, a leisurely tropical place with ceiling fans and walls opened to the elements—a bit of "old Hawaii," she told him, which still managed to have such things as a projection room and a thirty-two-track recording studio. Nicky paid more attention to the girl than to the surroundings.

"You're staring at me, Nicholas," she told him.

"Why didn't you tell me you were Billy Lion's daughter?" he asked.

She was about to open the front door to take them outside again. Nicky's words stopped her motion, left her paralyzed for one brief moment, and then she carried on as if she had not heard him.

"Come on, I want to show you the aviary," she suggested.

"You like caged birds? Perhaps you identify with them."

There was a sideways flash of violet. She took his arm and led him along a maze of paths, past the tennis court, through a grove of strangely shaped papaya trees, to a clearing where there was a metal cage fifty feet across and several stories high. This was no mere bird cage. Inside the enormous structure was a jungle habitat with several brightly colored parrots, a mynah bird, and a spider monkey frolicking in the branches. Unity opened a metal gate and took him inside the cage. They sat down together on a wooden bench by an artificial stream.

"Hi, Thelonius," she said to the mynah bird.

"Rock and roll!" Thelonius called back shrilly.

"And hello, Mick," she said to the monkey—which swung down through the upper branches and crawled into her lap. In her brightly colored blouse, Unity looked as if she belonged in this exotic cage, part of Bo's private zoo.

"Well?" he asked again.

"Well, what? Why didn't I tell you I'm Billy's bastard? It's not really something I advertise, Nicholas, for a lot of reasons. Anyway, it's no big deal. Do you know there were *twenty* paternity suits against my dear old dad during his lifetime? There's probably a platoon of us out there."

"Yes, but you were born almost exactly nine months after Billy died. If one were inclined to be mystical—or just plain fantasize—you might say you are a continuation of Billy. A reincarnation. The true heir."

Unity was making a show of playing carelessly with Mick the monkey.

"I stopped in Kamuela on my way over from Hilo," he told her.

214

"I saw where you grew up, talked to an old teacher of yours, and some people in the community. I'm beginning to get a pretty fair picture of you and your mother."

"I should be flattered, I suppose. All this attention," she said, making little smooching sounds at the monkey.

"I'm sorry about your childhood. It wasn't very nice."

"Oh, I survived."

"Did you? Your mother should have been institutionalized—you know that, don't you? She never came back all the way from the acid she took in the sixties. Of course, a small rural town in Hawaii didn't know that. The people in Kamuela didn't have a very enlightened attitude, did they? Your mom was just the town whore. The crazy hippie chick from the mainland who was too stoned to know what was going on. Some nights, there would be a party going on outside your house—all the guys drinking beer, waiting their turn. Crude local guys from the cane fields. Some of them could hardly speak English. Sometimes there would be fights, and they would slap her around, and the cops would have to come to break it up."

"I told you my mother was crazy, didn't I, Nicholas? It's not very pleasant talking about it like this."

"No, it's not pleasant," Nicky admitted. "Not now. Not then. Do you know how I see you, Unity? You were a very bright and sensitive child who had the misfortune to grow up in this terrible situation. You didn't have any friends, because your mother was trash—and you were white, which didn't help either. What do they call you over here?"

"Haoli," she said.

"Right. So added to your other problems, you had some racial prejudice against you as well. A bright, sensitive child, completely isolated—all you had were your fantasies and daydreams. That's where you lived your real life. Then, of course, you had your big secret."

She laughed. "My big secret! You make it sound so melodramatic, Nicholas."

"Oh, it is. Almost like a fairy tale. Everyone around you might treat you like trash, but you had something inside of you they didn't know—you were a princess. Your father was a very famous man. A king, of sorts. Which made you something special, however dispossessed. I believe you clung to this idea for dear life, until it became an obsession."

Her eyes expressed great wonderment. "This is really something," she said, "being analyzed like this. I feel like an amoeba on a slide. But honestly, why all these questions, Nicholas? What do you really want? Me?"

Nicky smiled gallantly, feeling the reassuring weight of his .38 beneath his arm. Actually, his being in Hawaii was a joke, against all known police procedure. He had no authority and no backup if he got into trouble—just the hope that if he kept stirring the pot long enough, some piece of evidence would emerge to justify his trip —and suspicions—and send someone away for a long, long time.

He consulted his notebook, looking up at the girl knowingly. "Now when you were seven, Bo Daniels came into your life," he went on. "Here we have a very interesting situation. Bo knew who you were, of course—the daughter of his oldest friend and greatest enemy. The way I see it, quite honestly—Bo and Billy together added up to a complete person. They needed each other terribly. It's no use, you see, being a creative genius without an ounce of practicality—just as it's terrible to be only practical without a spark of genius. Bo and Billy had a very symbiotic relationship, and not a very healthy one. So Billy dies—or is murdered, perhaps—and years go by, until, lo and behold, Billy Lion's daughter makes an appearance in Bo's life. Of course, you would become very, very important to him. I can understand now why he adopted you, gave you your own TV show—he even bought you that house in Laurel Canyon, didn't he? In a way, you represent Bo's chance to rewrite his own personal history."

Unity was shaking her head. "This really is amazing. Do they teach you this kind of stuff at the police academy, or are you just naturally imaginative?"

Nicky paid no attention to her. "You see, for Bo you were Billy brought back to life again—only he could dominate you this time, because you were a child. You were in his power. He could even have sex with you, since you were a girl. You're just part of a dialogue that goes way, way back—long before you were born. Unfortunately, Bo made a rather serious miscalculation."

"And what's that, Nicholas?" she inquired airily.

"It didn't occur to him that Billy Lion's daughter might take up her father's battle where it left off. He didn't realize how strongly you would identify with Billy's point of view—that you would take it upon yourself to destroy the man and tear down his corrupt little empire."

She laughed. "But, Nicholas, why would I wish to destroy my

216

great and noble benefactor? He's taken such good care of me most of my life. He gives me everything I want."

"That's part of the reason, isn't it? You hate him for that. He gives, and worse—you receive. You actually need this man. You don't have quite the strength to make it on your own—a little like your father, in fact. People often despise the vehicle of their own dependence. It's the way a three-pack-a-day smoker feels about cigarettes. That's how you feel about Bo Daniels. It's amazing how history repeats itself—that's how your father felt about Bo, too."

Unity was shaking her head, more vigorously now. Nicky was beginning to feel he was breaking through.

"Most of all, you hate Bo because he took your father's dream and your father's money and corrupted everything he stood for. You also hate him because all this is really yours—isn't it?—this estate, the entertainment conglomerate in Los Angeles, the works—all the fruits of your father's genius, *your* inheritance, but taken from you, stolen from you by Bo."

Unity had turned away from him so he couldn't see her face. "What a waste," he told her left shoulder sadly. "I used to think you were idealistic, but you're as greedy as the rest of them. Aren't you, my dear? You only want the plunder—just like Bo."

She jerked around. Her face was rigid and strange. "That's not true," she whispered. "Anyway, I can stay here—you *see* how they all treat me. If I want this life, it's mine any time I choose."

Nicky appeared skeptical. "Sure, you can stay here—as a guest. And Bo gives you little presents when you're good, doesn't he? But you had to sit on his lap and let him put his hands all over you, the dirty hands of the man you hated, your father's enemy, creeping up your dress."

Nicky was unprepared for the hand that slapped his face. It was a quick, vicious movement, so swift he hardly saw it coming. Then she immediately tucked both her hands into her armpits and smiled demurely.

"I'm sorry, Nicholas. I didn't mean to do that—but I really wish you'd stop talking like this."

Nicky's left cheek was stinging and partly numb, but he had no intention of stopping. "And now this man, your father's enemy— probably his murderer, in fact—is keeping you here like some exotic pet. Just like the parrots in this cage. You're like a trophy, Unity— a symbol that Bo got the better of Billy in the end."

"Nicholas! Stop it!"

He was getting through to her all right. She put her hands over her ears, as if this would help. It made her look younger than seventeen. Nicky took her wrists and forced her hands away.

"You're the Ghost of Rock and Roll, starting rumors, sending nasty letters. It's you, Unity. You've been looking for revenge a long time now, and you've found it—subtle, adolescent, but poisonous nevertheless. Without hardly lifting a finger, quite a few people have died. But it's over, Unity. It's going to stop right now."

"No, you're wrong," she cried. She was breathing hard, her nostrils flaring like some frightened thoroughbred horse. Nicky held on to her wrists, feeling that if he let go, she might scratch his eyes out.

"You *are* wrong, Nicholas," she said again. "Believe me."

He didn't know if he was wrong, she was not the Ghost of Rock and Roll, or wrong, he wasn't going to stop her.

This was how Bo found them, walking down the path to the aviary.

"Oh, there you are," he said. "What's going on here?"

Nicky felt the girl relax. A sly smile came to her lips. The violet eyes were laughing again. Unity had a tough facade and a quick recovery for such a pretty flower. Probably it had been essential to her survival.

Another five minutes, and he might have had her.

Unity stood up and walked out of the cage. Nicky followed quickly. He had a feeling both of them would just as soon shut him up with the birds and the monkey.

"I was just inviting the lieutenant to stay in one of the guest cottages while he's here," she said lightly, not even remotely like a mad killer.

"Now, darling, I'm sure Lieutenant Rachmaninoff has his own plans."

"Now Bo-Bo, honey—where's your aloha spirit? Just think of it as good karma to take care of a policeman wandering so far from home."

5

One of the servants showed Nicky to a guest cottage that had a bedroom, small kitchen, living room, and screened patio—or lanai, he supposed they called it over here.

Nicky wasn't sure about Hawaii so far. The weather was too hot, and everything looked like a Technicolor postcard. He felt homesick for the murky brown skies of L.A.—its air scented with exhaust fumes, its choked freeways, its snarling faces.

He lay down for a moment to rest on the giant bed in his room and awoke several hours later, drenched in sweat and not knowing where he was.

Someone was knocking on his door. "Dinner is served in half an hour," came a singsong voice.

"Yeah, yeah," he replied. He got into a cold shower to try to wake himself up, but the tropical air was enveloping and clung to him like a liquid dream. Night had fallen, and the outside paths were lit with propane torches stuck in the ground on long wooden poles. It managed to look a little hokey, like an entranceway to Trader Vic's. Nicky walked to the main house with the growing certainty that Unity and Bo would be dressed in white, as if they had just stepped out of some Somerset Maugham short story. Sure enough, he was right.

The dining room was lit by candles and hurricane lamps, with one wall completely open to the scented ocean breeze. Unity and Bo, in their tropical whites, sat at a round wooden table with a plate of lobster before them and a bottle of wine in a silver ice bucket. It was a touchingly domestic scene. Unity had a copy of *Rolling Stone* open in front of her, and Bo was making notes on a pad of paper.

"Very snug," Nicky remarked. "But where is Mrs. Daniels tonight?"

Bo looked up from his pad of paper and seemed to make a conscious decision not to take offense. "Kitty's gone to London for a few days," he explained. "That's how we keep our relationship so fresh, you see. Lots of space. Lots of freedom."

"Yeah," Nicky replied, taking in Unity Sphere. She was radiantly sexy tonight in her simple white dress—barefoot with a garland of flowers in her hair. No killer ever looked half so sweet.

"Nicholas was married once," she said to Bo.

"That so?" Bo didn't look up from his pad. He was clearly not greatly interested in the life, death, or marriages of a mere policeman.

"Nicholas was married to Susan Merril," Unity explained.

"Yes?" Bo looked up and seemed to see Nicky—really *see* him—for the first time. Being connected with a celebrity, however obliquely, raised him to the ranks of the visible. Fame was a strange

thing. In this overpopulated world forsaken by God, it was about all Hollywood people had to cling to. Nicky had to admit it certainly changed his image of Unity to discover she was not just a pretty face, but Billy Lion's daughter.

Billy Lion's daughter poured him a glass of wine and passed him some tender bits of underage lobster, which melted in his mouth. Dinner was a fish feast. After the lobster, a large Hawaiian woman served them something she called *opakapaka,* then later some grilled *ono.* The wine changed with each fish, from a Piesporter to a Vouvray to a nice Pouilly-Fumé. Bo was certainly not the sort of person to stint on his personal pleasures.

About halfway through the Vouvray, Billy Lion's daughter started playing footsie with him under the table, her bare toes creeping up the inside of his leg.

While Unity was feeling him up under the table, Bo was making a list of who he thought would win the Grammys Tuesday night. Apparently he and Unity did this every year before the awards, betting heavily on the results.

"Okay, we're at Best Original Song for a Sound Track. Here are the nominations. . . ."

Unity was extremely agile. While Bo read the list of films and songs, the girl's toes gently worked their way into Nicky's lap. He showed her what a world-weary sophisticate he was by not responding.

"Tell me, what do you think of the Grammys, Nicholas?" she asked him, interrupting Bo's list making.

Nicky shrugged. "They're okay. Only they should be held a lot less often. Like maybe once every ten years. I think the eighties should be skipped altogether."

Bo tried to smile, like a Moslem fundamentalist trying to make light of someone insulting his religion.

"Anyway," Bo announced loudly, "I'm putting two hundred bucks on Phil Collins. What's your pick, my dear?"

"I want Phil, too," she told him.

"Lamb chop, *you* can't have Phil. He's *my* choice, darling."

"But I want him, Bo-Bo. You can't have him just because you spoke first."

Bo-Bo sighed. "All right, my dear. I'll pick someone else." He put the end of the ballpoint pen in his mouth, studied the list, and then a smile crept over his face. "Okay, Madonna!" he cried, clapping his hands together. "And I'll raise you fifty. How about that, sweetheart?"

"He takes this very seriously, Nicholas," she explained.

"Damn right," Bo said in his own defense. "She still owes me nine thousand seven hundred and fifty dollars from the Grammys last year. Anyway, this is a good exercise, trying to figure out the trends before they happen. Know what I mean? Keeps you on your toes."

Speaking of toes, Nicky was getting an erection despite his best intentions. He reached beneath the napkin in his lap and held on to the bare foot there to stop its insidious wiggling.

"All right, we've come to Best Country Vocalist, Male. Here are the choices. . . ."

"What do you think, Nicholas?" she asked. "Does anyone give a damn? On a cosmic level, does any of this really matter?"

"Well, on a cosmic level, I'd say the Grammys are a bit like pissing out of a spaceship into a billion light-years of empty space. But the industry takes them seriously, that's the main thing. And for the rest of the country, they get a variety show, at least, and a chance to see their favorite stars."

"Damn right the industry takes 'em seriously," Bo echoed. "It's the field of play, man, where you win or where you lose."

"You see, it all comes from insecurity," Nicky said. "That's the real reason for all these ceremonies, one after another—the Academy Awards, the Emmys, the Grammys, the Golden Globe Awards, the American Music Awards—you name it. They seem to add a dozen new award shows every year. Deep down inside, everyone knows it's a second-rate con job, but the feeling is, if you get handed enough trophies, you might actually fool yourself into thinking you're doing something good. The way things are going, I expect pretty soon they'll throw the Grammys once a week."

Unity was delighted. "That's right, Nicholas! But they do, in a way. Once a week. Haven't you ever listened to the Top Forty countdown on Sunday mornings? I mean, in his entire life Beethoven never received one-tenth the hype and adoration your average pop song gets these days."

"Well, that's inflation," Nicky said. "In a sense, the sixties were about cooperation, while the seventies and eighties—it's all competition so far."

Bo was not looking pleased. "Don't bite the hand that feeds you," he warned the girl. "And you'd better not be saying anything cynical on Tuesday night."

"Trust me, Bo. Tuesday night, I'll be acting like the most important question mankind has ever faced is who will win Best Album of the Year. But I *am* allowed to have my private thoughts, after all. You can't deny me that."

"Don't doubt too much," Bo said sourly. "If you want to be a winner, you can't let things eat at you like that."

"A winner," Unity repeated vaguely.

"What are you going to be doing at the Grammys?" Nicky asked her.

She made a deprecating gesture. "Oh, not much. I'm going to be there, that's about all."

"Don't let her fool you," Bo said proudly. "This little girl's going to steal the show."

"Yes?"

"Really, Lieutenant—she's going to be great. Unity's taking a small crew with hand-held cameras around the auditorium as the show's going on. Get some real impromptu stuff."

"For The Rock Channel?"

"Yeah. The network won't let us broadcast it that night in competition with their own coverage, so we're going to run our show the next day. But the off-the-cuff stuff will be timeless. Like maybe a close-up on Phil Collins, his actual comments, right after Madonna wins—ha! ha!—for Best Original Song for a Sound Track."

Unity laughed, but there was something brittle in her voice. Laughter like the sound of breaking glass.

After dinner, they had coffee and cognac outside on a terrace underneath the stars.

"Don't lock your door tonight," she whispered when Bo was giving orders to a servant. "You're going to have a visitor tonight, Nicholas."

"Gee," he said. "Life in the tropics."

6

The room was dark, and his gun made a hard rock beneath his pillow. Nicky was lying on top of his bed, fully dressed, when the door opened and Unity slipped inside. From the light of a small digital clock, he could see it was 2:13.

The girl glided into his room like a wet dream. There seemed something unreal about all this. She was wearing a light robe of shimmering material. She stood in the moonlight by the bed and let the robe fall off her. She wasn't wearing anything underneath.

Then she was sliding next to him on the bed. Nicky felt warm skin and graceful curves. She reached for the belt on his pants, but Nicky stopped her, taking her wandering hands firmly in his own.

"Let's talk first," he said. "I have to make sure you'll respect me afterward."

"My philosophy is fuck now, talk later," she said. "Anyway, I've been waiting for this too long."

"I was expecting you earlier," he admitted.

"I had to wait for Bo to fall asleep."

"I thought you told me you didn't sleep with him anymore. Why does everyone lie to me?" he wondered.

"I wasn't lying, Nicholas. I said I don't let him touch me anymore. Sometimes we just sleep in the same bed."

"Isn't that tempting fate?"

She giggled. "Well, sometimes I take my clothes off and let him get excited while he watches me. He can look but not touch—that's the policy."

"You take your revenge quite seriously, don't you?"

Unity made a vague gesture, as if she couldn't be concerned with Bo's boring fascination with her. "Actually, I am beginning to look for a more satisfying relationship," she told him, gazing meaningfully at his belt buckle.

Nicky guarded his virtue. She thought this was funny. She spent a few minutes rubbing, tempting, and offering her naked self before she got the idea that Nicky was really saying no. It brought a pout to her pretty lips.

"Nicholas," she complained, "I can't believe you're turning down this magical moment of happiness."

"Yes," he said with a sigh. "It's murder, though. Somehow it gets in the way of my sexual desire."

She whispered in his ear: "You certainly had a wonderful big erection at the dinner table."

"Yes, but that was for the food," he said. "You have to understand that at my age you can get awfully turned on by a well-prepared piece of fish."

She regarded him solemnly. "I wish we were on the same side, Nicholas. I look at you, and I almost feel we are."

"I look at you, and you know what I think of? I think of Theo Oshimoto."

She had the decency to avert her eyes.

"I'm sorry about Theo," she said. "Was he a close friend?"

Nicky shook his head. "Actually, it was hard for me to be in the same room with him for more than five minutes. Theo was just a funny little guy with an immigrant mentality. What really gets me, you see, is the thought of a funny little guy like that getting squashed between big powerful Technicolor people like you and Bo. That bothers me a lot. It's like he didn't count."

Unity sat on the edge of the bed, naked and repentant.

"I'm also bothered about Tommy and Ginny and Marilyn, if you want to know the truth—more accidental victims in your game. Nancy—well, she was a killer herself. But J. J., he didn't deserve to die like that, mutilated at the foot of the stairs, all because you think he betrayed your father."

"He *did* betray my father, along with the rest of them. They sold him out."

"Yeah? Well, your justice has a pretty blunt edge to it, taking the innocent as well as the guilty. I think you're in a dream world, Unity. It's like you don't really understand the seriousness of what you've done."

"Look, suppose I wrote a few letters and started some wild rumors, like you say—I'm not admitting it, mind you, but just suppose —all right?"

"Okay. I'm supposing."

"Well, then—is that really a crime? I mean, I didn't actually kill anybody—I only sort of . . . well, I brought out people's natural tendency for evil. With *that* group, it wasn't hard—that is, if I actually did such a thing."

"You don't get it, do you? You take a rock, you throw it into a pool of water, and you've caused the ripples that spread outward to the shore. If there's some little ant walking along the side of the shore who gets drowned in the tidal wave you've caused—well, you've killed that ant. If that was the reason you threw the rock in the first place, then it's murder. You're responsible for what you do, Unity."

"Yes, Nicholas, that's all very moral and abstract. But have I actually committed a crime?"

"It's a possible felony to write threatening letters," he told her. "Depending on a lot of things."

"A possible felony," she said. "Well, say you arrest me and I have to stand trial—what kind of sentence do you think I'd get?"

"Mmm, if you had a decent lawyer, maybe six months. Suspended, most likely, because you don't have a previous record and everyone would be sympathetic with your lousy childhood and being sexually molested at an early age."

She stared at him. "Jesus Christ, six months' suspended sentence! Is *this* why you've been hounding me? Six lousy months' suspended sentence?"

"It's more than that, Unity. Much more."

"Yes? What is it, then? Maybe you'd like to spank me, Nicholas. It's all right. If it'll make you feel better, go ahead and do it."

Unity turned on the bed and offered her provocative rear end.

It was a tempting target. Nicky reached back and hauled off hard, open-handed, upon her bare butt. It sent her sprawling across the bed. She looked up at him with resentful tears in her eyes.

"Nicholas, *that* wasn't too damn sexy."

"It wasn't meant to be." He threw her robe at her. "Now put on your damn clothes and listen to me, girl. You killed those people, however obliquely. You know it and I know it, and I'm going to put you on trial for murder, even if the case is thrown out of court—just so everyone will know what you really are. That's the first thing I'm after—you hear me?"

She was massaging the spot where his hand had landed and looking at him sullenly.

"Do you hear me?" he asked again.

"I hear you," she said.

"Good. The second thing is that your days of playing God are over. There will be no more letters, rumors, or plots. The Ghost of Rock and Roll is retired, from this moment on."

"You think I'm planning something more?"

"I *know* you're planning something more. You've still got Donny and Rick to take care of. And then there's the person you hate most —the person you really want to destroy—your guardian and some time lover, Mr. Bo Daniels."

"You think so, do you?"

Unity slipped her robe back on and moved to the door. She was still rubbing her ass. Nicky had really hit her hard. She turned and looked at him before she left.

"You know, I take it back. That really *was* sexy, Nicholas. Maybe the most sexy thing anyone's ever done to me."

She smiled serenely and slipped out into the warm night.

Nicky sighed and lay back on his bed. This was ridiculous. He wasn't getting anywhere at all.

The damn tropics. The air was soft as a caress, and the sheets of his bed still retained the fragrance of healthy young girl.

He got up and took another cold shower.

7

Monday came, another Technicolor morning: blue sea, waving palm trees, bright flowers, dazzling beach.

Unity was standing in a flowered shift that barely covered her hips. She was eating a papaya with a spoon and staring meditatively at a small sailboat that was sitting unattended by the edge of the water.

"Well, good morning, Nicholas," she said with a smile. "Look what you've done to me. I'm a marked woman."

Without the least self-consciousness, the girl pulled up her shift and downed her underpants to show him the red outline of his hand spanning her rear.

"Jesus, pull up your pants, will you," he told her. He wasn't awake enough to face such a dazzling sight. "I'm sorry about spanking you," he added. "Generally I don't do that sort of thing."

"It's okay. I sort of like having your hand there."

Nicky accepted a papaya from her. Unity looked disgustingly pretty this morning, healthy and tan and young. Not at all like someone who was about to break down and confess.

"Why so gloomy?" she asked. "Anyway, I've decided to take you sailing this morning," she told him, glancing at the boat waiting on the beach. "You've come all the way to Hawaii, you might as well do something local."

"I don't know. I didn't bring a bathing suit."

Her eyes opened wide. "You came to Hawaii without a bathing suit?"

"Yeah, well, I'm not here for the water sports," he said. He was also not here to put himself totally at the mercy of a prime suspect. Unfortunately, Nicky knew nothing about sailing.

She came closer. "Please, Nicholas, there's a spot I want to show you, down the coast a few miles. It's . . . it's where my mother died," she managed.

"Fine. Why don't we drive there?"

"You can only get there by boat. It's a small bay, guarded by cliffs. Look, I know you think I'm some kind of homicidal maniac—

but you *do* like me, don't you? Just a little? No, don't answer—I *know* you do. No one in my whole life has ever really cared enough to spank me before—though God knows, there were times I deserved it."

"I'm an affectionate sort of guy," Nicky told her.

"Then give me a chance to explain myself, okay? Maybe you'll see we're not so far apart after all—maybe you'll be able to understand me once you see how my mother died."

Nicky was torn in two. The detective in him very much wanted to hear what Unity would tell him, but he also wished to survive the encounter.

"You trust me, don't you?" she asked, her violet eyes close and pleading. "*Please* say you trust me. I'd be heartbroken if you don't."

"I do, Unity. I do." He smiled back.

Unity went to borrow a pair of trunks from Bo. They were green and orange with bright yellow parrots on them. Nicky took them back to his room to change and fetch his gun. Somehow he felt he wouldn't be able to relax without it. Where to hide a gun on a small sailboat, wearing only a gaudy Hawaiian swimsuit, presented something of a challenge. He finally wrapped it inside a towel, tying the bundle up with his belt, the way he used to when he'd go swimming as a boy.

When he got back to the beach, Unity had the sailboat halfway into the water and had the ropes all rigged and waiting. She laughed, seeing the towel. "Afraid I'll get you wet?"

"Better safe than sorry," he told her.

Unity took control of the sail and rudder, and Nicky pushed them off from shore. The boat was a small catamaran, a Hobie Cat, she called it—with a canvas deck stretched like a trampoline between two pontoons and a colorful sail that was blue and orange and white. Unity seemed to know what she was doing. She guided the little boat skillfully out of the lagoon, past a coral reef where waves were breaking, and out into the open water. The breeze was gusty and erratic, but Unity seemed to be able to make the most of it. She tacked once, pulled in the sail, and the small boat was suddenly skimming along at a great speed. Nicky was a little alarmed at how quickly the land fell away. Beneath them, the ocean changed from a milky green to an unimaginably dark blue. Nicky didn't know how deep it was, but it was definitely above his head.

A wave splashed over the side and caught them full in the face. Nicky got a mouthful of salt.

"Isn't this fun?" she shouted.

"Wonderful," he said. He wished he had a life jacket. For the next half hour it was almost too fun for words. Nicky and the girl sat on the pontoon that was trying to lift out of the water, leaning against the thrust of the wind, while the boat sliced through the rolling swells and waves broke down upon them. Unity seemed to think this was what sailing was all about.

"What happens if we flip over?" he shouted.

"Don't worry, it won't sink," she shouted back. "We just stand on one of the pontoons and get it right-side up again."

Nicky sighed. He wasn't sure how far they were from land now, but the island had faded into an indistinct blur of clouds and mountains—not a good sign, he thought.

Then, without warning, the wild roller-coaster ride through the waves suddenly stopped. The wind stopped. They were becalmed on a flat, motionless sea. The sun baked down upon them and dried the salt to their bodies. Nicky felt like a potato chip.

"Aren't we a little far out?" he asked, squinting at the distant land mass. "Where's this small bay you were telling me about?"

She laughed at his nautical ignorance. "Nicholas, we have to come out this far so we can get around the far side of Captain Cook Bay in one long tack." She pointed up the coast, far away. "See, that's where we're going. Honestly, I know what I'm doing. I once sailed to Maui on a boat only a few feet longer than this. When the wind comes back, we'll be there in fifteen, twenty minutes."

"You, uh, think the wind will come back, do you?"

"Eventually," she told him, grinning. "You know, there's really no one else I'd rather be becalmed with. You and me. Stuck in the middle of nowhere. Maybe the wind won't come back. Maybe we'll just drift slowly off to China. Wouldn't that be fun?"

"Well, it would give us a chance to get to know each other," he said.

Unity had a small waterproof day pack tied to the mast. She pulled out a bottle of sparkling water and they each had a drink.

"I have suntan lotion in the bag," she said. "If you lie down, I'll rub some on you."

"I think I'll take my chances with the sun."

She studied him with scientific detachment. "Funny, I've never had trouble seducing a man before. You're making me feel maybe I'm getting old, Nicholas."

"Yeah, seventeen's pretty ancient all right. From here on in, Unity, you're going to have to get by with just the goodness of your character."

"The goodness of my character," she said dubiously. "That does it, then. Guess I'll be an old maid."

"You're that bad, are you?"

"Worse," she told him. "Nicholas, help me trim the sail, okay? If the wind comes up too suddenly, I don't want it to blow us out of the water."

"But there *is* no wind," he reminded her.

"Nicholas, *I'm* the captain here. I know these waters. What I want you to do is pull down the canvas when I loosen the rope. You'll have to stand up by the mast."

Standing by the mast, even in a becalmed sea, seemed a perilous sort of thing. Unity, however, insisted it needed to be done. The boat lurched when Nicky stood up, and he had to grab hold of the boom to keep from falling overboard. He made his way cautiously forward.

"Okay, pull down on the canvas," she told him.

Nicky pulled, but the canvas wouldn't budge.

"Harder!" she shouted.

He gave another yank, but nothing happened. "Are you sure the rope is . . . oh, I see," he said flatly when he turned to face her. Unity was holding his .38 revolver, pointing it his way. "I don't suppose we need to trim the sail after all."

"Of course not, silly. You only trim the sail when there's wind, not when you're becalmed. See how bad I am—I lied to you."

Nicky sighed.

"Come, sit down," she said. "Let's have a nice talk."

"Perhaps we could talk better back on land?" Nicky suggested.

She didn't seem to hear him. "Funny, no one's wanted to know about me before," she said. "Not really. Men especially take me at face value—a little sex object they want to get their hands on. And women, well—they're a bit defensive and competitive because of the way I look. Even my mother didn't really want to know who I was. And then you come along, this fatherly middle-aged cop, and you want to know about the real me. It scares me a little."

"It scares me a lot," he admitted, glancing at his gun. He wasn't too happy about being a dozen miles from land on a small, drifting sailboat with an attractive young killer who was about to confess.

Nicky knew all the signs. There was an earnest quaver in her voice, deeper than the surface banter she was still trying to maintain. She was in labor right now, feeling the first contractions. Truth looking to be born.

Only this was not a very good time. Back at the academy, it was considered a truism that when someone was about to confess it was a good idea if you—not the suspect—were the one holding the gun.

Nicky looked off to the vague swirl of land, now half hidden in the clouds. He sure as hell wished they were closer to shore.

8

"You're a very perceptive person, Nicholas. You know that?"

"I am, rather. It's true."

"No, I mean it. Of course, no one's ever looked at me real hard, the way you have. Most people think, hell—Unity sure scored having a big tycoon like Bo Daniels taking care of her. Giving her cars and a house in L.A. and a big break on TV, her own show even. All that shit. As if it mattered."

"It doesn't matter," he agreed. They were sitting across from each other, she on one pontoon, he on the other. Unity held the gun languidly, but she seemed to know how to use it, firing over his head once when he tried to get too close. Since then, Nicky had tried several times to convince her to give it back, but she would not part with her new toy.

"I mean, Bo stole it all from my father anyway," she was saying. "Everything he has, he took from Billy. By all rights, it should be mine—*my* inheritance he's handing out to me, if I smile right. You're right, Nicholas—when I was young I would sit on his lap, and his slimy hand would start creeping up my leg, and I'd think to myself, One of these days, Bo, I'm going to get even. And when I do, look out!"

"I can understand that," Nicky said.

"You can?"

Nicky nodded sagely. As compassionate as Buddha. As forgiving as Jesus. *Confess your sins, little girl, but relax, please, just long enough to let me get that gun from you.* "Tell me about your father," he said. "When did you find out you were Billy Lion's daughter?"

"I was maybe five or six. It's one of my earliest childhood memories, actually. I was riding in a car with my mother and 'Streets of Love' came on the radio. And she said to me, 'That's your daddy, Unity Sphere.' 'Daddy?' I asked. I knew what a mommy was—that was a stoned selfish bitch who forgot you were alive most of the time. But a daddy, now there was something I hadn't encountered. So she told me—what a daddy was, who Billy Lion was. The way she described him, Billy Lion was maybe the best person who ever lived. 'Too good to survive on this plateau'—that was the kind of metaphysical jive my mother liked to hand out. A couple of weeks later we were at Longs Drug Store in Hilo, and she bought me a copy of the first album—the one that had the really sexy picture of daddy on the front, looking like a Greek god. Of course I played that record until I wore it out, and then I thumbtacked the cover on my bedroom wall, just so I could look at my daddy's picture."

"I wore that album out, too," Nicky told her. "By playing it over and over again."

"Yes? Well, I didn't need much encouragement, you know. The idea of having a daddy went over very big with me—especially since Mommy was *not* so wonderful. I guess I fantasized a lot. I talked to the picture on the wall. For years I had this running daydream—do you want to know about my daydream, Nicholas?"

"Absolutely."

"Okay. Well, first of all, my daddy was *not* dead, as everyone said, but merely hiding. You see, he had been the king, but his wicked brother had stolen his crown, and he was forced to run for his life. So he came to me for help, and I gave him shelter. I was the only one my father trusted. Together we plotted how to get his kingdom back and punish the wicked brother. Then my father would marry me, you see—I would be his queen and together we'd live happily ever after."

"Makes sense," Nicky told her. "Tell me about Bo. When did he come into your life?"

"It was around the same time, when I was six or so. That's when Bo built his little retreat here. My mother took me to see him. She bought me some new clothes, I remember—it stands out, because she had never spent money on clothes for me before. She told me Bo was a very important man and that he had been my father's best friend. She said I was supposed to be nice to him. Yuck!"

"Why yuck? Wasn't Bo nice to you?"

"He was too nice. He was weird, you know. Wanting to kiss me and things. I knew he couldn't have really been my father's friend. I hated having his hands all over me. Instinctively, I knew he was a slob."

"Did you ever tell your mother he was molesting you?"

Unity flashed her violet eyes. "You think she'd care? Christ, Nicholas, my mother would have said, Go with the flow. Don't be uptight. I was supposed to be liberated, you see. Like her. Anyway, there was something else."

"What's that?"

"Well, I was no fool. I hated Bo, but I sure liked his house and all the servants and everyone taking such good care of me. I liked the feeling of . . . order. I mean, at my mother's you never knew what was going to happen. Who would show up. Half the time she'd never even remember to feed me. But at Bo's, everything was orderly and taken care of. I liked that. I liked that a lot," she said defiantly.

Nicky agreed. "A nice orderly home," he recapitulated. "All you had to do was be nice to Bo."

"Yeah. So I was nice. If I hated him, I kept it deep inside. The funny thing is, I even fooled my mother. After a time, she started getting jealous that I liked Bo more than her. Can you believe that? The woman does nothing for me, throws me to the wolves, and she expects me to *like* her. Anyway, I started spending more and more time at Bo's, and my mother started getting very bitchy about it. When I was twelve, she found me on the beach with Bo—we didn't have our clothes on, and we were doing things to each other, you know—and the shit really hit the fan."

"I thought you said she was 'liberated'?"

"You don't understand. I'm not talking about morals, Nicholas, just plain jealousy. My mother was so self-centered, you see. She wanted to be the only sexy one in the family. But when I reached puberty, men started hitting on me more than her, and she just couldn't stand it. It bothered her so much that Bo preferred me to her that she told me the truth about Bo and Billy, hoping it would turn me against him."

"What's the truth about Bo and Billy?" Nicky asked, scanning the horizon for sharks.

"Bo paid my mother to kill Billy in Rome. Mommy dearest drowned my father in the bathtub. They were having sex, and she held his head underwater until he was dead."

"And Bo paid her to do this?"

"Yeah. That's what she told me. He gave her money the rest of her life."

The wind was changing, uncertain which direction it wished to take. The ocean reflected restless currents. Nicky had a feeling he was getting fried by the sun. He tried to arrange himself in the shade of the sail.

"So I killed her," the girl said, looking out to the horizon. "I killed my mother, Nicholas. You understand, don't you? I really had to."

9

They were sailing again with the wind at their back, though not nearly as quickly as before. Nicky was relieved to see they were angled back toward land, though Unity kept his revolver quite handily in her lap.

A dozen feet off the bow, two dolphins burst through the water, looked at the sailboat with friendly interest, then disappeared back beneath the waves. Nicky hoped it was a good sign.

"So how did you kill your mother, Unity?" he asked about as casually as a question like that could be asked.

She laughed suddenly and mimicked his tone: " 'So how did you kill your mother, Unity?' Jesus, Nicholas, you really are a funny man. Admit it, you're shocked by what I've told you. And you're also a little nervous to be so far from land with me holding a gun on you. I mean, here I've just confessed to murdering my mother, and you're at my mercy, aren't you?"

He smiled. "If you want to shock me, Unity, you're going to have to try a lot harder. Besides that—I hate to tell you this, my dear—I got a pet dolphin out there, come and rescue me any time I whistle, you see. I came prepared."

She didn't smile.

"It's important you think well of me," she told him earnestly.

"I do. And I'm going to help you get this straightened out," he said soothingly. "Let's get back to how you killed your mother."

"It was easy," she told him. Nicky didn't like the brightness in her eyes. "It was a rainy night. It had been raining for three days. I knew my mother was driving down to Kona to meet some guy at midnight to buy cocaine. She'd been drinking beer all day, and smoking dope, which she could handle pretty well. Around eight o'clock she asked me to bring her another beer from the fridge. I pretended I didn't hear her right and brought her a screwdriver instead. One that was about eighty percent vodka. When she finished that, I made her another one without her even asking. You can see what a dutiful daughter I was."

233

Unity stopped confessing and looked to Nicky for applause.

"That's it?" he asked. "You made two strong drinks?"

"It was enough. I knew exactly what vodka did to her. Believe me. From bitter experience. She could drink a case of beer, a gallon of wine, smoke a lid of dope, drop acid, and everything would be cherry. But add vodka and she was gone, Nicholas. Like outer space. Kamuela to Kona's a pretty healthy drive, and she didn't get more than fifteen miles before going off a cliff."

"Hmm . . . I doubt if any jury in the world would convict a twelve-year-old child for making her mother two drinks."

"That's right. It was beautiful, don't you think? But I killed her, just the same, just as I intended to. *I* know it. You know it. If the legal system can't deal with such subleties, who am I to complain?"

"Pretty clever," he said, giving her the applause she was waiting for. "So you killed your mother and went to live with Bo. Wasn't that hard for you? After all, he was the real person behind your father's death."

"Oh, I was just biding my time," she told him serenely. "Looking for a way to destroy him. I think I told you, I wouldn't let him have sex with me anymore. *That's* been a sort of constant punishment over the years, to look but not touch."

"I'm surprised he put up with it."

"Oh, he had to. I have quite a lot of power over him, you know. Mostly he's frightened I'll leave him if he doesn't do what I say."

"Okay, why *don't* you leave him, Unity? Why not put about ten thousand miles between you and Bo and everything connected with your past?"

"Ah, one likes to stay close to one's prey. Doesn't one?" she asked.

"Tell me about it."

"Oh, there isn't much to tell. Over the years, I've become sort of an expert on Billy and the band, using my access to people and materials to find out everything I could."

"What were you looking for?"

"I didn't know, exactly. Everything and nothing. The key to unravel the empire. Some way to destroy Bo and what he's built and what he stands for. I've been very patient, you see. I didn't want to do anything until I knew I would succeed."

"You hate him that much?"

"Look, Nicholas—over the years I've had a chance to watch Bo up close, see how foul he's made everything he's touched. It's obscene, you know, how he's taken my father's vision and gradually debased it until he's turned rock and roll into just a profitable venture for organized crime. I thought for a while the Mafia connection might be the key I was looking for. I was still trying the indirect approach, you see. Incidentally, I liked what you said yesterday about dropping a rock into a pool of water. That's exactly what I've been doing. It's been quite a fascinating experience, a study of cause and effect."

"Very successful, too," he added.

"Mmm, yes and no. I got rid of J. J. pretty good—getting Bushy to believe he was about to talk to the FBI. Then there's Marilyn, of course—and I would have had Rick Elsmore, too, only you interfered. A pity. You should have been having a good time with me instead, on the sand."

"How did you set up Rick?" Nicky asked uncomfortably.

Unity smiled sweetly. "I told Bo that Rick told me *he* was sending the anonymous letters. Bo told Bushy, of course, who told Greg, his bodyguard, to take care of it. Did you ever play post office as a kid? It was sort of fun, really, but it wasn't as easy to tear down Bo's empire with rumors as I thought. Fortunately, I think I have it figured out now, how to do it."

"Yes? How are you going to do it, Unity?"

She laughed merrily. "Ah, if I told you, you'd know."

"I have a bad feeling I'd better know."

"No, I think not," she said, adjusting the sail in an attempt to make the best of the erratic wind. "Though I'm dying to. I think you would find . . . well, it's not quite as subtle as I'd like—but I think I've found a way to make a very strong statement."

Nicky suddenly got a very good idea. "It's the Grammys, isn't it? The whole industry's going to be there to watch Bo get his special achievement award. You're going to pull some damn stunt at the Grammys, for chrissake!"

She blinked innocently. "Now, Nicholas, it's naughty of you to try to guess."

"Unity," he began, "this may be difficult for you to understand, but what you're doing is very wrong."

"Don't you believe in justice?"

Nicky sighed. "Look, what if Bo didn't actually have anything to do with your father's death? Have you ever considered that?"

The girl's smile hardened. "It's not worth considering. Remember, my mother told me what happened."

"Yes, but what if your mother lied to you? No, listen to me," he said when she started to object. "I've been looking into this. My partner Charlie made three calls to Rome last weekend—I've talked with Donny about this, Rick, even Bo. I had to know myself if Billy had been murdered."

"Well?" she asked. "So now you know."

"No, I don't. And no one ever will. Look, there was no autopsy, just a death certificate and a brief police report, all of which are inconclusive. The two Italian policemen who came to the hotel, the doctor who saw the body, and the assistant manager who was called —all these people are dead, just as you told me, along with Billy and your mother. Exactly what happened in that bathroom in the Grand Hotel is going to stay a mystery forever."

Unity didn't like this very much. She had been holding the .38 only loosely in her lap, but now she picked it up and pointed it his way with a rapturous intensity Nicky didn't like at all. A pity. His left leg had been only a few feet from her lap, and he had been angling closer, hoping to kick the gun out of her hand.

"No, Nicholas," she told him. "I *know* what happened in that bathroom. My mother told me."

"You said yourself your mother was jealous and trying to make trouble between you and Bo. At the very least, she lived in a fantasy world. How can you trust what she said?"

"No, in this one case, I believed her."

"Since we don't have any real evidence, all we can do is use common sense," he told her, model of reason that he was. "Look, whatever you say about Bo, you have to agree he's a shrewd businessman. Can you really imagine a man like Bo putting his life in the hands of a spaced-out acid queen like your mother?"

Unity shivered, though it was very warm. She had also become very pale. Nicky was trying to shake the foundations of her world, and she didn't like it. "No!" she said again. "I know what I know. And I thought you were on my side, Nicholas."

"There aren't sides to this," he told her, trying to be calm and fatherly. "This is real life, Unity, where everyone's a villain and everyone's a hero, all meted out in equal measure. Bo's a pathetic son of a bitch, but in his own way he probably loves you. You're part of this, too, because you liked the nice comfortable things Bo could give you, like security and a big house. So you share some of the guilt, too—you should think about that."

"You think a child is responsible for being sexually abused, Nicholas? Is that what you're telling me? That's like saying a woman's responsible for getting raped, just because she goes around looking sexy."

Nicky shook his head. "I'm not saying you were responsible, only that you contributed to the situation. Life taught you to be a uniquely manipulative child. You had to be to survive. But you can't remain a victim of your childhood forever—that's what growing up is all about."

"Oh, is *that* what it's all about?"

Nicky kept at her. He tried to show how her life could have been different—that the choices you make affect what you become. He tried to tell her that we are all eventually responsible for our lives, and that—above all—we have the power to change.

It sounded pretty good. Very stirring. The girl nodded every now and then—a little blankly, perhaps, but seeming to agree.

"You know, you're quite deep, Nicholas," she told him.

"Way over my head," he agreed.

"But do you think *I* could change?" she asked hesitantly.

"I know you can," he assured her. "You're only at the beginning of things, Unity. You have your entire life in front of you."

She sighed and considered this awhile. "Okay," she said finally. "What do you want me to do?"

"Let's start by handing over the gun," he suggested.

She regarded the .38 wistfully, then handed it over. Nicky slid on the safety with a feeling of great relief. Unity hugged herself nervously and peered aimlessly over the water.

"So what now, Nicholas? Are you going to arrest me?"

"I want you to come back to L.A. with me, go to a grand jury and tell them everything you've told me. We'll get a hot lawyer for you. As I told you, you're a sexually abused juvenile—the court's going to be sympathetic, especially since everything you've done has been indirect and open to interpretation. If it's done right, you could walk away from this with maybe a suspended sentence, maybe some court-ordered psychotherapy thrown in. It won't be too bad."

"Then why do it?" she asked, bewildered.

"To clear the past. So you can have the future."

Unity seemed to consider this. She had lost interest in sailing, and the little boat was rocking uncertainly on the waves.

"This future you're talking about," she asked finally. "Are you going to be in it with me?"

"I'll be your friend," he said.

"Not my lover?"

He shook his head. "You're too young for me, Unity. It wouldn't work. Anyway, I'm kinda spoken for."

She thought about this some more. "Okay," she said at last. "I'll do what you say."

"You're going to stop playing God?"

"Uh-huh. The Ghost of Rock and Roll has just gone into retirement—if that's what you want, Nicholas."

"It's the right thing," he told her, trying not to set himself up as a new father figure in her life.

"How about a kiss?" she suggested. "Just to seal the bargain?"

He decided to give her a nonfatherly, nonsexual, chaste, and friendly hug with a little peck on the mouth thrown in for good measure. After all, she had agreed to come a long way for him. Her body was warm from the sun, velvety in his arms, but Nicky had a tight lid on his lust. In fact, he was feeling awfully good about himself—supercop and savior of lost girls—when a wave hit the side of the catamaran, and they were both tossed head over heels into the warm Hawaiian ocean.

Something, maybe the mast, hit the side of Nicky's leg. He came up to the surface sputtering for breath and feeling very disoriented. The gun in his hand was gone, probably to the bottom of the ocean, and the Hobie Cat was a dozen feet away, lying on its side. Unity was already pulling on the raised pontoon, trying to get the catamaran upright with the weight of her body.

"You okay?" he called.

"Yeah. How about you?"

"Fine," he said. "Just a little surprised. Here, I'll help you with the boat."

"I got it," she told him.

The sail came out of the water, and the boat flipped upright with a splash. Unity pulled herself up on the deck and took the rudder and the ropes in hand. A blustery wind had come up, and Unity and the Hobie Cat were moving away from where Nicky was treading water.

"I'm going to come around for you," she called.

The catamaran was now twenty feet away, and the distance was increasing every moment. The girl adjusted the sail, and the boat jumped forward in the water, sailing away.

"I'm sorry about this, Nicholas," she shouted without looking around, "I really am."

He was more sorry than she was. So much for being a supercop and savior of lost girls. In a few minutes the brightly colored sail was a dim memory moving into the sun.

10

Nicky swam.

And he swam.

He alternated the traditional Australian crawl with swimming on his back, as a way to regather strength when he was tired. The Hawaiian ocean was warm and extremely buoyant, which was his only source of optimism. Occasionally he dared himself to look and see if land were any closer, and the optimism would vanish.

It must have been an hour later when his energy level began to sag that some distant memory of a TV show filtered through his mind.

In the TV show, a plane crashed into the ocean and a passenger was able to survive by following a procedure he had learned in the air force. Now what was that procedure? Nicky wondered. He wondered about this for another twenty strokes on his back, and then it came to him. You do a dead man's float, facedown in the water, requiring no energy. Every now and then, turn your head to the side and take a nice deep breath of life-giving air.

Nicky gave it a try. It was quite relaxing actually, like floating on a waterbed. Of course, when he did the dead man's float he wasn't making any progress toward shore, but he began to see that if he alternated swimming with resting, he might survive a considerable time out here.

He worked out a routine: seventy-five strokes on his stomach, a hundred strokes on his back, then count to three hundred doing the dead man's float. Every five cycles, he allowed himself to see if land were any closer. It never was.

In the rhythmic boredom of his endless swim, Nicky's mind was free to wander upon the greater questions of Life and Death. Like, for instance, which TV show was it he was watching when he learned about surviving on the ocean with a dead man's float? He couldn't quite remember. It bugged him for hours. Eventually he narrowed the contenders to "Quincy," "Magnum, P.I.," and "Miami Vice." He had a feeling it was "Quincy." This was funny

239

because he hated "Quincy" mostly because he despised men who whined, and Quincy was the champion whiner of all time—high-pitched, nasal, self-righteous, a real complainer. The fact that he was always right did nothing to make him any more attractive.

So here was this TV show he hated. And lo and behold, it looked like "Quincy" might just save his life. What sort of sense did this make?

Sometime later he thought about the girl. Lovely Unity Sphere, so young and perky-breasted. It certainly had been a mistake to kiss her. Nicky thought about all the other girls over the years he shouldn't have kissed—and had.

What did it all matter now? A lot of sperm and motion.

He swam and swam. He was getting a little crazy as the hours passed. Strange thoughts came and went. Land did not look any closer. He had to rest more often, finding solace in the dead man's float.

Hand over hand, Nicky continued through the sea. The sun changed position in the sky. His eyes stung with salt, and his fingers became wrinkled beyond recognition. A time came when he had to admit to himself he wasn't going to make it. He was going to die out here.

Killed by a kiss.

At last, Susan came to mind. His lifetime mate, mother of his child. Susan drove him nuts in many ways. God knew she wasn't perfect. But he loved her. He even loved her funny imperfections. Susan was going to be devastated if he died out here. It gave Nicky a whole new burst of energy that kept him going another few hours, until the sun was casting long shadows across the swells.

He treaded water and looked. Land actually was considerably closer. Electric lights from the shore were beginning to sparkle in the fading twilight, maybe three or four miles away.

Too far. Still too far. Not even the dead man's float would get him there. Every muscle in his body ached with fatigue. The cycle had become absurdly shortened: five desperate, flaying strokes on his stomach, a few moments of gasping for breath on his back, and then the dead man's float—which was becoming more and more the real thing.

He felt the vibrations when his head was still in the water. He let the pulse massage him before he realized what it was—a boat's engine shuddering through the waves.

He looked up to see an unlikely sight: a great Viking ship with fake red sails and a diesel engine, maybe fifty feet away. On deck, people were dining and drinking cocktails. A Polynesian girl was doing a hula, accompanied by a ukulele and guitar.

The boat was passing to his left, lit brilliantly with colored lights. Nicky raised a tired arm and waved feebly. A fat woman on the deck seemed to see him. She was wearing a print dress, and there was a camera around her neck. She waved back quite pleasantly, and the boat continued on its way.

Nicky had to laugh, which wasn't wise. There is laughter that restoreth, and laughter that taketh away. This seemed to be the latter variety. Nicky swallowed a mouthful of salt water and sank down into his dreams.

The Ghost of Rock 'n' Roll (4)

Hello, this is Unity Sphere inviting you . . ."

The camera is tight on girl's face. Makeup hides freckles, adding several years of age and sophistication. Violet eyes peer outward into America's living room.

Camera pulls back slowly, revealing Unity in vast empty theater. She is expensively trashed in an outfit of incongruous parts: blue-jeans jacket with spangles, overlapping shirts, dress with tight pants underneath, pink jogging shoes.

"Tomorrow night, these empty rows will come alive, as this now darkened theater becomes the setting for the climactic event of the musical year—the Thirtieth Annual Grammy Awards Presentation, live from the Shrine Auditorium in Los Angeles. Join me Wednesday night at The Rock Channel for an intimate look at those who have won and those who have lost. The glory and the disappointment. The laughter and the tears. 'The Grammys: The Day After.' "

NEW ANGLE.

Close-up, Unity.

"So be sure to join me, Unity Sphere, with my special friends—"

CAMERA PULLS BACK TO REVEAL:

"—Lionel Richie and David Lee Roth. Only on"—all three in unison pointing at camera—"The . . . Rock . . . Channel!"

NEW ANGLE. Unity, Lionel, David. Arms linked.

"Brought to you by McDonald's. The official hamburger of the Thirtieth Annual Grammy Awards. Pepsi-Cola, the choice of a new generation. And Stri-Dex medicated pads."

Screen goes dead.

Part Five

The Big Cancellation

1

*I*t was between social studies and Latin that Tanya Rachmaninoff made a quick dash to the pay phone near the school cafeteria. She put her coins in the slot, dialed a number, and heard a message that was becoming all too familiar.

"Hi, this is Unity Sphere. I can't come to the phone right now, but if you leave a message at the sound of the beep . . ."

"Hi, it's me again," Tanya said when she was able. "I *hate* to keep bugging you, but if there's *any* chance you can get me that ticket to the Grammys tonight, I'd just about *die* with happiness. I'll be home from school around four-thirty, so you can reach me then. Thanks an *aw*fully lot! Bye.

"Damn!" she shouted, slamming down the phone. She had been trying to get Unity all day Monday, and now it was Tuesday, the day of the show. There wasn't much time left. Tanya made one more call to The Rock Channel. She was shuffled around from secretary to secretary until she finally reached someone on Unity's production staff. Unity had returned from Hawaii, she was told, but had not come into the station yet today.

"This truly sucks," Tanya said dispiritedly, hanging up a second time. Unfortunately Sister Georgina was just passing by. It was that sort of day.

"Miss Rachmaninoff! Please have the goodness to remember you are *not* in the gutter—not yet, at least, though you certainly will end up there if you insist on using language like that."

"Sorry, Sister," Tanya muttered. *Old bat!*

"Say you're sorry to God, my dear," the sister reminded her. "*He's* the one you've offended."

"Sorry, God!" Tanya cried, and ran away from the old nun, down the hall toward her Latin class. "But, God, just get me into the Grammys tonight!" she pleaded. "*Please!* Just one lousy ticket! Is that a lot to ask?"

Latin was hell to sit through. Some days you really didn't care if Julius Caesar ever went to Gaul or not. Kirsten was in the row behind her, beaming with joy because *she* was going to the Grammys tonight—with her family, though her father was just a TV producer who made dumb game shows. Even Patsy Kronenberger, a total airhead, would be there tonight, because her father had done some tax work for Whitney Houston, and for the past week nearly every word out of Patsy's mouth was Whitney *this* and Whitney *that*—all ridiculous, of course, because if Patsy Kronenberger was ever on a first-name basis with Whitney Houston, Tanya would be willing to eat her Calvin Kleins. But there it was. The social life in this town was hell and depended entirely on what you were invited to and what you were *not* invited to. It was a real jungle out there, and Tanya was getting her first taste of defeat.

Sister Emily, the Latin teacher, had her back to the class while she was writing irregular declensions on the blackboard. Tanya felt a tap on her arm, and a note was passed her way. It was from Kirsten: "My dad says there's space for you in our car if you can get a ticket. But we can't go to the party afterward at Spago's—he says we're too young. That sucks, doesn't it?"

Tanya wrote back: "I'll say! I'll have to think about this. If we can't go to the party, I mean I'm tempted not to go at all. Face it, the awards themselves are b-o-r-i-n-g."

Tanya braved it out, though there were times she had to gulp back her tears. She managed to reach Unity's answering machine after Algebra and again after lunch, always to get the same recorded mesage. She was getting a very sinking feeling about the whole affair, especially after lunch when Kirsten's mother came and drove her away, to get ready for the gala event. Tanya started fantasizing George Michaels showing up at Marymount to rescue her from P.E. and escort her personally to the show. Tanya would accept the award for him, maybe. Kirsten, up in the last row in the balcony, would pee green with envy.

A nice fantasy, but the joy of it faded with the afternoon. Tanya rode the school bus home in dreary silence, not even laughing when Maureen Hudson threw a package of condoms at two guys in a Mustang convertible. Under the circumstances, it struck her as very immature.

No one was home at Sunshine Terrace. Her father was off in Hawaii working on a case, and her mom was still at the studio. *I've become a latch key child,* she thought glumly. She dumped her books on the living room couch, poured herself a glass of grape juice in the kitchen, and wondered if it was worth trying Unity one more time. That's when she noticed that the red light was blinking on her dad's answering machine. She took her grape juice over to where the machine sat across the living room, rewound the tape, and pressed playback.

There were half a dozen calls. There seemed to be a whole bunch of big-shot cops—captains and majors and chiefs—trying to find her father. Tanya had some fun fast-forwarding their voices, turning them into squeaky, high-pitched chipmunks. Then, just when she was giving up hope, there it was—a message for her from Unity. It was a funny sort of message actually, and Tanya played it several times trying to figure it out:

"Hi, Tanya—it's me, Unity. Sorry I haven't gotten back to you earlier, but I've been ridiculously busy—you know how it is, hardly time to breathe. Anyway, double sorry, *triple* sorry—I know you'll be disappointed—but I *can't* scare up a ticket for you tonight, not for love or money. They're just not to be had this late. The whole place is going to be crazy, as a matter of fact—I think you'll be *much* better off watching the show at home this year. Tell you what, sweetheart—watch carefully and I'll send you a little message over the air. Okay? You'll know what it is when you see it. Actually I'm dedicating the entire evening to you. I want you to remember—"

And there it was. Her father's answering machine was set to record only thirty seconds, and Unity's voice broke off midsentence. Tanya never did find out what Unity wanted her to remember.

2

Charlie had a good laugh when he saw Nicky coming past the security check at LAX.

"What'cha do, brah? Roll a three-hundred-pound Samoan who was down on his luck?"

Nicky frowned but made no answer. He had made a rapid descent down the social ladder over the last twenty-four hours. Getting off the plane, a little blond kid with a freshly scrubbed face wandered too close to him, and his mother pulled him away. This was the way people treated someone who was unshaved, dressed in rubber sandals, a pair of stained synthetic slacks five times too large, and a

247

ragged T-shirt on which was written in faded letters I GOT LEI'D IN HAWAII.

Charlie, for his part, was dressed to kill: black dinner jacket, waistcoat, ruffled shirt, studs, black shoes with funny little tassles. The works. He seemed disappointed Nicky hardly glanced at him.

Nicky looked up at a digital clock on the terminal wall. It was 5:22, Tuesday afternoon. "You have my things?" he asked.

Charlie handed him an overnight bag with what Nicky had requested in a hurried phone call that morning from Kona. He took the bag and charged into the nearest men's room. When he emerged a few minutes later the corner of Charlie's mouth twitched spasmodically, then sputtered into a renewed laugh.

"The damn thing seems to have shrunk in the closet," Nicky admitted.

"Clothes will do that," Charlie told him, "especially around the waist."

Nicky scowled, glanced again at the time, then led the way swiftly down the long terminal artery toward the exit. Charlie had to jog to keep up. The late-afternoon airport crowd gave Nicky some worried looks and kept out of his way. It wasn't only that his evening clothes were too small, sitting unused in the back of his closet for nearly a decade now. They were also unpressed and slighty moldy. The pants' zipper went only halfway up, then branched out in a wide V, held in place by the belt—giving him the look of a sex offender, especially when combined with the two days' growth of beard on his face.

Then there was the ill-concealed gun, a heavy .45 automatic from Charlie's collection, outlined perfectly beneath the too snug dinner jacket, with the pistol grip protruding like some malignant tumor. If his sartorial taste were open to question, at least no one would do it openly.

"You do lead an exciting life," Charlie remarked. "Naturally, I won't mention how a certain person gave his partner a very hard time for becoming temporarily separated from *his* clothes and gun."

Nicky sighed. The past twenty-four hours had not been a whole lot of fun. He had been fished out of the water, barely conscious, by a tourist boat—a sunset dinner cruise—and had spent last night in a hospital in Kona. This morning he'd been able to convince a nurse to get him out and even lend him some of her brother's clothes—to spend the next five and a half hours in the narrow economy seat of a jumbo jet, squeezed between a teenage surfer and an overweight secretary from Kansas, hoping he wouldn't be too late.

"You have the girl in custody?" Nicky asked, riding the escalator down to street level.

"Well, ah . . ."

It had seemed an easy-enough request over the phone that morning—Charlie was to get a warrant to arrest Unity Sphere for the attempted murder of a police officer. Nicky didn't even care if they could make the case stick, as long as the girl was kept from attending the Grammys that night.

Simple? One would think so. But he could tell from Charlie's face that it had not happened.

"Shit, you didn't get her."

"No, I was going to tell you about it."

"Well?"

"Okay, Nick—first off, I went to the chief and the D.A., seeing if they'd go to bat for us and try to get a quickie warrant. I told them Unity assaulted you with intent to kill, etcetera, etcetera. They responded, That's very tough—we can't have seventeen-year-old girls assaulting our policemen. But under the circumstances, what with our Lieutenant Rachmaninoff being on suspension and all, one shouldn't be too hasty. Especially as said lieutenant wasn't supposed to be in Hawaii working on the case in the first place. The chief, as a matter of fact, has requested your immediate presence in his office. I am to bring you to him."

"Fuck," Nicky muttered.

"Exactly," Charlie agreed. "Tell me, Nick—did that sweet little pussycat really try to do you in?"

Nicky was pursing his lips. "What time do the ceremonies actually begin?" he asked.

"They've already begun—at five," Charlie told him. "The Grammys are broadcast live to the East Coast, then delayed to California so they can begin here at eight."

"Swell," Nicky said. 'Let's get there quick."

"Ah, Nick, I hate to mention this—but how about a little detour to the chief's office? I mean he'd be so impressed to see us in evening clothes, especially since he was so emphatic about wishing to chat with you."

Nicky gave his partner a long stare. "Give me the car keys, Charlie. You don't have to get involved in this."

"Hey, brah! Did I say I'd abandon you? I'm just trying to be reasonable that's all."

They reached their squad car, which was parked in an unloading zone with police I.D. in the window.

"Siren, I presume?"

"Go for it," Nicky told him.

Charlie wove skillfully in and out of traffic, a ballet of high-speed driving, emergency light flashing, using the siren itself only sparingly—the way a great chef might use a pinch of salt. In a few minutes they were out of the airport complex and on the freeway racing downtown. Nicky stared thoughtfully out the window at the amorphous skyline of the city. There was a time yesterday, bobbing up and down on the swells, when he thought he might never see Los Angeles again.

Charlie was saying something he didn't hear.

"What?"

"I said, hell, Nicky—all kidding aside—the great McGroder is deeply pissed at you. He got that narrow squinty-eyed look of his. His mouth got real mean."

They were cruising in the far left lane at ninety-five miles per hour. A Porsche got out of the way a little too slowly, and Charlie had to cut around him.

"Better keep your mind on the driving," Nicky suggested.

"Yeah, well, what I'm saying, Nick, is what the hell—how about me turning off the old red light, slowing down to a nice mellow fifty-five. We can see McGroder, have a good dinner somewhere, maybe find a masquerade ball to go to afterward, so we can say we didn't get dressed up for nothing. I mean, up to now—people are pretty pissed at you, but you have your twenty years of distinguished service, you have a lot of successful cases behind you. So you'll be on the chief's shit list for a while, but what the hell. You'll still have a job. However . . ."

"Charlie—"

"No, let me finish. *However,* if we go to the Shrine Auditorium and cause some sort of fuss at the Grammys, for chrissake—well, that's it. You see that, don't you? Like, brah, you'll never work as a cop again."

"Just drop me off there," Nicky said. "I've already told you—you don't have to be involved in this."

"That's not the point!" Charlie cried. "Listen, you're going to make a lousy civilian. I know Susan's a wonderful lady—I've always thought you guys should get together again. But if you lose your job, Nicky, you're just going to be *Mr.* Merril. Hollywood husband. That woman's going to put you on a leash, good buddy. She's going to turn you into a . . ."

250

"French poodle" Nicky agreed. "Well, what of it? Maybe I'm ready to take it easy."

"Oh, sure! Just look at you: Portrait of a Compulsive Cop. Sitting here clenching your teeth, probably working on an ulcer. Wanting me to drive faster because you have some damn hunch, you don't know what—but *something's* going to happen at the Shrine Auditorium tonight. I mean, who are you trying to kid? You're going to go crazy as a civilian. I'll come visit you in five years and find you've gained twenty pounds and drink vodka all day. That's if you don't eat your gun one morning because you couldn't take the good life anymore."

"Aw, it won't be like that," Nicky told him. "Just shut up and drive, will you."

"There won't be any more beautiful young women for you, Nicky," Charlie told him.

"I've had quite enough beautiful young women."

"You think so?"

Charlie told him with passionate conviction that you could *never* have enough beautiful women, but Nicky tuned him out. "You know what I think?" he said to Charlie. "I think she's going to wait until Bo's up on stage accepting his special achievement award. That's when she's going to pop him. Perfect justice. With fifty million people watching, right there on network TV."

3

The Shrine Auditorium was old and vast and ugly. It was a place that had seen generations of L.A. schoolchildren traipsing through for their one encounter with opera or ballet—a neoclassic building of ponderous proportions.

Unity Sphere stood in the grand main lobby, microphone in hand, a dazzling smile set permanently on her face. She was conscious of being at the height of her powers, as beautiful as she'd ever be, dressed in white to contrast with her Hawaiian tan—a space-age evening gown that wrapped around her body and left one shoulder bare. Men looked at her. Women, too. A rock star she'd interviewed earlier had tried to pick her up on camera. He was up for Best Male Vocalist of the Year. While they had talked, he'd kept trying to peer down the front of her dress. A real gentleman. He'd been convinced

251

he was going to win. He had invited Unity to a small party afterward to help celebrate his impending greatness.

"Maybe," she'd told him demurely.

Right now, she and her small crew were experiencing a moment of confusion. A particularly aggressive publicist was trying to convince them to interview Tiny Tim. The publicist was saying that this was the year Tiny Tim was going to make his big comeback. America wanted to see how Tiny was doing after all this time.

Unity's producer said, "Fuck Tiny Tim. We don't have time for this shit." Instead, he placed a pale young man by her side. The young man had teased hair, a wolfish mouth, and wore more makeup than she. He was the keyboard player for a British group that had broken up but was rumored to be getting back together.

"How are you, darling?" he asked her. There wasn't much heat to his question. He seemed stoned and vaguely bewildered.

The producer—a young man with a worried expression—was consulting with Dan, the cameraman.

"Come here a sec, Unity," he called.

Unity left the British rock star and joined the two men in a huddle.

"Tell her," the producer said.

"I was just saying I think maybe there's something wrong with the camera," Dan told her, his fingers caressing the portable video recorder resting on his shoulder.

Unity's fixed smile disappeared. "What do you mean, *maybe* there's something wrong? Is there or isn't there?"

"I don't know. Everything seems to be working, but . . ."

"But what?"

"It doesn't feel right. It's making a strange sound."

"Christ, Dan! I had them check out all the equipment back at the studio. So let's grab this interview, okay? Or what's-his-face is going to wander off."

Unity rejoined her star, who was a little sullen at having been left alone.

"We going to do this or what, darling?"

"Right now," she told him brightly.

The producer was counting down with the fingers of his right hand. He gave her the signal: They were rolling.

Unity crinkled her nose with intense teenage excitement. She had a private name for her TV personality: Sally Starfucker, teen queen and virgin whore. She had not been doing her show long—less than two weeks—yet America was already falling in love with Sally Starfucker. The letters were pouring in. Bo said it was fabulous. Declarations of love from men of all ages and the adulation of young girls who, like Nicky's Tanya, wished to be just like her.

Well, it would all be over soon. Sally Starfucker went on to ask the right perky questions: Was it true he was about to do a movie with Ringo Starr? What about these rumors of the band getting back together? What were his choices for Best Album? Best Song? And this was a cute one—Best *Female* Vocalist—asked with giggling innuendo, for whatever you do, bring it back to sex so the pubescent hordes will have something to get itchy about.

Unity found she could set Sally in motion, then retreat into her own separate thoughts. Just as she could sit on Bo's lap when she was young, keep one thing going on the surface and something else inside.

She had been worried there a moment, about the camera. Cowboy had assured her the job was perfect, undetectable from the outside, and that all the video equipment still worked as designed.

Cowboy, of course, was a real find. She had learned of his existence from one of her father's old diaries, for Billy had really gotten a kick out of Cowboy and wrote about him often—an AWOL Green Beret, rock and roll soldier, bringing the war back home. Toward the end of his life, Billy became convinced that Cowboy was the one with the right ideas. Rock and roll was not leading to the spiritual revolution he intended. All it was doing was making people like Bo Daniels very rich. Maybe it was best just to blow things up. Better living through dynamite, Billy wrote.

Unity had a luxurious feeling of power standing here now, listening to this pompous, vain, absurdly self-centered English musician explaining his next project—"some serious poetry, you know, about the world condition. And the music is not just rock—more a fusion of classical and jazz, with some Chuck Berry overtones."

Unity pictured the musician splattered in pieces around the inside of the Shrine Auditorium.

Sally Starfucker, however, was breathlessly mentioning how all the members of his ex-band were now married to world-famous fashion models. Was that what it took these days for a poor girl to land such a fine man as himself? she wondered.

"Well, we *do* like the beautiful ladies, don't we?" He tried to leer.

"Do you?" she asked, getting dangerous for just a moment.

Or are you all flaming homosexuals, and perhaps your manager set up your marriages so thirteen-year-old girls would continue to buy your records?

The rock star flirted a little to show his randy masculinity. Unity

253

thanked him and wished him good luck inside tonight. She added he would probably get exactly what he deserved.

The red light went off the front of the camera.

"Listen, I like your look," the musician told her. "Yeah, I like it a lot. Maybe you'd like to be in the new video I'm doing? You see, I have this one scene where I have a whole roomful of beautiful girls trying to keep me away from the one I really love."

"Yourself?" She smiled. He didn't get it.

The rock star waved and disappeared into a crowd of mutual admirers. There was a nervous, semihysterical feeling in the air. People demurred from going to their seats until absolutely necessary —especially since the coast-to-coast broadcast had not yet begun and they were only handing out the awards no one cared about, for classical and jazz. The lobby was full of people kissing and hugging and telling each other how great they looked.

Stevie Wonder had just come in, and Unity's producer was talking to one of his people, trying to steer Stevie his way. Unity had a moment to look into her Gucci bag, pretending to consult her notes.

There it was: an ordinary remote-control device, such as millions of people used to adjust their TVs when they were too lazy to move from their armchairs. Near the remote control, there was a gun. It happened to be Nicky's .38 Smith & Wesson, which she had been able to rescue as the Hobie Cat was about to capsize.

To detonate the explosives, Unity would first have to press the on button, then the button for channel 2. It was as simple as that, and the Grammy Awards this year would be canceled in a big way.

4

Outside the auditorium, great searchlights scanned the twilight skies, pointing to the stars. An armada of limousines disgorged their cargo of beautiful people, while the hordes of unbeautiful people— kept safely behind police barricades—screamed, cheered, pulled their hair, and wept in ecstasy. Like some strange religious cult, Nicky thought. There was riot in the air, and the police seemed a tad nervous as they protected the pagan gods from being torn apart with love.

Nicky and Charlie parked across the street, police I.D. in the window, red light left flashing on the roof. Since they were in evening clothes, people in the crowd gave them the quick once-over.

Were they *somebody?* Nicky almost looked like he might be, un-shaved and strangely dressed.

A girl grabbed him by the arm. She was breathing heavily. "Bruce?" she asked, not quite sure—but desperately wanting to believe he might be. "No, you're not Bruce Willis," she declared angrily.

"Sorry," he told her.

They managed to cross the street with difficulty. The situation in front of the auditorium was deteriorating rapidly. A Rolls-Royce had just let out a very nordic and beautiful young man in a glittering white satin tuxedo. Nicky didn't know his name, although he had seen Tanya staring dreamily at his picture in *Rolling Stone.* The crowd went wild breaking through a weak spot in the police line. A young woman with a wild look in her eye ripped open her blouse, offering her bare breasts to the young man's gaze—while another girl, sobbing, threw herself at his feet, wrapping her body around his leg.

The cops had to beat the girls off with their nightsticks. The beautiful young man smiled vaguely, accepted all this as his due, and he and his date continued inside the auditorium.

"Who *are* these people?" Nicky asked in awe.

"Well, you have to believe in something," Charlie told him.

Nicky found it all very disturbing. The end of the world could not be far away. Charlie showed his detective's shield to a uniformed cop and asked who was in charge. Fortunately, it turned out to be someone they knew, an L.A.P.D. lieutenant named Walter Engler —a middle-aged black man with gray in the hair, who at this moment was clutching a walkie-talkie and looking as if he were about to have a nervous breakdown.

"Rachmaninoff," he said, coming up to them. "Hey, Charlie Cat. What are you guys doing here? I suppose you're fans, huh?"

Nicky explained himself as briefly as possible: "Look, Walt—I have a suspect in a murder case who has a big grudge against someone who's getting an award tonight. I think she's going to attempt something dramatic."

Lieutenant Engler was looking at Nicky's evening clothes. "Jesus, Rachmaninoff, that's quite an outfit you're wearing. Tell me, is it stylish? Myself, I wouldn't know."

"It's called being in a hurry," Nicky said pointedly. "What's the security like inside?"

"The network's taking care of the inside, we're doing the outside. . . . Hey, Nicky, didn't I hear you're on suspension or something?"

"The network has private cops?"

"An army of 'em. The place is tight as a nun. Now answer my question."

"Question?"

"Yeah. Is this some unofficial thing you got going, or what?"

"Charlie's the one here in an official capacity," Nicky said. "As for myself, I've interrupted a short vacation to give my partner the benefit of wise counsel."

Lieutenant Engler looked from Nicky to Charlie and back again.

"You're sure about this? Something's really going to come down here tonight?"

"I'm almost certain," Nicky admitted. "Now tell me, do you have any of your people on the inside?"

"A few, but just as a liaison with the network's security. I guess I'd better get you boys inside there, huh?"

"Please," Nicky asked.

Sometimes being polite paid off. Lieutenant Engler hesitated only briefly, wondering if he were putting his ass on the line, and then he gestured for Nicky and Charlie to come with him. At the entrance to the auditorium, an elderly lady stood collecting tickets, flanked by a squad of security guards in blue blazers, each with walkie-talkie in hand.

"These are policemen," Lieutenant Engler told them. "They're with me."

And so they were in. The nature of Hollywood was very much a matter of those on the outside trying to get inside, just as Nicky and Charlie had done. Nicky felt the difference right away. The enormous main lobby was crowded with splendid clothes and well-formed people. There was high-pitched laughter, animated conversation, people hugging and appreciating each other madly while flash bulbs popped, immortalizing little vignettes for next week's magazines.

Everyone was trying to look as though they *really* belonged here, and no one completely succeeded, with the exception of the security guards.

Lieutenant Engler was talking to one of the blue blazers about getting Nicky to someone named Al Hendricks, an ex-cop who seemed to be in charge of security. The blue blazer got on his walkie-talkie.

"Al, there's a Lieutenant Rachmaninoff here who needs to talk with you. . . . Okay. Right. I'll bring him down."

This was when Nicky saw Unity. His eyes were scanning the lobby, and there she was—standing near the water fountain, microphone in hand, in the bright wash of portable lights.

She looked older than when he had last seen her. Maybe it was the makeup or the expensively revealing evening gown. Tonight she could definitely pass for an adult. In a room full of many beautiful women, Unity Sphere stood out, the most beautiful one of all. Nicky overheard someone asking who she was. Many eyes, scanning the room for celebrities, came to her and stopped. She seemed to know it, too. There was confidence in the way she was standing there, a complete self-assuredness.

Almost as if this night were for her alone.

5

"I'm glad you're a strong swimmer," she said.

"Me too."

Nicky had cut across the lobby to where Unity was standing. She was waiting for Stevie Wonder to finish a quickie interview with *People* magazine so she could get her hands on him.

"I bet you're awfully mad at me," she said with a pretty little pout.

"*Mad?* Hell, what's a little attempted murder between friends?"

"Almost lovers," she reminded him. "I'm sorry, Nicholas. By the way, I like your tux. And that salty unshaved look? Mmm, so masculine."

He took her arm. "Look, whatever it is you're planning tonight—I'm here to tell you, don't do it."

"Whatever do you mean?" She blinked innocently.

"It's the moment Bo accepts the award, isn't it? That's when you're going to do something."

He got a reaction out of this, but only briefly. She covered herself fast with her coy-cute look.

"I'm deeply dismayed, Lieutenant, by your insidious insinuations."

"Cut the crap," he told her. "We're way past pretending and fancy language. I tell you what—you hate these people, don't you? You hate this whole scene? Okay, well, so do I. So what you should do right now is shout '*Fuck you!*' As loud as you can. Tell everyone in this room what you think of them, and then we can find Bo and you can tell him, too. And then, hell, I'll take you out to dinner and we'll have a good laugh about it."

"Shout *'Fuck you!'* and walk away? Goodness, is that what a mature person would do?"

"Exactly."

"Oh, Nicholas, I *do* like you. I wish I had met you at another time of my life."

"Unity, you're seventeen years old. You have lots and lots of time."

She shook her head. "No . . . no more time. So do yourself a favor —go home, Nicholas. You don't belong here. You have a lovely daughter who needs you, and as for me . . . well, I have my destiny."

Nicky never liked it when people started talking about their destiny. A young man with little hair and an irritating voice came up to them.

"Okay, darling. Stevie's on his way." The man gave Nicky a furious look. "Come on, we're working here. We're doing a TV show —can't you see? Who is this guy?" he asked, turning back to the girl.

"He's a friend," Unity said, "but he's leaving. Bye, Nicholas. The show must go on."

The young man led Unity to where Stevie Wonder was advancing, brilliantly arrayed in African robes, his long black hair braided with jewelry, smiling to his own inner groove. Unity took his hand and his smile deepened.

Nicky was suddenly surrounded by Lieutenant Engler, Charlie, and two blue blazers.

"Jesus, Rachmaninoff—I turn around and you're not there. The head of security is waiting to see you."

Nicky was rerunning the girl's words. *No time left. Go home, Nicholas. You don't belong here.*

And worse: *I have my destiny.*

Yes, it worried him a lot.

"Hey, Earth calling Lieutenant Rachmaninoff!" Walter Engler was waving a hand in front of Nicky's eyes. "Is anyone there, buddy?"

"What?"

"Jesus, Nick. Come on, I gotta take you to Al."

Nicky turned to Charlie before he left.

"Stay right here with the girl," he ordered. "Whatever you do, don't let her out of your sight."

6

A blue blazer led the way: an elevator ride down to a subterranean level, along a maze of bare, brightly lit corridors, and at last through a door marked SECURITY into a large, windowless room.

Al Hendricks, head of security, was sitting behind a large desk, facing a wall of television monitors that showed him what was happening in his empire. There were half-eaten sandwiches on the desk, a full ashtray, several telephones, and papers scattered at random among the debris. Al was as disheveled as his desk, a great bulldog with a wide face, loosened tie, shirttails sticking out, unruly gray hair. A retired cop, Nicky had been told.

Al greeted the two lieutenants without getting up, told them to sit down, and turned his shrewd eyes on Nicky.

"Rachmaninoff, huh? Your father was Sam Rachmaninoff, I bet."

Nicky was surprised. When he first joined the force, people mentioned his father a lot—because his father had been popular. But by now, people who had known his father were a dying breed.

"Yeah, I knew your dad," the security man told him, leaning back in his swivel chair. "Back when I was on the robbery squad in North Hollywood. Good man. A tough old guy, but he had a big heart. They don't make cops like that anymore."

"No, they certainly don't," Nicky admitted, thinking this was both a good thing and a bad thing.

"Yeah, I've heard about you," Al said, shaking a finger at him in an accusatory way. "They say you're a real hot-shot homicide dick, but kinda flaky. They say you're not as solid as your old man."

Nicky shrugged, as though this didn't bother him. "No one's as solid as my old man. I do my best."

Al Hendricks was scowling at his appearance. He didn't have to say it: Nicky knew—Sgt. Sam Rachmaninoff would never have been on duty unshaved in an undersized tuxedo.

"So what do you have to tell me, Rachmaninoff?" Al asked grumpily. "Right now, I got a majority of the nuts and kooks and drug addicts in the English-speaking world right here under my roof. I need another problem like I need higher taxes."

Nicky laid it out, as simply as he could, but in more detail than he had to Lieutenant Engler: how there was once a rock star who

259

died young, who had a daughter who wished to destroy the world that destroyed her father. Nicky described how this daughter was doing pretty well in the revenge department, indirectly responsible for quite a few murders, yet untouchable from a legal point of view. And last, he spoke of how this pretty daughter was here tonight doing interviews for The Rock Channel, but with something a touch more dramatic in mind.

Al Hendricks was a practical man, not given to flights of fancy. He listened to Nicky's story with obvious skepticism.

"So what are you saying, Rachmaninoff? The girl is going to start shooting up the place or something?"

"Or something," Nicky said. "I wish I knew exactly. But tonight is an opportunity she's been waiting a whole lifetime for. The man she believes responsible for her father's death is going to be honored with a special award. Everything she hates is gathered together in one spot. She even has most of America watching. I can't believe she'll pass up this chance."

Al Hendricks sighed. "I don't know. When I was a cop, we didn't have all this psychological crap to worry about. What do you think Walt?" he asked the other man. "Do we have a problem here or not?"

Lieutenant Engler had been sitting quietly, hands folded in lap. "Maybe, maybe not. I have to say this—I'm sorry, Rachmaninoff —but the lieutenant's own people don't buy this. He's been taken off this investigation, and he shouldn't really be here at all. On the other hand, Rachmaninoff has a record which demands some respect. I don't think we can completely write him off."

Al was staring at the TV monitors on the wall. In the auditorium the televised part of the ceremonies was already under way. Frank Sinatra was on stage telling some humorous anecdotes about how the Grammys came to be.

"Jesus, if anything *did* happen here . . . " Al began. He was not a man to finish sentences, though he made his meaning clear. "Okay, Rachmaninoff, what do you want to do?"

Nicky leaned forward. "Stop the Grammys," he said. "Evacuate the building."

Al gave him a stony look. "Next suggestion," he snapped.

"Okay. Get rid of Unity Sphere. Tell her she can't do her interviews. Make certain she's out of this building until after the ceremonies are completely over."

Al crinkled his forehead in deep thought. Not taking his eyes off

Nicky, he picked up one of his several telephones and pressed a button.

"I need to speak with Pierre. This is Al Hendricks." There was a slight pause. "Pierre? We have a possible security problem. There's a girl named Unity Sphere who has clearance to go around with two hand-held cameras doing some stuff for The Rock Channel. I'd like to get rid of her and her crew."

Nicky could hear the explosion of angry words coming through the receiver. Al had to move the phone away from his ear.

"Yeah," he said, "okay . . . yeah, I understand. I *know* you're busy. Sorry to bother you."

He put the phone down.

"No deal, Rachmaninoff. The Rock Channel's paid nearly a quarter of a million bucks for the rights to have a crew here. They got a valid contract, the works. That was the producer you just heard, having a cow at the thought of the lawsuit that would ensue if we interfere with them in any way. Next suggestion?"

"Well, I guess we stay close and watch—shadow her every move. Pray we can stop her if she tries to pull anything."

The security chief smiled. "Yeah," he said. "Congratulations, Rachmaninoff. I think you've just created yourself a job."

7

Unity was in the left aisle, halfway between the stage and the lobby: Paul, her producer, was with the second camera two aisles over. They were in touch by walkie-talkie. There was still perhaps an hour to go, but she wanted Paul not far from what would be his final position.

Getting the explosives properly positioned, Cowboy had said, would determine the success of the operation. There were five devices in all, three of them already in place—two apparently empty battery cases toward the rear of the auditorium, one by the left exit, one near the right, as well as a silver equipment box on the stage itself, which looked as if it might contain patch cords or lenses. With all the network TV equipment—cables and boxes, cameras and lights—Unity doubted if her own things would cause much notice.

The two remaining bombs were the cameras themselves. At the climactic moment, she would be closer to the stage. Cowboy had assured her that this configuration would achieve a maximum degree of destruction. The auditorium itself would survive, but not many of the human beings either on stage or sitting in the celebrity seats orchestra level. Blood was going to flow.

Hers too. Unity was celebrating her final hour. The remote control in her Gucci bag would function from half a city block away, so she had a choice in this matter. By why live after you've accomplished your life's goal? She was not afraid to die young, follow in her father's footsteps. Life should be an intense, brief flash to be remembered. Not a long slow decline into oblivion.

Look at Bob Dylan—he was here tonight, still putting out music to a dwindling audience, but with no real influence, not like in the sixties. All anticlimax, after the magic was gone.

Now if he had died young—like Billy, like Janis and Jimi—his work would have remained pure, undiluted by the years. John Lennon would have a place in history forever, but Paul McCartney would not. So Unity decided to go for the greatness. She'd made her final decision sailing the catamaran home after leaving Nicky to drown. Better to be pure, and go out like a Lion. Anyway, to survive the cleansing flash of fire she was going to provide tonight would make the event somehow shabby.

With the decision made and the end approaching, Unity felt an immense calm. She continued to make her Rock Channel special that no one would ever see. Right now she had her camera trained on Michael Jackson, who was with an actress twice his age. Poor Michael. He was looking intensely uncomfortable behind his wall of dark glasses, perspiring a little in the ridiculous outfit he wore—a white jacket with gold epaulettes, in which he might lead the band at Disneyland or start a right-wing coup in Argentina.

Watching him very closely, she saw his lower lip tremble. The actress by his side patted his hand reassuringly. The contact, without warning, made him jump.

Yes, another victim of rock and roll: picked up by a wave, held high for just an instant—then dashed against the rocks.

Peace, Michael. Soon we'll all be free.

8

"What time does Bo Daniels get his award?"

"I'll check," said an assistant director, punching the request into a computer.

Nicky was backstage, standing in a control booth that was the size of a long trailer. Color monitors showed what each camera was seeing—at this moment, various angles of John Denver—while other, larger monitors showed how these angles edited together into their final release to the world at large—the ongoing live presentation of the Grammy Awards.

The atmosphere in this narrow room was like being in the cockpit of a jumbo jet that was preparing to crash. A host of anxious technicians, shirtsleeves rolled up, headphones in place, were fussing over the monitors and issuing terse commands to the cameramen on stage. Nicky suspected this part of the population was especially prone to nervous breakdown, suicide, and divorce.

He had walked in wearing a gold security pass on his lapel, accompanied by his own personally assigned blue blazer, a young man named Daryl. No one looked very happy to see him. They seemed to have a basic misunderstanding that what they were doing was more important than what he was doing. They were wrong, of course, but that was show biz.

Nicky persevered. The gold security pass he was wearing was ultimate authority. He could go inspect the women's restrooms, if that's what he wanted, and he certainly wasn't going to be bad-vibed out of this control booth just so these technocrats could concentrate better on showing John Denver's best side to the world.

Eventually an overtaxed assistant director thought it would be more expedient to deal with this unwanted interruption than resist the inevitable. Perhaps he sensed Nicky's determination was greater than his own.

"Here it is," he said. "The Daniels award. Between seven thirty-five and seven forty, immediately following video cue twenty-three A—that's a ninety-second prerecorded history of the Perceptions. We have a five-minute leeway at this point of the show. More than that and we're in damn big trouble!"

The assistant director was breathing hard. He was a fairly young

263

man—late twenties, early thirties—but there was a look about him that suggested if *one* more person asked *one* more thing of him, he might go stark raving mad.

Nicky had a feeling he was going to be that person.

"Could I see this ninety-second video on the Perceptions?"

The young man became incoherent. "Could you . . . take it out of sequence . . . how do you expect . . . rewind the whole fucking thing . . . *are you mad?*"

"Calm yourself, please," Nicky said soothingly. "Tell me this, have *you* seen the video?"

The assistant director nodded, taking several deep breaths.

"Can you describe the contents? Perhaps this will save me from actually having you run it for me."

"Yes," he said, latching on to this thought but unable for the moment to go any further.

"Well?"

"Well, it's sort of a brief history, focusing mostly on the lead singer —what was his name?"

"Billy Lion."

"Yes, that's right. Mostly short clips from concerts and old interviews."

"I see. I appreciate this a lot, by the way," Nicky told the young man. "Can you tell me, is there anything . . . peculiar about this video? That's right. Take a few deep breaths if you need them."

"In my opinion?"

"Yes, that's all I'm asking—your opinion."

"Well, it *did* seem peculiar, actually. The one guy, Billy Lion, comes through like he's some kind of saint. Of course, adulation's the big thing around here, but this video, well—it almost seemed too much."

"I see," Nicky said. And he did see, too. "Anything else about the video strike you as strange?"

"Yeah, now that you mention it. Billy Lion's just about wearing a halo in the thing. But the others—the rest of the band, especially Bo Daniels—come off a bit like they betrayed this great visionary. Sold him out for gold. It was just a few subtle negative remarks, you know—but frankly I thought it was a damn peculiar point of view for the Grammys. Especially since Bo Daniels is the one accepting the award."

"Thanks. You've been a big help."

"That's it? That *all* you want?"

The assistant gratefully turned his back on Nicky just in time to join his colleagues in cuing the eagerly awaited, brand-new Pepsi-Cola commercial, shown for the first time tonight.

Nicky looked at the clock on the wall to make certain he had the right time. It was five fifty-nine on the West Coast, eight fifty-nine in New York—nearly one hour into the show.

Nicky was almost certain he now had the *when*. Whatever Unity was planning, she would wait until after America had a chance to see her ninety-second piece of propaganda. Immediately after the special video, the two remaining Perceptions—Rick and Donny—would walk up on stage with Bo Daniels. Nicky was willing to gamble this was the time Unity would seek her big moment.

This gave him from thirty-five to forty minutes to figure out what she was planning and how he was going to stop her

9

Charlie was standing near the top of the aisle, trying to find a compromise where he could keep an eye on Unity and yet also stay out of the way of the ongoing show. It wasn't easy. He had already nearly been run down by Barbra Streisand as she swept down the aisle, summoned to accept an award.

A platoon of angry blue blazers had descended on him and demanded he return to his seat. Charlie showed his police I.D., narrowed his eyes in his most menacing way, and told them to bug off. He suggested that anyone interfering with an officer in the performance of his duties might very well be sent to prison to be sodomized by brutal convicts and beaten by guards with rubber truncheons. The blue blazers backed off a little. But they were keeping an eye on him.

Charlie was relieved when Nicky returned. The Grammys were an event where a simple policeman needed the support of his colleagues—even if only one of them was impeccably dressed.

Nicky pinned a gold security pass on Charlie's lapel and introduced him to Daryl, their personal blue blazer. Daryl was very young and sleepy-looking, probably a good indication that Al Hendricks did not take Nicky's mission too seriously.

"What's the girl up to?" he asked.

"Just going up and down the aisle with her cameraman, getting impromptu shots of celebrities. Occasionally interviewing someone. Like right now. See—she's talking with one of the Beastie Boys."

"The *who?*"

"No, the Beastie Boys, Nicky. You're about a decade behind the times, aren't you?"

"You keep up with all this, I suppose?"

"Hey, to stay young, you gotta remain in fashion," Charlie said.

Nicky gave an old man's sigh. On stage right now, fifty dancers were going through ecstatic motions as the orchestra played a symphonic medley of old McCartney-Lennon tunes. At the climactic moment of a rousing version of "I Want to Hold Your Hand," Paul McCartney himself in white tails and top hat emerged through the line of dancers to thunderous applause. Las Vegas never put on a show half so grand as this.

The entire audience was moved to stand up and cheer for Paul McCartney. Here was reputedly the richest rock star ever.

Nicky looked back down the aisle toward Unity. She was moving away from the Beastie Boys, pointing to her cameraman to show him something she wanted to capture. Nicky was curious what had attracted Unity's eye. He walked partway down the aisle to see what she was up to.

Ah, clever girl! She had found Yoko Ono in the crowd, looking not as ecstatic about Paul McCartney as the others around her. Yoko Ono apparently was unaware she was on the wrong end of a TV camera. Her scowl deepened as Unity continued to nail her with the lens.

The girl certainly had a knack for locating dissension, isolating it, and using it to her advantage. She held Yoko Ono in her predatory gaze, then touched the cameraman's arm to break away, when the ecstatic furor greeting Paul McCartney died off—probably within the proscribed time limits allowed for it.

Unity picked up her Gucci bag and continued down the aisle closer to the stage. Nicky had noticed how she kept the Gucci bag very close to her. It was beginning to make him wonder.

Charlie came up behind him. "Look, Nicky—Daryl says you can't just stand here in the middle of the aisle. We've got to move back toward the exit."

"He says that, does he?" Nicky made no motion to retreat. "What would you like to bet sweet Unity has a gun in that Gucci bag of hers?"

Charlie was getting nervous. "I don't know, Nicky—and there's no way we're going to find out, not here on live TV."

"No? If she's carrying a concealed weapon, we could throw her pretty ass in jail."

"Yes, but you can't just go down there and search her, my friend. Please, you have to have a little respect for the occasion. Can you imagine the fuss you'd cause, particularly if she *didn't* have a gun in there?"

"Hmm, but we can't let her commit violent murder, either. Can we?"

"Come on, Nicky. Let's move back toward the exit."

Nicky looked at his watch. Less than fifteen minutes to go. He was beginning to come up with a tentative plan. He allowed Charlie to lead him back toward the top of the aisle. No sense in blowing it by acting too soon.

10

Whitney Houston was being called up to the stage for the third time. She had a cute "What? Not again!" look on her face as she basked in her glory. The crowd cheered, applauded like crazy, and rose again to their feet.

Billy Lion would probably not have been happy here tonight. His daughter, meanwhile, was busy examining the event with her small crew and two cameras. Nicky watched how she used her walkie-talkie to position the camera in the far aisle. She seemed to be after the more intimate details of audience reaction. Anyone scratching or looking less than glamorous had better beware. Nicky noticed that Unity was focusing on the losers rather than the winners.

Whatever she was up to, she was going about her business with calm, professional self-assurance. She certainly did not look like someone about to commit a heinous crime. At one point she looked up to see Nicky at the top of the aisle. She smiled sweetly and waved. It bothered him she was not more upset by his close proximity. Was she so certain of herself that his presence was not a worry? Or was he all wrong? Maybe this would be a night like all the others, just the usual Hollywood orgy.

Daryl, his personal blue blazer, had been gone for a few minutes. He reappeared with a copy of the timetable Nicky had requested.

At 7:30, he saw, there would be a two-minute break for local stations to identify themselves.

Seven thirty-two would find Bruce Springsteen on stage. Mr.

267

Springsteen had precisely thirty seconds to fix Billy Lion and the Perceptions' place in the history of rock and roll.

At 7:32:30 came video cue 23A, the ninety-second spot Unity had put together about her father and his merry band.

Then 7:34, return live to Springsteen on stage. The Boss had a few seconds to introduce the survivors—Rick Elsmore, Donny Meredith, and—the mastermind behind the scenes—the great Bo Daniels.

The network cameras would then reach into the audience, where these gentlemen would be rising from their seats in the eighth row, preparing to come on stage.

And then . . . what? Pretty Unity pulls a pistol out of her Gucci bag and commences to fire? Nicky was not going to give her the chance. It was a good thing Susan had plenty of money to support him, because after tonight there wasn't going to be a police department in the country that would give him a job. His plan, such as it was, was absurdly simple.

While cue 23A was playing on the large monitor above the stage, Nicky would sneak down the aisle and steal the girl's Gucci bag.

That was it. Nothing fancy, but if the girl didn't have a weapon, there was not much damage she could do. If she put up a struggle, he was prepared to simply wrestle her to the ground and hold on to her until Bo and company had accepted their awards, expressed their heartfelt gratitude to the academy, and sat down again. At the end of it, Nicky Rachmaninoff would conceivably not be the most popular human being in the Shrine Auditorium, but bloodshed, at least, would not mar this splendid event.

It was coming up fast. Given more time, perhaps Nicky would have come up with something more artistically subtle. But time was what he did not have.

The seven-thirty station break had just begun.

II

Unity looked up the aisle one minute into the station break. This time she did appear slightly anxious that Nicky was so close. He flashed her his most harmless smile. She smiled back, but Nicky could sense the strain.

On the large monitor above the stage, a young woman in a leotard was discussing her new freedom to ignore her menstrual flow. This was followed by a commercial for a catsup that came out of the bottle slowly—which seemed an unfortunate juxtaposition of sponsors.

Harmless Nicky Rachmaninoff began to saunter down the aisle. Just a friendly sort of person, enjoying the Grammys, maybe taking advantage of the commercial break to say hello.

Thirty feet . . . twenty-five . . . twenty . . . fifteen . . .

Unity was speaking on her walkie-talkie to the second camera the next aisle over, apparently telling him to move closer to the stage. She glanced up to see Nicky approaching, and now there was definite alarm in her eyes. She ended the conversation with the second camera and put the walkie-talkie into the Gucci bag, clutching the bag—Nicky thought—a bit too tightly.

"Hi," he said, advancing slowly. He had a cat once that advanced upon little birds just like this.

"This is really a hell of a show," he told her. "So many rich and talented people gathered together in one spot. I must say, I'm tremendously impressed."

"I'm working now, Nicholas," she said. "I really can't talk."

"Well, how about dinner afterward? Maybe a little Chinese food to go?"

"You're on," she said, barely listening. "After the show."

They both looked up simultaneously to the monitor. The catsup commercial was over, and the screen was filled with the face of a local newscaster telling everyone to stay tuned immediately following the Grammys to the late newscast. Nicky sincerely hoped the man would not have anything too special to report.

"Go away, Nicholas," Unity hissed at him.

He pretended he hadn't heard. He was just a few feet away, nearly close enough to make his lunge. The violet eyes were blazing at him.

He should have moved faster. Unity did an unexpected thing. She left her cameraman and skipped away from Nicky's reach down the aisle, up the ramp to the stage, past a security guard, and into the backstage area.

Nicky bounded after her, but she had taken him by surprise. He still might have caught her, except for a little bad luck. Rod Stewart had been chatting with a friend and was returning to his own seat across the aisle just as Nicky came bounding down.

Nicky cut right, thinking the rock star was going left. Mr. Stewart, sensing the imminent collision, simply froze. Probably he didn't believe this was really happening to him: run down at the Grammys.

They met breast to breast with a thud.

"Idiot!" he swore. Rod wasn't used to being treated like this. Not for a long time.

Nicky danced with him a moment, trying to get past. In despair, he finally flung the rock star out of the aisle and into the nearest seat —which, unfortunately, was already occupied by Janet Jackson. This little fiasco was beginning to garner some attention.

Nicky kept going, down the aisle and up the ramp. He had a final glimpse of Unity disappearing behind a black velour screen, still clutching her Gucci bag. He was stopped again as soon as he was up on stage by two burly blue blazers who looked a lot less sleepy than his own Daryl. They stared at his all-purpose gold security pass as though there had to be a mistake.

"Can't let you through here now," one told him. "We're on the air live in twelve seconds."

"Police emergency," he said. Then added, "I'll stay out of the way. Promise."

They wanted to stop him but were confused by his security clearance and his insistence he knew what he was doing. Nicky ran up the stage in front of the bewildered TV crew—past Bruce Springsteen, who smiled wanly as if he had seen it all before—and came to the black velour screening where Unity had disappeared. He could not see where she had gone. The backstage area was enormous, as vast as an airplane hangar with curtains and scenery on ropes and pulleys high above.

Behind him, he heard applause as the ceremonies started up again. Bruce was talking about what a big influence the Perceptions had been on him and all the musicians who followed.

Nicky decided it was time to take out his gun—Charlie's .45—as he gazed about for signs of the girl. He was in the dark netherworld of flats and curtains masking the side of the stage. There were hundreds of places to hide. Farther off stage, he could see a platoon of blue blazers coming his way with grim and determined faces. They looked as if they might take his gold security pass away. However, they stopped abruptly when they noticed Nicky was holding a gun and conferred frantically on their walkie-talkies.

Time was running out fast. Nicky tried to empty his mind as he turned slowly in place: looking, seeking, listening. Springsteen's introduction was finished, and he heard now the familiar opening riffs

270

of "Streets of Love," the Perceptions' biggest hit. This meant he had ninety seconds left until the video was finished and Bo, Rick, and Donny came up on stage.

It also meant Unity couldn't be very far away. Whatever she was planning, she would need to be close to center stage ninety seconds from now.

He could not actually see the video from where he stood at the side of the stage, though he could hear its progress. At this point, Billy Lion was chanting improvised lyrics from some long-ago concert. The tune was "L.A. Lovers," one of his later hits, but now transformed with new words he seemed to be making up on the spot. The lyrics were vintage Billy Lion—insidious, snakelike, reaching into the dark spaces of the human soul.

Nicky walked back slowly toward the audience, keeping just out of the sight line. Then he saw it: a shape concealed in a black curtain. The shape moved and was still.

Nicky's thumb quietly let off the safety catch of the .45. He crept forward, took hold of the curtain with one hand—took a deep breath —then ripped the curtain back, gun pointed, ready to blast.

There was a gasp and a little cry. Nicky was fairly startled, too. Instead of Unity Sphere, he had uncovered the Grammys' principal host this year—a very famous man—and a girl, a dancer judging from her costume, who was kneeling in front of the famous man's open zipper. Nicky had the .45 held to the famous man's forehead, and they all stood in a frozen tableau, speechless.

"Ooops," Nicky said, letting the curtain fall back in place.

He wasn't making many friends tonight. He heard footsteps and turned to see Al Hendricks, head of security, marching toward him from the wings with a blue blazer on either side. Ahead, a few feet away, Bruce Springsteen was leaning against a wall, waiting for the video to end.

Nicky made some instant calculations.

If he were wrong, he certainly would be making an ass of himself. But that was the way it was sometimes. A true cop warrior shouldn't worry about such things as looking silly.

When you felt in your gut that something terrible was going to happen, you had to try to stop it, didn't you?

It was a matter of priorities. The Grammys were all right, he supposed. No real harm in people handing out tons of awards to all their friends and business associates. But lives were at stake. Maybe.

Nicky decided it was time to stop the show.

12

Back at Sunshine Terrace, Tanya was still extremely depressed she wasn't at the Grammys. Thank God she was going to the Academy Awards next month, which would restore some lost status—though, face it, the Oscars weren't nearly as rad as the Grammys.

Sullenly, Tanya tried to soothe herself by eating Godiva chocolates and watching rock videos with the volume full blast. Some days, though, life's a real bitch. Her mother came in from the kitchen, took the chocolates away, and changed the dial from The Rock Channel to the local news.

To add insult to injury, the local newscaster was announcing a few Grammy winners from the ceremonies now in progress—though the show itself would not be aired in Los Angeles until eight their time. Tanya heard who got Best Pop Vocal (Male) before she had the presence of mind to cover her ears and loudly recite the Shakespeare sonnet she had had to memorize last week for English.

All these circumstances combined to make Tanya say something really bitchy to her mother:

"So, Mom, how long are you going to be staying here, anyway?"

Susan was cutting the ends off string beans on the cutting board in the kitchen. She put down her knife and looked at her daughter with hurt eyes.

"I thought you liked me and Nicky and you all together again."

"I *do*, Mom. Christ!"

Tanya was regretting her bitchy remark. Especially since her mom was coming into the living room now with the obvious intention of having a Talk.

"Then what is it? You think I don't belong here? Maybe you want to have your father all to yourself?"

"Jesus, Mom, it's *none* of those things. I was just asking, that's all. Just a simple question."

Susan had brought a glass of wine with her from the kitchen. She sat on the couch and looked at her daughter thoughtfully. Tanya hated to have her mother study her like this.

"It's just I don't picture you here, that's all," Tanya said. "I mean, your bedrom in Bel Air is bigger than this whole house. Your fur coats alone wouldn't fit into this living room."

"Aren't you exaggerating a little, dear?"

Tanya was pouting too hard to answer.

"Look, darling, I spent a lot of my life being poor. There were years we could hardly afford to go to Europe on vacation."

"That's tough," Tanya said. Her mother missed the sarcasm.

"Ah, but it was wonderful, too. I lived in this house for eight years, you know—until you were two. We didn't have a maid or a fancy car, we couldn't afford to go out to the chic places—but your father and I loved each other, and there was a time when we were very happy."

There was a somewhat misty look in her mother's eyes. Tanya always found it fascinating when Susan spoke of the past.

"So coming back here now . . . well, the house *is* too small. And the bathroom—we won't even go into *that*. But for me, dear, this is like coming full circle back to my roots. When you're my age, Tanya, you'll understand what I mean. Maybe you'll live in Paris or London—wherever. Someday you'll come back to Bel Air, or up here on Sunshine Terrace—you'll wander through your memories, and you'll try to figure out your life."

Tanya had trouble picturing herself grown up. She was convinced she was going to die young, so this idea of coming back to her roots was very foreign to her.

Susan gave her a hug and went back into the kitchen to finish dinner. Tanya watched a game show on TV, but her mind wasn't really on it. There were big changes in the wind and many things to think about.

She was so absorbed in her thoughts that she didn't notice when the game show was interrupted for a special news brief—not until she heard the name Nicholas Rachmaninoff coming from the TV.

"Ah . . . Mom?"

"Yes, sweetheart?"

"I think you'd better come here and take a look at this."

13

Bruce turned out to be a pretty reasonable guy. He took one look at the two days' growth on Nicky's face, as well as the .45 in his left hand—and he cheerfully agreed to everything Nicky asked of him. When the lights went up on stage after the video clip was over, it was Lieutenant Nicholas Rachmaninoff who stood before the gathered luminaries of the music industry, not Bruce Springsteen, as they had expected. He had reholstered Charlie's gun at the last moment so he wouldn't frighten anyone.

"Ladies and gentlemen, I am Lieutenant Rachmaninoff of the Beverly Hills Police Department. We have received a threat that a bomb will be set off in the Shrine Auditorium tonight," he said boldly—simply the first thing that came to mind. "Although there is every reason to suppose this is only a hoax, we would appreciate your cooperation in immediately evacuating the building. Please proceed in an orderly fashion to the nearest exit and continue to the street. The award presentation will continue as soon as the bomb squad has ascertained the building is safe."

The effect of his words was an instantaneous human traffic jam in every aisle, those in back blocking the progress of those in front. There was shouting and pushing and clamoring to get through.

"Please do not panic. This is the police. Proceed in an orderly fashion to the nearest exit. Thank you."

Nicky stepped away from the microphone just as Al Hendricks, chief of security, took his arm. Al was very red in the face. His eyes were popping out of his head. A blood vessel along his forehead pulsed furiously.

"Damn you, Rachmaninoff! Damn you, damn you, *damn you!*"

"Al, I *am* sorry. But I had to do it, you know."

"Get this man off the stage!" the outraged security chief screamed to his blue blazers. Nicky opened his jacket to reveal the .45—not that anyone could miss the bulge in his undersized tuxedo.

"Remember, I'm a police officer," he warned them. "Anyone who touches me goes to jail for a long time."

This stopped the blue blazers cold. They might be security men, but they were not cops. Nicky had a feeling the cops would be showing up soon enough. He had managed to stop the show, but he had still not stopped the clock.

Where was Unity?

If she were going to do something, this would be her last chance.

Nicky had a glimpse of Charlie and Lieutenant Engler trying to make their way down the aisle toward the stage against the crowd moving in the other direction. Al Hendricks was trying to address the audience, but someone had turned off the microphone, apparently deciding cops and security people didn't tell very funny jokes.

"There is no bomb," Al was shouting. "Please return to your seats. I repeat, the bomb scare is a hoax. Please, everybody . . . "

Only the first dozen rows heard him, and to have a red-faced man no one recognized shouting at them only made matters worse. The mood of the well-dressed crowd hovered just on the safe side of blind panic.

Nicky tried to forget all the distractions. He turned slowly in place, looking for Unity Sphere.

He saw her almost immediately. Unity was standing in the wings just off stage left. She looked like an apparition in her white dress against the black masking material behind her. An avenging angel, holding a gun in one hand and a small plastic box in the other.

She was looking at Nicky, a strange, piercing look.

Nicky heard a commotion behind him. Bo Daniels had managed to get up on the stage.

"What the fuck's going on?" Bo shouted. The poor man seemed to want his Grammy. He couldn't understand how his moment of glory had arrived and not materialized. He saw Unity in the wing and walked toward her.

"Unity, what the fuck's going on? Tell me, babe!"

There was an unpleasant whine in his voice. Bo was used to getting what he wanted.

Nicky could have warned him that his arrival at just this moment was not wise. Unity began firing her gun, sending everyone on stage for cover. Nicky rolled to the left and came up behind a statue of Venus that seemed to be part of the next set. He pulled out his .45 and got a good aim on Unity. Bo was down on the floor, and the girl kept firing into his body, which jumped spasmodically each time a bullet hit him. Nicky had the girl lined up, but he just couldn't pull the trigger.

Unity fired six shots into the late Bo Daniels. When the gun was empty, she threw it with great force against the corpse. It was a fairly convincing statement for the way she felt about the man.

Nicky stood up and walked toward her. Charlie and Lieutenant Engler were on the stage now as well, guns drawn, approaching Unity very cautiously. She still might have some weapons left.

She did.

She held the plastic box in front of her. It appeared to be a remote television control.

"Don't come any closer!" she screamed. "I have five bombs planted in the auditorium. I'm going to blow you all to hell!"

Her voice was very shrill, not the pretty little lisp she had when she announced videos on The Rock Channel. Nicky, a dozen feet away, could see the whites of her eyes.

Charlie and Lieutenant Engler stopped their forward progress, looking to Nicky for advice. In the auditorium itself, the gunfire had sent everybody to the ground or hiding behind their seats. Nicky could see many guns drawn. Apparently it was quite fashionable to carry a pistol to award shows.

"It's okay," Nicky told Charlie and the lieutenant. "Unity's my friend. I'll just have a little chat with her."

He moved closer, two cautious steps, his gun pointed to her breast. She looked at him with fascination, as though seeing him for the first time.

"Well, well, sweet Unity—you got your revenge at last. Bo's dead. You did it, kid. Now you can put that little box down and come with me. I'll make sure you're treated well."

"Don't come any closer, Nicholas. Or I'll blow up the whole damn building."

Nicky stopped. "Where'd a cute girl like you learn about explosives, anyway?"

"A friend of my father helped me," she said proudly. "The revolution's still alive. I told you to go home, Nicholas. You should have listened to me."

"Look, Unity," he said. "Why don't you just sort of stop all this. There's going to be a SWAT team arriving any moment. Snipers and horrible people like that. They're going to kill you, darling, if you don't let me help you. You'll never get out of here alive."

"I don't intend to," she said radiantly. She had the mystical look of someone closing in on destiny. Nicky didn't like it at all.

He managed to move a few steps closer as he talked.

"Unity, I wish I could tell you all the things in my heart. I believed we were friends, you know. The thing is—you're so young. You have so much ahead of you. A lot more handsome devils to kiss on the beach in the moonlight."

She shook her head.

"Oh, Unity, such a child! Yes, the world *is* horrible, corrupt, and very nasty. But there are private pleasures. Laughter, friendships, children. Even lovers. All sorts of small joys that get better with the years."

Nicky had managed to get gradually closer, until he was only a few feet away. A great part of his attention was on the small electronic box she held in front of her, her thumb resting on a button.

"So what do you say?"

"Bullshit," she told him.

And he thought he'd been rather convincing.

He saw her thumb press downward on the button. Nicky fired simultaneously, the .45 making a deafening explosion, nearly as loud as a bomb.

Unity dropped the electronic box, a look of great surprise on her face. The force of the bullet drove her backward against the wall. She slid downward in slow motion, clutching her stomach until she lay on her back on the stage floor. A small amount of blood trickled from the corner of her mouth.

She was still alive. Her right hand was searching blindly for the electronic box, a few inches away. Nicky rushed to her side and took her wandering hand in his own. He cradled her head in his arms.

"She's going to be okay," Nicky said. "Get an ambulance fast."

Charlie seemed skeptical, but he went to do as he was told.

The girl was breathing shallowly, looking up at him with stunned eyes.

"This is such a waste," he told her. "Such a fucking waste."

She was trying to speak. Nicky had to put his ear close to her lips to hear her.

"It's a two-part command . . . press channel two. Do it, Nicholas. The bombs can still go off."

"Shh," he told her. "Enough talk of killing and dying. Just hold on, Unity. An ambulance is on the way."

Her eyes focused, and she seemed to have more strength.

"Nicholas, you're the only one who ever tried to understand. Do you like me . . . a little?"

"I like you a lot," he told her.

"Then press channel two . . . wipe the slate clean. A whole new start—and you and I'll be together forever."

He kissed her hand. He told her to hang on. He told her living was more difficult than dying, but worth it in the end. He told her the future had all kinds of wonderful things in store for her that she couldn't see now. He told her to live.

But young people never listen.

With a little sigh, she died in his arms. Nicky held her, rocking her gently, until Charlie came to pull him away.

Out Like a Lion

On a warm spring day in May, Nicky stood on the great rolling lawn outside Frank and Susan's Tudor mansion in Bel Air. The place was only a shell now. The last of the furniture had gone off two days earlier, and the new owner would not be arriving for a month—an Indian mystic, who was starting a meditation institute for stressed-out celebrities.

Nicky had joined Susan here for one last sentimental look at the place. She was dressed in blue cotton pants and a matching loose shirt that had a wide V neck. Her long blond hair fell luxuriantly over her shoulders. She looked as lovely as a spring day in Bel Air.

They walked around the grounds in silence, then entered the empty house. Susan sighed every now and then and mentioned the things she would miss: the library, the kitchen, the Olympic-size swimming pool.

"This house is like a fairy tale," she said, passing the projection room. "Funny, I thought I was so secure living here. But it was just a dream."

"The only real security is inside yourself," said Nicky Rachmaninoff, man of many wise sayings.

"It's hard to tear myself away," Susan admitted. "But I'm looking forward to New York."

Susan was going to New York to do a play on Broadway. "Something serious," was how she'd put it. At this point, she swore she would never do television again, though Nicky had a feeling she would change her mind if the right deal came along.

They walked up the wide curving staircase to the second floor.

"Have you heard? Frank's getting married again. And this time he swore he was going to stay a bachelor."

"Frank just can't say no," Nicky told her.

Susan chuckled. "The girl's twenty-three years old. Can you believe that? Some Swedish model with a funny name. Uga or something."

"Ula," Nicky corrected. "And she's a masseuse."

"Oh, have you met her?"

"We all went bar hopping last week. Frank, Ula, and I. It was quite an adventure."

"I bet. So tell me, Nicky—are you becoming some kind of major party animal, now that you're so famous and everyone thinks you're the greatest cop who ever lived?"

He shook his head, smiling at the thought. "No, I just made an exception for Frank."

They wandered along the second-story hallway until coming to Susan and Frank's old bedroom, which seemed even bigger now that it had no furniture in it.

"I heard a rumor the academy's going to present you with a special Grammy next year, Nicky. Do you know that?"

"That would be ironic."

"Well, you deserve it, after all. You saved the music industry from extinction."

Nicky shrugged. The subject did not give him any joy, but Susan was not going to leave it alone.

"I hope you buy yourself a tuxedo that fits better than the one you wore this year."

"Oh, they'll drop the idea," Nicky said. "If not, I'll pull a Marlon Brando."

They stood looking out a window in Susan's old bedroom toward the swimming pool below. Nicky felt a nagging melancholy. He and Susan were not going to be together. She had let him out of his promise, had even torn up the paper he had signed. Upon mature consideration—as reasonable, middle-aged adults—they had decided this was the right thing. Susan would go to New York in search of serious theater, and Nicky would remain in Los Angeles, where his own career had taken a decided upward swing. There was even talk of a promotion in store for him to captain. Tanya, as always, would go back and forth: with Nicky during the school year, with her mother on vacations and in the summer.

So nothing had really changed. Nicky wondered why he felt about a hundred and five years old.

"Hey, I got an idea," Susan said. "Let's take a bath."

"A bath?"

"Sure. One more time in the old Jacuzzi. Come on, Nicky, I won't bite."

Susan was already taking off her clothes, leaving a path of blue shirt, blue pants, bra, and underwear on the way from the bedroom

279

to her ultimate Hollywood bathtub, nearly the size of a swimming pool.

Nicky still hesitated.

"Come *on!*" she cried.

Well, hell. It had been a long time since his morning shower. It was a dirty city, L.A. He followed Susan into the bathroom, leaving a trail of his own: jacket, holster, gun, shirt, shoes, pants, underwear. Susan was already in the tub with the water running.

"I'm going to miss this old tub," she said mournfully.

"Yeah, well, life flows on," said the aging philosopher.

"Doesn't it?"

She flowed right into his arms. When their lips met, the hundred and five years began peeling away. Nicky had always liked the clean, fresh way she tasted. They began petting shamelessly.

As large as the tub was, it filled fast. Susan pressed a switch on the wall, and the water churned into motion. It was an energetic Jacuzzi. A bit like being inside a Waring blender or riding the rapids down the Colorado River.

They had a tickle fight for a while and did a few other mature things—like diving for the bar of soap and finding it every time (somehow) between each other's legs.

"Hey, you know what I haven't done to you in a long time?" Susan asked. She was grinning wickedly, looking about sixteen.

"What's that?"

She told him. It sounded like more fun than diving for soap, so he stretched himself out on his back, floating on the churning water, holding on to the side of the tub with his hands to keep his head up.

Susan moved so she was between his legs, holding up his ass with her hands. After some preliminary licking here and there, she took him fully in her mouth.

Life certainly was amazing. A hard road to travel, with a few monkeylike pleasures along the way: some primitive scratching and licking and grunting that made everything all right.

Nicky could get quite philosophical at times like this. It was nice for your mind to float wide and free. Delve upon the mysteries. Being in a bathtub, however, reminded him of one mystery he would never solve—the exact manner of Billy Lion's death, so long ago in Rome.

It would probably always bother him, not to know that—if Billy had died a natural death or if he had been murdered.

Right now, though, Nicky found he was increasingly not bothered by anything. The sensory experience was enough. Susan's tongue was sheer artistry. Like a Beethoven symphony, in a way—the last movement of the Ninth—building up to a mighty climax; then, when you'd least expect it, the horns and strings would cease and you'd have just a few measures of the solo bassoon.

Quite close to ecstasy, Nicky's hands slipped off the edge of the tub. His head slipped beneath the bubbles.

Susan pulled him up, laughing like a sunny day.

"Careful, Nicky," she said. "Gotta keep your head above water!"